"[A] fast-paced and intricately plotted tale of danger, deception, and desire that is perfect for readers who like their romantic suspense adrenaline-rich and sizzlingly sexy."

—*Booklist*

"Adair has done it again! The chemistry between Hunt and Taylor is red-hot, and the suspense is top-notch."

—*Rendezvous*

"A very sexy adventure that offers nonstop, continent-hopping action from start to finish." —*Library Journal*

"Get ready to drool, sigh, and simply melt. . . . Fascinating characters, danger, passion, intense emotions, and a rush like a roller-coaster ride." —*Romance Reviews Today*

Also by

CHERRY ADAIR

Stormchaser

Undertow

Riptide

Vortex

Hurricane

CHERRY ADAIR

St. Martin's Paperbacks

This is a work of fiction. All of the characters, organizations, and events portrayed in this novel are either products of the author's imagination or are used fictitiously.

HURRICANE

For information address St. Martin's Press, 175 Fifth Avenue, New York, NY 10010.

ISBN: 978-1-250-01636-2

Our books may be purchased in bulk for promotional, educational, or business use. Please contact your local bookseller or the Macmillan Corporate and Premium Sales Department at 1-800-221-7945, ext. 5442, or by e-mail at MacmillanSpecialMarkets@macmillan.com.

Printed in the United States of America

St. Martin's Paperbacks edition / April 2017

St. Martin's Paperbacks are published by St. Martin's Press, 175 Fifth Avenue, New York, NY 10010.

10 9 8 7 6 5 4 3 2 1

ROMANTIC SUSPENSE AT ITS BEST!

Praise for Cherry Adair . . .

"Cherry Adair writes for those of us who love romantic-suspense fast and hot." —Jayne Ann Krentz

"Adair leaves readers eager to dive into the next novel in her Cutter Cay series." —*Booklist*

"*Undertow* is the beginning of an exciting and witty new series enriched with fun characters and action-packed drama. I literally could not put it down!" —*Fresh Fiction*

"Adair returns to her romantic suspense roots with an underwater treasure hunt that is thrilling and hazardous! Nonstop action plays off the treachery and danger. When you add in the sensuous sizzle, you have the full Adair package." —*Romantic Times* (4 stars)

"Grips readers and never slows down as the protagonists struggle with perils, including to their hearts, with every nautical mile they sail. Fast-paced, Cherry Adair opens her Cutter Salvage series with a strong sea saga."

—*Genre Go Round Reviews*

"Full of action and suspense! Cherry Adair did such a great job making the reader feel as if they were part of the experience. I felt like I was right there diving into the water looking for the buried treasure with Zane and Teal." —*Hanging With Bells Blog*

"A relentless page-turner with plenty of enticing plot twists and turns." —*Seattle Post-Intelligencer*

One

Fuck. Could this week, month, goddamn *year* get any worse?

Small camera monitors in the owner's cabin revealed his ex-wife's arrival aboard *Tesoro Mio.* This was the closest Rydell Case had been to Addison in over a year. Gliding his fingertip over the cold glass image of Addy's face was no substitute for touching the real flesh-and-blood woman.

Control tightly leashed, his entire body ached with . . . *yearning*—yeah—*yearning* just looking at her. Dragging in a hard, painful inhale, Ry acknowledged he hadn't taken a normal breath in thirteen months, eleven days, and ten hours. And he might not ever again.

Pinpricks of pain coursed through his body. As with a limb fallen asleep, the pain of reawakening hurt like hell. Numb felt better.

Everything. Everyfuckingthing in his life hinged on the next two weeks. No more options. Fourteen days. This was it. Do or die. Every ball he juggled for the duration came with its own inherent dangers. A minefield of things to go wrong at every turn.

He snatched up the phone on the first ring.

"Miss D'Marco and the prince just boarded." Captain

Anthony Seddeth sounded as wide-awake as Ry felt at three in the morning.

Miss D'Marco, not Mrs. Case. Got it. "I see them." His wife and her date for the evening. About damn time she showed up. He'd been sitting in the dark waiting for the past. On board for several hours before that. Now that Addy was aboard things could start moving swiftly.

Ry narrowed his eyes at the dude in the tailored tux. Prince Naveen Darshi. Well, fuck. *Knowing* she was with someone else didn't have the same blow-to-the-chest impact as *seeing* her with her old flame. Ry rubbed at the sore spot just behind his sternum with a clenched fist. "Thanks, Tony."

Replacing the receiver, he stared at the monitors, checking their progress through his ship. *Hell.* Reality check. *Her* ship. Addison had scored it in the alimony settlement, and what was "ours" had become "hers" before Rydell had even seen his dream ship completed. This was the first time he'd set foot on her.

The *Tesoro Mio* was everything he'd hoped she'd be, and more. First-class all the way. One hundred and sixty feet of perfection, tri-deck, top-notch luxury and function combined.

On the plus side, all his dreams had gone up in smoke at the same time, so the loss of a multimillion-dollar ship was barely noticeable. An indication of the shit year it had been. There was something to be said for getting it all dumped on him at once. One giant, seamless pain had to be better than multiple slowly fatal stab wounds.

That's what he'd thought, until now, as he stared into the monitor. The camera captured Addy's sweet, oval face, the sophisticated sweep of her glorious apricot-colored hair, the way her lips curved as she smiled at another man. That smile rubbed salt painfully into wounds that had yet to heal.

As for her dickwad of a companion? Well, that was Ry's own damn fault for asking God what the fuck else could go wrong. Years ago he'd stolen Addy from Darshi, and all the sucker had to do was stand back and wait for Rydell to fuck up so she could fall right back into his arms. Which she'd bloody well done before the ink was dry on the divorce papers.

The lights of Cannes sparkled copper-gold in the diaphanous mist drifting off the water behind them. Much as Ry hated to admit it, they made an elegant couple. They . . . matched.

Unlike *their* pairing. Addy had always been way the hell out of *his* class.

The subtle vibration of the ship's powerful engines traveled up Ry's outstretched legs to shake a little of the knot in his belly loose. Action. At last. But phase one didn't come without its own hazards.

Glittering shoulder-dusting earrings tangled in the loose strands of Addy's glossy, strawberry-blond hair, picking up the pinpoints of illumination from the strings of white lights surrounding the deck. Darshi slipped a proprietary arm around her slender waist. Casual, intimate. Too goddamn familiar for Rydell's already strung-out nerves.

Prince Naveen Darshi. Even though Ry knew through several crew members that Darshi was around again, seeing them together made his belly cramp. So they *were* lovers again. The torque in his chest twisted deeper, a corkscrew winding into his heart. He picked up the bottle on the table beside him. The beer was flat—he'd been waiting down here for more than an hour. He drank anyway.

For a man whom many claimed was a robot with nerves of steel, his steely nerves were shot, his temper hair-trigger. That's because before, he hadn't needed this so fucking badly. Now he needed this—*all* of it—to go right. He had so many balls in the air, one fumble would decimate everything.

No fumbles.

No margin for error.

He drained the bottle, then returned it to the watermark on the table as, eyes intent, he drank her in. A year . . . She hadn't changed. Beautiful. Lean, athletic body, small high breasts, marmalade-colored hair. Those three freckles on her nose that she hated, and he loved.

His Addy.

Only she wasn't. Not *his*. Not anymore. He couldn't compete with a multifuckinggazillionaire prince, even if the rift between himself and Addison weren't as deep as the Mariana Trench.

Ry gave a mirthless laugh. "Yeah, asshole, and you're going to attempt to dive it with just a snorkel and bloody fins. Good luck with that."

Addy's long, body-hugging gown of shimmery, creamy fabric dipped precariously low in front as her long strides carried her across the deck, Darshi at her side. Only half of the double doors stood open, necessitating her disengaging from her escort's hold. Ry's fingers dug into the nubby linen of the chair arms as he observed them entering the salon where another discreetly placed security camera picked up their progress. Darshi kept his hands to himself this time.

The owner's cabin, designed for *them*, looked even better than it had on the drawing board. The room smelled of her. Sophisticated. Assured. Complex. Despite Darshi's presence on board, the room showed no evidence of male occupancy. Thank God.

Like the absence of a male presence, there was no indication of Addy sharing her life on board with anyone. *Tesoro Mio* was her home. Their cabin on board the *Sea*

Dragon had been filled with silver-framed pictures. But here, no pictures, no small mementos of the life they'd made and shared. No—

For a moment Ry shut his eyes as his chest squeezed. "Don't go there. Do not fucking go there." Instead, he prayed to gods who didn't give a flying fuck about his wishes and pleas for Addy not to invite the prince into her cabin tonight.

Ry'd hate to add a murder rap to his long list of woes, but at this point maybe it would give him a roof over his head and three squares a day if the rest of his world went to hell and he lost what little remained. Which amounted to bugger-all.

He got up to pace. The time alone in her cabin told him she'd dressed leisurely, as she always did, before leaving the ship. Addy loved being female and everything that went into the mysterious rituals of womanhood. Cast-off gowns, long and slinky and short and sparkly, lay over the bed. Rejected shoes, with heels nosebleed high, were scattered between the bed and the enormous walk-in closet.

Once upon a time he'd settled back to enjoy the show before the evening started. Addy loved parties and events, and dressing was part of her fun. Many, many times, they hadn't made it to whatever function Addy had been trying to drag him to. Ry would rather spend an evening in bed than anywhere else when they were together.

"Yeah, well, get that thought out of your head," he muttered to himself. If she had the chance, Addison would use one of the discarded shoes as a lethal weapon. He didn't doubt that she'd be happy to pin him like a butterfly with a spike through his heart. Not that he'd feel it. That useless organ had bled out a year ago. Dry as dust, it beat the required beats, but there was nothing more than blood and tissue. His emotions had flatlined, and it would take more than he had left in him to jump-start it back to life.

He doubted she'd be in a more receptive frame of mind now than she'd been a year ago. And while it fucking irked him no end to have to come to her, hat in hand, knowing how she felt about him, he had zero choice. He'd just have to make this as bloodless as humanly possible.

There'd be no cake. And no eating it. One thing at a time.

He'd done a thorough reconnoiter when he'd boarded several hours earlier. Everywhere he looked was a design feature they'd chosen together. From the sleek, sophisticated pale-gray leather sofas to the high-backed leather chairs in the dining room. Every single thing on board, large and small, reminded him of where and when they'd been together, the laughter, the long talks late at night, the way they'd resolved disputes with kisses and lingering touches—and usually in bed. The memories hurt. He returned to the chair in the dark corner to wait.

Addison Case had once been the most cheerfully open and forgiving woman Ry had ever met. Not anymore. Her anger was so deep, a scar ingrained in the fiber of her being, he knew unequivocally she was *not* going to be happy to see him.

Keeping an eye on the monitors, he watched their progress as they strolled leisurely through the salon. Darshi murmured sweet nothings in her ear, making her laugh as they headed for the stairs leading down to the lower deck.

"You've seen that she's safely on board, dickwad." Ry's jaw clenched so hard, if it were glass it would've shattered into a million shards. "Now bugger off."

Their images moved from one security feed to the next. They were a handsome couple. The same height. Addy wore her usual five-inch heels—he winced at what those heels were doing to his teak deck—so her head was on the same level as the good old prince.

Blue blood, rich as Croesus. The man looked just like you'd imagine a prince would look. Dark and swarthy, the guy was too pretty, too well dressed. Too rich. Too fucking *here.*

Ry couldn't take any more. His entire body felt as taut as a bowstring as he flipped off the small monitors. He didn't need to *see* them say good night. Just *goodbye.*

Braced to see if Addy planned on bringing the man to her bed to finish off the evening, Ry straightened in the chair, drawing his long legs in, ready to stand again. Only the light beside the bed across the room cast a rosy glow over the cream-and-gold comforter and piled pillows, the jumble of silks and gleaming satins, the lace and chiffon. The rest of the room, and the chair in which he sat, were thrown into the velvety, Addy-scented shadows.

In his mind's eye, Ry saw them traversing the gracefully curved staircase as his heartbeat pounded like a metronome with each footstep. He imagined them walking in step, side by side, in the narrow corridor. With a flip of the switch he could watch them in real time, but his jangled nerves couldn't handle it anymore.

The heavy cabin door opened right on time, placing her in a wedge of golden light from the corridor. Rydell's heart double-clutched. The low-light images on the monitor hadn't done her justice after all. The reality of Addy, in the flesh, shocked him. God, he'd forgotten how beautiful she was. The heavily beaded gown swirled around her feet as if she were floating on creamy clouds. Lit from within, her skin seemed to glow.

Addison.

Every atom in his body leaned forward as if magnetized. Electrified. His skin hurt, he wanted to touch her so badly.

"That was fun, Naveen, thanks." Addison's naturally husky voice traveled through bone and tissue to resonate deep inside Ry. His nails scored the fine fabric on the chair's arm.

God he'd missed her.

"Night," she told Darshi, who lingered hopefully at the doorway. "See you in a couple of days." Shutting the door in his face, she turned, the beadwork on the dress picking up the lamplight. "Shit. Shit. Shit," she muttered under her breath as she slipped the slender straps off her shoulders. The weight of the dress and gravity made it drift to the floor and left her in nothing but a barely there thong, fuck-me heels, and two flowery pasties over her nipples.

If his life depended on it, Ry couldn't move. He couldn't even breathe. She was all sleek golden skin and gentle curves. Perfect as the day he married her, as if nothing bad had ever happened. The pain in his chest ratcheted up another excruciating notch.

Stepping out of the pool of fabric, she started to cross the room, headed for the bathroom.

Freezing for a second as if she sensed him sitting in the shadows, she backed up, grabbed the crystal lamp from beside the bed, and held it aloft. The cord yanked out of the wall as she approached him, the cabin plunged into inky darkness, "Who the hell are you and how did you get into my cabin?"

No maidenly shrieks of terror. Fearless, still wearing her shoes but stark naked, she walked toward him. Ry got to his feet. "It's counterproductive to leave yourself in the dark with an intruder inside the room."

"I'm armed! Don't come any cl—*Rydell*?"

"Addy." Ry reached over to click on the light beside his chair as he drank her in.

She tossed the crystal lamp on the bed. Addy didn't hurry, or fumble to cover her nudity. Merely backtracked, dipped her knees, and shimmied back into the gown, all while giving him the stink eye. He'd never met a woman with more self-confidence. It was a hell of a turn-on. Even now when her anger was palpable.

"What the hell are you doing here?" she demanded, adjusting the slender strap on her shoulder. Glossy, more-gold-than-red hair draped cape-like around her shoulders and trailed tantalizingly over her breasts. The strands would smell intoxicatingly of gardenias and feel heavy and cool, like expensive Chinese silk, draped across his body.

"You didn't take my calls," Rydell pointed out, drinking his fill while he had the chance.

Cocktail-olive-green eyes narrowed. "I have a restraining order against you."

"Only in the UK."

"Don't split hairs. It's the spirit of the law."

"I need *Tesoro Mio*."

"*My* ship."

"Technically, half."

"No. You have *Sea Dragon*. I have *Tesoro Mio*, and never the twain shall meet."

Yeah, her lawyers had enjoyed that little bit of negotiation. Rydell hadn't fought Addy getting her hands on his dream ship. He'd instructed *his* lawyers to make it quick and give her anything she wanted.

She'd taken his dreams. All of them. "*Sea Dragon* was hijacked."

She shook her head, creating a small breeze of gardenia. "No way. You'd never allow that to happen. What's really going on, Rydell?"

"*Sea Dragon* was in port. Nicaragua. North Pacific. Went into town. Came back, the ship was gone."

"My God." She rested her hand at the base of her throat. "You're serious. The crew?"

His crew—those remaining on board—were found piled up like cordwood on the docks behind a fishing boat. The memory still made him want to puke with a combo of sympathy and pure, unadulterated, impotent rage. "Everyone on board was killed."

She started to reach out a hand, then thought better of it and dropped her arm to her side. "I'm so sorry. Was it the Cutters?"

"No. As much as I'd like to stick this on one of them, it was apparently a bunch of terrorists doing a con near Peru. The ship was expendable and was blown up in the process."

"Did the authorities find the bastards?"

Ry shook his head.

"That's a hell of a financial loss, Rydell."

That was the understatement of the century. "Yeah, big time." That was just the second sucker punch. They'd kept on coming.

Removing an earring, she held it in her palm, gaze steady. "You were insured, of course."

"Self-insured. The cost of premiums for salvage ships operating in waters subject to terrorist and pirate attack are astronomical. But then you already know that." He paid the premiums for *Tesoro Mio.*

Ry's heart hurt badly enough that he thought he might be having a heart attack. Wouldn't that be in-fucking-convenient right now? He'd thought—hoped—that seeing her again, after more than a year, would lessen her impact on him, would stop the constant ache. He'd hoped that his memory of her was exaggerated by his hurt and anger over what she'd done.

But no. She was more achingly beautiful than he remembered, and her impact on him was more severe than he could ever have imagined. It didn't matter that what she'd done was unforgivable. He still wanted her with an intensity that made his jaw hurt; made his chest feel as though his heart were being cut out with a rusty knife.

Shoving his fingertips in the front pockets of his jeans helped him not reach out to touch her. The familiar scent of her filled his senses and fogged his mind. Neither of which he could afford to indulge in when his life was going to hell in a fucking handbasket.

When he was around her he felt like a goddamn drug addict. Addy had always been his drug of choice.

"Too damn bad," she said without inflection as she removed the second dangly earring and let it pour into her palm like dripping water. "Not my problem."

"Yeah. It is. If I don't have a ship, I can't salvage. If I don't salvage, I can't afford the upkeep on the *Tesoro Mio*, or anything else for that matter."

"Then my selling her will solve both our problems, won't it?"

"You can't sell her. Not without my signature. Or my dead body."

She arched a brow. "I can hope for either."

"And you'll get neither. I have a lucrative salvage near the Maldives. I need *Tesoro Mio* now." Needed his ship, his wife, his fucking *life* back on track. Had to salvage that silver. Had. To.

She set the earrings on the mirror-topped bedside table, then returned the lamp to the table, straightening the elegant black-and-gold lampshade. She gave him a cool look. "Then you're ship out of luck, 'cause you're not getting *Tesoro Mio*."

"Addy . . ."

Her eyes darkened, and her shoulders tensed. "Get off my ship, Rydell. You can leave on your own, or I'll have you dragged off. Your choice."

The smooth vibration of the powerful engines was in counterpoint to the erratic throb as his blood coursed through his body. Just *looking* at her. And that was with ten feet and powerful emotions pulsing between them akin to the 4,250-meter span over the 8,000-meter drop inside the fucking Kermadec Trench.

He stuffed his fingers farther into the back pockets of his jeans to keep from grabbing her. His life was so fucked now, he had to put out one fire at a time. "We've set sail," he informed her flatly.

Two

Rydell's gaze swept over her in a heated stroke that made Addison's hackles rise. She adroitly ignored the way her treacherous heart skipped several beats.

Born and raised in Minneapolis, he'd made his home base in London where he kept a flat. But home had been *Sea Dragon*. When he was pissed off his British accent became more pronounced. Like now.

He was pissed off?

He. Was. Freaking *angry*?

Talk about a day late and a dollar short. He was the last damn person on the *planet* who should be pissed off. Just *looking* at him made *her* feel homicidal. It made her feel other things, too. Things she had no business feeling. Rydell Case radiated sex appeal in spades. Thank God she was immune.

Her brain computed what he'd just said, and with horror she felt the throb of the engines beneath her feet. She'd thought the sensation was just the speed of her blood racing through her veins and pounding in her ears at the sight of him. "What the hell? Damn it. I didn't give my captain permission—"

"Seddeth takes his orders from me now, Addy." His lips thinned as he crossed his arms over his chest. At least he was fully dressed; the man was fond of walking around the ship semi-naked half the time. Tonight he had on his favorite jeans, worn almost white over his thighs, and a black T-shirt that stretched over his six-pack as if painted on his body. Not an ounce of fat on him. Just tightly honed muscles from hard physical labor. *Get a bigger shirt!*

She felt feral. Caged. *Don't,* she warned herself. *Just don't. Don't stoop to his level. Don't hit or bite or show fear.*

She wanted to do all of it. Fight dirty. Hit. Bite, and God only knew, seeing him again made her heart race and her palms sweat with fear that she'd succumb to the same lust that had swept her away the first time they met.

Loving Rydell Case was dangerous to a woman's mental health. Thank God she felt nothing for him now other than a strong desire to shove him overboard into shark-infested waters.

Irritation spiked and spread in a heated rush as he stood there as if he owned the ship, her, and everything he surveyed.

I hate you.

Tall, he had shoulders almost as wide as the doorway, huge hands, strong muscular legs, and big . . . everything in between. His dark hair, always finger-combed, hung to his shoulders, and he'd needed a shave two or three days ago. Everything about Rydell Case was large and dark. Addison's skin felt hot and too tight.

Usually taciturn and very private, he never wore emotion on his sleeve. It had always maddened her, until she learned that just because he didn't show feelings didn't mean he didn't have them. His favorite place to show her how he felt was in bed. When they were both naked, he let his feelings fly.

He could be charming and would, if he put his mind

to it, even be amusing. But under that were dark corners even the sunlight couldn't reach. She'd had glimpses in the two years they'd been married, but she saw not even a sliver of light in him now.

Addison had never felt as safe and loved as when she'd been in Rydell's arms. And never so scared and lonely as when their divorce had become final. A pang squeezed the air from her lungs.

"We're en route to pick up my divers, then going directly to the Maldives. Your choices are limited; be glad I'm giving you a choice at all. We could've set sail while you and Darshi were having that cozy dinner at Le Louis XV Alain Ducasse."

Her heart kicked into overdrive as fury built and adrenaline surged through her entire body, making her hyperaware of him standing there so freaking sure of himself and his place in the world. Not her world anymore. But he was like a damn five-hundred-pound gorilla, sweeping back into her life as if nothing had happened and he could do any damn thing he wanted.

She narrowed her eyes, wanting to go for his throat but standing her ground, hands clenched at her sides. "Did you have someone *spying* on me at Hôtel de Paris?"

"I had an aperitif at the bar there before boarding."

That had been four damn *hours* ago. "That's outrageous!" Damn him and his bulldozer ways. Even though she hadn't heard from his family about his ship being hijacked, she believed him. That didn't mean she wanted him on board *her* ship. Or anywhere near her. Just looking at him was an agonizing reminder of all she'd lost.

Rydell Case could go to hell. She straightened her spine and gave him a look that would've made her haughty, superior mother proud. "Then I guess you'll be swimming back to Cannes."

"Sorry, sweetheart. Not gonna happen. There's a chopper on standby to take *you* back to the city if *you* want to leave. I'm staying."

She saw the lights of Cannes twinkling goodbye through the large window behind him.

"This salvage is more important than you hating my guts."

She swiveled her attention back on him. "Nothing is more important than me hating your guts, Rydell Case. Not a damn thing. And I don't see that changing in the next century."

He looked right at her, but as usual she couldn't read any emotion behind his steel-gray eyes.

His voice dropped several octaves and a muscle jumped in his jaw as he said harshly, "We have to talk about Sophia sometime, Addy."

The blood drained from her head, leaving her dizzy and sick to her stomach. Wrapping her arms tightly around her waist was little comfort. "Don't. You. Ever. Mention. Her. Name. Not ever!"

"I feel the same pain."

Pain. Such a mild word for how she felt. He had no freaking *idea.* "Impossible. Don't—" She held up her hand to stop what he was about to say. "Just. *Don't.* All I have to do is yell, and *my* crew will be in here in seconds to bodily remove you." Only because she knew she didn't have the physical strength to kill him herself.

"I'll shoot the first person coming through that door." He looked grim and deadly serious.

"You're armed now?" she asked, appalled.

"My ship was just hijacked. Hell yeah I'm armed."

"Is your intention to take *Tesoro Mio* at gunpoint then? Hijack her? Hijack me?"

"Everyone on board has accepted the reality. Like the

crew, you've been given the option of declining and returning to Cannes."

"I'm not going to wrestle you for possession. And I'm certainly not leaving you to do whatever you please with my ship! I have plans. Plans that don't include you, or a side trip! I'm hosting guests for the trip to Australia. It's all arranged—"

"You'll get to Australia—eventually. Your sainted mother and the prince also have the option of not coming on this voyage, or they can opt to spend quality time sunbathing in the Maldives on a salvage operation."

Rydell and Hollis did not get along. The list of reasons he and her mother disliked each other was endless. "No. We're leaving for a leisurely sail to Sydney on Wednesday. I have an appointment there that I can't miss." Selling *Tesoro Mio* for one thing; appeasing her mother for another. And she'd promised Naveen an answer when they arrived in Sydney. He'd been pretty insistent on coming in with her tonight to "seal the deal." He'd keep trying in the weeks leading up to Sydney.

Shit and double shit.

"You'll miss it." Rydell's voice was hard, his expression closed and, as always, impossible to read. The Sphinx had nothing on Rydell. "You can't sell her, Addison. It's in the legalese. Read that again. And you won't be in Sydney anytime soon, unless you take a commercial flight. This ship is going back to what she was built for. *Salvage.* It's either take the chopper back to Cannes or come with me to the dive site."

How had he known about the pending sale? Her fingers tightened on the door handle, breasts rising and falling with her agitated breathing. She hated being cornered. Hated, hated being bullied, and she hated how sexy and appealing Rydell looked. Apparently hating him with all her heart didn't mean her body felt the same way. She'd beat it into alignment as soon as he was out of her cabin and she didn't have to look at him or smell that fresh sea air on his tanned skin.

"You denigrate hijackers, yet that's exactly what you're doing. This is despicable and low, even for you."

"You have no idea how low I'd go for something important to me."

"No. I really don't. Probably because it's impossible to tell one damn way or another *what's* important to you. When the chips are down, when it really counts—you're gone so fast you're a damn *blur*." Sucking in a shaky, oxygen-necessary breath felt like dragging in tiny slivers of lacerating glass. Let him feel the cold shoulder and see how he liked it.

"Once I gave a damn. Now? Not so much. I'm going to Sydney, and I'm not taking any freaking detour to India *or* the Maldives to get there!"

"We're both traveling through the Suez Canal."

"We're scheduled to go through in a *week*. You aren't going anywhere without permission from the Suez Canal Authority prior to transit. And they won't change the date so close to sailing." Unless of course he bribed them.

"Already taken care of."

He'd bribed them.

There was something—*something* she couldn't read or even decipher about his expression that made Addison stop pushing back. They'd never had a clean break. He'd left, no communication until she'd received the notice of divorce. He hadn't felt that warranted an explanation. And now he was back? Still no explanation. Rydell Case was a law unto himself.

Maybe this was about his ship being hijacked. That would be an enormous financial slam to anyone. He wasn't just anyone.

The financial trouble would be a bigger loss for him because it meant more than just him going broke. Losing his ship meant more than not having a beloved vessel.

His ship was his whole life. Treasure hunting and sailing the seven seas was Rydell's lifeblood. It's what got him up in the morning, what allowed him to subsist on five hours of sleep a night. So yes, she got that he needed to do this salvage, whatever it was. But was she reading more into his inscrutable expression than really met the eye? "What about divers?"

He didn't huff out a deep breath, but his very stillness implied that that relieved breath was being held tightly inside him. "Picking them up in Mangalore in a few days."

India? "Why didn't you find a wreck in the Mediterranean?" *Why don't you tell me what's really going on? Why is this trip so important?* Because it was important, Addison was sure of it. "Why do you have to commandeer my ship to go halfway around the damn world?"

"Because my wreck is two hundred miles from the Maldives."

"Rent a dive boat—"

"I *have* a fully equipped dive boat. This is it. There's no point arguing, Addy. I'm not forcing you to accompany me. You can get the hell off anytime you like. I told you, I'll have someone fly you back to Cannes in the chopper. It's not too late."

As taut as a bowstring, Addison shot death rays from her eyes when he taunted, "Go if you're too chicken to share space with me for a few weeks."

Even knowing what he was doing, she stepped right into it. "Abandon my ship? Not just no, Case. Hell no!" She hesitated a beat. "Is Callie coming?" she demanded, referring to his sister-in-law, and one of her best friends, and one of the best marine archaeologists around. Having her friend there would make this bearable . . .

"She defected to the Cutters," he said coldly. "So no."

"Oh, for heaven's sake, Rydell! She didn't *defect.* You sent her there to *spy* on Jonah Cutter and sabotage his dive. Serves you right that they fell for each other." Addy threw up her hands. "*Who* then?" she demanded through clenched teeth. Entire body rigid, she braced for an emotional blow.

Shit. She didn't want to see any of his regular team, he must know that.

"I need my best, and I'm damn fortunate to get them for this job. Len, Sam, MoMo, Georgeo, Kev."

The same people who'd been on board that fateful worst day of her life. Addison dropped down on the side of the bed and pressed her fingertips against her mouth for a moment, then dropped her hand into her lap, feeling cold and hollow, as though she'd been crying for months. "You sadistic bastard," she whispered through numb lips. "I'll hate you forever for this."

He shrugged. "What's new?"

She got to her feet, body rigid with anger. The heavily beaded dress swished and hissed like sea serpents around her legs as she stalked to the door and wrenched it open. "I want to see you as *little* as possible," Not sure if her heart was even beating, Addison's voice dripped icicles as she tried to hold it together. But her eyelids prickled, and the pressure on her chest wound tighter and tighter.

It was too soon to relive that day. Too damn soon. Just as it was much too soon to see Rydell again. A flood of mixed emotions rushed her like a tsunami as she held on to the solid door to ground herself.

"Fine by me. All I want is the ship." He walked to the door. Smelling the salty sea air on him mixed with the spicy soap he favored made her stupid, stupid heart do flip-flops.

"Do whatever the fuck you want." His deep voice sounded impersonal. "As long as it doesn't impact what *I'm* here to do."

She didn't flinch at his hard tone, just tilted her head to meet his gaze head-on. "I presume you've already settled in?" said the woman who wished him stone-cold dead and gone.

"Next door. The dive team will need the other cabins when they arrive."

"What am I supposed to do with my guests?"

He shrugged.

Her lips tightened. "How long do you expect this to take?"

"It's a simple salvage." He stopped a few feet away from her, nostrils flaring like a stallion scenting a mare. "Ten days."

That was pretty precise. Tilting her chin pugnaciously, she indicated the open doorway with a regal sweep of her hand. "I'll set a countdown clock."

Sitting at a small outdoor café on the Via Venti in Genoa, Addison sipped a cappuccino, waiting for the shops in the Via Soziglia—the Medieval District—to open.

The sun had yet to climb from behind the buildings, and she snugged the lightweight black cashmere cape around her shoulders. Even with the short covering, it wasn't nearly warm enough to wear the sleeveless white linen, Riccardo Tisci, or the Louboutin five-inch heeled sandals with bare legs. But she was dressed for war and willing to use every weapon in her arsenal. Even if she had goose bumps.

Okay, maybe it was childish to reroute the ship while Rydell slept, but she didn't care. He had no right to commandeer her property. And certainly no right to kidnap her. Just because *he* was on a timetable didn't mean she had to comply. She'd scheduled this quick buying trip today long before her ex-husband decided to barge back into her life in his typical bulldozer way.

There was a darling little shop with beautiful clothes from a talented, as-yet-undiscovered new designer. The velvets were exquisite, but the last time she'd been here, the shop was about to close for the day. Despite everything, she still had a job to do. Her weekly fashion blog attracted hundreds of thousands of followers all around the world. Her books on where to shop for the best bargains from top designers and where to find the hidden shopping treasures in major cities were national best sellers. She was currently writing book number six: *Hidden Style Treasures of the Liguria Region*.

Her readers wanted to know what, where, and how much, and Addison made sure she delivered. She was a success. A success with a gaping hole in her heart that nothing and no one would ever fill again.

Right now, vapid worked as insulation for her. Maybe she'd *never* feel excitement and hope ever again. She rotated her foot to admire the bright-orange polish on her toes, and the way the sculptural harness of white-and-bone-colored crossover straps wrapped around her ankle. Nothing gave a woman more confidence than a great pair of shoes and a good pedi. But the reality was, some days her writing was the only thing that got her out of bed every morning.

Nothing infuriated or scared her more than seeing Rydell face-to-face again. A year hadn't done a damn thing to heal her wounds. She'd never forget. And having him right in her face was akin to ripping a Band-Aid off a still-festering wound.

She didn't want him anywhere near her. His presence

made no sense at all. Knowing how she felt, he should be renting a dive boat. He could afford it. Rydell wasn't going to tell her what was behind this sudden and unexpected trip, but his sister or Callie might know. Addy had struck out when she tried calling her best friends and ex-sisters-in-law Callie and Peri.

In the last year her friendship with Rydell's family had deteriorated, too. They blamed her for the divorce. In the last few months a tenuous return to their friendship was starting to bloom again. Addison missed them.

Peri was Rydell's younger sister, and Callie had been married to Ry's brother. Adam had died of leukemia before Addison had met any of them. Ry was very close to both women, and considered Callie family. Another sister. Addison loved both of them, and the rift, on top of everything else, had broken her heart even further.

As usual, Peri's message box was too full for her to leave a message. Addison tried Callie next. At least she'd been able to leave a message for her.

Until she spoke to either of her friends—or Rydell told her what was really going on—she'd have to play it by ear.

Just as she was about to return the phone to her purse, it rang. Addison jumped as if she'd been goosed. Crap. It wasn't a ranting Rydell, but rather the absolutely *second*-to-last person she wanted to talk to. The opening ominous tones of Ozzy Osborne's "Mr. Crowley" warned her that it was her mother calling. "I Hate Everything About You" by Three Days Grace indicated a call from her ex.

Not that he'd bothered to ring her in the past year and one damn month. Not *once*.

Addison hit ANSWER, even though she'd rather throw the damn phone hard against a wall. "Hello, Hollis." Because her mother had the nose of a bloodhound for anything she could use to her advantage, Addison modulated her tone. "You're up and about bright and early."

"I just got in from the Rothman gala."

At eight in the morning? God, Addison thought with part humor, part dread. She hoped her mother hadn't latched onto husband number six. She was not a woman who liked her own company. It was parties, galas, and rich men's beds. And of course clothes. The only thing they had in common.

"The prince tells me the ship is no longer docked in Cannes," Hollis accused petulantly. Her Minnesota accent had been obliterated several husbands ago in exchange for a pseudo-European accent that was part British, part French, and wholly fake.

"Where did you see Naveen?" He'd only left *her* five hours earlier. That must've been the call she'd missed after Rydell had left her cabin in the early hours.

One problematic male at a time.

"He came to the gala after he dropped you off. Where *have* you hared off to now, Addison? I really don't have the emotional wherewithal to deal with you gallivanting around before breakfast. I'll be joining you in a week, and whatever you're doing, I could enjoy doing with you if you'd just consider my fragility and *my* needs for a change."

The count had tossed her mother aside and married a young American heiress the week before. That said, Hollis was the least fragile person Addison had ever met. She wasn't hurt, just furious that she wasn't a countess, and tweaked that she'd been pushed aside by someone younger. A title was her mother's brass ring. Which was why she was so desperate for Addison to marry Naveen.

"I'm just doing a quick trip to that little shop in Genoa with those exquisite velvet gowns I told you about. I'll be leaving in a few hours, Mother." *More or less. Depending on how long it takes for Rydell to find me.* "You can come here another time."

"The Italian Riviera! Addison, how could you go to the best shopping destination in Liguria without me? Typically selfish. I'll have the prince bring me when he joins you." It wasn't a question. Her friend and her mother were tight as thieves. Addison wasn't looking forward to *that* conversation, either. Naveen was joining her for the trip to Sydney. Her mother had invited herself along for the last voyage on the *Tesoro Mio* before the ship was sold.

"I won't be here."

A heavy pause. "Then when *will* you be back in Cannes?" her mother demanded, not keeping the testiness from her voice. "Babette has me almost packed, and I must tell you, Addison, selling that lovely ship is a foolish mistake. If that man is paying the bills as penance, I say let him do so. He can certainly afford it."

She and her mother had circled this drain so many times, Addison didn't even have to listen to respond. "I don't care whether Rydell can afford it or not, Mother. It's ridiculous for a single woman to live on a hundred-and-sixty-foot megayacht unless she's a rock star, which I'm not. I don't need so much space, I don't want a full crew tending to just me, and it's becoming an albatross around my neck." *And I only insisted I got it in the divorce because I knew it would kill Rydell to lose his dream ship.*

"You're still welcome to come, but stop insisting I not sell. Naveen's arranged everything, and I'm grateful to get out from under the weight of owning and running what's basically a floating hotel. I just want a nice condo centrally located—Milan, perhaps."

"Be sensible and marry Naveen. He's a prince, for God's sake! Lord only knows, the man adores you, and he has a healthier bank account than that uncouth sailor you were smart enough to jettison. You've kept him on ice long enough, Addison. If you don't say yes, he'll find someone else. You're not getting any younger, you know."

Rydell was a sailor, Addison supposed, but he wasn't uncouth. Or not very. "I'm twenty-seven, Mother, not seventy-two. Naveen and I are just friends now. Not even friends with benefits. Platonic buddies." *More than Mother needs to know.* "Look, I'll call you to see where we can meet. There's been a slight change of plans, and we're heading to the Maldives, before going on to Sydney." She figured there was plenty of time for her mother to find out Rydell had decided to play pirate for real and commandeered the ship.

"I've *done* the Maldives," her mother said tartly. "I was there with the Archambeaus after my divorce, remember?"

Which one? "No problem. Then you can join me in Sydney if you like."

"I want a *cruise*, Addison. I'm completely shattered by that nonsense I had to endure while visiting the Fouseks. I need rest and relaxation, I need to feel *safe*, for God's sake! I need *fun*. Wait for me in Genoa. I'll meet you there, and we'll go on together. I'm *utterly* bored with Paris, and I don't want to join the Davenports in the Caribbean. They offered to send the jet, which has *the* most uncomfortable seats, and I swear, they don't keep the caviar chilled properly. I'd much rather be there with you and Naveen, darling."

Lucky Naveen and Addison.

Her mother hadn't been married and divorced five times because she didn't know how to get exactly what she wanted. If Addison hadn't put both feet down when she was fifteen, she'd have the tire tracks all over her back from her mother's riding roughshod all over her.

"You're welcome to come here," she said coolly, looking out over the almost empty square as the sun slid across the far-corner cobbles in an interesting golden triangle. "But I'll be gone. We stop at Mangalore, if you want to meet the ship there."

Please don't. Having Rydell on board was about all she could handle right now. "But honestly, Hollis, instead of leisurely as we planned, this trip is going to be fast. There won't be any time for shopping excursions and sightseeing. Go ahead and join the Davenports, and have fun. Why don't we go on a commercial cruise when I get back from Australia?"

"Mangalore, *India*?" Her mother went straight to the meat. "Addison, what on earth is going on?"

Hollis hadn't taken the hint, and had skipped the irrelevant parts. "I have to go, Mother. I'll keep you appri—" Addison's eyes clashed with those of the man striding across the piazza.

Rydell.

Three

Long legs closed the distance in no time flat. Dark hair fluttered in his movement, creating a false softness around his face—which was all harsh planes and angles in the early-morning light.

Hollis was still talking as Addison disconnected the call, then dropped the phone into her purse, which hung on the back of her chair. Recrossing her legs, she picked up her cup. She'd given Captain Seddeth the order to put into Genoa just after dawn, just to piss off her ex, and by his expression she'd done just that. Taking a sip of her now cold coffee, she signaled the hovering waiter as Rydell cast a long shadow over the table.

Addison lowered the cup to look up at him. "You're up early," she said dulcetly, repeating what she'd said to Hollis. Earlier than she'd expected, since he'd been up when she'd returned at three a.m., and she'd seen the light in his cabin reflecting on the water until the sun came up.

"What the *hell* do you think you're doing?"

She raised a brow. "Drinking a cappuccino before the shops open."

She couldn't see his eyes, but his jaw was tight. He needed a shave and a damn haircut, but he was still the sexiest man she'd ever laid eyes on. It was so much easier to hate him when she wasn't sitting three feet away from his crotch. The jeans weren't that tight, but they cupped his package like a loving hand. Her heartbeat kicked up several notches. Forcing her gaze to travel up his body, she glanced at her watch. "It'll be about an hour."

"There isn't time for shopping, Addy. I have divers to pick up."

His sunglasses hid his emotions, but Addison saw herself reflected there and was proud of her cool demeanor. She'd left her hair loose around her shoulders, dressed with care in a deceptively simple sleeveless white sheath. "You know I hate being rushed, unless there's a good sale on." She sounded exactly like her mother, which gave her pause. Is that what Rydell had reduced her to? Sounding and behaving like Hollis English-D'Marco-Payne-Smithe-Belcourt-Moubray?

"Woman—"

"I'll be back after lunch . . . ish." She waved him away, then smiled at the waiter delivering a fresh cup of frothy cappuccino. "*Grazie*."

"Not a problem. You just stay right here, sipping coffee, and enjoy the shopping. When I get back to *Tesoro Mio* we set sail. With or without you. Makes no difference to me if you're on board or not." He turned on his heel, then paused and turned turn around. "Preferably not."

A lie.

Ry cared, damn it. Cared too much, which scared the living crap out of him. It wasn't good to want anything as bad as he wanted . . . *all* of this.

For a year he'd existed in a bubble of pained indifference.

Indifference didn't rip out your heart. Indifference didn't kill you like an insidious poison. For a year he'd been little more than a zombie. Going through the motions with nothing penetrating the dark cloud he'd lugged around like a fucking leaden cloak.

Coming back to life was as painful and unpleasant as a limb falling asleep that you didn't miss until you tried to move it, and then the pain shot through your body in lacerating sharp stings.

World suspended, heartbeat painfully slow, he waited. His entire world hanging on Addy's next action.

It was no idle threat. Any delay here was a delay he couldn't afford when they reached the Maldives. But just as urgent as his need to scoop up that silver and take care of his business problems was the need to resolve the bitterness between himself and this woman who could bring him back to life with a mere touch of her hand and a smile.

He ached just looking at her. Her bare skin glowed with a healthy, light tan, set off by the plain white dress and a soft, black wool wrap thing. Gold hoops glittered amid the glossy strands of her marmalade-colored hair, which draped around her shoulders like a cape of finest Chinese silk. All the ornament she needed. A wide, pagan-looking beaten-gold bracelet cuffed each slender wrist.

In counterpoint to his internal angst, she looked cool, calm, unutterably beautiful, and completely indifferent. An ancient goddess, completely unattainable and dispassionate as stone.

He missed her fiery temper. Missed the fights and the making up. Missed the physical contact. Missed—God—he missed *her*. He should be used to feeling like the exposed nerve of a broken tooth. But he wanted to feel joy again, wanted to feel love, wanted to be loved. He craved light instead of this perpetual darkness. "Well?"

"Don't be so damn impatient." She set down her cup. "A few hours won't kill you, Rydell."

A little heat? Progress. Perhaps. "Last chance, Addy." His voice was hard and glacial. The numbing protections he'd erected were melting just by being this close to her—like a glacier against a supernova. Fuckit. He hated coming back to life. And clearly, *she* didn't give a damn if he dropped dead where he stood. He shrugged one shoulder, half turning away. "So be it. I'll have Oscar pack some of your things and leave them. Where would you like?"

"In my cabin." She got to her feet. The scent of sultry summer afternoons in her perfume, heated by her skin, made him dizzy. "Nobody is touching my things," she informed him, queen to serf, as she swathed the black wrap around her shoulders against the morning chill, then slung the straps of her handbag over one shoulder. "I'm not allowing you to steal my ship from under me. If you're on board, I'll be on board."

Ry almost dropped to his knees in relief. Instead he shoved on his sunglasses and said flatly, "Your call. Get a move on, we're wasting fuel. I've already got approval from the Suez Canal Authority, and the security team will meet us in Port Said this evening. The convoy leaves at five tomorrow morning. We'll be part of it."

"You bribed them."

Of course. "I did what had to be done." His life had already been a goatfuck; adding pirates to the mix had certainly made it that much more interesting. And now, as if the already ticking clock wasn't enough, he'd had to scramble to rearrange schedules and paperwork to accommodate the earlier departure. Everywhere he looked the window of opportunity was slamming shut. Karma was a raging bitch.

He tossed a handful of euros on the table, then turned

and started walking back the way he'd come. People were starting to cross the piazza on their way to work in little shops and restaurants lining the square. A dog barked a series of happy, excited yips. Talking with their hands, two elderly women shouted insults companionably as they carried limp shopping bags on the way to the market around the corner. The bells from Basilica San Siro and Duomo di San Lorenzo each rang nine times in perfect sync. Sunlight cut a wider swath across the cobblestones as it rose to warm the shadowy alleys feeding into the piazza.

Ry's heart muted the sounds. Every atom in his body listened for the only sound that mattered: Addy's heels clicking across the cobblestones behind him. He kept walking, not slowing his pace when he didn't hear her.

Addy didn't do ultimatums. Fuck. Neither of them did.

But he would not look back.

He was halfway across the square when she caught up with him. He almost sagged with relief. She could run a marathon in those heels. "Keep out of my way, Rydell. I mean it. There's no need for us to even see each other, let alone communicate."

"You're going to take all your meals in your cabin?" he asked as she fell into step beside him, her long legs matching his strides. "Awkward."

"You can just tell the others I have a deadline."

"I'm not your message boy, Addy. Tell the dive team yourself when they board. If you don't want to socialize with anyone, say the word. Though why you wouldn't when they're your friends, too, is ridiculous."

"They saw me at *the* worst moment in my life. I never want to see them again. Ever."

This dive team had seen him at the worst moment in his life, too. And as much of a dick as he'd been to them, he was grateful for their friendship and support when he'd finally emerged back into the world.

"Maybe they need closure—"

Olive-green eyes narrowed to slits, Addy whirled on him like a feral cat. "*They* need closure?" She stopped dead in the narrow alley. "Ask me if I give a flying fuck that *they* need closure! You're putting me in an untenable position. Stay the hell out of my way, Rydell. Do it, or I'll figure out a way to toss you overboard in the dead of night. No one would blame me."

"It might be a fucking relief." The black-clad grandmothers who'd been arguing gave them a wide berth, and the evil eye for their bad language.

"So you're back with the prince," he said apropos of nothing, except that last night was stuck in a loop in his brain. "Hollis must be—" A strand of her hair fluttered in the breeze to tangle in the stubble on his jaw. It slipped free as she moved, but Ry still felt it there. A taunt. A visceral memory. A silken, binding tie. "—thrilled," he finished.

"My mother likes the idea of a title for me."

Yeah, he was well aware. "She'd be better off wanting *happiness* for you."

"I'm happy with Naveen."

"Trouble in paradise?"

"Absolutely not. Why would you say that? We're going to Australia together."

"Why didn't he stay last night?"

"Because I didn't ask him to. We'll be spending the next month together. He had things to do."

"So he wouldn't have stayed even if you'd invited him in?"

"Don't twist my words. Naveen had business to attend to."

"What kind of business does a wealthy playboy have? Count his money then ride his polo pony before the ball?"

Addy gave him a fulminating glance. "Naveen has absolutely nothing to do with you. Stay the hell out of my affairs, and I'll stay out of yours."

Ry had met Addy three and a half years ago in Cape Town when the prince had been interested in investing in one of his dives. That investment never happened, but six weeks later Addy had called him. The rest was history. "Were you still sleeping with him after we were married?"

She spun on him so fast he couldn't dodge the flat of her hand as she slapped him. It didn't hurt. Not physically anyway.

"Stay here," she said through clenched teeth. "Give me a ten-minute head start. I can't bear the sight of you."

She was going back to the ship.

It was a start.

He felt like an ant pushing a fucking boulder up Mount Everest as he watched Addy stalk away with long, sure strides across the uneven ground. Even in high heels she was sure-footed, walking as though she floated an inch off the ground on a fashion runway.

Three suited men turned to look. Rydell didn't blame them.

He wasn't sure he could survive the next few weeks. And suddenly he realized that now he *did* give a damn whether he survived everything or not.

He gave her seven minutes, watching her walk away, her long-legged stride taking her farther with each step as his face tingled from her slap. He smiled, really smiled, for the first time in a year. Her slap had knocked some sense into him, proving to him that—goddamn it—he was so desperate for her touch, he was willing to do anything to get it. Okay. He got it.

He'd been hit with a game changer.

Time to play by different rules.

Addison managed to block out Rydell for the rest of the day, making excellent headway on her new manuscript. Unable to return to the little shop with the amazing velvets, she'd incorporate it into the book anyway.

She stopped typing when her stomach grumbled, a reminder that she'd skipped both breakfast and lunch. Something she wouldn't have done if she hadn't been avoiding another confrontation with her ex-husband. Time for a break and a snack before dinner. The mini fridge in her cabin was stocked with water, sodas, and fruit, but she wanted real food.

Rubbing her eyes, she got to her feet with a stretch. She'd check the galley to see if chef Patrick O'Keefe had any chocolate cake left. Better yet, she'd change into her running shoes and do a few laps around the deck. It wouldn't satisfy her hunger, but it would make her feel too sanctimonious to eat a large slice of sinful cake.

It was midafternoon, and a warm salty breeze blew through the open window, so it shouldn't be unbearably hot. They'd be docking in Port Said pretty soon. Better run now, before she lost the opportunity because they were in port.

Addy headed to the walk-in closet, a large square room with shelves and hanging space ceiling-to-floor, with an entire wall with special shelves designed by Rydell just for her shoes and purses.

Usually she took a moment to enjoy her collection, but today she was too distracted. Pulling out her favorite jogging shoes, she sat on the padded bench in the middle of the closet to put them on. Something was . . . off with Rydell. She couldn't put her finger on it. Perhaps because her annoyance, and her own pain, obscured her interest in what he may be feeling like a foggy mask.

Tightening the laces, she chewed the corner of her lip as she considered whether she was prepared to work up the emotion needed to delve more deeply into why he was so determined to commandeer the ship, or if she didn't give a damn one way or the other. It wasn't like her to be apathetic, but it had been more than a year since she'd allowed herself to feel anything other than numb.

If it was all true, and *Sea Dragon* had been pirated—well, Rydell was a wealthy man, he could've rented any number of dive boats and continued his track record of not wanting to talk to her or see her. He'd done a damn fine job of that for the last year.

It was clear he felt about her the same way she felt about him. So this wasn't a ruse to rekindle what they'd had before.

Their divorce was final. He'd instigated it. She'd merely signed the paperwork and sent it back without a word.

Incapable of giving a damn about their daughter's death, he'd chosen to deal with it by *not* dealing with it. In those intervening three months, when she'd been at her lowest point, *he'd* been too busy with his salvage business to race to her side. Too damn busy to pick up the phone. Too busy to come to their daughter's funeral.

He'd found the time to file for divorce.

That said it all.

Addison's phone rang in the other room, and she left the coziness of the closet to pick it up from the small desk under the window. Her sister-in-law Callie. Sophie's death had inexplicably caused a rip in Addison and Callie's friendship as well. God only knew what Rydell had told her friend—or his sister, Peri, for that matter. The three of them had once been as close as sisters, but for a year now both women had been extremely cool. The fact that, like Rydell, Callie and Peri refused to discuss what had happened hurt Addison deeply.

Callie's job with the Cutters wasn't turning out quiet the way Rydell had planned.

"Ry is furious with me," Callie said without preamble as soon as Addison answered.

"Screw him, who cares?" Addison sat on her desk chair and finished tying her shoes. "This is your life and your happiness."

"I love Jonah. I've never been happier. Will you, at least, come to my wedding? It'll be in Switzerland. Neutral ground."

Addison smiled. "I wouldn't miss it. I'm happy for you, Callie, I really am."

"Ry will never forgive me. He's pissed that I've found love again."

"Come on. You know him better than that. He loves you as much as he loves Peri. He knows you loved Adam, but you weren't *buried* with him. No, it's marrying a *Cutter* that has his shorts in a knot."

"I know. But it's something he's going to have to adjust to. Although I have to say, in the mood he's been in for the last few months, maybe not."

Ah. Perhaps Callie knew what was eating him. "What's going on with Ry?"

"Other than his ship being hijacked then blown to smithereens, you mean?"

So that part was true. At least Callie hadn't brought up Sophia. Knowing what a proud man Rydell was, Addison knew having someone steal his ship was a blow to his ego as well as his pocket. The baby's death was personal. Too personal. "Rydell bounces back from adversity." Tucking the phone between chin and shoulder, she scooped her hair up into a rough ponytail, then opened the drawer for a covered rubber band. "Trust me, this I know."

Neither woman was ready to discuss Sophie's death. A good thing because Addison was still too raw to be rational. She didn't *want* to hear anyone else's point of view when the pain was still just as raw as it had been when she'd died.

"That's unfair, Addy." Callie's voice was sharp. "His pain is no less than yours. You needed each other, and things fell apar—"

"We dealt with it in our own way. Our ways were opposite. That topic is off the table. I mean it, Cal. I can't handle Rydell and Naveen, *and* pick at that barely healed scab as well. I just can't."

"Fine, but it's like a festering wound that won't heal until it's lanced."

Addison winced. "Jesus, thanks for that disgusting visual."

"Sorry." There was a lengthy pause. "Addy, have you spoken to Peri recently?"

"A few months ago, I guess. Actually I called and tried to leave a message last night. Her mailbox was full as usual. You know Peri." Rydell's sister was often incommunicado for months on end. They'd all learned not to worry. Too much. "Why, have you?"

"Not for months. I do think there's something going on with Ry. I could hear it in his voice when I spoke to him a few weeks ago. Maybe Peri knows."

"He's his usual Fort Knox of emotion."

"Just because he doesn't show it doesn't mean he doesn't feel deeply."

"His inscrutable mask is made out of titanium, believe me. Nothing permeates. No emotions go in, none come out."

"Talk to Peri."

Addison's heart skipped several beats, and her mouth suddenly went dry. About to stand so she could stretch before her run, she dropped back onto the chair. Hot and cold tingles spread over her body. "Is he dying?" It would be impossible to hate a dead man. She wanted him alive and, if not suffering, then at least as miserable as she was.

"What? No!"

"Are either you or Peri dying?"

Callie laughed. "Not unless Ry kills me before my impending nuptials, no. But I think Peri might know what's going on."

"What's going on is that he's furious his precious ship was hijacked, he's even more pissed that I own his beloved *Tesoro Mio*, and he doesn't like being inconvenienced. He'll get over it. And frankly, Cal, if he doesn't, I don't give a damn. We're not married anymore. Honestly, I don't think he ever really committed to marriage; he just wanted me in his bed badly enough to put a ring on my finger. The bloom dropped off that rose when—" Her throat closed up before she managed to push out the words she loathed to say out loud. "We stopped loving each other when Sophie died."

"That is *patently* untrue. I've never seen a man more in love with a woman than Rydell was with you. You were his everything, Addison. He thought you hung the moon and the stars and pulled the tides. That man loved you more than life itself. You needed to draw strength from each other, and you pushed him away."

"I didn't push him. *He* ran. As far and fast as he could. If he won't talk about it, and I don't want to talk about it, at least respect my wishes."

"Fine," Callie said calmly. "I'll shut up. I'm damn lucky that I found a man who feels that way about me. It's a once-in-a-lifetime kinda love."

I used to think the same thing. Until it wasn't. "Let me know where and when for the wedding. I'll be there."

"Addison—"

"It was great catching up, Callie. I can't wait to meet Jonah, I'm sure he's everything you say he is." And since he was part of the Cutter family—Rydell's archnemeses—the union was sure to cause all sorts of conflict. It remained to be seen if Rydell loved Callie more than he hated the Cutters. "Love you to the moon and back, honey. Talk to you soon."

Four

Addy was down in her cabin, pissed. So be it. Ry'd had no intention of leaving her in Genoa while he continued on to the dive site. Not unless that had been the only option. He'd counted on her stubbornness, and brought her back on board. But he was well aware that it could easily have gone south and he'd be continuing on without her right now.

So she was on board. A plus in the clusterfuck of it all.

The good news was that she was so angry having him there, she wouldn't want to rehash the past, and for that Rydell was pathetically grateful. He couldn't handle an emotional outburst on top of the rest of it.

Captain Seddeth leaned against the chart table, arms folded. "Everyone is on their way."

He'd asked the captain to call a crew meeting. Ry had hired Seddeth and several of the others, then left the rest of the hires to the new captain's discretion. Now he wanted them to know who was boss on this trip.

He scanned the horizon through the wide windows on the bridge. Clear skies, rolling five-footers hitting them on a beam. He filled his lungs. God, he loved this ship. He drew his focus back to the captain. "I need to know where their loyalty lies. They don't know me, but I need them to trust me."

"I've already spoken to them, Ry. I know and trust you. Yes, Addison is my boss, but you hired me, and while I don't know what's going on, I'll trust that you'll let me know when you're ready. Although God only knows you're a tight-lipped bastard, and hardly the guy to share any secrets. You hold everything close to your chest."

Rydell smiled. "For someone who barely knows me, you have a pretty good idea how I operate."

"I've worked for Addison for over a year. She's almost as tight-lipped as you are, but she's let me see glimpses of the life you shared together. I have no interest in getting into the personal, but as far as this ship goes, I'm your man."

Rydell wondered if Addy had told Seddeth about Sophie, but didn't ask. The lid had to stay on that Pandora's box until he was ready to open it. If ever.

"Thanks, I appreciate that. And thanks for coming," Ry continued, turning to the men cramming into the wheelhouse. "I helped design *Tesoro Mio*, but before I took possession, Addison was awarded it in the divorce." Not that she could do anything other than live on board without his written consent. If she ever decided to sell her, he had the right of first refusal. Under the circumstances that was laughable. At the moment he couldn't even afford a sailboat. "I didn't anticipate ever being on board *Tesoro Mio*, but things changed when *Sea Dragon* was taken."

Several of the men gave him sympathetic looks, whether it was for the loss of his ship or the fact that his ex-wife had been awarded this magnificent craft before he'd ever set sail in her. Hell, maybe they felt his pain over the divorce. Or maybe they were all thinking what an asshole he was for taking over his ex's ship, because their loyalty lay with Addy, not the man who'd just shown up out of the blue.

Still, their private opinions were immaterial. He'd do the best he could by them, but that wouldn't change what was coming down. "Now circumstances have forced me to take back control, at least until after the dive. The dive site is situated between the southern tip of India and the Maldives. We pick up the crew in four days in Mangalore. I don't anticipate any complications on this dive. I know where the silver is, I've scouted out the site, and I've done all the necessary paperwork. Everyone on board will get a percentage, and I don't anticipate the salvage to take any more than ten days. Two weeks at the outside."

The prospect of a percentage of the salvage changed people's demeanor almost instantly. Now they were really paying attention. "There's a possibility—slim, but a possibility—that we don't recover the silver. In which case—" He shrugged. *Nada.*

"What happens once you find your treasure?" First Mate Badri Patil asked. Small and wiry, he probably weighed in at a hundred pounds soaking wet. "Will things go back to the way they were with Ms. D'Marco in charge? Or will we basically report to you?"

Fair question. It was odd hearing Addy referred to by her maiden name; it gave Ry an unpleasant twinge in his gut. "Addison has found a buyer for the ship in Sydney. That's *not* going to happen. If she insists on selling, then I'll buy her out." A situation he hoped to bloody hell never happened because he didn't have the funds to do so. "But that's down the road. I just wanted to fill you in as to who I am, and why I'm here. Until such time as the ship docks in Sydney, you are all to report to Captain Seddeth first, as you do now, and then to me. No exception, is that understood?"

He waited for each person to give him an affirmation.

"Good. Now the main reason for this meeting. We're

going through the canal. None of you have done so before, and the captain and I want to make sure you understand just how perilous the transit can be—and probably will be. We're meeting a group of mercenaries, paid to protect the ship. I don't know these men; their reputation is all we have to go on. This is your chance to bail at Port Said if you're not willing to do everything necessary to keep the ship secure from pirates."

"I'm better with a frying pan than a gun these days. But I was in the Gulf. I know my way around a weapon," Patrick O'Keefe assured him with his strong Boston accent and a gleam in his eye as he looked out the assortment of weapons Ry and Seddeth had gathered for the trip. "She looks neat and nimble. Come here, my girl." He picked up a Sig Sauer and a box of ammo.

Each man picked up his own weapon of choice and a box of ammo.

Addison never did get around to the run. They'd been closer to Port Said Shipyard at the northern entrance to the Suez Canal than she'd realized.

Callie's words went around and around in her mind like a hamster on a wheel. Something was wrong. Very wrong if Ry's sister-in-law and sister were concerned about him.

"Damn you, Rydell Case! I do *not* want to *worry* about you. I don't even want to *think* about you!" It was all very well snarling at him from the privacy of her cabin. She needed to get her emotions in check before she went out on deck, because the last thing she wanted to do was show even a sliver of feelings for him to his face.

She considered going into town once they docked, but decided against it. Rydell, ever impatient, and freaking cranky as hell, would just come and find her and make her return to the ship again. Or worse, set sail without her this time. Possession was nine-tenths of the law. She wasn't going to give him the chance to take over completely.

Still, she wanted at least to look at the city since they had to wait for the security people to show up.

Dressing conservatively in her lightest-weight white cotton pants and a sheer, pale-blue long-sleeved tunic over a skimpy white tank top, she made her way up to the third deck to join the captain.

"You're just in time to get the first look at our security guys." The captain indicated a large military-looking truck as it pulled up close to the boarding ramp. Rydell, clearly waiting for them, jogged down to greet the first man to emerge. Addison's throat tightened. She was filled with so many conflicting emotions seeing her ex again, it was hard to contain them.

She placed a wide-brimmed straw hat on her head to shield her face from the brutal sun. "He's lucky they could come at such short notice." Because *Tesoro Mio* was setting sail a week earlier than scheduled, the private maritime security company had to hustle to supply the necessary men before they departed in the morning.

The transit from Port Said to the Gulf of Suez in the south, and from there through the Red Sea, was under fifteen hours. Some of the most dangerous—and expensive—hours that Addison had ever heard about. Transit fees, bribes, and the astronomical cost of the mercenaries added up and up and up. Because Naveen's Australian friend was going to buy *Tesoro Mio*, he would reimburse her for all expenses. Or reimburse Rydell, since he was the one now paying.

Up and down the pier men loaded and unloaded ships of every size and description, securing cargo, taking on produce. If they weren't working, people milled about or lounged in the shade of huge shipping containers.

Color, noise, unidentifiable smells, heat, and flies.

The temperatures hovered in the high nineties, so hot and dry Addison's skin felt parched; every breath scorched the inside of her nose, burning all the way down to her lungs. There wasn't another female in sight. A trickle of sweat glided down her temple beneath her hat and over the bridge of her nose under her sunglasses.

Tesoro Mio would leave with the second southbound convoy, consisting of fifteen to twenty ships of various sizes, at five the next morning. A shiver of misgiving cooled off Addison's skin for a nanosecond. She'd read extensively about the dangers of pirates in the narrow canal, and she wasn't looking forward to the next few hours. She already felt nervous and tense, and they hadn't even left the dock yet.

Standing beside Tony Seddeth, Addison leaned against the rail watching Rydell on the dock as he greeted a dozen soldier-of-fortune-looking guys piling out of a large vehicle with black-tinted windows.

"Impressive." Despite his gleaming white uniform, Tony, a tall, rawboned Texan in his mid-fifties, looked as if he should be wearing a cowboy hat and a gun belt in the Old West. "They look like they can do the job."

They also looked as though they were enforcers for the Mafia. Lots of muscle, no visible necks, biceps the size of her thigh, and weighed down with a terrifying array of weapons in plain sight. No doubt a deterrent to anyone scouting out *Tesoro Mio* for later piracy.

Addison frowned as the men unloaded incredibly heavy-looking duffel bags from a large military-style truck with the assistance of some of her crew. Wearing black cargo pants and a black muscle shirt, Rydell looked just as hard-ass and tough as the mercenaries he'd hired.

But a small part of her brain knew his almost hidden tenderness, and how gentle he could be when he made love to her . . . *Stop it!*

Rydell glanced up to see her watching him at the rail on the third deck. She deliberately turned her back to speak to the captain. "You couldn't get another security company to send us the five men we're short?" Those five were on another job until the end of the following week—their original departure date.

"Not in this tight window, no. We were lucky those guys could join us. If they hadn't, we would've had to wait until the date they were contracted for, a week from now. We'll be okay. I've been to this rodeo before, so has Ry, and we have several crew members who are professional security."

Really? She raised her eyebrows. "We have security people on board? Who and for how long? How did that come about, and why wasn't I informed?"

Avoiding eye contact, Tony ran a hand over the back of his neck. "You'll have to ask Rydell about that."

Rydell hired Tony Seddeth before her life had fallen apart. At the time, Addy had just taken possession of the ship, letting Tony hire the crew as he saw fit. Now, she realized, Rydell had kept his nose in her business even when she hadn't been aware. "Believe me, I will."

It was hard to be pissed off that her ex had hired guns on board for her safety. But she was. Even when he hadn't been around, he had people watching her. Did they report back to him? Was he aware of everything she said and did, and who her guests were?

"But I'll ask you again: Who?"

"Addison—"

He'd always called her by her first name in private, Ms. De Marco in public. She and Rydell had been divorced by the time the ship was ready to sail; the captain hadn't known her when she'd been Mrs. Case. Now, with Rydell here, she wondered who Tony was loyal to. "Who, Tony?"

He sighed. "Jax Han, Oscar Vaccaro, and Patrick O'Keefe. He was watching out for you, Addy."

Jax was second engineer, Oscar the chief steward, and of course Patrick was their chef. No matter where she went on the ship, she could be watched. "I can take care of myself, and if and when I can't do that, I'll hire my own security." She pointed down to the dock with the earpiece of her sunglasses. "Just as I did for this trip though Suez."

Rydell had somehow managed to push through permissions from the Suez Canal Authority. She and the captain had submitted the paperwork a month ago, with the necessary letter from their flag state, Italy, endorsing the *Tesoro Mio* for transit. Addison wondered if the authority always worked on a dime, or if it had taken more than a dime to motivate them to push the permission through early.

Shading her eyes, she observed the men climbing on board. "They look like they can repel just about anyone." They wore regular clothes, but they were armed to the teeth and looked battle-ready. A shiver traveled across her skin. Going through the Suez was the most logical route to Sydney. But the chances of being attacked by multiple groups of pirates were very, very high.

They'd go with other ships of various sizes in a convoy, and everyone should be ready, willing, and able to deter pirates en route. Addison wasn't looking forward to any of it and had, in fact, requested that her mother meet her in Sydney instead of joining her on board. Her mother always had her own agenda, and made decisions based on God only knew what. Money for sure. Her own comfort certainly.

The pirate situation was so bad that leading think tanks had called for worldwide efforts to tackle it. Modern pirates were a far cry from movie stereotypes. Seaborne terrorism was now funded by millions and millions of dollars from ransoms and expensive cargoes. From what Addison had read when she planned this trip—most of the reading material unread, because she'd thought she had more time to bone up on it—she knew they were violent, efficient, and well stocked with fast boarding craft, GPS technology, and the latest weapons. They were a force to be reckoned with. And every one of the professional guns for hire was worth his exorbitant price to ensure the safety of the ship and everyone on board.

"They came highly recommended." The captain cast a critical eye over the battle-ready men. "I'd advise you to stay clear of them. Their reputation for violence is well documented. Good if we're threatened, but not good if they become bored and start looking for ways to entertain themselves. You're the only woman on board."

"I'll be careful." She'd read reports from various other ships' captains who'd used this same security firm. Former US Navy SEALs and special forces operatives not necessarily honorably discharged. The men were said to be well trained and lawless, but damn good at what they did.

Rydell talked to two men, who were clearly in charge, as the others went back and forth carrying their equipment, then returned for heavy sandbags, which they slung over their shoulders.

"What are those for?"

"They'll strategically line the railings so we can take cover behind them."

"God—" It looked as though they were preparing for war. And, she thought with a creepy sensation in her stomach, in a way they were. For fifteen hours they'd be braced for attack, *Tesoro Mio* a fat sitting duck ready for the plucking as she traveled slowly down the narrow canal. Even in convoy, pirates were known to lie in wait along the banks to attack from all sides as the ships passed.

The broiling sun shone on Rydell's uncovered head, making his dark hair shine as the long strands danced around his face and shoulders. She might hate him in the daylight hours, but her subconscious ached for him in her dreams. Hell, in her dreams anything was possible. And then she had to wake up and face the reality of what her perfect life had become.

Tony looked as though he was visually weighing the new additions for their worthiness. "They better be good as advertised. The best at what they do. We're going through Suez. Not safe by any stretch of the imagination. Pirates are thick on the ground. Professional security is a necessity, not a whim. You know our insurance company will fine us if we *don't* have additional security through the canal. Nevertheless, I'll take her through as quickly as they'll allow us. The lead ship sets the pace."

"We should be safe enough inside the convoy, right? We don't have anything valuable aboard." She realized as soon as the words came out of her mouth how naive she sounded. Hostages. A multimillion-dollar luxury vessel. Why *wouldn't* they try to take the ship and everyone on board? "Never mind. That was a ridiculous statement."

He rubbed the back of his neck as he glanced over at her. "Not that I want to get rid of you, but would you consider joining us in India?"

An argument Rydell had presented as they'd passed in the hall this morning. "I'm staying." And why did he have to park his ass in the cabin right next to hers?

The captain frowned and looked no happier than Ry

had when she'd told him the same thing. No doubt seeing the pack of muscle-bound, well-armed security men brought home the reality of just how dangerous the situation was. "Then arm yourself and stay sharp. The concept of a citadel is out unless we're fortunate enough to transit between two warships who'd protect us and engage the pirates quickly. But since we can't ensure that, the security people are our best bet."

Addison didn't like the idea of a citadel to protect passengers and crew anyway. The idea of being enclosed somewhere—however safe it might be—didn't sit well with her. She'd read last year about pirates who had set a ship on fire to smoke out the wealthy passengers enclosed in a citadel. She didn't want to be trapped on board, with no way out.

"The pirates don't care about the ship or anything else if they grab a high-profile hostage for ransom."

She was also aware that pirates had very little to lose, and would do whatever it took to capture wealthy passengers for ransom and, if they could, hijack the ship.

She waited until Rydell and the men disappeared inside before turning back to the captain. "I changed my mind about the trip into town. I'll be in my cabin if you need me." Which he wouldn't, because as soon as Rydell boarded Tony was *his* captain again, not hers. It wasn't fair. But then what in life was?

Addison took her time going downstairs, but she ran into the men in the salon anyway.

In days of old Rydell would've wrapped an arm around her waist and pulled her in tight against his hip. Now he left his hands in his pockets as he introduced her to the group. "My wife, Addison." His expression told her not to correct him, and in this case she didn't. No one shook hands, and they didn't introduce themselves beyond a short nod. "We're having drills twice a day until we're clear," Rydell told her shortly. "I've already spoken to Anthony. No one is exempt."

Rydell was many things, but he wasn't an alarmist. "Believe me, I'm hearing every word."

"Good. The canal is narrow—under three hundred meters at some points. Places where we'll have less than a hundred fifty meters on each side of us. Well within the range of any weapon they choose to use. They can take potshots at us from a lawn chair on the bank. The narrowness means one-way traffic only for most of the transit. Two convoys going south, one going north. Which is why we're going in the second of the southbound convoys."

"There's a ninety percent chance they'll target this fancy ship of yours." Crew-cut, earring, no neck, six six if he was an inch: Addison wouldn't like to meet this guy in a dark ally. The guy's eyes were hard and shifted constantly, as if he was waiting for attack from any quarter. Not jumpy, but on high alert. "The ship's worth a shitload, you and Case here are worth a hell of a lot more."

Rydell laughed, and Addison sent him a frowning glance. "Mayhem and worse isn't funny."

Rydell shrugged. "Too bad perceptions don't match reality."

"They'll try to help themselves to all of it. We're here to make sure that doesn't happen."

"Good," Addison said briskly. "I'll have someone take your things to cabins—"

"No cabins, and no sleeping for the duration. We'll spell each other when we can, but we're on watch twenty-four seven starting now. I'd suggest you change into dark clothing and stuff that hair under a ball cap if you venture on deck. Better yet, stay below and keep your door locked until we're though."

Rydell walked with her through the living room. "You don't like him."

Ry had always been able to read her. Before, it had been sweet and romantic; now it annoyed her that she was still so damn easy to peg. "I don't have to like him, or even see him. He's here to do his job." She was quite happy to lock herself in her cabin for the twenty-four hours it would take to clear Suez Canal. It would keep Rydell away from her as well.

Rydell took her elbow. Electricity sparked up her arm and suffused her skin with prickly heat. "I don't suppose you'd reconsider and fly out? You could meet the ship in Mangalore when I pick up the dive team."

"I'm not flying anywhere."

He dragged in a breath. "Don't take any of this lightly, Addy. Not for a second. The threat is very clear and present. Chaos in Somalia has kept that country ungovernable. Al-Qaeda-allied insurgents, spearheaded by the Taliban-style Islamic courts—"

Shaking off his hand, she took a step back. "I get it, Rydell. I'm not an idiot. I've read the official briefs." Certainly enough to know the gist, and to be suitably scared. "I'll stay in my cabin until we're given the all-clear. Believe me, I'm not the stupid girl who goes down to the basement to investigate a suspicious noise—I have my Glock and know how to use it." Thanks to Ry and his numerous lessons, which had usually turned into makeout sessions.

His darkening pupils told her he remembered, too. "Keep it with you at all times. Even going into the head. But frankly, if you need it, it'll be too late. If they board, we're screwed. They have faster boats, sniper rifles, rocket launchers, and more men. They know the area like the back of their hands, and they're determined. The convoys are scheduled, and they know when and who's in them because they're computerized. They know exactly where each ship will pass, and they'll lie in wait. Stay in your cabin for the duration."

"Fair enough." She curled her fingers over the satin-smooth teak railing leading down to the cabins. "Do we have our position in line yet?"

"Yeah. Dead fucking last."

The worst position to be in. Blocked by the ships proceeding them, and with no room to turn around in the narrow channel, they'd be sitting ducks should pirates come knocking.

Addison felt chilly fingers on the back of her neck and held Ry's gaze. "Shit."

"Yeah."

For a moment it looked as though he was about to reach up to touch her; then he shoved that hand into his front pocket. "Stay below."

"Not a problem." Addy took two steps down, then turned. Rydell, standing at the top of the stairs, hadn't moved. She hated him, but she didn't want him hurt physically. "Be careful, 'kay?"

"Wow. I'm touched. I thought you wanted me dead."

"Not necessarily," she told him sweetly. "Just in excruciating pain." But when Addison resumed walking downstairs, she knew that wasn't true. Unless she was the one inflicting the pain, she hated the thought of Rydell Case injured by exterior forces.

She went to her cabin to check how many clips she had for her Glock.

Five

Holding a small tray on one hand, Ry walked unerringly to the bed, despite the stygian darkness of Addy's cabin. The heady fragrance of skin-warmed gardenias almost brought him to his knees. Locking them to prevent him from falling on her like a starving wolf, he said quietly, "Addy, it's six a.m. Wake up."

Ry was adrift without her. Divorce hadn't made him any less insanely in love with her. His fucking stupid, refusing-to-take-a-hint heart physically hurt with loss as he longed for the achingly familiar taste of her. Silky fragrant skin and mouthwatering womanly musk. If only—

Her movement under the satin sheet sounded like the susurrus of an ocean breeze whispering over a calm sea. "Are we moving?" she murmured, voice thick with sleep. God, he loved her like this. Soft and vulnerable as she woke slowly. When she had loved him, morning sex with her in this half-awake, half-dream state had been one of the wonders of his world.

It always took her a good ten minutes to be fully awake, but they didn't have the luxury this morning. At least she wasn't attacking him for coming into her cabin unannounced. That was something. He felt for the lamp switch, and the room was instantly bathed with warm, dim lighting.

Today her sheets were leopard print. Ry knew how much she loved the feel of silk against her skin. Her long hair, more a deep, streaky blond than red in this light, spread across the pillow in a wild tumble of glossy marmalade-colored strands.

Ah, hell, she still slept naked. He would've put money on Addy wearing body armor because he was on board.

She was covered to her lightly tanned shoulders with the luxurious leopard-print sheet. The light followed the hills and valley of her body, spread out like a tormenting feast to his senses. The fragrance of her sleep-warmed skin intensified when she moved.

"Yeah, we departed an hour ago," he told her, wrenching his attention away from temptation. He walked over to place the tray on the desk across the room, noticed she had closed the drapes tightly, then returned to her bedside. He took several deep breaths to center himself and get his mind back to the impending situation as they transited the canal.

"Get up and dressed." His voice was thick, and he cleared his throat before continuing. "I want you awake and on high alert for the duration." The throb of the powerful engines vibrated through the soles of his deck shoes. The sheet, draped over her shoulder and hip, shimmered with the vibrations, looking like water flowing over her nude body.

She pulled the sheet up over her shoulder as if realizing that even that small curve of nakedness would have his heart thumping and his dick stirring. Addy knew him well.

She always woke up looking fresh and alert—but it took a few minutes to get her brain there. And it was those few minutes first thing in the morning, when she was soft and welcoming, that Ry missed most.

She gave him a cool look as he opened the drawer in

her bedside table. "I don't give a flying crap what *you* want. I had my alarm set. I'll be ready in five minutes. You can go now."

Bitchy when cornered or afraid. He knew her well. He wanted to see her up, armed, and secure behind a locked, heavy, watertight door. He handed her the Glock, then kneed the drawer closed. "Take this, keep it with you at all times, and do not leave the cabin until I come for you."

Freeing one arm, she took the gun and held it beside her hip on the lustrous sheets. "Already loaded and ready to use. Feel free to get the hell out of my cabin, Rydell."

She knew how to use the gun; he'd taught her himself. It was always wise to have a weapon on board, and the knowledge to use it. Addy had a steady hand and a sharp eye. He had to be content with that right now.

"Lock the door behind me and secure the windows."

"Where are you going to be?"

"Up top. No one is taking my ship."

She didn't correct him, but the sleepiness left as her eyes hardened. "You're paying professional military guys stupid amounts of money to protect us. Why risk your own life?"

"Because *Tesoro Mio* is my life right now. I have no intention of sitting twiddling my thumbs in my cabin if pirates decided to take my ship. I'll protect her with everything I've got." *Protect you with everything I've got*, he didn't add. Which right now was precious fucking little.

He indicated the tray. "Sandwiches and other stuff, and a pot of coffee to keep you going."

She wouldn't starve in fifteen hours, he was perfectly aware. But he'd needed to see her. Needed to ensure her safety before the shit hit the fan. Of course he had an overwhelming need to touch her. He refrained.

"Thanks. The mini fridge is full of snacks and drinks,

too." She made no move to get out of bed. "I'll be fine. It's only fifteen hours."

"Yeah," he said drily. "*Only.* Wedge that chair under the door after you lock it. I brought a bulletproof vest for you. Put it on when you're dressed. I'll give my knock when we're cl—*Fuck.*" The sound of gunfire peppering the glossy, navy-blue hull of the ship, made his heart trip. Addy flinched. "Up and at 'em, Addy! Now!"

She sat up, hand flat against her breasts like a Victorian maiden, holding the sheet over her chest. She jerked her head at the door, long hair slithering like pale amber satin over one bare shoulder. "We'll discuss how you opened my bolted damn door. Late—" A loud explosion made the thick glass in the window knock. "Holy shit." Her eyes shot to his face. "*Go!*"

Out of the corner of his eye, Ry caught a flash of pale leg as she threw back the covers. "Lock it," he yelled, running for the door and not looking back.

He paused on the other side for the seconds it took for her to engage the lock. "It goes without saying," he told Oscar Vaccaro—the chief steward and Addison's personal security guy—who waited outside in the companionway, "guard her with your life."

"Always, boss."

Rydell's heart pounded as if he'd just run a marathon. "Anyone comes down here—"

"Shoot to kill. It's what you hired me for."

"Right." Since he couldn't be in two places at once, and since he'd vetted the three men he'd secretly hired and put in place for Addison's protection, Ry hauled ass down the corridor, taking the stairs leading to the top deck three at a time.

His own Glock in hand, Ry paused at the top of the ladder to assess the situation. Wearing protective helmets and bulletproof vests, *Tesoro Mio*'s crew, stationed one deck below him, manned the fire hoses. Mounted on the railings, the hoses shot powerful jets of water alongside the hull from prow to stern to deter climbers. The sound was thunderous, yet it wasn't enough to block out screams, yells, and the *rat-a-tat-tat* of gunfire.

Ry winced every time a bullet struck the hull or gouged a path across the pristine teak deck. Thank God he'd opted for the steel-and-aluminum hull when he commissioned the boat. It had been the most expensive of the alternatives, but now, as the bullets pinged the sides, it was worth every goddamn fucking penny he'd paid.

Jesus, the pirates were determined. The banks of the canal, *both* fucking banks, were lined with men armed with rocket launchers, shotguns, rifles, and assorted other weapons. They were so close—thirty yards or less—Rydell saw the whites of their eyes. They hadn't wasted any damn time.

"Stay down!" second engineer Jax Han yelled from his position beside the hot tub at the other end of the deck. "These suckers are relentless as hell." He returned a volley of shots into the men running parallel to the ship.

On either side of the single-file convoy of ships large and small, the land was flat and sandy. Hardly any vegetation, but dozens of people followed the ships, shooting as they ran. Some were seated in lawn chairs, rifles across their laps, as if watching a hometown parade. Waiting.

Now they were up and motivated with the arrival passage of the sleek, 160-foot luxury megayacht.

Rydell's high-priced security men were doing their jobs, picking off their attackers one at a time with precise and accurate aim. The shooters on board were outnumbered twenty to one, but they had the advantages of higher ground and expert marksmanship. When they shot, they killed.

Ry ducked behind the bulk of the container of life vests and squeezed off a shot at a man wielding a rocket launcher like a pro. Skinny, barefoot, and wearing nothing but baggy jeans, the guy repositioned the rocket launcher on his shoulder, his focus the bridge behind Ry.

Without hesitation Rydell aimed and squeezed off a shot. His bullet was true, striking the man in the throat. Ry winced as the man fell to the sandy ground beside his ancient lawn chair, what remained of his head a gory mess. The fired rocket went wild, hitting several of the man's fellow pirates, and missing *Tesoro Mio* by a few yards. In response, the men around the dead guy scattered like pigeons, yelling and gesturing wildly. Others ran along the banks, seeking new positions.

Forward progress? Painfully slow. A brief pause in the assaulting fire gave Ry an opportunity to look back at what he'd done to the guy with the rocket launcher. Bloody hell. His stomach twisted. He didn't condone killing, and wholesale murder went against everything in him. Hell, the shooter's ribs showed through his sunbaked skin. Emaciated, desperate—it was no wonder they were trying for the brass ring. But Rydell wasn't going to allow his *Tesoro Mio* to be that prize.

The ship would be a trophy. But the pirates' main objective was to capture hostages for ransom. They could not be allowed to board. Ry would die to protect Addison. Do anything. Kill if he had to. Nothing and nobody would ever hurt her again. And that included himself.

Even though he knew he'd had no choice, he felt like shit for killing a man. But it had come down to the pirate or everyone on board his ship. No contest.

Spray from the hoses misted over him. Eyes constantly scanning the banks for danger, he swiped water out of his eyes and scraped back his wet hair.

From his vantage point on the top deck, he had a

bird's-eye view of the action. On closer observation, Ry realized that most of the men running alongside the *Tesoro Mio* were merely going through the motions. Scattershot with little hope of hitting anything. Quickly separating the noisemakers from those determined to do the ship harm, he joined the security men's effort in holding them off.

Ahead was the bulk of the barge carrying huge multicolored containers. Beyond *Tesoro Mio*'s wake, the narrow canal shone crystalline blue between the parched, sandy beige embankments.

He recognized the short-cropped black hair of one of his men, hunkered down beside the hot tub. Jax was one of the guys he'd hired a year ago to protect Addison. Ex-military, a sniper, and now in his element. Ry paused, crouching on his haunches behind his barricade as he tuned in on a new sound. Beneath the intermittent cries and loud bangs of battle, the throb of a small, powerful engine drew closer and closer.

"Hear that?" he yelled at Jax. Peering around the side of the metal storage unit, he scanned the deck for the behemoth with the crew cut, leader of the group he'd hired. Would've been damn nice if Klein had fitted him with one of the communications devices he and his men wore. Rydell saw him on the middle deck, midship starboard side. He and two of his men, protected by a barricade of sandbags, were firing at a group with a rocket launcher on the starboard side.

The air smelled of rancid smoke from something on the tanker ahead of them. Flames licked up the starboard side of the hull, quickly doused by their fire hose. The sound of radios communicating between the ships, men yelling—either in pain, or shouting rapid-fire instructions—added to the cacophony surrounding them. Gunshots and the periodic loud boom of a rocket launcher strike made the whole chaotic scene seem as though they were in a fucking war movie without a script.

The three mercenaries had their hands full fending off the group of determined fatigue-wearing soldier-pirates with their rocket launcher. It didn't look as though they'd seen the rapidly advancing skiffs coming up on their port side.

With the noise of gunshots, shouts, and hard pounding of the water jets, there was no way to communicate with Klein or his men. If he wanted to go down and yell in someone's ear, it was ten feet from his position to the ladder and down to the next deck.

"Not fishing vessels!" Jax's yell was almost lost in the noise. "Two skiffs, moving *fast*."

"Yeah. See them. Coming to you." Ry dropped to his belly and crawled across the warm teak deck toward his security guy.

The two small boats looked like fishing vessels, but their speed indicated high-powered motors. Hauling ass, they closed the gap, peppering the space between their boats and the ship with random bursts of gunfire. Automatic weapons. And limitless ammo.

Ry slid in beside Jax and, after a brief glance at his Glock, handed him a high-powered sniper rifle from the cache of weapons on the deck beside him. "Know how to use this?"

"We'll soon find out, won't we?" Ry peered through the sight and picked off a man in the back of the skiff on the left. Jax mimicked his action, taking care of the occupants of the skiff on the right.

From the deck below, Klein's men did their job in lightning-fast succession, dropping the remaining pirates in each small boat with mind-boggling speed.

Between Ry, Jax, and the small military group in the

stern position on *Tesoro Mio*, they made short work of the approaching danger.

Driverless, the two skiffs careened up onto the bank, plowing through sand and vegetation and scattering the men running along the bank. Amid yells and large dust clouds, the two boats burst into spectacular flame on impact.

Jax shot him a grin as they exchanged a fist bump. Like Ry, he was doused in water. "Fucking awesome, right?" His second engineer leaned back against the hot tub surround looking completely relaxed, yet his gaze strafed the banks of the canal. The pirates who'd been following the ship on foot had dropped back as the burning skiffs sent plumes of acrid black smoke into the clear blue of the sky.

Ry set the borrowed sniper rifle down between them, but rested his hand on the stock just in case he needed it again. Heart knocking, sweat mixing with droplets of water on his skin, he felt more alive than he'd felt in over a year.

Tempted to push aside the drapes to see what was happening outside, Addison refrained. The loud sounds of bullets hitting the side of the ship, and the manic shouting of the pirates, told her what she needed to know. She didn't need to actually *see* events as they unfolded.

She paced. Dressed in jeans, a black T-shirt, and her favorite running shoes, with the bulletproof vest on but hanging open, she walked from bedroom, to sitting room, to closet, to bathroom.

It was with relief that she snatched up her cell phone when it rang. If nothing else, reception was good. She sat on the tub surround to take the call.

"Addison." Prince Naveen Darshi always said her

name as if he were king to her serf. Mostly it amused her, but not freaking-well today. "What's this I hear about you departing without us?"

A loud *bang* caused Addy to flinch. "This isn't a good time, Naveen."

"What was that noise?" Clearly alarmed, his voice rose several octaves. "What on earth's happening?"

"We're transiting Suez."

There was a particularly long pause before he said coldly, "So Hollis was right. What impulse precipitated this, Addison? It's extremely inconvenient to change my plans at this late date."

Not: Oh, my God, are you safe? Her mother's priorities were apparently rubbing off on Naveen. It was no more attractive on him than it was on her mother. "You don't have to change anything but your flight destination, Naveen." Addison kept her tone cool with effort as she glanced around her luxuriously appointed bathroom. Warm creams and crisp whites. Marble and glass sparkled and shone, enveloping her in calm luxury. The thick fluffy white rug underfoot had been purchased a lifetime ago with the thought of after-shower hot, wild monkey sex with Rydell.

"You and Hollis are welcome—" *Not really.* "—to meet the ship in Mangalore tomorrow if you like," she told Naveen, who, like her ex-husband, had never had the opportunity to roll around on the thick, fluffy rug. "Or you can go ahead and met me in Sydney in a couple of weeks." She hoped to hell Rydell was telling the truth about this dive. She knew from experience that a salvage operation frequently took anywhere from several weeks to several damn *years*.

"Have you forgotten," he said, sounding extremely annoyed and very upper-crust British, "I brokered the deal for the sale of *Tesoro Mio*, and we're meeting the buyer in *Sydney*, in a *week*?"

She got it. There was a broker fee, a lot of money even for a man of Naveen's vast wealth. Still . . . There was a great attraction to alpha men. But there were many detractions that went along with them. "I'm sorry. But we'll have to postpone that meeting."

Time she'd need to convince Rydell that selling his half of the *Tesoro Mio* was in both their best interests. Addison ran a finger under her edge of the bulletproof vest where it chafed against her throat. She cocked her head to listen. The shouts and sounds of gunfire were petering out. Was it over?

"You're going to stand up someone willing to pay you your asking price," Naveen said, impatient and getting more annoyed, "in *cash*? On a bloody *whim*?"

"It's not a whim," Addison informed him tightly. She didn't like his dictatorial tone; nor did she appreciate being taken to task by yet another high-handed male. *Nor* was she prepared to explain herself to *anyone*. "Rydell needs the ship for a quick salvage in the Maldives. The buyer can wait a couple of weeks, surely?"

"You permitted your damnable ex-husband to *hijack* you?"

Naveen was still furious and resentful that Rydell had stolen her away from him the first time. Addison knew he wouldn't be happy about her ex's return into her life. "Not *me*. *His* ship was hijacked, and this treasure is easy to salvage. It'll be a quick side trip."

"I won't have it."

Oh, really? "Not your cal—" She angled the phone so she'd lose the connection in the marble bathroom.

"Addison? *Addison?*"

"—ear e-ou," she faked. "Mayb—" Always cut someone off when *you* were the one talking. It sounded more believable. With a devilish smile she disconnected him, midword.

"I hope you *do* meet me in Sydney," Addison told the absent prince as she got to her feet and returned to pace the bedroom. "Having you and Rydell on board together for several weeks will make me either suicidal or homicidal."

Going to her desk, she took her laptop to her comfortable easy chair across the room. Annoyingly, the chair smelled of Rydell. "Damn it." He didn't use cologne as Naveen did, but Ry's skin had always had a distinct fragrance that used to make her hot and bothered and want to nuzzle him. All over.

Not now of course. Now the sight and smell of him made her blood boil in a whole other way.

Annoyed, Addison got up and moved to her rumpled bed. There she settled in a nest of pillows and opened her laptop.

Might as well write a couple of blogs while she was holed up in her cabin. She was too distracted to go back to work on the book. But several short pieces would keep her mind occupied until she got the all-clear.

The weekly fashion blogs had become syndicated last year, and she'd built up a sizable following worldwide. Which in turn had placed five of her *Treasures Of* books on the *New York Times* and *USA Today* best-seller lists.

She'd made a life for herself. "A good life, damn it." Addison scowled at the blinking cursor on the screen; it was called a *cursor* for good reason. "It'll be odd not coming home every night to *Tesoro Mio*," she murmured to herself as her laptop booted up. But also liberating to find a lovely apartment. Milan? Perhaps Paris? Put down roots. With Naveen? He was certainly pushing for the happy ending he believed Rydell had stolen from them.

Hands resting on the keyboard, Addison pushed that aside for now. She'd promised him a decision after the ship was sold, buying herself a couple of weeks. It wasn't fair to string him along. He was a lovely man. Handsome, wealthy, titled, and amusing.

Midmorning sunlight, diffused by the soft white drapes, streamed through the large window. She loved early mornings. She and her ex-husband had had that in common. *Naveen* used to like waking up slowly, wanting a quickie before rolling over and going back to sleep. By the time he woke up again, Addison had already completed her five-mile jog, showered, started breakfast, and was well into her day.

Maybe he'd changed in the intervening years? She hadn't woken up beside him since first meeting Rydell, even though he was pushing her to resume their intimate relationship. He'd been doing his best to persuade her for the past year.

They'd have to work that out when they lived together—*if* they lived together. They'd have to—she grimaced—*compromise*. With Naveen there'd be plenty of those. Which was what had prevented her from marrying him the first time around.

A loud volley of gunfire, seemingly close, made her unable to concentrate on creating new content on her blog. She switched gears and went to her bookmarked news pages. Usually she started with the style pages, but a headline popped up, snagging her interest. She'd been following this particular news story for years, and was absolutely fascinated by it. The report was a week old, but news to her.

PROCIONI STRIKES AGAIN. FOUR PAINTINGS VALUED AT OVER €168 MILLION. BIGGEST ART HEIST RECORDED IN DECADES.

A van Gogh, two Monets, and a Degas were stolen from the home of Brigita and Emil Fousek in Devjice, one of the most affluent neighborhoods outside Prague.

The loss of the artwork wasn't detected for what could've been several weeks . . .

"Oh, shit! *This* is what Hollis was bitching about when I spoke to her in Genoa the other day." This time Procioni had struck close to home. Addison knew the Fouseks. They were good friends of her mother's. She and Naveen had accompanied Hollis to the Czech Republic for the wedding of Brigita and Emil's oldest daughter, Eliska, a few months ago.

The Fouseks' palatial home, set in hundreds of acres of rolling hills, was as big as a good-sized hotel, with hundreds of rooms and God only knew how many precious, invaluable works of art hanging on every wall. Artwork Addison privately thought belonged in a museum for everyone to enjoy.

Hollis treated the place like her own private hotel, and came and went at whim. Apparently she'd been there when the theft had occurred. Very inconvenient. Addison shook her head. Interrogated by the authorities? Confined to her room with her belongings being searched? The press? Yeah, Addison could see how traumatic that must've been, and why her dear mother needed a vacation from her perpetual vacations. She still preferred that her mother vacation elsewhere.

She scanned the article. Perhaps Hollis English-D'Marco-Payne-Smithe-Belcourt-Moubray had a mention—nope. How disappointing for her mother.

As in all the other heists, the paintings had been sliced from their frames, leaving no clues as to the identity of the thief. No signature tells, no fingerprints. Procioni—Raccoon—was the name Interpol and European officials had given to a deviously clever art thief who'd struck, frequently and randomly, over the span of five years.

Hundreds of paintings had been reported stolen. These latest were the most valuable yet.

Authorities suspected many more had been taken from private collections and *not* reported. Cézanne, Picasso, Degas—the thief wasn't discriminating, but every painting was highly coveted, and high-priced.

Procioni stole from residences, private collections, galleries, and museums with equal ease. So far to the tune of over one *billion* dollars. Whoever it was had yet to be caught. That was a *lot* of time to elude capture. Speculation was that the thefts were perpetrated by a gang, possibly organized crime. Others insisted it was an individual. The public's imagination had romanticized the robber to epic proportions.

When Addison thought *art heist* she thought of Pierce Brosnan in *The Thomas Crown Affair*, but she highly doubted the thief was that cool and sophisticated. The thefts had caught the public's imagination—and hers as well. But no matter the value of what he stole, he was still a criminal, and as such should be captured and punished.

Addison flinched as a muffled explosion seemed to come from very close, followed by shouts and a rapid volley of gunshots. *Rydell, I hope to hell you're not doing anything stupid out there. I'll be so pissed if you get hurt.*

Worrying about him was no longer her job, she reminded herself. She didn't care—oh, hell. Yes she did. Only inasmuch as she wouldn't want *any* of *Tesoro Mio*'s crew to get hurt. Or worse.

Out of my control. She tried to tune out the faint noises of warfare beyond her walls as she exited the news article.

She made a mental note to call Brigita once they cleared the canal. It must've been scary knowing someone had sneaked into their home and robbed them when the house—as big as it was—was filled with servants and their perpetual groups of revolving friends and no one had seen the thief. Pretty damn bold of the thief. Pretty damn scary for everyone else.

Addison switched gears to read some of her favorite society posts to see who had worn what to which function.

Six

Having worked so hard to tune out the sounds of shouting and gunfire, when the brutal cries and explosive sounds ceased, the sudden silence jerked Addison back to reality. A chill pebbled her skin as she lifted her head.

Silence.

"Good news or bad news?" Leaning over, she pulled the house phone into her lap, but before she hit the button for the bridge, there was a sharp rap at her door. Swinging her feet to the floor, she went to let Rydell in. No one else knocked that way. As if a brief, hard bang with the flat of his fist was enough to gain him entry.

She stood back as he pushed passed her. The smell of hot, sweaty male filled her senses. She held her breath until the moment passed. Damn him. Damn *her.* Why did she suddenly have the overwhelming urge to lick his damp skin? Clearly he'd run his fingers through his wet hair to get it out of his face. In contrast with Naveen's sartorial elegance, Rydell didn't give a damn what he looked like. Yet Ry's rough and crumpled look was vastly more appealing for some annoying reason. "Was anyone hurt?"

"Not anyone on board."

"Good to know. Damage to the ship?"

"Port side's a bit banged up, but other than that we

were lucky. I figured you'd need some fresh air about now."

"I do." Addison's heart ached as she scanned his familiar features, once so dear and precious to her. For a moment she wanted to wrap herself around him, feel the strong beat of his heart and the strength of his arms around her. She wanted to feel safe and loved. She wanted the yawning abyss of the past year to be washed away, and things to go back to normal.

She wanted Sophia alive.

That was a pain no one could ever fix.

"We'll have a late dinner in Mangalore with the dive team," Rydell told her. "Then head out again in the morning."

Addison hardened her heart, her foolish yearnings, and her voice. "I'll have a quiet dinner right here. Enjoy yourself. Goodbye."

"Addison . . ."

"No."

His chest lifted as he dragged in a breath. The wet cloth of his black T-shirt clung to his broad chest and defined his six-pack. As rock hard as his damn heart. "You don't know what I was going to say."

"I don't give a damn *what* you were going to say, Rydell. There's nothing you could possibly verbalize that interests me. I hope you find what you're looking for sooner than your allotted two weeks. Then the only word I require from you is goodbye."

The muscles around his eyes tightened, then he reached out. Addison flinched as he brushed a light finger against her neck. "The flak vest rubbed a red spot right here."

That brief, light brush of his fingers send a domino effect of rippling sensations through her nerve endings, shocking her to the core. His touch no longer had any business affecting her.

Stepping back, she removed the heavy vest, then held it out to him. "Thanks for this. Glad I didn't need it. You kept the castle safe, and the dragons at bay. Bully for you."

"I protect what's mine."

No, you bastard, you don't. "I'm not touching that line with a ten-foot pole."

His shoulders stiffened, as if he were braced for a blow. His eyes went flat. "Are you coming?"

Not only were his head and damn heart as hard as flint, he was impervious to the undercurrents swirling around them. "In a while. There's no need for you to keep track of me. I won't get lost." The *Tesoro Mio* was 160 feet long and 30 feet wide. Three upper decks, two lower. *Way* too big for a single woman. And way too damn *small* for herself and Rydell to share the space.

"Would you prefer we not eat on board tonight?"

"I don't give a damn where or *if* you eat, Rydell. Do whatever the hell you want. As long as you're nowhere near me when you do it."

"Hearing you loud and clear, Addy. But you can't avoid the conversation forever."

"Really? *You* managed to do just that just freaking-well *fine.* Now it doesn't suit me to rehash the past at your damn convenience, and it's too late anyway." She wasn't interested in his explanations. It would be too damn little, too late.

"Will you *ever* be recepti—never mind."

Right. Never mind. Sophie was dead. Talking about her was too damn painful, and talking about her precious baby with Rydell would be picking at barely healed scars with a rusty penknife. "In the quest for expediency: If you think of a question for me, the answer is always no.

See how simple that is?" Of course she hadn't thought that one through quickly enough. Rydell could easily phrase something in a way that her no would mean yes.

Devilish amusement now sparkled in his storm-cloud-gray eyes, but his lips remained sober. Yes, he'd come to the same damn conclusion. Jerk.

"I'll be sure to keep that in mind." Reaching for the door handle, he paused to look back at her. No trace of humor remained. His eyes looked flat and dull, an expression she wasn't accustomed to seeing in him. He was typically a man whose boundless energy was reflected in the shine of his eyes, whose laser-sharp focus seized each moment with verve and gusto.

She looked closer, then shook her head, refusing to believe that she glimpsed anything other than what she expected of him. Must be a trick of the light.

"Get up on deck," he ordered. "Go for a run. Breathe. I'll stay out of your way."

When the door snapped shut behind him, Addison stared at the space he'd vacated. She held the back of her hand to her mouth, trying hard to breathe calmly. He sucked all the damn oxygen out of a room. That was the only reason she felt breathless.

Hours later they docked in the bustling port of New Mangalore, India. The late-afternoon sky, a brilliant blue streaked with apricot and lemon yellow, beckoned Addison to run on deck and breathe in some fresh air after she'd been cooped up all day in her cabin. At Rydell's urging she'd had a long and vigorous run a few hours earlier. She'd chosen the treadmill in the gym, mainly because he'd told her to go on deck, but also because she didn't want his eyes on her as she ran. On deck there were any number of vantage points from which he could see her, and any number of places where she could accidentally run into him. At least in the gym she'd see him coming. But since she'd been braced for him to come in the whole time, her run had been neither fun nor relaxing.

Now, feeling like a prisoner in her own home, restricted, annoyed, and put upon, she wanted fresh air. "Oh, freaking get over yourself." She was starting to sound like her mother. Except *she* only got pissy when she was stressed or around her ex-husband, unlike her mother who was a raging bitch *all* the time.

Damn it, she wanted her old self back—the old self that was typically happy, the person whose default reaction to circumstances and others was something other than knee-jerk bitchy. She wanted to feel again the undying optimism and sense of adventure that had made life fun and exciting. Since her daughter's death she'd been diligently, *consciously*, working on regaining some of her joie de vivre—and then Rydell had shown up and stomped all over it.

She couldn't allow herself to backslide and fall into the darkness that had almost obliterated her. The last damn thing she wanted was to become her mother. Addison *hated* being a bitch. She hated . . . hating. But seeing Rydell again made it impossible not to backslide, because he reminded her viscerally of all she'd lost.

"I will not be a bitch. I will not be a bitch. I. Will. Not. Be. A. Bitch."

Today.

One day at a time. Hell. One hour at a time. She could do this.

Worse than disliking the bitchiness, she knew what waited should she slide back any farther. Bitchiness was just the armor for the darkest despair she had ever experienced, and if she allowed her backslide to continue, she was going to feel the acute, raw, and crippling pain that came with Sophie's death. If she slipped back into that level of despair once again, she didn't know if she'd ever find her way out. Worse still, she might stand on that precipice of not caring if she drew another breath or not.

One day at a time.

One hour at a time.

Fresh air.

If she had space and fresh air, she'd feel more like herself. She wasn't a prisoner, and she sure as hell didn't have to confine herself belowdecks just because her ex-husband happened to be on board and a thorn in her side. The *Tesoro Mio* was as much hers as his to do with as she pleased. And right now she pleased to go for another damn run without Rydell watching her every move like a lion watching his dinner.

Instead of racing up on deck, she waited for him to disembark. He'd be back soon, bringing with him the very last people Addison ever wanted to see again: the dive crew who'd been witness to her greatest sorrow. They'd been with her when Sophie died, and Ry had been nowhere to be found.

Through the large windows in her cabin she observed Ry's departure. He and the security people he'd hired parted ways with handshakes, them into a black, unmarked van, Rydell into a waiting taxi.

His too-long dark hair lifted in the breeze as he turned, hand on the roof of the cab. She swore he saw her there in her cabin watching him. He couldn't of course, the glass had a mirror-like tint on it, but she felt his gaze like a caress. Rubbing her bare arms, she stepped back but couldn't stop watching until he got inside the vehicle and disappeared from view. Did his heart ache as hers did? Did he sometimes—hell, all the time—feel as though he couldn't draw a real breath? Did he ever imagine he smelled the sweet, milky breath of his daughter on the breeze?

Tears burned and her ribs squeezed around her lungs in a vise as she waited for Rydell's taxi to move. The answer to her question was no. Rydell Case was too controlled, too contained, to let his imagination carry him into the abyss. Pragmatic and unemotional, he'd put the death of their child into one of his many emotional vaults, then not only locked the door but thrown away the combination and moved on.

He professed a willingness to talk about Sophie's death because he knew *she* couldn't. A win–win for Rydell. A safe bet, making him look like a grieving father and her like a coldhearted, unyielding bitch.

She was coldhearted all right. Her heart was frozen, and nothing would melt the icy pain of it. She was learning to live with that. Pinching the bridge of her nose to hold back the prick of tears, she waited until both vehicles pulled away from the dock before leaving the cabin.

She practically bumped into her chief steward when she opened the door. "Oops." Smiling, Addy did a little dance step to regain her balance. "I'm going up for a run." Had he coincidentally just been passing her cabin, or had he been standing guard?

"On deck, right?" he said easily. Now that Addison knew Rydell had hired Oscar to be her private security detail, she noticed things she hadn't noticed before. Oscar, Jax, and Patrick had all been with her since she'd commandeered the ship. None of them wore their white crew shirt tucked in as the other crew members did. From whom did Ry anticipate she'd need an armed guard's protection?

She gave her chief steward an assessing look. "Are you armed, Oscar?"

Sharp brown eyes scanned her face. "Always."

That was it. No further explanation. She left it at that. Oscar had always been affable without being overly friendly. Now she noticed his dark eyes were hard and ever watchful. His body language was alert rather than relaxed.

"I wouldn't recommend going ashore, however. The docks aren't safe. Especially here," he said, easily changing the subject as he fell into step beside her. "And never at this time of evening."

She was aware, and that wasn't why she'd asked if he were armed. But she had her answer. "Don't worry. I'm running on the deck." Eighteen laps would give her about a mile. She'd rather run flat-out on a soccer field for five miles, but she wasn't about to go and look for one in a strange city at dusk, and she'd run her requisite five miles on the treadmill earlier. She and Rydell were both runners, and together they'd designed a track on deck so that they could get their exercise outside when they were at sea. At the time they'd laughed that they'd get more exercise in the bedroom and had spent as much time picking a mattress as they had designing the track.

For inclement weather, there was the state-of-the-art gym, with its enormous windows and wide, sliding doors, but Addison preferred to be outside with the wind in her face.

"Want company?" Oscar asked as they started up the polished mahogany stairs.

Not really. But he'd watch her from the deck above anyway. He, too, was a runner, and she knew he'd enjoy a good run, even if it was in circles. "Sure."

They emerged onto the middle deck to the sounds and smells of bustling New Mangalore Port. Located along the coast of southern India, the area was a feast for the senses. The port itself was as unattractive and bustling as any other major port in the world, but beyond the prosaic, the area was surrounded by tall palm trees, with a backdrop of the hazy Sahyadri Mountains. The area showed its rich cultural heritage in the scents and sounds drifting to them on the warm breeze.

With the spicy fragrances of exotic foods and flowers filling her senses, Addison started jogging, Oscar beside her. The ocean zephyr brought with it the smells of brine, fish, curry, and fruit from a nearby market. Golden, late-afternoon sunlight glinted off azure water as brilliantly colored returning fishing boats wove their way through the pleasure craft dotting the harbor. A large oceangoing luxury liner gleamed white and brass as it disgorged passengers for a late tour of the prominent and sacred temples nearby.

The blurred sounds of voices, the throb of drums, and the faint clatter of a train on its tracks served as a backdrop to the rhythmic *thud-thud-thud* of Addison's steps as she broke into a steady run.

"Okay?" Oscar asked, giving her a concerned glance as her feet faltered.

Addison picked up the pace, because life went on despite the pain in her heart. "Sorry. Distracted."

She still had the option of disembarking, catching a flight to Sydney, and waiting for Rydell to bring the ship to her. And her buyer. But that could be weeks, if not months during which she'd be shelling out her profit to live in a hotel. Possession was nine-tenths of the law. As long as she remained on board she'd have some say when Rydell returned the ship to her control. As much as she didn't want to be here, Addison knew she didn't have much choice.

She'd worked up a good sweat, then return to her cabin to—not hide. *Retreat.* A sound plan. Until she heard the throb of helicopter rotors approaching. Shading her eyes, she observed the scarlet-and-gold chopper hovering overhead. She knew those colors and the logo of lions emblazoned on the crest under a crown. *Shit.*

"Prince Naveen is about to land." Oscar didn't sound any more pleased than Addison at Naveen's early arrival. Her mother must've lit a fire under him. Bracing herself, Addison held on to her ponytail as the helicopter hovered off their starboard side.

Always polite and urbane, Naveen would be oblivious to subtle undercurrents. She'd probably be the only person who noticed Ry's strong dislike for the other man. Still, the next few weeks weren't going to be pleasant.

Two dogs, one her.

Addison waved to the blurred faces in the helicopter before it disappeared to hover over the helipad on the upper deck.

"Does Ry know the prince is expect—" Oscar's voice cut off as the sound increased as the helicopter shut down.

"It'll be a surprise," Addison said wryly, heading toward the stairs leading up to the next level. Her steps faltered, and her fingers tightened on the teak handrail.

"Expecting company?" Ry asked directly behind her. She'd *felt* him as he came up behind her. Turning her head, her entire body stiffened even though he stood a good three feet away. He wore navy-blue board shorts and his favorite Oakleys. That was it. He hadn't gone on shore half naked, so he'd come back and changed at lightning speed. She glanced behind him to see where the dive crew was. He was alone. She swiveled to face him head-on.

Miles of tanned, hair-roughened skin gleamed in the bronzing dying sunlight, and his gray eyes were hidden behind his shades. His shoulder-length dark hair flew across his face, and he shoved the strands away with his left hand. A large hand that sported—damn him—a wedding band he no longer had a right to wear.

She hadn't noticed it before, but now it seemed to glow and glint with his movements. Mocking her. Annoying her. Damn it. She didn't want Rydell Case near her. Showing up as Naveen arrived brought a hurricane of emotions. Emotions she didn't want to have to take out and deal with. Out of sight could almost be out of mind. Almost.

I will not be a bitch today.

Seven

I'll try *not to be a bitch today*, Addison amended. "I told you I expected houseguests," she said as mildly as her clenched jaw would allow. She supposed the situation could be more awkward and uncomfortable, but she couldn't imagine how. She turned to go up the stairs to meet her guest.

She wanted Naveen here almost as little as she wanted her ex-husband here. And having her two ex-lovers on the same small piece of real estate surrounded by nothing but water promised to be a disaster of epic proportions. Addison considered jumping overboard now to avoid the fallout later.

Oscar melted away as Rydell fell into step with her. He smelled achingly familiar. Salt, wind, and his crisp-scented soap. "He'll be bored."

Addison tried to hold her breath. "He knows how to amuse himself," she snapped, annoyed that she was so annoyed, and wishing she could be as oblivious, as damn uncaring as Rydell clearly was. "You don't need to come with me. He isn't your guest." Dear God, she couldn't even make it five minutes without bitching at him.

"In a way he is," Ry said easily, not appearing offended by her tone in the least. But then he never was affected by anything she said or did. Emotions bounced off him like bullets off a Kevlar vest. "It would be rude not to at least say hey."

Her jaw ached. "Say hey, then get lost." She'd try for not-bitchy tomorrow. Anyone would be a cranky under these circumstances.

"Is he going to hide in your cabin with you for all his meals?"

None of your damn business. "I won't be *hiding.* I'm on a deadline. I'll be *working.*" They crossed the second deck and headed for the stairs to the top deck. His arm brushed hers, and Addison's steps hesitated for a second before she resumed walking. He was not going to affect her.

She was perfectly aware that her pissiness told him exactly how much he affected her. That had to stop. Her fault. She had to be more guarded around him—showing her pain, her anger, her unwillingness to cooperate would give Rydell the upper hand. She had a dozen valid reasons to be careful around him. His gravitational pull was powerful, and she was damned if she'd fall into that pit filled with spikes again.

The wind blew his hair across his face, and he reached into his front pocket and pulled out a rubber band, then haphazardly gathered his hair and wrapped it. He'd get split ends. Not that she cared. But damn it, with his hair off his face he looked like a modern-day pirate. Bare, broad, and badass. Her traitorous heart kicked up her pulse a notch.

"Where this time?" he asked, dropping his hands.

He was talking about her latest book. Knowing what he meant in shorthand was unnervingly intimate. *Hidden Style Treasures of Rome: A Fashionista's Guide to Shopping in Italy* had been published by a small press five years earlier. Her *Treasures Of* books were considered essential reading for fashionistas before any trip, and made her a very comfortable living. She was now writing book six. "Liguria Region. Genoa. Portofino, Nervi—"

"And your next can be the Maldives."

"I won't be there long enough to do any shopping or research possible cottage industries."

"At least a couple of weeks. But you can always stay longer or go back."

"I'll be too busy entertaining my guest." Subject closed. So much for not being a bitch. It just leaked out of her when she was in close proximity to Rydell. She wished that weren't the case, because that wasn't who she was—most of the time.

Side by side they reached the top deck.

The sleek red-and-gold helicopter looked like an elegant dragonfly as the rotors slowed, forcing them to stand well back from the blades. Addison bunched her hair in one fist as it blew around her face.

Being between these two was going to be like juggling a flaming torch, a watermelon, and a saber. Better if she did it alone. She figured she'd get a lot of writing done in the next few weeks.

Rydell shoved his fingertips into the pockets of his shorts. The drag on the fabric exposed the unbearably sexy V-muscles between his torso and thigh, and a faint hairline of crisp dark hair, proving he was once again commando. It annoyed the hell out of Addison how badly she wanted to touch him there. Just seeing a glimpse of an amusement park she used to have liberty to indulge in whenever she liked made her heart pound and her mouth go dry as her dopamine receptors lit up. That park was closed, damn it.

Returning her attention to the swirling blades, she concentrated on keeping her hair from giving her whiplash.

"You didn't send our chopper to pick up His Mightiness?"

Rydell's joke was combining Naveen's title, *highness*, and *majesty*. It had been funny when they were dating. Now it wasn't.

"He didn't want to inconvenience me," she said pointedly. *Tesoro Mio*'s helicopter, not as big or tricked out as Naveen's, was neatly folded up beneath their feet. "Do *not* shitstir, Rydell, please. This situation is already awkward."

She could see herself reflected in his glasses. Color high, eyes narrowed. Relaxing her shoulders, Addison wiped the anger off her face. The only person affected by her anger or any other emotion was herself. Rydell Case didn't give a damn how she felt one way or another. He'd proven that. For once she was glad he was a machine. Let him do his thing. She and Naveen would do theirs.

"Why would I make trouble just because your lover shows up on my ship?"

Before Naveen stepped out of the helicopter, she spun on Rydell, gripped his forearm, and said furiously, "Don't bait me. Do. Not. Bait. Me. Because whether he is currently my lover or not is none of your goddamn fucking business, do you understand that?"

He didn't try to pull her hand off him. He stood perfectly still, as though shocked by her sudden vehemence. And so he should be. She rarely swore, and she hated that he'd rattled her enough that it had slipped out now.

"And the reason it is none of your business is because that man—unlike you—was there for me when I needed someone. When I needed arms to hold me as I mourned the loss of *our* daughter, you were nowhere to be found." She jerked her head to the helicopter. "He was. So instead of being petty and prideful, think about the fact that he acted with human dignity, kindness, and compassion, while you, you—" She drew a deep breath, as an avalanche of words, dammed up inside her for a year, threatened to spill out and drown her. "—*you* didn't react at all. Think about *that* for a second and behave accordingly."

She spun around, seething, not caring how he reacted or even if he did. He had no right to say anything about . . . *anything*! Whether she and Naveen were actually lovers was none of Ry's business. Ry wouldn't believe the truth if it bit him on the ass. She and Naveen had been lovers—briefly—before she and Rydell met years ago. And as much as the other man would very much like to rekindle that flame, Addison wasn't ready. They were friends. That was it. Good friends. And none of Rydell's damn business.

She watched as Naveen bent to avoid the rotors. He wasn't alone. "Fortunately," she added, vocal cords achingly tight, "it's *my* ship he showed up on. Do whatever you were doing. I'll see to my guest."

Rydell wasn't one to leave until he was good and ready. As though she hadn't said anything of importance, as though her words had bounced off him unheard, he jerked his chin toward the men flanking her guest. "Who are the neckless guys?" he said. "Muscle?"

Naveen went nowhere without a phalanx of bodyguards. Addison barely noticed the three men with him anymore. "*That's* your goddamn reaction to what I just said?"

"This is neither the time nor the place to have a real conversation about that, Addy."

"Make up your mind, Rydell. Either you want to talk about—" *Sophie*, but she couldn't say her baby's name when she was so raw. "—or you don't. But don't pretend to me that you give a flying fuck about the *when* or the *where.*" Damn it, there she went again. Rydell brought out the absolute worst in her. "This suits you perfectly. Another excuse not to face the music."

"Fine. You want to talk about Sophia here and now?" He grabbed her upper arm in the vise of his fingers. "Let's do it. We'll talk. And perhaps this time you won't run like hell like you always do before I speak my mind. How about we try *that*, Addy?"

His finger felt hard and hot on her skin, gone cold with anger. She tried to shake him off. He was superglued to her arm. "Let go of my arm, Naveen is right there."

"What's the answer?"

Addison peeled his fingers from her arm. "Fine. We'll talk."

"When?"

He hadn't removed his sunglasses. Intentionally, she suspected, because he didn't want her to see his eyes. Her own face, reflected in the dark lenses, looked pale and tight. "When we're alone." *And hell freezes over.*

"I'll make the time. Will you?"

Her jaw ached from clenching her teeth, and she took a step to the side, away from everything he represented. "Yes."

They both knew they were lying through their teeth. Rydell because he didn't do "high emotion" and herself because talking about Sophie was too painful and wouldn't bring her back. And it was too late to repair what Rydell had ripped apart.

Able to switch gears a hell of a lot faster than she could, Rydell jerked his chin at Naveen and his bodyguards. "Who does he think he's in danger from aboard ship?"

She looked beyond Naveen to the three men following him with their arms loaded down with his luggage. "A question you should've answered yourself when you hired three men to be my bodyguards behind my back." Not giving him time to answer, she moved forward out of his force field.

"Naveen." Addison held out both hands in greeting as the prince straightened and strode toward her with the assurance of a man confident in his welcome, even if he was days early. "How was the flight?"

He was dressed in a crisp white linen shirt and loose-fitting, beautifully cut white linen slacks. With his even features, black eyes, short and immaculately styled black hair, he looked like a model in *GQ*. He *looked* like royalty. Taking both hands, he reeled her in for a kiss. Addison expertly turned her face so his cool lips fell on her cheek.

"Uneventful, my dear." He released her to give Rydell an assessing look. Naveen was too European and sophisticated to make waves, thank God. "Case," he said by way of greeting in his beautiful accented English. He didn't offer his hand, probably because he figured Rydell wouldn't reciprocate. "Addison tells me you'll be doing a bit of salvaging before we continue on to Sydney. A bit inconvenient and inconsiderate, don't you think? Addison has an important meeting scheduled in Sydney."

Without missing a beat he motioned to the three men with the luggage. "Take those to my cabin and unpack."

"You're in a different cabin this trip," Addison told him, hooking her hand through his arm as they headed down the stairs after his men. Rydell had commandeered the second-biggest cabin, next door to hers, for himself.

Naveen shot Rydell a cold glance without comment.

Rydell fell into step with them as they headed down the stairs, three abreast. Addison in the middle.

"Unfortunately," Rydell said easily, no *unfortunately* in his tone, "Addy can't sell this ship without my signature. And since I need her, that's not going to happen unless she allows me the use of the vessel for this salvage. Inconvenient, yes. But an unfortunate turn of events."

Since I need her . . . He was of course talking about *Tesoro Mio*, not herself. Then why did her heart skip several idiotic beats? God. She was going to be a *foolish* bitch for the duration?

Ry didn't like Prince Naveen Darshi. It wasn't because of his smooth, movie-star good looks, or the fact that he could buy a medium-sized fucking country with his pocket change. He loathed the man for having his hands all over Addy.

Again.

He'd won Addy from Naveen once.

Given her resentment over how he'd handled the aftermath of Sophie's death and how much she loathed him for his inability to comfort her—emotions that were now abundantly clear to him—he doubted his ability to win her back.

Usually he didn't fight battles he couldn't win.

Addy knew it, and he knew it.

Once the dive was over, they'd never see each other again.

The fact that Darshi was well aware of the seething rage inside Ry didn't help matters. He parted ways with the two of them to go back to the conference room where he'd left the dive crew when he'd heard the chopper overhead.

Ry knew where Darshi's cabin was—on the other side of Addison's. Which made her the filling in the sandwich. A revolting thought that Ry shoved out of his brain.

"Everyone settled?" he asked easily as he strolled into the conference/dining room, which currently smelled of spicy foods and beer. The long narrow room sported ceiling-to-floor windows along one side, a table that seated twenty-four, a wall of monitors, and a dozen computers. It had been designed as the command center of the salvage operation. He'd switched it from dining room back to its original purpose.

Hidden inside a sleek black console, the nerve center consisted of hard drives, backups, and a spaghetti of wiring. The surface was used as anything from a buffet to a holdall for dive paraphernalia and charts. It was currently surrounded by his team as they inhaled the food put out by chef Patrick O'Keefe.

"All's good," Lenka Swanapoel said around a large bite of litti—a deep-fried ball of wheat and powdered lentil filled with creamy chicken curry. He wiped butter off his chin as he chewed. The lanky South African could usually be found wherever there was food. Ry had no idea where the guy put it; his frame ran to string bean. The redhead always smelled of zinc and sunblock for his fair, freckly skin. An excellent diver, he'd been on salvages with Ry for close to ten years.

Samuel Hildebrandt, Shlomo Bergson, and Georgeo Arcuri, gathered at the far end of the table, had been with him almost as long. "This looks like a massive drop-off right beside her," Sam said to Ry without looking up from the charts layered and spread out on the teak surface of the table. He indicated the chart with a spread hand. He was missing the tip of his index finger, but his hands were large and competent as he slid one chart out of the way for a better look at the area.

"Hundred feet, give or take." MoMo took a slug from his bottle of Jaipur Pale Ale. "Do we have an ROV available?"

"Yeah." Ry grabbed a cold one from the cooler on the floor and strolled over to the group. "Although we might have to dust her off. She hasn't been used since she was loaded on board more than a year ago. I hope we won't need it, but our wreck *was* pretty precarious when I went down three weeks ago." Pretty precarious as in teetering on the edge of the drop-off.

"She shifted over the years as storms screwed with the currents. She should be fairly stable for now."

"Does it feel weird seeing her for the first time?" Kevin Hill asked as she came into the room and headed straight for the men. Deeply tanned, petite, muscled, and no-nonsense, she picked up Geo's beer and took a slug. With her blond hair in a short tousled pixie cut, piercing blue eyes, and smooth skin, she looked closer to thirty-five than fifty. She'd worked off and on with Ry's team for almost seven years.

She'd been with this group longer than Ry'd known Addy. He knew Kev wasn't talking about seeing his ex-wife again. He shrugged, cradling his beer as he scanned the topmost chart. "I spent so much time on the design, walked through her a millions times in my head—nah. It doesn't feel weird at all. It feels like coming home."

If the *home* was torn apart, dysfunctional, and filled with seething longing for something that had once had been perfect but was now shattered beyond repair. Yeah. Just like fucking home. The sad thing was that he felt better being there, even with Addy so clearly despising his existence, than he had in the year since Sophie's death. Even knowing he and Addy were marching to their inevitable, irrevocable ending, he felt better being in her presence.

Goddamn it, he was well and truly screwed.

Eight

Addison came to the dining room early, purposely sitting at the far end of the table, knowing Naveen would sit on her left. No one was on her right, because she'd asked Oscar to remove the two head chairs. She knew Rydell. At the end and foot of the table for the duration, they'd end up as "Mom" and "Dad" for meals. She'd taken that option off the table. Literally.

Normally Addison preferred eating all her meals outside on the middle deck where a small table was placed closer to the galley. When in port she liked to watch the bustle of happy human activity. When at sea she relished the peace. Tonight she anticipated getting neither.

Usually she had flowers and candles on the table even when dining alone. But tonight she'd instructed no frills. There was nothing romantic about dinner on board with this many people. The pale-turquoise place mats and simple white china looked just as pretty in the bright overhead lights.

With Naveen, Rydell, and the five-member dive team to feed and a hard rain pelting down, tonight they'd eat family-style in the dining room while the weather gods raged outside. She'd get even less peace inside with her ex-husband and current boyfriend in the same room.

She'd taken the time—forced herself—to go and say

hi to the dive team shortly after they'd arrived that afternoon. Reconnecting hadn't been as traumatic as Addison had dreaded.

Lenka Swanapoel had greeted her with a bear hug. He still wore his bright-red hair in a buzz cut, and his pale, freckly skin flushed when she hugged him back. He was as sweet and exuberant as a puppy. "You good, Skattie?" he asked, blue eyes concerned and South African accent thick with emotion. He'd always called her "Little Treasure," and tears stung the backs of Addison's eyes hearing the nickname again

She smiled up at him. "Getting there."

"My turn." Samuel Hildebrandt shoved Lenka out of the way and gave her a friendly hello kiss on the cheek. Shlomo Bergson was next, giving her a tight hug like a child seeing his lost teddy bear at last. Holding her away from him he scanned her face, his swarthy cheeks flushed with emotion. "We love you, Addy. All of us."

"Thank you, MoMo."

Georgeo Arcuri, sexy Italian that he was, let his lips linger as he kissed her hand with a flourish, and her friend Kevin Hill, with tears glistening in her eyes, hugged Addison tightly enough to squeeze the breath out of her.

It had felt good. Better than good. No one mentioned the last time they'd been together, and within a few minutes the trepidation disappeared. They'd all been friends. Once. She hoped they could be again. Having everyone in the dining room this evening would dilute what was sure to be an uncomfortable meal. She hoped that at the least, Rydell could remain civil.

Standing near the door, Rydell—dressed only in black board shorts and attitude—flaunted his broad, tanned shoulders, washboard abs, and impressive biceps. Really? Not even a nod to a freaking shirt? The man loved being naked or *almost* naked. The problem was, Addison lov—*used* to love his body. He had a *great* body, damn him.

She resented the fact that he *knew* she'd always had a weakness for his chest and arms, and back and abs and—damn it. He'd never looked better. Tall, with mile-wide shoulders, tawny skin stretched taut across his chest, and defined abs, the whole package that was Rydell Case looked . . . desirable.

Addison clenched her fingers in her lap as he disappeared from view to dig through the ice in the cooler while everyone milled around finding a place to sit for dinner.

He held a bottle of local beer aloft. "I'm sure there's wine, but anyone want a beer?" He passed bottles of the icy Kingfisher to those who held out a hand. The perfect host.

The only damn problem was her ex was *not* the host on this voyage. Not that it made any difference to the current company. The dive team had always looked up to Rydell. He was a born leader.

With the dark scruff on his jaw, and his hair tied back, he looked bad-boy-rocker cool, or sexy pirate. All he needed was an earring and a cutlass clamped between his strong white teeth.

He was relaxed as he joked with the team. What was he so damn smiley about? Addison wanted to stab him with her fork. But that wouldn't deliver the kind of pain she experienced on a daily basis. He'd never feel that kind of pain. Wasn't capable of feeling that depth of emotion. And oh, God, she resented the hell out of him for that alone. She hated that he had continued his life as if nothing bad had ever touched him.

He was healthy, happy, getting exactly what he damn well wanted without any freaking effort at all. While for her it was frequently more than she could manage to act like a normal human being, let alone *smile*. One day at a time. She'd been told that it became easier. Of course everyone saying that didn't have a damn clue because they themselves had never lost their child. But she didn't want it to be easier. Easier meant she'd forget Sophia. Forget the smell of her milky breath, and the powdery scent of her skin . . . It was an effort to breathe.

Addison gave herself a mental shake. *Be present.*

Chairs pulled out, beers opened, everyone found a seat. Naveen, who'd dressed for dinner in his customary white slacks paired tonight with an olive-colored silk T-shirt, skirted the table to come to her side. He smelled of Versace Eros cologne, a fragrance she liked, but not when newly applied with a heavy hand and in such close confines. In sum, not tonight.

A brief, involuntary glance across at Rydell reminded her of his pure, natural scent. Salt water. Fresh air. Clean skin. His pheromones. The most powerful aphrodisiac ever. She hated him for affecting her so easily.

"Are you settled in?" she asked Naveen under the sound of voices, furious with herself for reacting to her ex's nudity.

"Azm is unpacking as we dine," Naveen told her, indicating that Fahad could fill his wineglass. He waited for the steward to move away before he said, sotto voce, "I must say, Addison, I'm most displeased you chose to place Case in my usual cabin."

His "my usual cabin" sent up a warning signal that she chose to ignore. They were practically engaged, after all. "I'm with you. He should be in Outer Mongolia instead of here. But here he is. *I* didn't place him anywhere. He took over the space without permission. Consider him a squatter till we reach Sydney." She smiled to soften her tone. When Nav's eyes lingered on her smile, his scowl softened. His eyes returned to hers, with a trace less animosity. "It's only for a few weeks."

She accepted him for what most people didn't see. A generous heart and a kindness he hid very well. He could be arrogant, selfish, and childish when he sulked, but instead of his behavior annoying her, she just found it amusing and laughed at him to his face when he got carried away. Perhaps it was because in contrast with Hollis, Naveen seemed almost normal.

Addison was used to moving in rarefied social circles, and had been since birth. She didn't apologize for being born with platinum and diamond spoons in her mouth, either. Her wealth didn't define her the way Naveen's did; that wasn't who she was. She rarely thought about her net worth.

Georgeo, instead of Rydell, took the chair directly opposite her, thank goodness. Addison let out the little breath she'd been holding. The only empty seat left was at the other end of the table, far enough away that she wouldn't have to make banal dinner conversation or, worse yet, share intimate words with Rydell.

"You know I'd be more comfortable sharing *your* cabin, darling." Naveen leaned in close. His tone was intimate, but she was pretty damn sure everyone heard him and that it was more for their benefit than hers. He curled his arm around her shoulders and pulled her against him, his eyes carrying the pending question that no longer needed words. His chest was hard, his arms strong. He always dressed appropriately and adored her. Why was she having such a damn hard time telling him yes?

"I'm not ready," she said, quietly enough to reach only his ears. "I'll give you my answer in Sydney, I promise." She touched his smooth-shaven jaw with her fingertips. "Would you please be your usual, civilized self for the duration, Nav? That will really help. Having"—she was about to say *Rydell*, but changed it to—"all these people on board is stress enough without having tension between us."

He turned her hand, pressing a kiss to her palm. "Your wish is my command."

Addison extricated her hand from his as she shot him an honest look of gratitude. Naveen Darshi was a good, decent man. Proud, arrogant at times, as was natural for a prince, but good. He'd been with her in her darkest hours, and hadn't disappeared when the going got tough, even with all the times she'd gently rebuffed his advances. He couldn't understand why they'd been lovers before, but not now.

She could've told him that just because she didn't have Rydell's ring on her finger anymore, didn't make her feel less married to him. Still, she *was* a divorced woman. She should just bite the bullet and tell Naveen yes now.

Checking that her dinner guests were in place, she indicated that Oscar could bring in the meal, leaving the second steward, Fahad, to pour wine for those who wanted it. Most were drinking beer.

Annoyingly sexy and appealing, Rydell pulled out the remaining empty chair between MoMo and Samuel and sat down. Diagonally across from Addison, and almost at the opposite end of the long table. While they were at a safe distance for conversation, it did nothing to keep him from looking in her direction. Their eyes met.

Nothing warm and comforting and safe about *this* exchange. There was heat, regret, anger, frustration all mixed together into a storm behind sharp, stormy gray eyes.

Addison refused to play chicken and maintained eye contact.

"Why is this particular shipwreck so important that

you had to commandeer Addison's ship so precipitously, Case?" Naveen unfolded the paper napkin with care, as if it were the finest linen, and placed it on his lap. "Couldn't the salvage wait until you had your own ship? What happened to the *Sea Dragon*, by the way?"

Addison tore her attention away from Rydell. She imagined losing *Sea Dragon* had punctured his self-confidence, and he wouldn't want Naveen to perceive him as weak. "It was hijacked five months ago," Rydell told him, his tone flat. "And the reason we're salvaging the *Nicolau Coelho* is because it's there, and I've already staked my claim on it. Salvage is how I make my living, Darshi. I wasn't born with a silver crown on my head. Detouring to the Maldives is merely a short pause on the way to Sydney."

"If you were in such dire financial straits, all you had to do was call me. I could have floated a loan for an interest in the salvage," Naveen said, his words silencing the room. Lower, he added, "A partnership, so to speak. You on your own ship, even one that you rented, just seems like a better option than disrupting Addison's plans." Arm draped over Addison's shoulders, he pulled her a little closer. "Our plans."

Permafrost eyes sent Naveen a chilling look. Addison held her breath, waiting for Rydell's answer. "I didn't need an investor three years ago, and I don't need one now, Darshi."

Was that the truth? After her conversation with Callie the other day, Addy was beginning to suspect that this salvage was critical. He wouldn't have gone to such extreme measures unless he was over-the-top desperate. "Legally," he said smoothly, "this is my ship and I'm using it for its intended purpose." He gave the prince a slight smile, with not a trace of humor. "This will only delay your arrival by a few weeks."

"A few . . ." Naveen leaned closer to Addison so that Oscar could place the hors d'oeuvre course, a small plate of crisply fried samosa triangles, in front of him. The few seconds gave him time to modulate his tone. "It's terribly inconvenient, not to mention disruptive," he informed Rydell. "Your wreck has been at the bottom of the ocean for centuries. It's not going to move while you find another ship for your salvage."

"Fortunately I *have* a ship, so I don't have to waste time making *your* life more comfortable, Darshi. The *Tesoro Mio* is half min—"

"We have an important appointment in Sydney a week from Tuesday." Naveen made the mistake of challenging Rydell. A bad, bad move.

"You won't make it, if you insist on staying aboard *Tesoro Mio*," Rydell told him, his tone chilling several degrees. "And the impending storm could delay us by several more days. You'll just have to be stoic and enjoy our hospitality awhile longer." He paused a beat. "Or take your second option."

Naveen twisted his head to glance at the rain beating against the floor-to-ceiling windows at his back, then turned around again. "A little rain won't delay a ship of this size, surely?"

Rydell's lips twitched before he took a swig from his frosty beer bottle. "Captain Seddeth let me know earlier that we're in for a major storm in a couple of hours." This time he addressed the table at large. "Worst-case scenario, we'll hit the tail end before midnight."

Why was *her* captain telling Rydell about the storm before telling *her*? It was petty and small of her to be annoyed. She had bigger concerns than Seddeth telling Rydell instead of herself about rough weather. She concentrated on enjoying the crisp, pastry-wrapped veggies dipped in spicy tamarind chutney.

They were already experiencing moderate swells and a light chop, with pellets of rain lashing at the windows. Fortunately *Tesoro Mio* had excellent ballast and state-of-the-art stabilizers, but severe wave action would still be felt if the large ship rose and fell with rougher seas in the heart of the storm later.

The dive crew, having just met Naveen for the first time, looked from one to the other, as if expecting the big blowout swirling under the surface of the conversation to erupt at any moment. It wasn't just the impending storm making the atmosphere thick enough to chew.

"The *Nicolau Coelho* was a caravel, right? Not a balinger?" Kev adroitly inserted. Addison wanted to hug her for attempting to diffuse the tension by talking business.

"Yeah, a caravel." Rydell took a small bite of his samosa, which he liberally dipped in the tamarind sauce to obliterate the taste of curry. "It was a long trip from Portugal to India, and balingers were fragile with only one mast and fixed square sails." He took a couple of sips of his beer to wash down his food. He really hated curry.

He used his thumbs to push his plate away. "The Portuguese developed the caravel based on their existing fishing boats. They were agile and easier to navigate, with a tonnage of fifty to sixty tons. They had anywhere from one to three masts—the *Nicolau Coelho* had three. Being smaller with a shallow keel, they could sail in shallow coastal waters with lanteen sails. And with square, Atlantic-type sails attached, they were highly maneuverable and very fast. They were the best sailing vessels at the time."

"No Suez Canal back then, so they went around Cape Horn, right?" MoMo observed as Lenka indicated Rydell's samosa and gestured to himself. Rydell nodded, and the other man switched plates, almost inhaling Rydell's leftovers.

"To where?" MoMo continued, picking up his beer but not drinking. "Must've had something to do with spices, right?"

"The where, Goa, was located in the southwestern region of India." Rydell glanced fleetingly Addy's way. He was either looking at her or gauging Naveen's reaction to what he was going to salvage. "They were loaded with silver to buy precious spices, turmeric, ginger, pepper, cardamom. But word was they'd taken on diamonds while at the Cape."

There was silence as everyone digested that. "There are *diamonds* on board your wreck?" Naveen asked, sounding interested in Rydell's business for once. Maybe he really did hope to invest. Addison doubted that Rydell would want Naveen as an investor; besides, at this point of the salvage, investors would've already signed on and contracts been drawn up.

She wasn't crazy about the idea of the two men becoming partners on any level. Addison sipped her wine and let the conversation about the upcoming dive flow around her. It was a familiar scene: Rydell and his dive team, food forgotten, surrounded by piles of charts and the monitors ready to watch the action below the water when the salvage started. It was odd to be there. Part of, but apart from, the team's excitement.

Rydell leaned back in his chair and draped his arm casually over the back of Sam's chair beside him. "Diamonds are on the manifest, yeah."

The ship did a little roll, and a flash of lightning turned the room white for an instant. Addison loved storms, the majesty of thunder and lightning. Rydell's eyes returned to her face briefly. She remembered a night they'd stood, watching jagged flashes of light zigzagging in the sky, lighting the turbulent waters of the Gulf of Mexico, while wrapped in each other's arms. Some of their most passionate lovemaking had been during the most dramatic storms.

Naveen asked about the estimated value of the diamonds. Lost in her memories, Addison didn't hear Rydell's answer. A low-pressure system had settled over the Gulf. The stormy weather had prevented him from diving. They'd spent most of the following week in bed, or watching the rain as it pounded the waves. They'd conceived Sophia that week. Addison had never felt as safe or as loved.

She wished for a few moments of that bliss again. She wished . . . Closing her eyes she rode the pain until it became bearable. When she opened them again, Rydell was watching her again. Still? His expression was closed. She looked away, pretending to listen to Naveen.

Although the prince faced her and looked lovingly into her eyes as he spoke, she couldn't focus on him. His words had no definition, no meaning. It was like hearing a cartoon character speaking. *Wha wha wha wha wha.*

Oscar returned with a wheeled dinner cart, the smell of deliciously spicy curry wafting into the room as he approached the table. Addison's mouth watered, but when she glanced up, as if compelled to do so by a force beyond her control, it was to observe Rydell glancing down the length of the table, locked on Naveen with the intensity of a heat-seeking missile. "Captain says you'd be clear to use the chopper to get back to Mangalore if you leave within the hour, Darshi."

"Thank you," Naveen said politely as he absently stroked his pinkie across the back of Addison's hand lying on the table between them. "I prefer to stay here with Addison."

A nerve jumped in Rydell's jaw. "Suit yourself."

"I always do."

"If your insistence on staying, despite the storm, and

aside from Addy's obvious attraction, has anything to do with what the *Nicolau Coelho* was carrying, may I remind you, you're a guest on board, and therefore will have no claim on the salvage."

"Rydell!" Addison said, appalled. "That's unconscionably rude, even for you."

"I do not need your salvage profits, Case," Naveen said smoothly. "I assume Addison will receive her share as part owner of *Tesoro Mio*?"

"That's between my wife and myself."

"She's not your wife," Naveen pointed out.

"She's—right. She's not. Our financial arrangements are still none of your business, Darshi."

The air in the room crackled with hostility. Barely civilized, yet poised on the precipice of disaster. Addison was glad they were having fish for dinner, which meant there were no sharp knives on the table.

She did not enjoy seeing Naveen through Rydell's critical eyes. The fact that she also found Naveen's superior tones annoying, annoyed her.

This was the man she was considering marrying.

Rydell had only annoyed her *after* their divorce.

I will not be a bitch.

The mantra was starting to wear on her taut nerves. Maybe she should let it rip and let the chips fall where they may. The thought was tempting. She resisted. A declared war in such close confines wouldn't just punish the main players. Everyone on board would be affected. She bit her tongue.

"The curry is unpleasantly hot, and why are we having two curried meals one after the other?" Naveen asked her, ignoring Rydell's jibe, his annoyance evident as he reached for his wineglass and drained it.

Since she suspected he was more pissed at his old rival's remarks and tone than about the spicy heat of his dinner, she merely shrugged. "*I* like both dishes, and I requested the chef serve them as our first meal."

Rydell hated curried . . . anything. Give him the spiciest Mexican meal, however, and he loved every bite. Addison considered serving hot curry at every meal for the duration. Kevin leaned around Naveen to see Addison. She jerked her chin at Rydell. "Our boy here isn't a fan . . ."

Addison gave Rydell an innocent look. "You don't like curry? I forgot."

"Not a problem," he responded, still leaning back in his chair. Damn it, with his lower body hidden by the table it looked as though he was completely naked. It was disconcerting, and he knew it. She didn't expect formality for meals on board, but it would've been nice if he'd *dressed.*

He shot her a small smile. "I suspect I'll learn to—if not *like* it, at least tolerate it after this trip."

Addison wiped her mouth on her napkin to hide a smile. *Touché.* He knew her well.

Kevin knew Rydell better than Addison did. They'd been together longer than she and her ex had. The thought of Rydell and Kevin in a clinch made an ugly swirl start up in her stomach. Not jealousy. Merely the slight pitch of the ship. But once her thoughts went there, they continued, as she glanced down the table and got a glimpse of his biceps, chest, and brawny shoulders.

Geo, Italian and movie-star gorgeous, was tall, dark, and incredibly handsome. With bright white teeth and a swarthy complexion he was far better looking—not to mention more charming—than Rydell would ever be. Ten years Kevin's junior, he was so in love with her he could barely keep his eyes off her. Addison had never understood why Kevin didn't just admit to herself that she was just as much in love with Georgeo as he was with her. She was a stubborn woman.

Addison liked that about her.

The two women, the only females aboard the *Sea Dragon*, had been good friends once. Seeing Kev again, Addison realized how much she'd missed their easy conversations and laughter. Peri and Callie, her ex-sisters-in-law, were always traveling. It was hard to maintain a friendship over the phone.

Sophia's death had ripped apart more than just her relationship with Rydell. She'd lost all her friends because she'd never wanted to see anyone who'd witnessed her at her lowest point. They, in turn, had been uncomfortable, not knowing what to say and so eventually not saying much at all. Avoiding people, of course, didn't include Rydell, who'd been away at the time. He hadn't been there when she needed him the most.

But seeing the team tonight, Addison realized it wasn't hard at all. In fact, it helped. For the first time in a very long time she caught a glimpse of who she used to be despite the testosterone-fueled negative energy rolling off Naveen and Rydell.

Maybe there had been other women for Rydell since the divorce—or hell, *before* the divorce? God only knew, and so did she, that he had one hell of a sex drive. There was no way he'd been without for an entire year. Hell. Her stomach twisted.

Maybe there was *a* someone. One someone. Addison mulled that over until the thought of Rydell with another woman, someone important to him, made her favorite curry dish taste like dirt. She reached for her wineglass and sipped what she knew was a fine Chardonnay. It, too, tasted off. Sour. If the man would just put on a damn shirt, maybe she could think straight and not lose her appetite.

God only knew she wanted to move as far away as she could from her past and get on with her life. Instead, her past and future were sharing a meal.

"Think this is gonna get worse?" MoMo asked, jerking his chin to the weather outside even while he had his fork raised to his lips.

"So Captain Seddeth says." Rydell stabbed a piece of curried fish with his fork, clearly trying to pretend to his taste buds that it was a slab of rare steak.

Good luck with that, Addison thought.

"There's nothing to be concerned about, however," Rydell placed the loaded fork back on his plate. Clearly pretending it tasted like something else hadn't worked. "He'll take us around as best he can, and if not, *Tesoro Mio*'s displacement hull is state-of-the-art. She'll cut through the seas with strength and elegance like a knife through butter."

Addison heard the pride in his voice, and wondered how hard it must've hit him to hand his labor of love to her in the divorce, sight unseen. But then, for Rydell, *Out of sight out of mind* was a motto. Perhaps it was merely avarice and vanity rather than any real emotion that had affected him. She'd never know. She wished to hell she didn't care.

Nine

Addy rubbed two fingers across her temple. She had pretty hands, and favored a spicy ginger nail polish. He wanted her hands on him, and hurt from the lack of physical contact. God, it was jarring to see her without her wedding ring. Dropping her hand, she resumed eating the spicy fish curry.

Addy knew how much he disliked curry. In any form. *That's my girl. Hit me where it hurts. My stomach.* Ry grabbed another dinner roll and slathered butter on it. He already had heartburn.

Hell, heartburn. Heartache. Heartbreak.

Just looking at her made his chest torque with the pain of missed opportunities. *Damn it, Addy, when did you learn to hide in plain sight?*

Her hair, the glossy color of ripe apricots, was coiled in a deceptively simple knot at the base of her slender nape. It didn't matter what she wore, she always looked polished, elegant, and expensive. Tonight was a simple dress the color of ripe eggplant. The deep purply-aubergine color highlighted her smooth, lightly tanned skin, and made her hair more gold than red. The dress left her arms and shoulders bare, and showed nothing more salacious than her clavicle. Her collarbone turned him on. Her shoulders turned him on. Christ, who was he kidding? Everything about his wife turned him harder than stone.

Starting to bring the roll to his mouth, Ry realized if he ate anything on top of his regrets and pain, he'd choke. He tossed the crumpled roll back on his plate just as the chef walked in.

Dressed in spotless white shorts and white crew shirt, chef Patrick O'Keefe's bitter-chocolate skin showed his mother's African heritage, but his attitude and accent were pure Boston Irish. "And how's the food then?" he asked easily, tenting his fingers on the table.

"The curry is probably far too hot for an unfamiliar palate," the prince responded in his plummy British accent that grated on Ry's nerves like fingernails scraping on a fucking chalkboard. Jealousy aside, the prince was an asshole. Entitled, arrogant, and leaning against Addy like she was ballast.

O'Keefe checked their empty plates with a sweep of his gaze, not missing a thing. "I'm pretty familiar with the palates of my guests," he told Naveen politely. He glanced around. "Anyone else have a problem with the spiciness?"

There was a chorus of nos and sounds of appreciation.

"Let me know if you can't handle the heat," the chef told the prince with a straight face. "I'd be happy to provide a blander diet if you have dietary restrictions."

Kevin, sitting across from Ry, choked back a laugh. Even though his expression didn't change, Ry noticed that Darshi's fingers closed around the back of Addison's hand in a hard, annoyed clamp. "The heat didn't bother *me*."

"Excellent." Chef O'Keefe's expression remained the same, too.

Addy extracted her hand so she could pick up her fork again. It galled the living shit out of Ry that Darshi had

had Addy first. Goddamn it, and was having her *last*, too. Had she been in love with the fucking prince while they were married? While he'd held her in her arms and loved her more than he'd loved anything in his life? Had she dreamed of the prince when she'd whispered to *him* in the night?

Ry caught his friend Kev openly giving the chef an assessing look. In her early fifties, Kevin looked twenty years younger, with a petite, compact body and short, tousled blond hair. She had the laid-back disposition of a California surfer, but beneath her flirty persona was a shrewd businesswoman with an uncanny ability for finding buried treasure at salvage sites. Kevin was one of Rydell's favorite dive partners, and a friend he'd known pre-Addy.

Kevin had the smarts he liked, and the wit to make him laugh, and a sensuality that simmered just below the surface, which she didn't bother to hide. But there'd never been any sparks between them. Besides, his friend Georgeo was crazy in love with Kev, if she ever took the time to notice him.

No. Kevin wasn't the woman for him. Ry preferred sassy, grumpy strawberry-blondes, with long lean bodies and bee-stung mouths.

O'Keefe and Kev shared a smile. The chef was an interesting-looking guy, with a short, compact body, shaved head, and enormous hands; Ry liked him enormously. He'd hired him on before the christening of the *Tesoro Mio*. He and Addy had jointly hired the rest of crew.

She'd gotten all of them in the divorce. The plan had been to make *Tesoro Mio* their home, and the older, smaller *Sea Dragon* would be the start of their treasure fleet. With two ships he'd be in more of a position to thumb his nose at the Cutters, who were always trying to one-up him.

Now *Sea Dragon* was at the bottom of the Atacama Trench, 160 miles off the coast of Peru, and he was on board his dream ship, with his dream woman, in a nightmare of his own making.

Karma was a bitch.

"Chef, your meal is superb, I just love . . . *hot.* The hotter the better. If this is an example of what we'll be eating in the next few weeks, I'll be too happy to ever leave the ship." Kev smiled, eyes sparkling as she gave the chef a thumbs-up. The dinner was the first time the dive team was meeting many of the ship's crew, and Kevin was always interested in flirting with a new man.

Ry cast a sympathetic glance at Georgeo. His friend had been pining for Kevin for years, and despite every rebuff had never given up. He always watched her with a mix of adoration and frustration.

"Tell me what I'm eating." Kev leaned into chef and lay her hand over his on the table between them.

"It's meen gassi. Mangalore fish curry," chef O'Keefe clarified, smiling back at the blonde. He'd picked up on the flirt but was too professional to act on it. Smart man. Kev would eat him up like chum. "A specialty there. All fresh ingredients. Mr. Patil caught the seer fish himself earlier this afternoon. Can't get any fresher than that."

"Unfortunately the meal was not a success with me." Naveen inserted smoothly, indicating his half-eaten meal.

Yeah, dick, so you said already.

Addy rested her had warningly on the dickwad's arm. He'd already insisted the dish was too spicy; now what? "Naveen . . ."

"No, Addison. A good chef remembers the likes and dislikes of the people he serves. He forgot that I'm allergic to onions."

The prince neatly established he'd been on board often enough for meals that the chef knew his taste.

O'Keefe spared him a bland glance as Addison removed her hand. She looked as if she wanted to dig her nails into her boyfriend's thick skin.

Excellent.

"There are no onions in your portion of the meal, Your Highness. I don't forget."

Ry leaned back in his chair, rotating the base of his empty beer bottle on the table mat as he toyed with crispbread he had no intention of eating. The visceral memory of the exquisite sensation of cupping Addy's breast, and the flashing image of how his dark hand looked against her pale skin, gave him a full-body shudder. The bread he'd been holding as he watched all the currents swirl about the table crumbled between his fingers.

"Our dinner put up a good fight," Rydell inserted before Darshi opened his mouth and regurgitated another complaint.

He was damn sure the small smile Addy shared with him was unconscious, but he cherished it just the same. God, Addy—her green eyes met his, softening for a moment at the shared memory. First mate Badri Patil was all of five feet tall, and weighed a hundred pounds soaking wet. Which he'd gotten as he valiantly battled the fish for tonight's meal.

O'Keefe grinned. Patil's passion for triumphing over his catches was well known to Addison and the crew. "That he did. Tough little bugger."

"Fish or my first mate?" Addy asked. She shifted her shoulders as if releasing tension there.

Used to be Ry was the one she came to for release.

Crap. Was he going to have to listen to Darshi and Addy later? A crushing weight pressed against his diaphragm. Maybe he needed something stronger than a beer. No, he definitely needed something stronger.

"Both." The chef straightened. "I'll leave you to your dinner. Save room for dessert. We're closing the galley in the next hour due to this storm." He glanced over at the water speckled on the windows, looking like shimmering diamonds against the dark sky.

"Why aren't we circumventing the storm?" Naveen asked, his tone just short of demand. He'd already complained that the curry was too hot, his wine not sufficiently chilled, and the service subpar; he'd bemoaned the nonexistent presence of onions in his meal. Through all his complaints Rydell had done no more than tighten his fingers around his utensils. A nerve ticced in his cheek as he held on to his temper by a thread, chewing the words he wanted to spew and swallowing them down, all for Addy's benefit.

"You'll have to ask Captain Seddeth that question," the chef said evenly, sparing a fleeting glance at Rydell before nodding to the other man. "If we're still going through the storm come morning we'll serve a cold breakfast. Good night, ladies and gentlemen. Enjoy the rest of your evening."

Kevin waited until O'Keefe left the room and the sound of his footfalls disappeared under the drumming of the rain. "Is he married?" She leaned forward, past Lenka and Naveen, to speak to Addison.

"It would be poor form to seduce a member of Rydell's staff," Georgeo said tightly, his Northern Italian accent thick with annoyance.

"Did I say I was planning to seduce him?" Kevin said, tone sweet, eyes hard as she glanced at him across the table.

"He's not married," Addison told her with a small smile.

Ry wanted to lick that smile. He wanted to run his tongue across the seam of her lips until she opened for him—fuckit. There were shitloads of things he wanted. Wanted wasn't getting. He of all people knew that.

The million-dollar question was how, and the universal answer was before it was too late. But minute by minute as he watched Darshi and Addy he felt his opening at redemption growing smaller and smaller.

Kevin grinned, teeth white in her tanned face. "Hmm. A girl needs a project. I wonder how he feels about midnight snacks?"

"It's impolite to talk about seducing our boss's chef, Hill," Georgeo told her tightly.

"Oh, I'm not *talking* about it," Kev said cheerfully, taking a slice of bread to mop up the last of the spicy sauce on her plate. "Any man who can cook like this must have even more tactile skills I'd like to explore." She compounded Georgeo's annoyance by eating the bread with delicate greed as she held his gaze.

Ry wasn't sure whether to cringe or laugh at this added drama. It only underscored the tension between himself and Addy. Darshi compounded the problem of ever getting her alone. He didn't like this balance on the edge of a razor blade that would cut no matter on which side he fell.

If he didn't retrieve *Nicolau Coelho*'s treasure in two weeks he was fucked. Really fucked. Life was already not half worth living. But if he didn't get the treasure he'd be free of that option as well.

Selling *Tesoro Mio* in Sydney would cut the last tie between himself and Addy. Once the sale was finalized, money in her pocket, she'd continue the rest of her life, Darshi at her side. After that there'd no need for them to ever set eyes on each other again, and then he'd be lost. The thought made his heart thump painfully against his breastbone, and his stomach churn. Belatedly he realized it wasn't the curry so much as the company and anticipating a bleak future that soured his stomach.

With both Addison and *Tesoro Mio* gone, all his options would go to hell in a handbasket. Of course, with both gone, did he really give a flying fuck where he ended up?

The fathomless sea of darkness in which he'd been adrift since he'd learned of his daughter's death would end up swallowing him. Without hope of seeing Addy, coupled with the loss of his ship, he'd have nothing to live for.

Hope for a future with her had been his lifeline. Addy was a born mother. There'd be other children. He wanted them to be his, damn it. His children, like Sophia had been his daughter. The sweet, beautiful baby girl who had disappeared from their lives in one god-awful moment that had turned him into a running-scared, heartless monster. He wanted Addy to be happy again and *he* wanted to be the reason for their happiness.

Gold? Silver? Diamonds?

At one time nothing would have mattered more.

He glanced across the table at the woman who was his reason for living.

Seeing her at the other end of the table, remote and distant, not only from him, but from the world around her, gave him the answer in one heated lightning flash. *Not for one fucking second.*

This was about his life.

All the damn treasure maps and ocean charts in the world wouldn't help him with this one. He'd already found the only treasure that mattered. He just had to figure out how to reclaim her.

Tesoro Mio was capable of speeds up to eighteen knots in calm conditions. And God only knew, Ry wanted to get to the wreck as quickly as possible. But now with the sea running six to nine feet, Tony Seddeth had cautioned against using top speed. The wind was directly on the bow, the ship meeting the seas head-on at twelve knots. Ry trusted the captain he'd hired. While he himself knew every inch of the ship from plans, schematics, and detailed drawings, Seddeth knew her structure and performance from bow to stern.

The floor seemed to undulate beneath his feet as the ship pitched and rolled. Ry lifted his fist to pound on Addy's door, then hesitated before making contact.

Seddeth' s voice came over the PA. "This is the captain. This is not a drill. Passengers and crew please gather in the main lounge immediately. Repeat: Passengers and crew to the main lounge. Immediately."

The Indian Coast Guard had made it in record time.

In various stages of sleepwear, Kevin and Lenka, followed closely by MoMo and Georgeo, emerged from their cabins and headed for the stairs. As they passed him. Kev said, "What hell's going on?"

Ry looked beyond the small group. He frowned. "Where's Sam?"

"Here." Samuel caught up with the others, pulling a T-shirt over his head.

"Get up top," Ry instructed his dive team. "I'll be right there to fill you in." *They* were all okay, and he breathed a sigh of profound relief to see them looking sleepy and disheveled coming out of their cabins.

"Is Addy—?" MoMo demanded, face white as he looked from Ry to Addison's closed door.

Poor bastard had been in love with Addy almost as long as Ry had. "As far as I know she's getting her beauty sleep. Just came to hurry her along. Go ahead, we'll catch up."

After a few exchanged glances, they hotfooted it down

the corridor, then disappeared up the stairs at the end of the hallway.

Ry pounded his fist on Addy's door. God only knew, the dickwad could be in her bed. The last thing Ry needed was a memory of the two of them in a clinch engraved in his brain forfuckingever. Still, Darshi in her bed was a better option than discovering her gone. The hard *thump-thump-pause-thump* of his heart was pure fucking anxiety. Jesus—he really couldn't go there . . .

The heavy door snapped open. Abby, barefoot, dressed in bright-yellow shorts and a royal-blue tank top, face washed clean of makeup, hair brushed up into a high ponytail, looked breathtakingly beautiful and about sixteen years old.

"Why have we stopped?" Her hands shot out on either side of her to grip the door frame to keep her balance as the ship rolled. "I saw the lights, are we sinking?" No panic, just calm and composed. Her tank top had little yellow smiley faces on it.

Ry's relief at seeing her, whole and hearty, was profound. Mouth fear-dry, it took a moment to speak. "Coast Guard. Man overboard."

Olive-green eyes wide, she put a hand to her throat. "Holy shit, Rydell! Did you push Naveen over?"

He almost laughed. *Damn. Should've thought of that.* "No."

"Throw? Shove?" She gave him a suspicious look. "Otherwise persuade?"

At least he now knew Darshi wasn't in her cabin. "None of the above. Captain saw footage of two men in an altercation on the aft deck. One went over." He glanced at her bare, slender feet with bright-orange polish on her pretty toes. Ry almost groaned. He loved her feet. "Want to put on shoes before we go up?"

"No, I'm good. Let's go." She shot out a hand again to brace herself on the wall as *Tesoro Mio* dipped in a trough. Once steady, she shut her door. "Go ahead, I'll wake Naveen."

"If he isn't awake in this storm, he should be after that announcement." He was probably taking the time to style his hair. "The authorities want to talk to the owners first. That's us."

"The lights were the Coast Guard boat? All the way out here in this weather?" She fell into step beside him, the fragrance of her hair wrapping around him with sweet memories. Just the *smell* of Addy made Ry happy. Which was nuts.

"A man overboard?" she said in an unnecessary stage whisper. "Horrific. What a terribly way to die. Do we know who it was?"

"I've looked at the security footage half a dozen times. Impossible to tell who either of them were in the dark and rain. The ship's movement doesn't help." The fact that all the lightbulbs had been loosened prior to the fight was proof that this was no fucking accident.

Ry hadn't had a chance to meet with his security people, Jax and Oscar, yet. But Addy was first on his dance card. And he wasn't letting her out of his sight until the person responsible was caught. "All we know for sure was that two men came to blows. We'll see who's missing when everyone reports to the lounge. Most of the crew is gathered up top already, in anticipation of the arrival of the Coast Guard."

Unless the killer had joined the other man over the rail, he was still on board.

"Are you sure they were fighting? Maybe one guy was trying to hold on to the other when a wave hit."

"Then he was trying to hold him in a headlock." Ry's

tone was dry. They moved closer together to take the stairs. Wanting to touch her, he stuffed his hands in his front pockets.

"Shouldn't you get dressed?" she asked, tone snippy.

He looked down. "I'm dressed."

"Put a *shirt* on, I mean."

He'd stuffed a T-shirt into his back pocket on his way to the bridge, then not bothered to pull it on. "The only royalty on board is your prince, and he's already seen my chest. Didn't seem adversely affected by it."

"Have you been practicing being an ass?"

A loose strand of shiny hair fluttered beside her check. A year ago he would've thought nothing of tucking it behind her ear. Of turning her in his arms and kissing her senseless, there on the dim curve of the stairs. "Nah." He walked beside her, close but not touching. "Just comes naturally." Liberating the shirt, he pulled it over his head. "There. Happy?"

Addy just shook her head, sped up, and reached the lounge door two paces before he did. First Officer Badri Patil, who'd procured their fish dinner, was there with four men from the Indian authorities. They were speaking Hindi but switched to English for the introductions.

The crew stood in one group, the dive team in another.

Patil introduced the four men to Ry and Addy. Paras Sharma, the captain of police, was in charge. Patil offered to coordinate the one-on-one interviews in the dining room and a small library next door. Choudhri and Gollen went off with him.

"Captain is waiting for us on the bridge," Ry told Sharma and his second in command, Varma. "He has the surveillance tapes ready. I'll be interested in your take." Ry gestured. "This way, gentlemen."

Addy stayed by his side as they went up to the bridge. The two officers looked like matching bookends in their dark uniforms. They were almost the same height and build, and walked slightly behind them as they mounted the stairs to the bridge.

Rydell glided his hand up the satin-smooth mahogany handrail he'd had hand-carved by an artisan in a small town in Thailand. He knew every inch of his ship. Had lived and breathed every detail for the two years it had taken to build her. He could navigate every inch of her with his eyes closed. Every curve, every dip, every satiny—

Yeah. His mind went from silky wood, to silky skin. He knew every inch of *that* topography even better than he knew *Tesoro Mio*'s.

"Captain—" Ry announced them since Seddeth had his back turned. The bridge was brightly lit; the sleek bridge system—with its multifunctional workstations, selected navigational data, radar, ECDIS, and conning—gleamed in the artificial lighting. Flat-screen PCs with state-of-the-art components had been selected with particular focus on function, but, damn, it was also pretty.

The windows, pummeled by unrelenting rain-soaked night, were large black squares, reflecting the lights and the people inside. While *Tesoro Mio* sat still in the water, the Coast Guard ship was doing slow circles looking for the man overboard. Their bright lights strafed the room every now and then as they searched the dark water. An impossible task.

Since Ry had left Seddeth, the captain had changed into his formal whites. Looking grim, he turned to greet Addy and the two officers. "Bad business, this."

The slightly older of the two police officers, Sharma, addressed Seddeth after they'd been introduced. "Have you been able to identify the two men, Captain?"

"No, sir, and I'll show you why." Seddeth turned to the monitors. "I have the applicable surveillance video isolated. Location 7F—that's the second aft deck. Time; twenty-three-hundred-fifteen hours. Everyone was supposed to be secured in their cabins in anticipation of the storm."

The second officer cast an admiring glance at the immaculate task-oriented multifunctional workstations and high-tech equipment, then focused on the captain. "Which crew members were on duty at that time?"

"Several were tasked with securing the decks while the passengers ate diner. Haamid Malik, one of our deckhands, was the last to report in after his watch at twenty-two-hundred hours."

"How long has Malik been with you?"

Seddeth shrugged. "I'd have to look at his file, but about seven months or so."

"Anyone else on board for less than a year?"

"Everyone on board has been with us less than a year. The ship was taken from dry dock and put into operation in November last year. Omesh Chauhan has been with us the shortest amount of time. He's our chief engineer. Had to hire a new engineer last month because our other man broke his leg in five places ziplining in Spain."

The officer punched out the information into his iPad. "Anyone else?"

"No new crew members since we did our maiden voyage."

"Can you vouch for your dive crew, Mr. Case?"

"Absolutely. I've known all of them for more than a decade."

"What about the prince and his employees?"

Ry shook his head. "The prince—barely. His employees, not at all."

The officer looked at Addy. "He is your friend, yes?"

"I've known him well for more than five years. There's not a violent bone in his body," Addy assured him. "I don't know his men at all. Well, barely. They're always with him, but unobtrusive."

The man turned back to the captain. "What were your orders re the impending storm?"

"I ordered everyone to stay indoors for the duration as the storm increased." Seddeth finished keying up the video. "Here ya go, then."

"As you can see—" Ry walked up to angle the monitor so it didn't reflect the overhead lights. "—even state-of-the-art surveillance equipment is no match for this weather." Rain slashed in front of the camera lens, obscuring the two blurred shadows as they moved against the rail.

"You have no security lights in this area?" Sharma asked, eyes narrowed as he focused on the monitor.

"We do," Ry told him. "Come on automatically before dusk. The bulbs were all loosened. I imagine you'll find fingerprints."

"Yes, I imagine we might. If this was an accident. But if it was murder, then the killer was unlikely to leave any incriminating evidence. We will, however, check." He keyed up a walkie-talkie and spoke quietly in Hindi.

"If—*if* it was an accident?" Addison's bare arm brushed Ry's as she instinctively moved closer to him. "Dear God. Are you saying we have a *murderer* on board?"

Ten

The search went on for hours. They never did find the body. But then Addison didn't expect them to. The waves were massive, the ocean pitch-dark. The bright lights used to strafe the dark water seemed to be eaten by the blackness and the thrashing waves.

Addy shivered at the thought of the man being swallowed up by the unforgiving, angry sea. A man she may or may not know. Who'd been murdered? Why? And by whom? Did he have a family who would miss him? A son or daughter who would miss their daddy?

Addy couldn't think of that now. First they had to discover who the missing man was, and who had caused him to be missing.

It didn't take long for the entire crew, dive team, and an indignant Naveen to be accounted for. The missing man was one of Naveen's bodyguards, Azm Kapur. Forty-two years old, single, no children. He'd worked for Naveen for thirteen years. The two men had appeared to be inseparable. Addy had seen him dozens of times, always deferential to Naveen. She'd caught the guy giving her a cold, contemptuous look now and then, and wondered if she was imagining it.

Now she'd never know.

And it was the not knowing—how it had happened,

why, or what it would mean for all of them—that twisted her tummy into a Gordian knot. Naveen never publicly showed favoritism; he treated his servants like . . . servants, not acknowledging their presence other than to bark out orders. He wasn't the type of employer Ry was, the type of man who treated his employees like family. But considering how long Azm had worked for the prince, Addy presumed the two men had been—if not friends, at least closer than in the typical employee–employer relationship.

It was scary to know that someone had murdered the man. Scarier still knowing that person was still on board, someone they interacted with every day. *Tesoro Mio* wasn't *that* big. Naveen must be feeling awful.

"I should go and talk to Naveen." Addison got to her feet after she and Rydell had been questioned. Varma had gone down to help with the rest of the interviews. She, Rydell, the captain, and Paras Sharma were still on the bridge. Rain continued to lash at the large wraparound windows, drumming on the glass, making dull white stars out of the outside deck lights.

Despite the stabilizers, the ship dipped and rose at steep angles, making footing precarious. Stumbling, she had to grab the back of Ry's chair to maintain her balance. The heat of his skin permeated her hand, making Addison realize she was cold.

It wasn't cold in the room. Nerves, she supposed. Or Ry was just hotter than hell. The warmth of his body through the thin fabric of his red T-shirt so close to her hand was more marked than usual. Whatever the reason, she withdrew her hand from the back of his chair and spread her feet, better to brace herself for the ship's next rolling lunge.

They hadn't been able to skirt the storm because of the search, and now they were in the middle of it. By the feel of the swells, the storm was intensifying. The wind had strengthened and the swells were, according to the captain, nine to twelve feet. Thank God she wasn't prone to seasickness.

When Rydell had summoned her earlier, she had been watching the flashes of lightning and the undulating waves. Addison doubted anyone could've slept through this, and it had taken mere minutes for everyone to assemble in the lounge.

As she turned to see who'd banged into the door as he entered the room, Addison staggered with the rise and sudden drop of the ship as it crested a huge wave. Before she could grab something to keep from falling, Rydell grabbed her hand, tethering her in place beside him. "The police are talking to Darshi now."

"Yes, *shrimati*," the middle-aged officer told her. "*Raajkumaa* Naveen and his other two servants are all being questioned privately, and individually, as we speak. It might be some time now. You are free to go. If we have further questions for yourself and your husband, we will wait to the morning."

Addison wriggled her fingers free of Rydell's firm clasp. The tension lashing at her inside matched the storm raging around the ship. She hated that she loved the feel of his strong fingers clasped around hers. Hated that the sight of his broad chest still turned her on. Hated that she freaking hated him, because *loving* him had always been so easy. Hating him was such freaking hard work.

She hated this person she became around him.

"He's *not* my—This is *my* ship, and I won't be retiring until I know what happened tonight."

"The inquiry might take several days."

Rydell sat up straighter. "Several days?" He fisted his hands and then opened them again with great effort.

"This storm is already taking us out of our way. Delaying us by a full day." His voice sounded tight, and Addison shot him a sideways glance.

The hair on the back of her neck prickled as something stirred in her subconscious. *Why is this salvage so damn important to him? Why* this *salvage, why* now *on this tight time schedule?* His sister-in-law Callie was worried about him, and she'd urged Addison to call his sister Peri. Now Addison was sorry she hadn't tried harder to reach Peri. She knew enough about Rydell to know he did nothing casually. Everything he did had a purpose or an ulterior motive.

"Are you saying we can't continue our trip while you investigate?" her ex asked Officer Sharma.

"I've ordered our ship to accompany your ship to Malé," the older man informed him. "We will remain on board. No one may leave the ship until we've thoroughly investigated this situation. Unless you'd like to turn around and return to Mangalore?"

"No. This is more contained." Rydell got to his feet, towering over Addison beside him. As frayed as her nerves were, six three of mostly naked Rydell was almost more than she could take right now. "I'll have Oscar make sleeping arrangements for you and your men. If you need me, I'll be available. Captain Seddeth will contact me." He took her upper arm and practically dragged her from the bridge. "Come on, Addy."

It was like being swept up by a hurricane as he propelled her down the stairs. *Come on, Addy? Come on where?* "Where do you th—"

They headed for the forward lounge. Members of the dive team were gathered around the large slab of the American walnut floating coffee table, each with a steaming mug of coffee. They'd gone from asleep to wide-awake, and were in various forms of dress.

"There *is* nowhere for more people to bunk," she pointed out as they crossed the room.

"We'll figure it out." Rydell pulled her in after him as if she were a damn tug toy. "I need to speak to Oscar."

Addison half turned, trying to uncouple their fingers. He wasn't holding her tightly, but their hands remained clasped. While his grip on her was annoyingly possessive, it also reminded her of his strength, of the way he always protected the women in his life. Peri, Callie, and at one time herself.

But those days were gone. She didn't need Ry, or any other man for that matter, to protect her or be her champion. She was better off on her own. She never ran away; she never broke her own damn heart. She was always there when she needed strength. "Then I'll say good night now."

He glanced at her, eyebrow arched "Addy. Humor me. Please. There's a murderer on board. I can't have you going off alone. Not now. I'll walk you back to your cabin in a minute."

Suddenly, like a lightning bolt, Addison knew she could never marry Naveen. Or maybe there was nothing "lightning bolt" about the thought at all. If she loved Naveen, if she wanted to be with him always, she wouldn't have been putting it off—putting *him* off—for all this time.

Years ago they'd been lovers, and even back then he'd pressed for marriage, and even back then there was a small voice in her head that resisted. Maybe that's why, when she'd met Rydell, she'd been able to fall for him so hard and so fast.

Spending the rest of her life with Naveen wasn't an option, because she'd always be comparing him to Rydell, and he'd never measure up. Oh, in some ways, Naveen was a better man. But on the things that mattered to her, the things that made Rydell unforgettable, Naveen couldn't compare. Like how Rydell could inspire a roller coaster of emotions with just a glance of his fog-gray eyes. Like how Ry didn't bother to hide his opinion. Like how he was a man guided by instinct, and how he'd risk everything to follow his instinct. Like now—when his instinct told him to protect her, when really, all she'd done ever since he'd gotten on board was be a royal bitch to him.

What she needed, more than marrying Naveen, was to find another man like Rydell. She might spend the rest of her life looking for the man who could compare favorably with him, but nothing else was going to help her get over him.

God, what horrendous timing. She couldn't tell Naveen now, of course, but when the dust settled, when they reached the dive site, she would. Flexing her fingers, she tried to break free. She needed to be alone. Needed time to sort through the roller coaster of her emotions. She needed—damn it—to be away from the force field that was Rydell Case.

Her reluctance to be pulled along with him was, apparently, immaterial. His fingers remained clasped between hers, and her feet keep up with him because otherwise she'd fall on her ass.

Ry spotted Oscar across the room, talking with Kevin and Georgeo. "You'll wait for me?"

She nodded.

"Oscar, *tengo que hablar con usted.*"

Oscar came to Rydell's side immediately. They had a brief, quiet conversation. Addison, intrigued, watched the two men as if she were at a tennis match. She might not speak Spanish, but Rydell was emphatic, and Oscar seemed to be agreeing with him.

"Just need to talk to the team and fill them in." He

steered her over to where they sat. Without preamble, he said, "The man who went over was one of the prince's bodyguards. Surveillance footage clearly shows a fight. Someone threw him overboard. There's no question it was deliberate."

"Holy fuck," Lenka said, his buzz-cut red hair fiery in the overhead lights. Bare feet propped up on the huge coffee table, he wore a prison-striped blue-and-white pajama bottom and a white undershirt. He sat forward. "What kinda douchenozzle would do something like that?"

Rydell's biceps brushed against Addison's upper arm, sending an electrical current through her body. She felt an intense need for self-preservation and shifted in his hold again. But his fingers remained twined through hers, and he didn't release her. Her heart did a few calisthenics. She reminded herself they were no longer together, and why. Her heart didn't give a flying crap. It beat harder. A quick sideways glance up at his face showed that he was oblivious. Thank God.

"We have no suspects," Ry told his dive crew. "Which pretty much means everyone on board is a suspect."

"Come on, Ry." Samuel sounded annoyed as he gestured to the small group with the hand with the partially missing index finger. "Surely you don't think one of us had anything to do with this?" Unlike the others in their rumpled, just-out-of-bed attire, Samuel wore navy shorts with a neat crease, a light-gray T-shirt, and sandals.

"Of course not. But someone tossed that poor bastard overboard. And until the cops figure out who, we're all along for the ride."

Everyone sat forward in their chairs, eyes trained on Rydell. Georgeo, sitting on the arm of Kevin's chair, put a hand on her shoulder. She didn't shrug off his touch as she usually did, but looked up at him as he said grimly, "You're saying we have a killer on board?"

Rydell looked from one to the other and nodded. "I know *this* for sure. That man didn't *jump*. He wasn't even pushed. He was lifted and *tossed*. So yeah, we have a fucking killer on board. I suggest no one wanders around alone, and I sure as shit advise no one to go out on deck in this weather.

"The Coast Guard officers are remaining on board until we reach the Maldives. The alternative was to return to Mangalore and remain there until they finish the investigation. Cooperate in any way you can so that we can get this resolved as soon as possible. I trust each one of *you* implicitly, and you can trust both Jax and Oscar. Good men. Security specialists I hired last year to keep an eye out for Addy. They're both armed, and will be doing their own investigation. Go to your cabins, get some sleep. This storm should be behind us in about four hours. Either myself or Seddeth will keep you apprised as the situation is updated."

"You won't object to me carrying." MoMo didn't phrase it as a question.

"I don't object to any of you carrying as long as this doesn't turn into the OK Corral. Keep your weapons out of sight. For now."

"Kev, bunk with me until this is sorted out," Addison offered. She didn't like the idea of her friend being alone at the other end of the ship, and knew her friend had a similar stance on guns. Neither woman liked them around. But right this minute Addison was thrilled that so many people on board were armed and knew how to use a gun.

Georgeo's hand tightened on the blonde's shoulder. "She won't be alone."

Kevin peeled his fingers off her shoulder but didn't move otherwise. "I'm not having sex with you, baby boy."

Addison bit back a smile. Kevin wasn't rejecting Geo's offer. "My offer stands," she told her friend. It was good to have options.

"You good with that?" Rydell addressed Kevin. She gave a small nod, not looking too happy, but not rejecting the idea out of hand. He turned to Addison. "Georgeo will watch Kev's back."

And her front. But Addison didn't point out the obvious. They were adults, they should be able to share a confined space for a few hours without coming to blows.

"*Addison* will be alone," MoMo pointed out with a frown, his Polish accent thicker when he was tired. Short, stocky, and muscular, he already had a thick shadow blurring his lower jaw. His curly black hair stood up around his head like a halo. He had a habit of combing his fingers through it when he was frustrated or nervous. He was like a big, hairy teddy bear, and Addison gave him a reassuring smile. His cheeks flushed when he smiled back.

"She won't be." Rydell glanced at Addison with steely eyes glittering with certainty—of what? Promise? Threat? Voice suddenly husky, he said, "Ready?"

Oh, I've heard that *voice before. Ready? To be alone with you? Not just no, but hell no.* "I'd appreciate you walking me as far as my door," she told him pointedly.

His lips twitched as he extended his elbow like Fred Astaire. A buff, semi-naked Fred Astaire. She ignored it, and him, and after saying good night to the others left the lounge, footsteps even. It only *felt* as though she were running for her life on the inside.

Addison had no idea why her heart was pumping so fast as she crossed the lounge.

Fear? Logical. There was a killer on board, after all.

An anxiety attack? Unprecedented.

Anticipation? Un-freaking-acceptable.

She walked faster.

If Ry followed, awesome. He might save her from the killer. If he stayed in the lounge, yakking to his best buddies until sunrise, double awesome. She'd get to the safety of her cabin untempted. Either way she'd be happy as long as she got to close a solid door between them.

"Hey, hold up." So much for her strategic retreat. Rydell caught up with her as she started going down the stairs. She held on to the teak bannister to keep her balance as the ship rocked and rolled.

"You could've stayed up with them," she told him, feeling the heat of his all-but-naked body down her back. She fought the urge to step closer to him. One touch, and she wouldn't let go. "I'll be asleep the second my head hits the pillow."

"No, you won't." He glanced over at her. Damn him. He looked at her body like he was drinking her in, and her body responded to the touch of his eyes by tingling with anticipation, forgetting what her mind was ordering.

Not. Going. There. Not!

You'll stay up for the rest of the night and mull," he told her. "You'll analyze everyone on board and try to figure out who our killer is."

He was, of course, right, damn him. It galled her that he knew her so well.

"And I'll be doing the same thing," the arrogant bastard informed her. "We'll be doing it together, because until this guy is identified and caught I'm not letting you out of my sight."

He was aware of how high-handed he sounded, but didn't give a flying fuck. Addison gave him a hostile look. "That's not necessary. I'm no longer your concern. I'll lock my d—"

"Addison!"

Well, fuck. Good ol' Prince Darshi to the rescue.

Ry had the instant sensation of going from light to heavy. He fought the urge to tell the prince to go back to bed, because the words were going to sound just as petty and spiteful as he would intend them. And, yes, the words were going to reveal just how damn scared he was about losing. Like a sixth grader on a playground who knew he stood a damn good chance of losing a fight. Like he'd felt when his boat was seized by pirates he couldn't stop. Like he felt when he thought of the rest of his goddamn life without her.

Addy's my concern. Not yours. Not yet, not ever.

Cold sweat broke out on his chest. Yeah. She *was* his concern. She was his . . . everydamnfuckingthing. Addy stopped, turning to greet the prince with a smile that set Ry's teeth on edge and bored a hole straight through his core.

"Naveen." His wife held out both hands. "I'm *so* sorry. Is there anything I can do?"

Not his wife, Ry reminded himself.

Not. His. Wife.

Not anymore.

Yeah. That sucked the big one. He didn't pretend, even to himself, that he wasn't jealous as hell. It ate at him. Was a living, breathing, manifestation of all that was wrong with his world.

Masochist that he was, he stayed close enough to read their microexpressions, close enough to observe the prince's face.

Darshi gripped Addy's hands in his well-manicured fingers and reeled her in. Her ponytail bounced on her back, and one of the skinny straps on her tank top slid down her arm. Before he repositioned it, she did it herself.

Ry didn't step out of the way in the narrow corridor, so they were sandwiched in like sardines in a ménage à trois.

"Nothing, thank you, darling," the prince assured her. Like the rest of them, he'd been woken to report to the police at the butt crack of fucking daybreak, yet he looked shower-fresh, hair slicked back, eyes bright, white linen pressed. Hell, he'd even taken time to dose himself with cologne. And Ry was certain that wasn't for the local law enforcement's benefit.

"He had no family," the prince told Addy. "So there's no one to contact. It's troubling that we have a killer on board." He slanted Ry an antagonistic glance. "Nothing untoward happened *before* Case and his motley crew came on board. I'm sure once the Coast Guard investigates further they'll discover some nefarious connection between one of *them* and Azm. Trust me," Darshi drew one of their clasped hands to his face and kissed her fingers while looking deeply into Addy's eyes.

"Naveen—" she said warningly. But she didn't look annoyed or even mildly cranky that he'd cast aspersions on everyone else on board. It was just a polite murmur of correction.

Ry's chest hurt looking at them together. They were the unit he and Addy had once been. The unit he wanted back with every fiber of his being.

"*Nothing* is going to happen to *you*," Darshi told her. "I'm not going to leave your side until this matter is resolved, and even then . . ." His attention flicked to Ry, and his tone changed. "This is a private conversation, Case."

"And not that interesting. Addy and I were in the middle of a far more compelling convo when you showed up. Wanna fight for her?" Fuck. That just came out. Addy was going to turn around and punch him. Instead, she muffled a laugh.

Ry let out the breath he'd been holding for the last few minutes. She'd laughed. His world tilted sideways. He'd begun to think his memory had been playing tricks on him when it recalled how magical her laugh could be. It hadn't. Her laugh was even better than he remembered. Water on a dying, parched plant. And greedy bastard that he was, he'd do anything to hear more of it.

"Childish. But typical," Darshi said smoothly before turning his attention back to Addy. "I'll wait for you in my cabin, darling." He brushed her chin with his fingertips then slid between them and headed to his cabin one door down from Addy's.

Douchebag.

The prince thought he could have anything he wanted with a flick of his fingers. Including Addy. *I'll wait for you in my cabin, darling.* Hah. *Over my dead body.*

Addy slipped her keycard into her door. As the door clicked shut on the prince's cabin, the asshole on the correct side of it, Addy said lightly, "I'd pay good money to see the two of you rolling around on the floor fighting for my honor."

The door opened, releasing Addy-scented cool air and revealing her dimly lit cabin. He knew she'd been watching the storm before he'd knocked earlier. They both loved observing clouds boil and wind whipping the waves. For storm-watchers tonight was a doozy. The floor beneath his feet pitched with high surges, strong enough that he had to brace a hand on the wall to keep his balance. Unfortunately, he wasn't sure it was just due to the storm. Addy had him off kilter.

Preceding him into the cabin, she stopped just inside as he closed the door behind them. His heart stuttered when she didn't instantly give him a hard shove and order his ass out.

Walking partway into the cabin afforded him a delectable view of her ass in the yellow shorts that showcased her long, long legs. She turned, and they were a couple of feet apart in the dimness.

Ry's senses were overwhelmed by the nearness of her; by the clear oval of her face with her hair pulled back and swinging down her shoulders. "Who'd you bet on?" His voice sounded thick to his own ears, yet he managed to make it sound like he was joking. Her fragrance wrapped around him like gardenia-scented bonds.

Jesus. This was like prodding a sore tooth. He knew it was going to fucking hurt; why did he keep on doing it? Because pain when he was *with* Addison beat the shit out of the hell he lived in without her.

"Naveen would never resort to a fistfight."

"Swords at dawn, then?"

She didn't smile, but the tension around her eyes eased some. Her lips were the same color as he remembered her nipples were, a soft, pale pink. His mouth watered, and his dick stirred.

"Of course not."

Of course a physical altercation wouldn't happen. Darshi was a lot of things, but uncivilized wasn't one of them. He was probably a decent guy. Ry should really stop baiting him. It wasn't the most mature behavior. But when he was around Addy he felt like a randy sixteen-year-old with only one thought on his mind.

Mine. Mine. Mine.

"Not even for you?" He couldn't keep the joke in his voice. The stakes were too bloody high.

The almost-smile drifted from her face. "Not for anything."

"Then he's a fool. Because I'd fight for you like"—he drew a deep breath—"like my goddamn life depended on it."

She closed her eyes as if he'd struck her, and the color

left her cheeks. With words that were barely a whisper, she looked at him with pain-filled eyes. "But you didn't."

Her words couldn't have been more crushing if they were a five-ton anchor on his chest. Words screaming of her pain and anguish and all the hurt they inflicted on each other.

She was the one who wanted the divorce, but now wasn't the time to point out that that ball had been in her court. Yet he had to lock his knees to keep from falling to them and begging her to forgive *him*. For *anything*. Fuck, for everything. Who gave a fuck who was at fault? They were beyond that. "I'd kill to win you back, Addy."

Eleven

Ry stepped closer. Addy didn't retreat, but her eyes narrowed fractionally as she looked up at him. There was no anger, no heat, nothing. He had enough for both of them.

This close he saw things he'd almost forgotten: the small beauty mark she insisted was a freckle under her left eye. The three freckles on her nose. The tiny scar bisecting the outer tip of her left eyebrow that she'd gotten when she fell on the playground at her fancy Swiss boarding school at age six. The soft, rosy flush of her cheeks when she was either mad or aroused.

The need to map her contours again was overwhelming. His fingers flexed, but his hands remained at his sides. Unconsciously he leaned forward a little, as if drawn by a magnet. "I don't like him touching you," he said, voice thick with a need he didn't bother to hide. Because he couldn't help himself, Ry used a fingertip to rearrange her hair so it fell behind her shoulder. The strands felt cool, the scent of flowers intoxicating. He dropped his hand as if he'd been burned. It was too little. It was like seeing a delicious cake and not being allowed even a small taste.

Inhaling sharply, she bit the corner of her lower lip. Something he desperately wanted to do himself. A shallow exhale. Then no breath at all as she held it. Self-calming, he knew. He could've told her it wouldn't work. Because, just as acutely as he was aware of her, he knew she felt the same way. It was in the dilation of her pupils and the rapid throb of her pulse at the base of her throat.

Ry had never waited for permission for anything in his life, but even though it was killing him, he waited now.

She could've pushed him away. But she didn't. She could've stepped back, away from him. But she didn't. There were a dozen things Addy could've done that would've stopped him cold. Hell, she was capable of freezing him with a word or just a look. But she gave no signal for him to halt.

Instead, her gaze met his, direct, unflinching, as she said softly, "He doesn't."

Naveen didn't touch her? "Since when?"

How was *not* kissing her more carnal than stripping her naked right now? He craved her like a man with five minutes of air left in his tank, and ten minutes to go before surfacing.

"Since the day I met you on board the *Sea Dragon*. You were all scowly and gruff and needed a shave. And I'd never been attracted to a man with a ponytail before."

Yeah, there were about a hundred levels of class distinctions between high-society Addison D'Marco and salvager Rydell Case. She was as beautiful as a fairy-tale princess, and she'd already had her very own real-life prince.

He'd known just looking at her that he was outclassed and outmatched. He hadn't given a flying fuck. He'd wanted her as he'd never wanted another woman. Before or since. Nothing. Not a damn thing had changed.

"That was more than three years ago," he said gruffly. "You took my breath away. You were wearing a yellow dress with little black birds on it, and sky-high fuck-me pumps. I didn't give a shit that you were destroying my decks with those heels. I wanted to strip you in the sunlight and see if you were as perfect as my imagination insisted you were under your clothes." Unable to resist, he slid a strand of her hair between his fingers. "I wanted those high heels digging into my ass as I pumped into you. I had to be content with my imagination. You went home with him that day."

"I *left* with him, and broke up with him in the car, before he even got me home."

Yeah, he knew that. It had made Ry feel like a bloody king when she'd come back six weeks later. "You've been seeing him again this past year." He knew. His spies on board kept him apprised of Addy's comings and goings with the prince. His Mightiness spent a *considerable* amount of time on board *Tesoro Mio*. In the cabin Ry now occupied, as it happened. Right next door to hers.

"Seeing."

"No sex?"

"You have no right to ask me that."

Fuck rights. "No sex?"

The ambient light from the table lamp behind her cast a copper nimbus around her hair as she shook her head. Being alone with her made him feel alive again. Whole again. Feel hope again after their soul-sucking divorce.

He had no doubt it was temporary. He knew it. But fuckit, he didn't give a shit. He'd take the relief, the lightness, the cessation of the crushing pain that had dogged him for the past year even if it was ephemeral.

Somehow, hell if he remembered putting it there, his palm cupped her warm cheek. Silky strands of cool hair clung to his wrist. Her beautiful eyes looked fathomless.

"I never stopped loving you, love. Not once. Not for a nanosecond." The words, low and intense, were wrenched from deep in his gut, unfiltered and intemperate. He said them anyway, because he couldn't not. "I loved you from the moment I first saw you, and I'll love you until the day I die."

Throat working, she squeezed her eyes shut for a moment. When she opened them again they were all pupil. "Damn you, Rydell Case. I'm not strong enough to fight both of us." Stepping into him, Addy wound an arm around his neck, drawing his mouth down to hers. Her tongue touched his, and his body ignited in response. His thrashing heartbeat matched the intensity of the storm raging outside.

For now, this was enough. For now, it was everything.

When he reacted to her like this, with sheer carnality, Ry forgot how smart and sassy she was. He forgot that they had mountains of serious issues creating a chasm between them; he forgot that he had shit going on in his life that seemed insurmountable. He forgot everything other than the feel and taste of Addy. All the world narrowed down to just the woman he loved.

Her lips, slightly parted, moist and free of lipstick, had tempted him in his dreams for over a year. Now her mouth, damp, lips silky smooth and pliable, opened under his. *Addy . . .* Ry's heart beat triple time as he crushed her against his chest.

Bed; less than eight feet away. Too damn far.

She tasted of the coffee she'd drunk on the bridge earlier. The coffee that was going to keep her awake for hours. Which, under the circumstances, was most excellent.

Her mouth was as eager as his as they kissed ravenously. Teeth, tongues, lips. Familiar. Perfect. The wet slip and slide of their mating tongues caused his dick to stir, and he rubbed the hot, pulsing need into the juncture of her thighs, knowing how it had made her react once upon a time. Her low moan shot his arousal up another several notches.

He couldn't get close enough. The soft pillows of her breasts flattened against his chest as he gathered the silky mass of her hair in one hand to hold her. Tether her. Keep her.

A harsh sound of need came from his own throat as he tightened his arm around her, tasting her, memorizing the moment for the fleeting reality of it.

Her back hit the wall with a dull thud.

Her mouth was hot, the inner lining of her lips slick and sweet. He felt the exhale as her breath left her lungs in a ragged sigh. Tipping her head to rest on his shoulder, Ry crushed her mouth with his own, temperance forgotten. He kissed her as if it was their first kiss. The feverish intensity came back in a rush of emotions and a flood of greedy need.

The hard knock of her rapid heartbeat under his palm felt like a small trapped bird. Her nipple was already hard. He knew how sensitive she was, knew exactly how much pressure she wanted as he pinched the erect bud between his fingers.

He burned for her. Lusted for her to the point of insanity. Dropping his hand to her waist, he shoved his fingers up under her tank top with the happy smiley faces on it. Hot, silky muscles flexed beneath his touch. Her bra was no match for his desperate fingers, and he yelled a silent hallelujah that she still wore front-closure bras as he made fast work of the clip, to cup the heavenly weight of her breast.

She kissed him as if she'd die if she didn't. God, he could relate. God, he loved the sounds she made, a happy bliss-filled murmur. He wanted to hear more of it. It made him feel . . . Ry didn't have a word for it. He didn't even have a place for the feeling, but it spurred him to hold her more tightly as he kissed her again.

Lightning flashed behind his closed lids. The ship rolled. Thunder boomed. His heartbeat sounded louder in his ears. Everything he remembered about loving Addy flew out the window. The height and breadth of her sexual desire as she reciprocated sparked a heightened need in him that went beyond even the magic of his memories.

Aroused to a fever pitch, he knew no other woman could compare. He hadn't even tried. He burned for *her.* Craved only *her.* Lusted, with an unrelenting hard-on. *Only* for her.

His free hand slid over her arse, firm muscles tensed under his hand. Thin cotton the only barrier between him and what he needed. *Later.* Now he had to be tight inside her. Needed to drive into her to satiate this unbearable longing he'd held in check for so long. He slid his fingers to the zipper, and she shifted to grant him access.

Her arm uncoupled from his neck, and she shoved her hand down between them, fighting him to be the first to get her zipper down. Since her fingers were more nimble than his in this instance, Ry tackled his own zipper, shoving his board shorts down his legs and stepping out of them and into her. Addy only managed to get her zipper down; it was Ry who made short work of stripping shirts from their torsos and a thong down her smooth legs.

His hand went back to the clench of her ass. Smooth skin, living muscle.

Need.

Want.

Hunger.

She curled her leg over his hip. Gripping the flexing muscles in her ass, Ry yanked her even closer, thrusting up inside her in one powerful stroke. He was home. This joining was familiar . . . what he'd wanted for so long . . . now he had it . . . at this moment . . .

The sensation was exquisitely painful. So sweet, so sharp. Almost unbearable, but he stopped moving, sweat slick on his skin to say hoarsely, "Look at me, love."

Addy's lashes fluttered open, eyes glazed with lust.

"I want you to *see* me. Want you to know who's loving you."

"I know." Addison managed to push the words out. Her lungs felt constricted, her breathing erratic. He started to thrust and she made a deep husky sound she didn't recognize as her own as her body clenched tightly around him. They found their rhythm together. She clasped her hands on his butt and settled into a deep, wonderful plunge-twist swivel-slide that made her gasp with pleasure as she lifted herself to him.

She cried out and her world turned upside down as they climaxed together.

Addison's internal muscles still pulsed as Ry, still hard inside her, carried her to the bed. The punishing grip of his fingers supporting her butt cheeks notched up Addison's arousal, which hadn't abated despite the powerful orgasm they'd just shared. That was more than physical. It had been emotional and psychological as well.

Somehow a sliver of light had broken through the darkness.

Burying her face against his sweaty neck, she tasted the salt on his skin. A flavor she'd thought she'd never savor again. Tears stung her closed lids. *Don't leave me.* "Don't let me go."

He braced his knee on the mattress. "Never. Never again."

If only . . .

With her cradled safely in his arms, they dropped onto the bed with a small bounce that drove him deeper. Spreading her, he pumped into her. Faster and faster. She wrapped her legs around his waist and framed his face with both hands, pulling his mouth down to hers for sweet poignant kisses.

Sweat slicked their bodies together. The slap of skin on sweaty skin filled the dimly lit cabin. Addison arched her neck for his kisses, gripping his long hair in her fist as he bit gently on an extended tendon, then ran his teeth from her ear to her shoulder and back again. The sound of his ragged breath, the heat and intensity of his breathing, made her breath come faster. The wonderful weight of him on top of her, combined with the driving power of his thrusts spreading her wide, made her thrash and arch beneath him.

Hot and cold shivers rippled from her head to her toes.

Perfection.

Heat. Lightness. The absence of everything but feeling.

She wanted this moment to last forever.

Ry reached between them and massaged her clit with his thumb as he plunged his hips. Sweet agony, intense pleasure. Arching her back, her strong internal muscles squeezed him, drawing him in even deeper. Breath sawing, she followed his quickening pace, grinding herself against him, heels gripping the flexing muscles of his ass as he drove into her like a man possessed.

She felt her next orgasm starting to crest, but clever Ry held her there, hovering on a pinnacle of release, then tempered the pace so that the wave flattened out, allowing her to breathe, to explore the muscles of his back, to brush the damp hair from his eye. He brought her to the very edge, pulled back. And because she knew this dance, her body wasn't fooled by the lull; it was already coiling for the next crest.

"Wait for me," he ordered as his hips pistoned against hers in a pounding rhythm that had her head thrashing on the mattress and her nails digging into the supple skin of his back.

"Can't—" Eyes squeezed shut, she pushed the word out as every nerve, every tendon, every muscle and joint in her body came together in a climax that rendered her deaf and blind.

Several minutes later her heavy lids flickered open and she found Ry frowning down at her. He traced a finger beneath her left breast. He met her gaze, his eyes shiny and filled with emotion. "This is one of the most beautiful things I've ever seen, Addy."

He'd finally seen the white-ink tattoo of tiny angel wings right over her heart. No one else ever had. "Sophia is always with me."

Without a word, Ry pressed his warm mouth to the delicate wings.

Twelve

Addy sighed in her sleep, a small broken sound that tore at his heart. The movement drew his gaze to the slope of her breasts. Her cleavage looked shadowed and velvety, her breasts small and absolutely perfect. Ry wanted to press his open mouth there. He knew that the merest touch of his tongue or fingertips would rouse her awake. But she needed her sleep so he touched with his eyes alone.

When she was awake Addy was fierce, but in the moment of calm after their storm, he lay beside her, marveling at her delicate features in repose. He loved how the soft white moonlight turned her skin to warm marble, dusting her cheekbones and the tips of her lashes with silver glitter, turning the fire of her hair to frost. He loved the way her dark eyelashes fanned on her cheeks, still flushed from their lovemaking. Her normally sassy mouth with the full, sexy lower lip lay soft, her lips slightly parted.

Now her mouth looked vulnerable, bee-stung. She loved to kiss, had taught him the pleasure of taking his time when they kissed so that now it was almost as much a turn-on as having sex. Almost. He loved her kisses when they were soft and deep, he loved them when they were hot and wild. Kissing Addy was a miracle.

Instead of touching, he looked his fill to store the picture away for later. The pleasure and pain of being with her again was almost unbearably perfect. He didn't want to ruin it. Yet he understood that he could very well do so.

The question was: Would he do this right? Could he say and do the right thing this time when morning and reality came knocking?

Every muscle in Ry's body tensed to the point that he thought he was having one fucking hellish cramp. Sweat beaded above his brow, over his mouth, down his back. "Crap. I've got to be better or leave now before I make it worse."

He loved Addy. Did love give him the right to ruin her life . . . again. Or, did love give him a chance to make it right?

"Fuck."

How each of them had reacted to Sophia's death lay at the heart of their history; pain too deep, too profound to share. When tragedy should've brought them together, it had, instead, ripped them apart. Had anything really changed from those days?

Or did making love to her confirm what his broken heart had told him? He would do whatever he needed to do to get her back.

In a few hours, with the harsh light of day, they'd talk. They *had* to fucking talk. It was past time. Or had so much time already passed that he had to leave her the hell alone . . . because he loved her that much.

Ry stayed until the cold light of the moon filled the cabin, then slipped quietly out of her bed.

It's a dream. Wake up. Wake. Up.

Addison shifted restlessly as fear and oppressive, cloying darkness surround her. *Wake up!* Arms were too heavy to lift. Surrounded by dark spears of tall trees, the starless night sky was just a shade lighter than the dense foliage pressing in around her. Unable to cover her ears to block out the hideous sounds of pain, she tried in vain to run.

The air, humid and somehow malevolent, curled around her, making her flash hot then cold. Goose bumps pebbled her skin. Every hard knock of her rapid heartbeat caused piercing pain in her chest, making it hard to breathe.

Just a dream. God. It *felt* real.

She loved animals, and somewhere in the dark forest where she stood, naked and alone, a wild beast cried out in torment. The agony in the guttural sound made the fine hairs on her skin stand straight up, and caused her heart to pound even harder.

Her legs moved, and she ran, not knowing to what, or how to get there; all she knew was that she had to help. *Now.* But no matter how hard she tried to break into a full-out sprint, she moved in slow-mo. Sharp grasses slashed at her legs, cutting deep, stinging. She sped up at last—now running faster than she'd run in her life. Dark shapes blurred with her passing. The agonized cries tore at her own throat, although she knew she wasn't the one making the sounds herself.

Close. Getting closer.

Panting, struggling to draw oxygen into her constricted lungs, she had no idea where she was going. She only knew getting there was imperative. She paused to listen, attempting to get a directional cue. Blackness pressed tightly around her. Blood from a million lacerations on her feet and calves trickled warm down her cold legs. The sting was nothing compared with the animal's tortured screams.

There! "Coming!"

Suddenly she was hip-deep in viscous quicksand. Trapped. Barely able to move. Other than her own frenetic heartbeat throbbing in her ears, the forest was silent. The flutter of the leaves on the branches didn't make a sound, yet, she felt the brush of the breeze on her cheeks. Warm. Damp. She shook her head, trying to clear her ears to the sound that had to be around her . . . it had to be there. Trying to step forward, her feet dragged heavily through the gluey sand and waist-deep water.

God. "I've got to get out of here." She didn't hear her own voice, only that awful animal scream from afar. She knew if she didn't get out of the sucking earth beneath her feet, she'd die.

Frantically scanning the area immediately around her, Addison tried to reach a dark distant bank. But the more she tried to move toward it, the farther away it seemed to be . . . it was far, too damn far away . . . and getting farther as she inched slowly toward it. Her thighs burned with each dogged step.

Wake up!

Rydell? Help me!

From quicksand to her moonlit bedroom aboard the *Tesoro Mio.* From the sharp smell of pine trees and earthy loam to the soft scent of gardenias. The sounds of the ship's powerful, vibrating engines as they sliced through calmer seas filled her head now.

Awake? She sucked in a shaky breath. Yes! Thank God.

Reaching for Ry, she needed the solid heat of his reality.

His side of the bed was empty. The rumpled sheets cold.

Gone. *Again.* Dear God. Did she never learn? Wrapping her arms tightly around her body, Addison shivered.

He'd gotten what he wanted. Didn't he always? she

thought, too hurt, too crushed to acknowledge that she'd gotten what she wanted tonight, too. Now, having had sex with her, he'd slunk off in the dead of night, leaving her alone. She didn't know him anymore. Maybe she never had.

Her eyes burned. Pain crushed heavy on her chest, making it hard to drag air into her lungs.

Damn him. Damn him. Double damn him.

And double damn herself, for giving in when she should've resisted and told him to go to hell. Maybe she needed this final blow to be done with him once and for all. Now she knew what her subconscious dream mind understood before she did.

He always was competitive with Naveen and wanted to stake his claim on her first. Coldhearted son of a bitch. Did he have no feelings? No conscience? Apparently not. Her throat ached with tears she was damned if she'd shed.

Eyes squeezed shut, Addison sat up, letting the silky sheets fall to her waist and the cool air wash over her skin as she dropped her clammy forehead to her up-drawn knees.

She'd always had vivid dreams, but never nightmares. Not even after Sophia died. This one shook her to the core because the sounds and smells were so real, so immediate, it was hard to separate dream from reality. The pitiful awful animal screams must have been her own. The final death of her love for Rydell?

Sweaty forehead pressed on her knees, she waited for her erratic breathing, and the hard knock of her heartbeat, to return to normal.

Dreams were a manifestation of the sounds and images experienced during the day. God only knew, after an action-and tension-filled day it wasn't surprising that her dreams were filled with all sorts of imagery. But she had no idea what *this* dream symbolized. Being trapped? Probably. The animal crying out in pain? She had no ide—

An anguished cry, vivid and clear, ripped through the moon-washed room. The same harsh cry that had filled her dream. Her head jerked up. Dear God. *Not a dream.* Real.

Flinging off the sheet, she sprang from the bed and followed the muffled sound to Sophia's room. The room her baby had never occupied.

Decorated in anticipation for the life the three of them would share on board, she'd almost forgotten until she'd walked into the fully decorated nursery her first day on board. Seeing it, seeing the future, when the future was dead, almost killed her. Addison had removed the changing table, and the crib, but the walls were still covered with the white-and-pale-pink toile wallpaper, and she hadn't been able to part with the velvet-covered glider hunched in the far corner. She'd never held her baby there, but when she needed to feel closer to Sophia, she came into the room and sat alone in the dark, Sophie's baby blanket pressed to her face.

Losing a child was the loneliest, most desolate journey a woman could take. She was a mother without a child; grief was a constant sharp knife at her throat, her lungs, her heart. There was barely a moment in her waking hours that she didn't think of her baby. And when, for those brief moments that she didn't, she felt guilty as hell for forgetting her precious little girl for even those few seconds.

She always felt numb and cold. But tonight, Ry had made her feel heat and light and *alive*, again. It was all she'd get. It had to be enough. She had to *make* it enough.

Addison crossed the soft carpeted floor from shadow, through moonlight, back into shadow and soundlessly pushed open the door. It had been locked. How had Rydell gotten in?

On the outer edge of a swath of moonlight filtered through the large window, a naked Ry knelt in the shadows, his body bowed over his knees.

Oh, Ry—The harsh sound emanating from him ripped out Addison's heart.

The room smelled of baby powder. Her imagination. Sometimes it brought her a small measure of comfort. But not tonight. Tonight she knew the soft, baby scent was a figment of her imagination. A lie.

Dry eyes burning with unshed tears, she dropped to her knees beside him, the lump of misery in her throat restricting her breathing. Her own pain was still so huge she couldn't shed the tears constricting her lungs and heart. And Ry's pain amplified her own unbearably. Addison stretched out a hand to touch his shaking shoulder, then withdrew it and clenched both hands on her knees.

Throat and chest impossibly tight, close enough to feel the heat of his body, she bowed her heavy head. And waited.

Ry knew the hideous wrenching sounds came from his own throat, but he was incapable of quieting them. Grief ripped up from the depth of his soul, so dark, so deep it bowed his body and ripped out his heart.

When he'd found out, *three fucking months* after her death, that Sophia had died of SIDS, he'd gone bloody apeshit, then dived headfirst into a dark pit.

Now, being in her room reminded him poignantly and painfully of the hours he and Addy had spent choosing the furniture, pondering the softness of the carpet for little crawling knees, researching the best brand of diapers. *This* was a reality that hadn't hit him last year when he'd heard the news of his baby's death thirdhand.

Now he knew he hadn't succumbed to even a tenth of the iceberg that lay below the surface of the pain.

Now the loss of their baby was profound and far too real.

He'd thought he'd reached his lowest points this year. Coming into Sophia's room was the topper. She'd never slept in this room they'd so carefully prepared for her, never crawled on the rug or taken her first shaky steps to her father's outstretched hands. But the entire room was filled to brimming with the hopes and promises of her.

He wasn't sure how long they sat there in the middle of the floor in the dappled moonlight. Minutes? Hours? Ry's throat ached. Fuck, his entire body ached as though he'd been thoroughly beaten and left for dead.

Sitting back on his haunches, he looked at Addy. Her head was bowed, and her shoulders shook. But she wasn't making a sound. Seeing her pain made him feel worse than shit. Her pain was the only thing that pulled him to the surface of his own misery. He focused on her, on soothing *her* pain.

With an agonized cry, Ry gathered her in his arms. Her naked breasts against his chest. Stroking her slender back, rocking her, murmuring against her hair as the tears on their cheeks mixed.

After what seemed like an eternity, he got to his feet, picked her up in the cradle of his arm, and strode back to the rumpled bed and set her down as if she'd break. Sitting across from her, he took her hands in his. Her fingers were ice-cold, clammy; his shook.

They stared into each other's tear-drenched eyes.

Lost. Destroyed. Inconsolable.

"Jesus, love." Ry's voice sounded choked. "How the bloody hell did we get here?"

She shook her head, tears swimming, mouth trembling.

"We have to talk."

"Y-yes."

Not releasing her, he grabbed the box of tissues off her side of the bed. "Water?"

She shook her head, wiping at her wet cheeks with a handful of tissues.

"Wine? Whiskey?"

She shook her head again. Cheeks pale, nose pink, her lips slightly swollen, she'd never looked more beautiful. Her red-gold hair was a mess from his marauding fingers, still damp at her hairline from their energetic lovemaking earlier.

Ry crawled up the bed to sit directly in front of her. The lamp was on the desk across the room behind him. Illuminating parts of her beautiful body like a glorious, perfect jigsaw puzzle. The soft curve of her waist, the pink tip of her left breast, the slope of her shoulder. The sheen of tears on her flushed cheek.

They were still naked, and for a nanosecond he considered suggesting they grab some clothes and cover themselves. But so much had been hidden this past year, he figured their nudity was symbolic. Laid bare to each other at last.

Knees touched knees. Squeezing her hand, Ry said quietly, "It's time to talk about Sophia, Addy. Past time. I'm not going to interrupt, although I suspect I'll have to eat my tongue to resist. Get everything out. This wound needs to be debrided, the infected parts cut out so that it no longer festers. The way we've been going is killing both of us. We have to heal. Together."

He brought their clasped hands to his mouth, then returned them to her thigh. "Want the light on or off?"

A small shake of her head. "I'll ugly-cry. But I don't want any more darkness between us." She used her free hand to run the damp, balled-up tissue under her eyes. Ry took it from her and replaced it with a dry one.

"I don't know where to start."

"March eighteenth."

"Her three-month-old birthday. Sophie was such a good baby. S-sweet. Happy. When I walked into her room that morning she actually rolled over onto her tummy and lifted her head. I captured the moment to send to you—I videoed her as she smiled and gurgled up at me, so proud of her new trick. I thought it would cheer you up when you were dealing with all that Cutter legal stuff in South Africa. I heard the stress in your voice every day about the trial, and knew seeing her sweet little face would help."

Ry wanted to see that video *now*. Wanted a glimpse of his daughter. Later. He squeezed Addy's hand, her fingers curled into his.

"We had breakfast, dressed, went up on deck. She gurgled and wrapped her little starfish hand around Mo's, and spat up her breakfast on my mother's new Galliano. Pissed off, Mother handed her back to me as if she were a bundle of dirty laundry. She'd only taken Sophie because Naveen had offered to feed her, and he handed her to the closest person when she was wet."

"Your *mother* with a baby? Wet or otherwise. The mind boggles." Ry's lips twitched imagining Hollis holding a wet baby. She was the least maternal person he knew.

"Sophie had been a little cranky the night before, and neither of us had had much sleep. I took her down for a nap at two, brought her carry crib beside me so I could hear her if she got fussy . . . I can't—"

"I need to hear this, Addy. All of it."

She closed her eyes, her lashes a dark spiky reminder of her tears. For several moments she couldn't speak. Seeming to gather herself, she opened her eyes. What Ry saw there, even in the semi-darkness, gouged another hole in his heart.

Pain. Agony. Doubt and fear. Worse, *guilt*.

"I woke up and it was six thirty-seven. She should've been crying for her dinner. For a moment I closed my eyes again and lay there, happy because I thought you'd come back from Cape Town and had sneaked in to take her so I could sleep a little longer. But—I-I looked, just to ch-check . . ."

Addy's face crumpled and she buried it in her hands as her body shook with her sobs. Ry gathered her onto his lap, rocking her as she cried. The tears, wrenched up, seemed to come from her very soul. They wet his chest and arm, burning like the acid of recrimination.

He stroked her hair back where the strands stuck to her cheek, then rubbed a path from her shoulder to the small of her back with the flat of his hand. God, she felt deceptively fragile under his touch. Skin slick with perspiration, pebbled as if she was cold. He stroked and rocked, murmuring how much he loved her, how much he missed their baby, his own voice broken and thick.

After what felt like hours, or seconds, she lifted her head. Addy wasn't a woman who looked beautiful and dewy when she cried. Her skin was red and blotchy, her eyes rid-rimmed and swollen. To him she was the most beautiful woman he'd ever laid eyes on.

Ry lay a gentle kiss on her damp, swollen mouth. "Need a break?"

Dragging in a ragged breath, she shook her head.

"Okay to hold you?"

"God, yes. Can you reach the tissues?"

Pulling her across his lap, Ry buried his face in her hair. Needing to hold her. Desperately needing to be held. He felt the hot soak of her tears against his throat, and his own throat closed as grief prickled behind his lids. Taking her face in both hands, he lifted it, died seeing the ravages of her grief, and brushed a gentle kiss to her swollen trembling lips.

Holding on to her, Ry leaned back so he could reach the box on her bedside table. He brought the whole container back as he steadied them back into position.

While she dried her face and blew her nose, he rearranged their limbs so that they were both comfortable, but still as close as they could get without being behind each other. "Whenever you're ready."

He felt her large, shuddering inhale against his chest before she resumed talking. "The rest is a blur of hysteria. My mother took charge, did what had to be done. She brought in a doctor because I was—frantic. He had to sedate me, against my wishes I might add. They took Sophie away. Mother made the arrangements."

The only time in her life that Hollis did something for someone else, Ry thought, knowing how she'd always treated her daughter like a bloody designer accessory.

"Honestly, I couldn't have m-managed any of it without her, I was inconsolable. Out of my mind with grief. And God. Self-accusations. Self-recriminations. Self-loathing. What had I done wrong? How could I have prevented it? If I hadn't fallen asleep would I have been able to save her?

"What kind of mother lets her baby die?

"For once I was grateful Hollis was on board.

"The days passed in a blur. I wanted you desperately.

You didn't come. Days and nights blended into a massive swirling black nightmare."

Addy looked down at their clasped hands, her words low and agonized. Just looking at her made Ry's chest ache with empathy.

"Naveen comforted me, held me as I sobbed, looked after me when I slept. Encouraged me to eat and drink. He never left my side. We returned to port. I couldn't handle being drugged and stupid anymore. The pain was almost welcome, because it meant I was alive and could mourn my precious girl.

"You didn't come." She mopped the tears pouring down her face, dripping off her chin, making her voice thick. "I l-left messages, but you never came. Never returned my calls. I had days when all I could do was sleep and cry. I took whatever the doctors prescribed. Nothing worked. I didn't know how many times I called, or how many hysterical, raving lunatic messages I left. You never called me back. It was all a hideous blur. All I knew was that I wanted you, and you weren't there.

"Everything faded to a dim gray existence where I stopped caring. Stopped feeling anything for anyone. Stopped wanting to live. So I stopped calling."

A serrated, dull knife twisted in his heart, making it fucking impossible to breathe. Words dammed up in his throat, unspoken.

Lashes, dark and spiky, lifted as Addy's olive-green eyes rose to meet his. The knife pierced deeper. "I couldn't live without Sophia, but I learned I *could* live without you and survive. Mother and I moved to Naveen's villa in Paris. I got the p-papers. Then I weaned myself off the meds. *Sea Dragon* was my home. I lost my b-baby, my husband, and my home. My entire life fell apart. And all *you* did was expedite the divorce papers so that it went through uncontested."

Ry waited several minutes to gather enough resources to speak. Throat and lungs constricted, it felt as though someone had poured acid in his eyeballs and ripped out his heart without an anesthetic.

"On March eighteenth," he said in a rush, and without preamble. "I was sitting in the courtroom in Cape Town while the Cutters decimated my character, honor, and stole my salvage rights from under me. I was getting my ass handed to me on a platter, and my lawyers warned me that I could end up paying all their court costs as well as my own if I lost. They pretty much assured me I was going to lose my shirt.

"I left the courtroom while the jury was out for the night. The minute I hit the hotel I called you. The first officer told me the prince was with you and you'd asked not to be disturbed. It was fucking *five a.m.* I ordered him to go and knock on your door; maybe your phone was off the hook. Knowing you'd never bring that dick onto my ship considering our history. After half an hour of dropped calls, and being put on hold, your mother—yeah, your *mother*—came on and told me you'd instructed her that you didn't want to talk to me. Now, I figured, knowing you as I do, you'd never have sex with His Highness. Hell no. Not in our *home*. In our *bed*. I was exhausted, stressed, scared shitless quite frankly, so maybe I wasn't thinking as clearly as I could've." He paused, gave breathing a shot, found he couldn't manage more than a sip of air and kept going.

"I figured Sophie had kept you up, and you were so tired your mother was trying to protect you. After a week I dismissed that as bullshit because Hollis English-D'Marco-Payne-Smithe-Belcourt-Moubray had never done an altruistic thing in her selfish life, up to and including covering for her daughter.

"I tried to think of what the fuck I'd done to piss you

off. Couldn't think of a damn thing. For weeks I called you in every recess, at the end of every day a dozen fucking times. I called you every morning. You refused to take my calls—"

Wordlessly she shook her head, allowing her hair to curl around her breast like an amber question mark.

"Then I lost my ass. The Cutters got control of that wreck, and I was fucked, holding the bag with none of the loot. It was a bitter pill. The day the ruling came down was the day I received your divorce papers. It was a one–two punch. I was KO and I didn't fucking know why. I signed whatever they put in front of me. Against my expensive lawyer's advice. I signed you away, signed *Tesoro Mio* away, too. I tried to contact Peri—her damn voice mail is always full. I tried Callie, but she was undercover with the Cutters and it was impossible to have a private convo with her. I was beside myself.

"It was only three months later that I managed to get in touch with Kevin. Ostensibly to see if I could hire the team to go to Peru with me. But really to find out if she knew anything. She started crying and gave me her teary and heartfelt sympathy about the death of my daughter."

Addy gasped, her head jerking up. "You knew."

"No, Addison. I didn't."

Thirteen

Steady, red-rimmed storm-gray eyes met hers. "I swear on my life. Until Kevin told me about S-Sophie, I didn't know."

It killed her that his voice broke when he said their baby's name. And yet—God, it was good to hear Sophia's name spoken out loud. Everyone else tiptoed about, as if she'd burst into tears if she heard her baby's name. She might, but hearing it kept Sophie alive.

She must have flinched when his fingers tightened even more, and he immediately loosened his grip. Ry stroked his thumb over the back of her hand. "I demanded to know why none of them had called me. She said you, through your mother, asked my crew, my friends to respect your privacy. Said we'd had marital problems and needed time to work it out without interference. A lie, I now know. Didn't then. I was gutted by the news."

Addison had never seen this expression on his face. Raw grief reflected the same gaping black hole she'd felt since March 18.

Turning one hand, her palm brushed his and she curled her fingers between his, supporting his large hand in the smallness of her own, braced on her knee.

Ry drew in a harsh breath, his chest expanding as he held it. Centering himself. "My grief was a cavernous hole, impossible to fill. You, gone, devastated me; the news of our precious child's death hit me in way I could never have imagined. My grief was profound, and terrifying in its intensity. Made worse because I had no one to share it with. I went through all the stages of grief I'd had for our divorce, all over again."

"You didn't instigate the divorce."

"Fuck no. I thought you—" He shook his head. "I went into a dark cave and wanted to hibernate there. Didn't help worth shit. I realized just how goddamn alone I was, and needed answers. For months it was almost impossible to function—hell, even to breathe. The devastation I felt was chest-caving. I was in the deepest, coldest part of the ocean treading water, barely keeping my head above the surface as I drowned in my grief."

His hand held hers so tightly, Addison thought he was going to break her fingers. She kept her hands in his, this time not indicating how painfully tight his grip was.

"I knew if that's how *I* felt, it's how *you* must have felt. Must *feel*. I needed you with every fiber of my being. Needed to see and touch you. Hold you. Wanted you to need and want me in the same way. But clearly you didn't. Because all I'd heard from you was through a Parisian lawyer I'd never fucking heard of."

"Naveen's lawyer."

"Yeah, I figured. One more nail through my heart. I called you. Your number had been disconnected. I went to see your mother in Milan. She told me I was dead to her and slammed the door in my face. I put a private detective on her to see if you were staying with her. I tried calling the prince's residences. Paris, Mumbai, New York. Messages were taken. No one knew where you were. I went to the prince's penthouse in Paris. Was told Miss D'Marco and His Highness were on a trip to Scotland and not expected back for a month. I flew to

Scotland. Thirty thousand square miles, over five million fucking people. I walked, I drove, I called hotels and rentals . . . I hired private detectives there, too. You were nowhere to be found.

"I left for the dive in the North Pacific. A good wreck, with plenty of gold to replenish my wallet, and enough work to prevent me from drinking myself to death. New crew. Went into town for supplies, and when I got back *Sea Dragon* was gone, hijacked by a bunch of terrorists. Left most of my crew and divers dead on the wharf. Police, investigators . . . A shitload more trouble—

"Understatement," he said, his voice bitter. "It has not been a good fucking year. For the past thirteen-plus months my life has turned to shit—"

"You think everyone—" Addison's voice cracked as though she'd been crying for a month. She had to start again. That water would've been welcome now. But she didn't want to get up, refused to leave him. "—conspired to keep Sophie's death a secret from you?" she finished. "Why?"

His hesitation was almost imperceptible. "Put together your truth and my truth. What do you get?"

She didn't hesitate. "Hollis."

"You called and left messages?" He looked as grim as she felt.

"Dozens of them. And a hundred texts." He let go of her hands, and the blood flowed back in sharp pinpricks. "Where are you going?"

He leaned over to the bedside table on her side of the bed and retrieved her cell phone. Turned it on. "Delete any of the messages?"

She hadn't been able to look at them, and somehow deleting them would make what they had shared evaporate, too. "No."

The light from her phone illuminated the dark side of

his face as he scrolled through RECENTS. He held the phone up so that she could see all the incoming and outgoing calls. She knew what was there. Most of her outgoing calls and texts had been to Rydell's number. His lashes lay on his cheeks as he looked down, scanning some of the text messages she'd sent over several months. There were hundreds of them.

"God, Addy." His voice broke, and his throat worked.

"I told you."

"I swear I never received any them." Holding her iPhone where she could see the screen, he went into CONTACTS and found his name. ICE RYDELL CASE. In Case of Emergency. "This isn't my number."

"Of course it's your number!"

"No. It's *programmed* with my contact name on it, but this isn't my phone number, never has been."

She blinked, her mind stumbling over the truth. "I never looked at your *number*. In fact I doubt I'd even remember your number. I *always* use speed dial."

"*Everyone* does. Someone," he said dangerously, "reprogrammed your fucking phone."

Her chest ached. "Someone hated 'us' so much, they sabotaged us when we needed each other the most."

He stroked her wet cheek. "We have to forgive each other, Addy. It's the only way we can hope to heal. Especially now we know there was an explanation for the miscommunication."

Addison wanted to rip off the face of whoever had manipulated her phone, with her fingernails. Then stomp them with her favorite Christian Louboutin five-inch stilettos and chain them to the anchor and drop them over the side of the ship, *then* haul them above the surface and stomp them again.

She and Ry had barely slept for the rest of the night.

Instead, they'd curled together, emotionally and physically spent, and talked.

Telling her, *showing* her, how damn sorry he was that he eventually stopped trying to find her because he was convinced that that was what she wanted didn't take away the hurt that he'd given up. On her. On them.

Addison hoped one day to forgive him for that. Knowing how stoic and unemotional he could be was no excuse. He shouldn't have given up. Ever.

Now, an hour after they'd parted ways in her cabin, she was dressed and having breakfast like a civilized human being. Screams lodged in her throat, and her stomach churned. Closing her eyes behind her dark glasses, she breathed in slowly, willing her racing heart to slow the hell down and give her time to plan some sort of strategy.

She'd deal with her mother via telephone.

Naveen was right here beside her.

Since ripping off a face was not only a disgusting visual, and she wasn't going to ruin her favorite pumps, nor was she going to throw someone overboard—especially not, she thought with a glimmer of amusement, with the Coast Guard still on board—she was going to sit here and make nice until she formulated a viable plan to deal with Hollis. And if necessary, Prince Naveen Darshi as well.

Breathe in. Breathe out.

The stormy night had provided a fitting backdrop for her intense conversation with Ry. A conversation for which there should've been no need. On so many levels. As unsettled as the conversation had left Addison, the storm should be continuing, but not a cloud remained in the Wedgwood-blue cloudless sky.

Breathe in.

Breathe out.

Ry had asked to keep her phone for a few hours. Her

heart hurt for both of them knowing that right now he was in his own cabin, reading all those heart-wrenching, desperate text messages.

Breathe in.

Breathe out.

Reliving Sophie's death had been heartbreaking. But it was heartbreak shared. She hated, hated, *hated* her mother for what she'd done to both Ry and herself. It was an unconscionable crime, for which Addison could—would—*never* forgive her.

Sunlight glinted off the smooth, dark-blue water, making sunglasses necessary. *Tesoro Mio*'s powerful engines drove the large ship smoothly through the water, leaving a trail of frothy white lace in its wake. From Addy's vantage point at a small table in the shade on the middle deck, Mother Nature had painted a day that was picture perfect, while her own mother had painted a life—Addison's life—that was filled with high drama, and not in a good, enjoy-the-opera way.

The air smelled of ocean, bacon cooked minutes earlier in the nearby galley, and Naveen's Versace Eros cologne.

Breathe in. Breathe out.

She was going to need a flat-out, balls-to-the-wall run after this.

Naveen sat at the table with her. Choosing the seat right next to her, even though no one else was around. It was damn hard for her to be civilized after the revelation about her phone being reprogrammed. Had Naveen known what her mother had done? Had he been part of it? Hollis had never made any secret that she wanted her daughter married to royalty.

While her only child had been dazed with profound grief, had the two of them colluded to irreparably split her and Rydell?

The thought ate at Addison as she watched the prince's handsome face while he sliced into his eggs Benedict. Was he capable of that kind of deceit? Was anyone? *Yes.*

Her mother was certainly not only capable, but *motivated.* The knowledge chilled Addison to the bone. She loved her mother, but she wasn't blind to her faults. And she didn't *like* her. Hollis was a terrible mother, forgetful, vengeful, manipulative, and careless. But this topped anything she'd ever done. This was pure evil.

"It's a good thing I'm here to protect you and your interests," Naveen said as he took a sip of coffee.

He was dead serious, and she appreciated the sentiment, if that was his truth, if not the reality. If she needed or wanted protection physically, she'd take Ry's brute strength and tenacity over Naveen's sophisticated verbal volleys. Each had its place she supposed, but when the chips were down, she wanted Ry in her corner. He'd fight for her to his last breath.

She'd decided to let Naveen down easily. His ego would be bruised, but stringing him along was not only unfair to him, it was wrong. She could never care for him the way she did for Ry. Never. Everything about him paled when compared with her ex-husband.

Now . . .

If he'd had *anything* to do with Telephone-Gate—even if he'd *known* and not told her—she was not going to let him down *easy.* She was going slam-dunk his ass overboard.

She stabbed a slice of pineapple with the tines of her fork and set it on her plate beside the rashers of bacon she shouldn't be eating. "From my ex-husband?"

Perfect opportunity to ask if he knew about the phone tampering. He'd stuck by her through some harrowing times, and at the very least been a good friend. It was only fair that she give him the opportunity to say his piece about the changed phone number. On one hand there was a possibility—a *remote* possibility—that he'd had no idea. On the other, he very well may have been her self-absorbed mother's willing accomplice in the diabolical scheme.

Addison's heartbeat sped up. If that *was* the case, he must've been deaf, dumb, and freaking blind, because he'd been with her almost night and day for three months under his own roof. It was hard to believe he *hadn't* known.

In the heat of the moment last night, Ry had told her how much he loved her. He'd shown her with his body when they'd made love again, after they had talked.

In the past, returning the sentiment, saying how she felt in return had never been an issue. Now a small part of her—a small, petty part of herself—couldn't manage to get those words out. She wasn't sure why. Even after they'd bared their hearts earlier. She just couldn't. Not yet. And as if her heart hadn't been wrenched enough, Ry had seen the hesitation, knew the words weren't coming anytime soon, and he had placed his fingers on her lips and said, in a choked, harsh whisper that told of endless pain, "*I understand. It's okay, I can wait.*"

"Addison? Where'd you go?"

She blinked Naveen back into focus, thankful for the sunglasses that hid her red eyes, and also the look of suspicion he'd be able to read if her whole face was exposed.

"I was thinking about your man, and how terrified he must've been." Not quite a lie. That thought was in there somewhere with the rest of the stressors. The Coast Guard had told them that recovering the body would be next to impossible, but they'd searched for hours in the storm to no avail anyway.

They'd disembark when the ship reached the Maldives tomorrow. Hopefully taking the killer with them.

Naveen was closemouthed about the incident, and now his lips were set in a thin line. He didn't want to talk about it. Not with her anyway. Officials had questioned him at length the night before, and were still on board, going through every inch of space on board looking for clues. He apparently didn't want to talk about that, either.

"I was referring to having a murderer on board." Naveen's eyes narrowed. "*Do* you need protection from Case?"

The dive crew and Rydell were down in the dining room, which was now more of a staging area than a place to eat. Addison knew exactly what it would look like this morning. Gone would be the pretty place mats and flowers. In their place would be charts and research material—Ry liked to print out everything. All four of the monitors would be in play as the dive team planned their first dive, which was to take place in a couple of days. He was capable of compartmentalizing his life. He'd sink himself into the dive and push aside what he'd learned last night. She wished she could do the same.

Thinking about the dive reminded her that Ry was still hiding something from her. What, she had no idea. But if they truly wanted to clear the air, he was going to have to share with her why this salvage was so damn important. Why this one? Why now?

Or was she seeing problems where there were none, because the rest of her life was off kilter?

And if, and when, Ry found his treasure, what then? Where did they go from here?

Addison was just fine with not seeing him for breakfast. In the light of day she was more confused than angry. Sex between them had always been spectacular.

Last night had been no exception, but the last year proved that life wasn't just about sex. She needed space to think things through. Time, to come to terms with his explanation and rationale. Time to decide how to handle Hollis, and what to do about Naveen.

She had to be sure when she said she forgave Rydell that she really, really meant it. Finding him undone in Sophia's room had given her a glimpse of what it had been like for him to lose his daughter. It had also cracked the wall she'd firmly installed between her heart and any feelings she had for him.

"Darling? Come back to me, I asked whether you feel you need protection from Case?" Naveen's words were clipped.

She didn't blame him for being impatient with her inability to focus. The fog that her swirling thoughts created suddenly lifted, and with crystal-clear clarity, she knew she needed protection from her own bad judgment, not from Ry. "Of course not. Sorry. I didn't get much sleep last night. Rydell is just as worried about this as we are. But we've got all the Coast Guard officers on board. I don't think whoever did this will act again, do you?"

"I don't know *what* to think," Naveen told her, pouring her another cup of fragrant coffee. "All I know is there was never any trouble before Case and his divers came on board."

Exactly what Ry had said about Naveen and his men. Addison raised an eyebrow. Naveen had hurled that accusation at Ry last night, too. If that's what he believed, it would make the trip even more uncomfortable. "Why would any of *them* throw your bodyguard overboard? None of them knew him before yesterday."

Addison noticed a sheen of sweat on his suddenly pale skin. It wasn't that hot outside yet. Barely seventy. She gave him a look of concern. "Are you okay?"

"Of course, why wouldn't I be?"

"You look—" Agitated. Annoyed. Scared? "Worried."

"Not in the least, darling. Just a small issue with a business matter. Nothing that a phone call won't resolve." He smiled. Nice white teeth, zero joy in the gesture.

A business matter? Not concern about the death of his man? Or demands that the killer be found *immediately*? None of his usual bombastic, royal decrees that his subordinates—and to Naveen pretty much *everyone* was a subordinate—hop to it, and get the job done. Immediately?

Very out of character. And the fact that she *knew* it was out of character bothered Addy. She knew this part of his personality; why hadn't it bothered her before now? She'd known Naveen for five years. Slept with him for God's sake. Why see him now without blinders on when she'd never really registered it before?

Because Rydell was in the picture again.

Because she'd almost forgotten how an honest, honorable man behaved with everyone he encountered. Ry didn't have one way of talking to his crew, and another when talking to his friends.

Naveen never was, never could be, Ry.

"I don't trust Case," Naveen said. "His sudden appearance is suspect, and so is his urgency to salvage this wreck. Which just *happens* to be on our route to Sydney. He's up to something. And that something has everything to do with getting back into your good graces."

Getting back into my bed. "He just wants the use of *Tesoro Mio*, and he assures me that the salvage should only take a week or two . . ."

"You believe him?"

I believe his need is urgent, and specific, and that he has some sort of time line. I just don't know what or why. After what I saw last night, I know, with every beat of my heart, that he'd only have come here if he had no other choice. No person would have willingly walked through the hell that he walked through last night.

Something had Rydell running scared.

"Naveen, did you reprogram my iPhone after Sophia died?"

He frowned. Or gave every indication of frowning, but the Botox in his forehead prevented anything that extreme. "Why on earth would I manipulate your phone? Even if I knew how, which my tech people would tell you I don't."

Reprogramming her phone was simple. He certainly *could've* done it. But had he? "Rydell's phone number was altered in my list of contacts."

He glanced at her before picking up his coffee. "To what purpose?" He took a sip, watching her over the rim of his cup.

"So that every call I made to him after Sophie's death went somewhere else."

"You must be mistaken, darling. Surely if that was the case, when you called and voice mail picked up it wasn't Case's voice."

"It was. His *recorded* voice. I think someone taped it from his real message, and changed the number so I thought I was calling my husband, and instead my calls and texts went—God only knew where." It sounded positively Machiavellian and absurd in the light of day.

Naveen put down his cup. "Good God. That's outrageous!"

Addy saw her own reflection in his sunglasses. Her expression was tight, which was certainly how she felt. Confused, angry, hurt, vengeful. "Yes," she said tightly. "It is. The question is, who would do a thing like that?"

"Hollis," he said without hesitation.

Dear God, was her mother so vile that even someone

who detested Ry would immediately see her as a potential culprit, without questioning that Ry had never received the calls?

He covered her hand with his. "But *why* she would do something so vile is beyond me."

"She wants you and me to be married."

Naveen picked up her hand to play with her fingers. "As do I. But by fair means, not foul."

"You swear you had nothing to do with it?" God, she wished she could see his eyes, gauge what he was really thinking.

"Darling, I swear. You must confront Hollis."

"Oh, I will, you can count on that."

But Addison knew she had to get in touch with Ry's sister first. There was another piece of the puzzle he hadn't shared in the early hours of this morning. If anyone knew what was eating Rydell, it would be Peri. The siblings were close. Or as close as someone like Rydell would allow himself to get to a person. Even family. "Rydell is many things, but he isn't dishonest."

A rueful smile lit Naveen's handsome face, and he brushed her jaw with his palm. "I trust *you*. Doesn't mean I won't be watching your back every second of this trip." His hand slipped under her loose hair at her nape, and he drew her closer. His breath smelled of strong coffee. She was mildly alarmed at her lack of any emotion at his touch. More alarmed that after a second of dullness, she had to fight the urge to brush his hands off her. "I could do a better job of that if I shared your bed."

Addison disengaged his hand by shifting in her chair. Scanning his face as a shiver ran over her skin. An errant breeze and nothing—okay, a *little*—to do with Ry leaving her bed just hours earlier. "We already discussed this. I won't sleep with you, Nav."

"I can wait until we reach Sydney."

She had to tell him the only thing that was going to happen when they reached Sydney was that they would part ways. Had to find a way to let him down easily. Had. To. She opened her mouth, but the words escaped her.

"You must know that you drive me mad, Addison. I want you desperately, but I feel that with each passing day you pull away instead of drawing closer. And even more so now. Case stole you away from me once. I won't allow him to do so again."

"He didn't *steal* me, Nav," she told him gently. "I went willingly. I know that hurt you, and God only knows it wasn't intentional. It just . . . happened." Love at first sight. Like a lightning bolt.

"You were mine first, and as long as you're mine last I must be content." He nodded. "Until we reach Sydney."

He pressed a quick kiss to her mouth, then released his hold and picked up his glass of orange juice. He gave her a mock toast. "I've done everything in my power to change your mind." His smile was wry and charming, reminding Addison what had attracted her to him in the first place. It wasn't his fault that as soon as she'd met Rydell Case, Naveen's smooth, sophisticated charm wasn't enough. It was like the moon challenging the sun.

He drank his juice and swirled the last inch in his glass, dark eyes intent on her face. "Everything short of clubbing you and dragging you by the hair to my cave. So I'll be patient and wait a few more weeks. We have the rest of our lives to make love. I want a life with you, darling. Children to take the place of the girl you lost."

Her name was Sophie. Is Sophie. Will always be Sophie.

"I could have a *hundred* children, and none of them could replace Sophie." Addison's voice broke. Children. Her heart pinched. All she could see was Sophie's sweet little face, the wisps of black hair, her soft gray eyes.

"I know, darling. I misspoke, of course not. But you'll have other children, and the pain of loss will fade."

He had no idea. Would never have an idea. That on the day she held another baby for the first time, she'd still remember Sophie, as though not a minute had passed since she'd held her lifeless little body.

And it was exactly because Naveen couldn't comprehend the depth of emotion that would guide the rest of her life, her decision not to marry him was the right one. Knowing that, with as much crystal-clear certainty as she'd ever have in her life, it was cruel to string him along. She had to *tell* him. Now. Not later.

"I'm sorry, Naveen. I've made a decision. Rydell and I—"

Fourteen

The phone on the table behind her rang. Her heart did a little jog. News from the Coast Guard officials? Perhaps they'd caught the man? She stretched out and took it off the cradle. "This is Addison." She mouthed *Sorry* to Naveen, who didn't bother hiding his annoyance at the interruption.

Saved by the bell. She hadn't *planned on* blurting out anything right now, but words had been on the tip of her tongue. *God help me.*

"Badri, Miss Addison." Badri Patil was first mate. "We have Miss Persephone on the ship-to-shore for you. Do you want it connected there?"

Finally. She'd called her sister-in-law as soon as Rydell had left her cabin that morning. Thank God Peri had finally decided to return one of her calls.

"No thanks, Badri, I'll run down to my cabin. Give me a few minutes." Pushing back her chair, Addison got to her feet. "Thanks." At the moment of disconnection she snatched up a slice of bacon. "I've been waiting for this call. Don't let your breakfast get cold waiting for me. I'm not sure how long I'll be."

Naveen grabbed her wrist, his mouth a thin angry line. "Finish what you were about to say, Addison. You and Case—what? Fucked last night?"

His vehemence, and the fact that she'd never heard him swear, made her go cold. "Let go. I have to take the call."

"Did you fuck that son of a bitch behind my back again?" His shackling fingers tightened like a hard vise around her wrist. "Did you?"

Addison wrenched her arm free of his grip. His fingers left red marks on her wrist. "Do *not* manhandle me, Naveen. I'll take my call and then we'll discuss where our futures are going to part ways."

"Addison!" Naveen called after her as she flew down the outside stairs instead of winding her way through the main room. She ran down the corridor to her cabin just as Fahad, second steward, exited with his arms loaded with sheets and towels. He stepped aside and Addison flashed him a smile before closing the door and racing to pick up the phone on her desk.

"Put her through please, Badri." There was a click as the line connected. She realized she was shaking from the confrontation with Naveen. It was as if someone else had suddenly invaded his body. She was partially at fault. She hadn't handled that well, or diplomatically. Naveen was a proud man. She'd left him once for Rydell, and he was astute enough to know she still had unfinished business with her ex. Still, the look on his face had scared her, and him grabbing her like that pissed her off.

They'd have words all right, and he could go ahead to Sydney without her. Addison realized her heart was beating fast, as if she'd encountered danger and only narrowly escaped. Silly.

"Hi Peri?"

Without preamble, and ignoring the fact that the two women hadn't spoken in months, Peri said, "Ry told you."

Addison, slice of bacon raised to her mouth, sat down. "Told me what?"

"Shit."

"Oh, *that* instills me with confidence and not fear. What the hell's going on?"

"Hasn't Ry been on board for several days?"

Addison wasn't in the mood to be combative with anyone else today. Especially not with her ex-sister-in-law, whom she adored. "So?"

"So you need to *talk* to each other, Addy!"

"We talked about Sophie last night."

"Thank God! But no, not about Sophia, Addy."

Holy freaking crap. What the hell else? "What's he supposed to have told me?"

"It's not my place—"

"Bullshit. What else is going on with him, Peri? I know about *Sea Dragon* being hijacked." Her heartbeat stuttered as her mind raced with every dreadful scenario imaginable in her fertile brain. "Is he sick? Please don't tell me he has some terminal disease—"

"As far as I know he's healthy as a horse, and going to live well into his nineties like Grandpa Paul. It's the Cutters."

Swamped with relief, Addison made a rude noise. "I wish they, and Ry, would just leave each other alone. Why does every damn little thing have to be a contest between them?" She nibbled the crisp, salty bacon. "Who did what to whom this time?"

Rydell was always in conflict with one or more of the Cutter brothers. The problem was, the men were so much alike that they knew which buttons to press. Sometimes Ry ended on top; sometimes one or all of the Cutter men did. It was a lose–lose situation. "You would think that with over seventy percent of the earth covered with water there'd be enough room for dozens of salvage operations at the same time without them all falling over one another!"

"Daniel Cutter and our father were partners," Peri said flatly. "A long time ago. There was a third partner. Some French guy named Antoine Baillargeon. He died about nine months ago, apparently."

Addison digested the fact that the two archenemies had once been not only partners but friends. "Ry never mentioned it."

"We didn't know until we go a letter from Baillargeon's lawyer in England five months ago. Right when the *Sea Dragon* was hijacked. So Ry was a little occupied at the time."

Right when Ry had been fighting to find her and out of his mind with grief. Addison tossed the rest of her uneaten slice of bacon into the trash. "The three men were full partners?"

"More like venture capitalists, but in essence, yeah. Dad needed an infusion of cash for a major salvage. In short, Baillargeon lent him the money and gained an ownership share of Case Enterprises as collateral.

"Ry learned about it when Dad died, and he suddenly found out we had to make payments. He was already planning on buying them out, but over the course of years—many years. Unless he made an incredible salvage sooner. Now the Frenchman's heirs want to sell their share. They want fast money. A shitload of money."

Addison frowned, rubbing the tension at her temple. "Rydell *has* a lot of money."

"No, actually, he doesn't. Not *this* kind of money, Addy. *Two hundred and fifty million euros.* The Baillargeons have to honor the right of first refusal that was in the contract. Without *Sea Dragon*, Ry hasn't had an income for a year. That big lawsuit in South Africa brought by the Cutters cost him—and us—pretty much everything. Supporting you, and a full crew on board *Tesoro Mio*, has eaten up everything he had left. Even with every cent to both our names—Ry and myself—we can't come up with two hundred and fifty million euros in eight days! There's just no way." Peri dragged in a ragged breath.

"Ry will kill me for telling you all this. And I'm not telling you to make you feel bad. At any damn time, my muleheaded brother could've told you, and knowing you, you would've done everything in your power to alleviate the financial burden. Which was exactly *why* he refused to tell you."

That was Rydell in a freaking nutshell. Protect and serve.

He took care of the people he cared about. No matter what. "If the Baillargeon heirs are the majority owners of Case Enterprise . . . no wonder Ry is so freaking cranky and bad-tempered. No wonder he's so desperate to salvage the silver from this wreck fast." Addy paused a moment before continuing. "So he has to buy them out? That's why he needs this silver salvage so badly."

"Yes, and yes. But it's worse than that, Addy. Everything has to be paid back and finalized in a week. The heirs won't give him an extension. We're talking multimillions of dollars here. Ry wouldn't tell me the details. They want their money, or they'll sell. Ry and I have the right of first refusal. We don't have anything close to the amount they're asking for."

Addison's mouth was dry. "What happens if we can't pay?" It would kill him to lose the business he'd built from the wreck his father had made of Case Enterprises. Where his father had been an adventurer and a dreamer, Ry was pragmatic, and had worked hard and invested well. But now, according to Peri, that was all going to be lost if he couldn't come up with this enormous lump sum. Eight days? Impossible.

"If Ry can't pay by the stipulated date, the *Cutters* will have a chance to make an offer."

Addy knew that would be a disaster as far as Rydell was concerned. The final win for the Cutter brothers. It would kill him to lose *Tesoro Mio* on top of everything else he'd been through. "They'll own Case Enterprises outright. Lock, stock, and barrel."

"Yes. Worse, they know all about this will and the stipulation. The Baillargeon heirs have them waiting in the wings like birds of prey just in case Ry can't pay. That fricking bastard Logan Cutter has been secretly driving up the bidding to make it all but impossible for Ry to meet the astronomical asking price. By this time next month the damn Cutters will own everything Ry and I have worked for since Dad died."

"Is there anything I—"

"We're working on it. This isn't your concern. Not anymore."

Hurt beyond words, Addison choked back a cry. "That was uncalled for!"

"Sorry. Honest to God, I didn't mean it to come out like that. But the reality is, much as I love you, you're not part of this family anymore, Addison. That was your choice."

Tears stung her eyes. "Who are you, and what have you done with my best friend?"

"You wrecked our friendship when you divorced my brother instead of telling him that Sophia had died. That was cruel and heartless." Addison had never heard Peri's voice sound so cold, so disinterested. "That baby's death affected *all* of us, not just you. I only returned your call because I thought—hell, I *hoped*—that you'd do the right thing and that Ry had talked to you."

"We did talk. Last night. My mother reprogrammed

the wrong number for Ry into my cell phone. All that time I was calling, leaving him messages—he never got them, Peri. Not a single one. I think she changed my phone number as well. We couldn't contact each other, no matter how hard we tried. She made that impossible."

"Shit on a shingle, Addy! The bitch! Have you killed her yet?"

"I haven't *spoken* to her. Yet. But I assure you, it won't be pleasant. It will also be the very last time I see *or* speak to her. Ever. But first things first." She paused to drag in a ragged breath. She was so damn pissed, she was barely breathing between words. "I was going to sell *Tesoro Mio* in Sydney this week."

"You can't. Ry still owns half of it."

"Would us selling it jointly be enough money to pay off the debt?"

Peri made a rude scoffing noise. "It would be a great chunk of cash, but wouldn't get us where we need to be. Not after the year Ry just had."

Addison's throat ached with unshed tears. "What can I do?"

"Keep away from Ry—"

"Hard to do when we're on the same boat—"

"Then for crapsake don't break his heart again." Her ex-sister-in-law, ex-best-friend disconnected, leaving behind a monumental void.

Talk about a one–two punch. She hadn't realized that she'd lost her friend in the divorce. She'd thought, hoped, that Persephone would remain neutral. But clearly Peri sided with her brother. Tears sprang and Addison's chest hurt. It took fifteen minutes for her to move and function again.

As Rydell always said: One thing at a time.

She picked up the phone and gave Badri a number to connect her to her financial adviser in Milan.

When Pia Naletti answered the phone, Addison gave her the bare-bones information in rapid Italian, then finished with, "Liquidate everything. *Sí*, I realize I'll lose—that much?" Addison shrugged away the loss of at least a third of her assets. "Yes, I'm dead serious, and no, I don't have six months. I need my assets liquidated in less than week." She paused to listen to Pia's expert, always sound recommendations. For once, Addison wasn't going to take Pia's advice.

"I appreciate your concern, and I do hear you. I have the royalties from the *Treasures Of* books to live on. And if necessary, I'll get a job."

Addison listened to Pia try to talk her out of this "financial folly" for a few more minutes.

"Even my trust fund. All of it. Everything I have. I'm on board *Tesoro Mio* on my way to the Maldives."

Pia's concern ratcheted way up. "Think about this for a few days. You cannot liquidate your assets on an impulse. Besides what this may mean to your future, I need to assess market timing. I strongly advise you not give this more thought, and at least wait until—"

"I don't have the luxury of time. Please do as I ask. Call me with a number and how soon everything is liquid. *Molte grazie*, Pia."

"Sure, stay. I've asked Oscar to meet me here, but we have a few minutes. What's up?" Ry asked MoMo, who hung back as the dive crew departed the dining room. Through with breakfast, the dive crew was leaving to check equipment for the next day's first dive. Ry had asked Oscar to meet him in the dining room to go over additional security plans. Jax was belowdecks, stationed outside Addy's door.

He hoped to hell Shlomo Bergson didn't have some insurmountable issue, because right now Ry had enough fucking crap on his plate.

"I hope this isn't inappropriate, but as your friend—as *Addison's* friend—I have misgivings I want to share with you."

Ry was pretty sure MoMo had fallen for Addy as quickly as Ry himself had. Mo's feelings for her might have once been something romantic. In the early days, Ry had been aware of the looks of longing the other man sent Addy when he didn't know anyone was watching. Now MoMo seemed just to have a soft spot for Addy. "You have an issue with Darshi." Not a question.

MoMo looked startled, then nodded. "Yeah. I do. There's something—squirrelly about the guy. Look, I know this is none of my business. He's your guest, and Addison likes him, but—" MoMo spread expressive hands. "—I just don't like the guy."

"Join the club," Ry said drily. "What brought this on?" Was MoMo as jealous as he was himself? Probably. Neither of them was exactly impartial as far as Addy went.

Mo shoved his hands in the front of baggy green board shorts. "I was watching him the other night at dinner. That wasn't the look of a man in love." His swarthy skin flushed, and the tips of his ears, visible through his thick, curly black hair, turned bright red. "Not even the look a man gives a woman he lusts after."

Thank God. Not his imagination then. "Darshi watches her almost clinically, right?" Ry leaned his hip on the table and folded his arms. "Like she's some sort of science experiment. Believe me, I notice. Must admit, at first I chalked it up to pure, unadulterated jealousy. But then I started really listening to the way the guy speaks to her. More telling, and a crapload more subtle, is the guy's body language."

"Exactly!"

Contrary to the international playboy image he projected, the prince wasn't into Addy. Something Ry couldn't comprehend. Unobserved, he'd watched them from the deck above while they shared breakfast earlier.

Even when talking to her, Darshi's eyes flickered around the deck. Looking for what? For whom? Or, hell, no one. He was distracted, when his gaze shouldn't have left Addy's face.

Darshi had cradled Addy's head, dragging her in for a kiss. But where Ry himself would've filled both hands with her, Darshi's free hand lay relaxed on the table. Darshi wanted *something* from Addy, but not because she was Addy. Ry couldn't imagine what else there was.

"Addy's—*everything*. Beautiful, sexy, articulate, independent, and when she's not bowed down with grief, *funny*. What's not to like?" MoMo asked, looking miserable. "And yet—" He shrugged. "I don't get it. Is he after her *money*?"

Ry shook his head. "Addison's wealthy but she's not in the same financial bracket as the prince. She comes from a wealthy family, and her father left her a sizable trust fund. But Darshi's loaded. He doesn't need her money."

MoMo looked even more miserable. "So if it isn't attraction, and it isn't money, what the hell else is there? Look," he said quickly. "I know I have no right to have a voice in who she sees, but honest to God, *not* Darshi. He's—hell, he's *fardekhtik*, suspicious. Skeevy."

"No shit. You're preaching to the choir. I'm going to tell him he can't stay for the salvage. No reason for him to be here."

"Right," MoMo agreed with alacrity. "Sorry if I overstepped . . ."

Ry clasped the other man's shoulder. "You didn't. And thanks for watching out for Addy."

"Are things—Did you—Everything okay now?"

"Yeah. We talked out some things last night. I think we're going to be good."

"Good. That makes me happy. Rather you than that putz. Seeing them together again must be tougher than shit on you, Ry. I hated to add to that. But I couldn't just let it go. Addy deserves better. I'm happy you're working things out. Real happy." MoMo sucked in a breath, looking slightly uncomfortable about the exchange. "I'll go help Georgeo with the tanks."

After last night's revelations, as far as Ry was concerned, watching Addy and the prince having breakfast mere hours later had sealed the fuckwad's fate. The guy had to go. They'd reach Malé by noon tomorrow. He'd make sure Darshi's feet were on terra firma and not *Tesoro Mio* within minutes of the first sighting. Addy had looked distracted at breakfast with the prince and, her distraction had given Ry a small measure of satisfaction. *No shit.* They'd been making love like there was no tomorrow just an hour earlier.

Ry hated that the lips *he'd* kissed had touched Darshi's an hour later. Hated it, with every fiber of his being, yet with the realization of heart-wrenching grief that had come in the stormy night, he knew it was a penance he deserved.

He'd taken their kiss like a man. Though he'd prefer to walk slowly over hot coals, he'd stood there at the upper rail, silent. And let it happen, then made a strategic retreat before the urge to throw His Mightiness overboard became overpowering.

He didn't want the guy dead, but he'd draw a great deal of satisfaction when His Royal Pain in the Ass was in a fucking galaxy far far away, preferably with a crapload of broken bones. Just thinking about the fucking prince had made Ry feel feral and homicidal.

Cut him loose, Addy. Tell him to fuck off. And if you don't, I'll do it for you.

The man overboard had been put on a back burner in light of the revelations in the early hours of this morning. Ry still felt raw and off kilter. Partially hopeful, but also deeply troubled by Hollis's actions. Addy's mother—and possibly Darshi himself—had changed the course of their lives.

He'd spent an hour reading some of Addy's texts, starting on March 18 and working his way through the days, weeks, and months of anguish, despair, and finally anger. Her pain, her need to have him at her side was all there in print. *Oh, Addy.*

Ry decided he'd take her ashore tomorrow when they reached the dive site. Let the crew start the setup, persuade Darshi to fuck off, and ban Hollis from ever boarding his ship again.

He and Addy would go for a romantic dinner. Walk along the beach at sunset. Make love, talk—fall in love all over again. Ry's heart lifted.

Yeah. Great plan. At any other time in his life, when he had the world in his hands. He'd broken her heart. Their daughter was dead and he hadn't even had the decency to grieve with her. On top of that, he was staring down almost certain financial ruin. It would be better for Addy if she got off the ship and walked away from him without looking back. Ever.

Damn.

If he had any decency at all he'd let her to go. But not with Darshi. He might be royalty and wealthy beyond belief, but Addy was still too damn good for him.

Oscar walked in. "Addy's been in her cabin. Alone, for the past hour. Jax is outside her door. The prince is in his own cabin."

"Excellent. I want both of you to be like white on rice with Addy until such ti—"

"Excuse me, Mr. Case?" The senior police officer interrupted as he and one of his subordinates came into the room. With them was Captain Seddeth. "We've made an arrest."

Fifteen

Still reeling from sensory overload in the early hours, Ry hadn't forgotten that a man had died yesterday. He glanced at Oscar, then back to Sharma. "That's good news. Who is it?" *Please. Tell me you arrested Darshi's ass and are going to throw him into prison for the rest of his sodding life.*

"The prince's bodyguard, Okito Van Engen. As you know, the camera was disabled on that section of the ship at the time of the incident. But we spent several hours looking at *past* recordings, searching for anything that might give us a clue. May I?" He indicated the control for the monitors and picked it up when Ry nodded.

The center monitor flicked for a moment, and Seddeth said, "We watched several hundred hours of footage in the early hours. Fortunately, when I replaced some of the defective cameras about six months ago, I didn't bother erasing prior recordings, and I had the disks in a drawer. I isolated the relevant footage. See for yourself."

Ry and Oscar turned to watch the screen. All the images were of the prince with one or more of his bodyguards.

I knew it! Damn that fucker for bringing danger to Addy's door. I'm going to kill him.

"This was the most telling," the senior officer said,

slowing the video. "Fortunately, Varma here has some knowledge of lipreading. Here is the first exchange between Prince Darshi and Van Engen, dated only nine days ago."

The footage was taken in broad daylight, with crisp, clear visuals. Darshi and his bodyguard, Van Engen, stood with their backs to the rail; Cannes Marina and a string of luxury hotels lay in the background. The *Tesoro Mio* had been docked there for several months.

Goddamn it, *Addy* had been on board at the time. Ry's blood pressure rose to throb behind his eyeballs, and his fingers flexed as he imagined them wrapped around the fuckhead's neck.

"Varma," his commander said, "if you will?"

The younger man nodded. "Here the prince is telling Van Engen, 'You work for *me*'—I believe the word here is 'asshole.' "

Clearly not a friendly exchange. The prince's handsome face was contorted with anger, and he pounded his chest for emphasis.

Van Engen shoved the prince's shoulder, his face clearly visible as he gave his boss a smug look. "No I don't, dickhead," Varma lip-read. "If I don't make my regular call in, he'll come down on you like flies on shit."

Ry's fury rose. "Who's *he*?"

Sharma shrugged. "This we do not know. Yet. With this new information, we will of course interrogate His Highness again. We wanted to bring this to your attention first."

"Is it possible it was the *prince* who was meant to go overboard, and not Azm Kapur?" Oscar asked.

Ry shook his head. "The two men couldn't have been confused, even in the dark. Kapur was fifty pounds heavier and at least six inches shorter than Darshi." The prince was tall, slender, and Indian, with a British accent.

Kapur had looked Asian, was built like a sumo wrestler, and had a strong Australian accent. No confusion possible. He looked back to the officers. "Why arrest Van Engen and not the prince?"

"Out of deference to His Highness, we interrogated Van Engen first, knowing the prince is, technically, at our disposal as long as we are at sea. Van Engen confessed, with some persuasion."

"Okay. So now we know Van Engen worked for someone else, and we presume killed Kapur."

"It would appear so. Although it isn't out of the realm of possibility that he confessed to cover for someone else," Sharma agreed. "Here is another interesting section that we found, dated the day before *Tesoro Mio* set sail with you on board."

The view switched to a location aft, near the hot tub. "As you see, they have their backs to the camera, and therefore we could not read their lips. This exchange was once again impassioned, and not . . . friendly."

To say the least. Van Engen seemed to be the one talking, and the prince, shoulders tense, stood and listened. When the exchange was over, the bodyguard walked away.

Darshi's handsome features showed fear before he turned to grip the rail with white knuckles. So the threat had scared the shit out of him. Good.

What struck Ry was that this was filmed the same evening Darshi had taken Addy to the Hôtel de Paris for dinner that first night Ry had come aboard to wait for her.

What the hell was Darshi mixed up in? More important, what was he involving Addy in? One man that they knew of was dead. A man connected to Darshi, and killed on board Ry's ship. Darshi was clearly shit scared of *something*—or *someone*. Whatever it was, whoever the fuck it was, it couldn't be allowed anywhere near Addy.

Ry felt a start of alarm. Darshi and Addy were both belowdecks. "Now we know why," Ry said tightly, only remaining where he was because he knew Jax stood guard outside Addy's door. "To get the *who* Van Engen was talking about, we have to speak to Darshi. Get him up here. I want answers, and I want them *now*. I want to know who ordered the hit, and if or what it has to do with Addy and *Tesoro Mio*."

Ry had never liked the fucker; instinctively, he'd always known the guy was a sleazeball. Now he was even more sure that Darshi had been involved in Addy's mother's deception. Hell, he was probably the one to reprogram Addy's phone. He'd certainly whisked her away so her frantic husband couldn't find her.

Ry tried to stay focused, but he still felt raw after the night and early morning spent with Addy. "What does Van Engen have to say?" *One fucking problem at a time.*

"With a little *persuasion*, Okito Van Engen admitted he was hired to kill Kapur. It was *not* meant to look like an accident," the senior officer told them. "He claims he was ordered to deliver a message."

"The message was intended for Darshi," Ry said. " 'If I can kill your bodyguard, I can kill you.' "

The police captain nodded his agreement. "Van Engen will not say for whom the message was intended, nor will he tell us the name of the person who hired him. What we do know is that he carries a New Zealand passport. Residential address is in Tasmania. When we ran background checks on everyone yesterday, his didn't raise any red flags. He appeared to be who he claimed to be. Worked for the prince for six months. Freelance security for the last ten years. Some high-profile clients. No complaints. The prince told us his staff ran a security background on Van Engen before he was hired. He was not only cleared, but came highly recommended. Of course," he said drily. "Under the circumstances we'll dig deeper. Look at his connections, et cetera."

"Will you send him back to New Zealand?" Oscar asked. Since the "event," Oscar, Jax, and Ry had all been carrying guns in plain sight. The captain's weapon was concealed under his white dress shirt, but it was there. No one was letting down their guard until this matter was resolved.

Paras Sharma shrugged. "If they ask for extradition. They might try him separately. But since the crime was committed in Indian waters, we're taking him back with us to Mangalore to stand trial for murder."

"Van Engen confessed?" Oscar asked, looking like Ry felt. Incredulous. "Makes no sense at all."

The taller officer shrugged. "He claims he'll be safer in prison."

"Presumably he did what he was hired to do. Why would he think he'd be safer in prison in a foreign country rather than just disappearing? That makes no sense, either."

Varma, the younger, shorter officer, glanced longingly at the coffeepot and the pile of pancakes—cold—beside it. They'd taken their meal in the galley hours earlier. "Hopefully we'll know more when we have him in interrogation and he realizes the severity of his actions. Though the death penalty is rarely imposed in India, capital punishment is an option for murder. We will advise him of that fact."

"Van Engen confessing is—odd," Ry said. "I'm not sure that few-second video would hold up in court. A threat? Sure. But leading to tossing someone overboard? Maybe not. We're about to reach the Maldives. *Land.* He could've split. Disappeared."

"Our thoughts exactly," the senior officer said. "Hopefully we'll know more after we've spoken to

Prince Darshi again. He might be able to give us some insight."

"Or he's involved in some way himself," Ry pointed out.

"This is true," the police officer admitted. "Although, given the prince's celebrity and wealth, even with the tapes, it might be impossible to prove he knew what the killing was about. It remains to be seen."

Removing Darshi and his men sooner rather than later would resolve Ry's more immediate problems. Finishing that conversation with Addy would, hopefully, if not resolve things then at least ease them even more. Finding that silver—in time—would take the boulder off his chest.

"Oscar? Go get Darshi, so we can get this over with. Whether he was directly involved or even aware of what was going on, both men worked for him; he's got to have insight into their backgrounds and habits." And if he discovered the fucker had colluded with Hollis, Ry would kill him himself. Oscar left quickly to go belowdecks.

"What did you do with Van Engen?" Ry asked.

"Secured in one of your storerooms until our helicopter arrives in a few hours. If the prince wants to accompany us as we take Van Engen to Mangalore, we will, of course, accommodate him."

Hell, yeah. Arrest his ass, and bloody take him the hell away.

Sunset on the water was always magical, and this evening was no exception. The massive storm seemed to have washed the air clean. The orange-and-raspberry-sorbet-colored sky bled seamlessly into the water surrounding *Tesoro Mio* in a wash of soft watercolors, making the wavelets look like gentle brushstrokes.

Addison inhaled the balmy ocean breeze, which carried with it delicious aromas of barbecued meats and beer.

She'd missed evenings like this. She and Ry sharing a meal with friends under the stars. Laughing, teasing, going back to their cabin to make love . . .

After supervising the table setting—purple place mats, white china, and an amethyst glass bowl filled with fat yellow lemons—Addison walked over to the rail and leaned her elbows on the polished teak to watch the unfurling froth as the hull cut through the water.

She'd dressed with care in a high-necked, white cotton sundress with wide straps that crisscrossed over a low back, showing off her light tan. The warm breeze wrapped around her bare skin like a soft, diaphanous shawl, and teased strands of loose hair to tickle the back of her neck and shoulders.

She'd coiled her hair in a simple, just-got-out-of-bed updo. Ry loved her hair up. She shivered, remembering how it felt when he kissed her nape before taking it down. Diamond studs Ry had given her for their first anniversary sparkled in her ears, and trio of diamond and gold tennis bracelets adorned one wrist. If push came to shove, she'd sell every last piece of her jewelry if that would help him.

She was as nervous as a teenager on a first date with the prospect of talking to Ry again after the emotionally charged exchanges—plural—in the early hours of the morning.

After returning to her cabin after breakfast to take Peri's call, she'd remained there until it was time to come up for dinner. There was a lot to digest. Ry. Naveen. Peri's new information . . .

The daylight hours hadn't been wasted. She'd completed a new blog post, gotten a good handle on the new chapter in the book, and mulled over, and examined, the conversation with Ry.

Truth be known, it wasn't Ry she was avoiding. It was Naveen. It was the honorable thing to do to tell him she and Rydell—were what? Not reconciling. Not yet anyway. Sleeping together? None of his business. She settled for *talking*. Naveen could interpret that however he liked. The bottom line was she'd let him down as gently as possible. She knew his pride would be stung losing her to Rydell twice.

God. Why the hell was she so worried about hurting Nav's feeling when it was almost a certainty that he'd been involved with deceiving both herself and Rydell? Hollis was smart, and sneaky, but she didn't have the tech skills to manipulate the phone. Naveen had denied doing it, but Addison wasn't sure she believed him. It was a despicable thing to do, if he had been involved. Was he capable of doing that to her? The woman he professed to love and wanted to marry?

Addison turned her head instinctively when she heard Rydell's voice. He and the others were gathered around the grill at the far end of the aft deck. Thirty feet separated them, and the wind allowed her to hear snippets of their conversation, easy enough to block out.

The dive crew and two Coast Guard officers were in the area with the bar, grill, and hot tub with Rydell. Their laughter—*his* laughter—carried on the breeze, making Addison's heart pinch with emotion. She wished she could blink away everyone else. Be alone with him.

He glanced up, and their gazes locked. Her heart fluttered, much as it had when they'd first met. Rydell started to move, but she gave a small shake of her head. She needed a few minutes alone. He nodded, but continued to hold her gaze like a tractor beam. Addison let out the breath she'd been holding. Reprieve for a little while longer.

Typical Ry, got her like no one else ever had.

MoMo asked him a question, stealing his attention, and the eye caress connection was broken.

Naveen wasn't with the others, she noticed. She was still annoyed at their exchange over breakfast. Yes, under the circumstances, his expectation that she'd say yes to his proposal was logical, so she understood his anger. That said, he had no business manhandling her. She twisted the bracelets on her wrist, worn not only because she loved the bling, but also to cover the faint bruises left by Naveen's fingers when he'd grabbed her this morning.

Ry had grabbed her, too, yet he hadn't left a mark on her. Not on her skin anyway.

They'd be in the Maldives in the morning. Like it or not, Naveen would disembark with the others. It would be a relief to have him gone. Guilty or not, he was guilty by association. She'd never look at him the same way ever again.

As for Rydell—they were good. Okay, not *good*, but considerably better than they'd been twenty-four hours ago. There was more to say, more to tell, more to heal. That required time, more specifically time alone. Something they wouldn't get in the next few weeks as Ry tried to retrieve a treasure that could mean the difference between saving his company and losing everything to his archenemies, the Cutters.

She knew him. He wouldn't lie down without doing everything in his power to win. And she'd do anything she could to help him. Whether he asked for or wanted her help was beside the point. She was here. She was damn well going to figure out a way to help.

"Hey." Kevin walked over to stand beside her. Short strands of her yellow-blond hair ruffled in the breeze as she inhaled deeply. Like Addison she was barefoot. Wearing a fire-engine-red bikini top and frayed denim shorts, she looked as wholesome as the girl next door.

This was the first time since the dive crew had boarded in Mangalore that they'd had a chance to be alone. More, Addison admitted, because she'd spent a lot of her time alone in her cabin instead of socializing.

"Are you having a private moment communing with nature," Kevin asked, "or can I join you?"

"I'd love for you to join me. We can commune together."

Letting out a small sigh, the blonde leaned her elbows on the railing beside her and looked across the water before turning her head to face her. "Can I just say one thing and then change the subject?"

Bracing herself, Addy said, "Anything."

Cheeks flushed with high emotion, Kevin's eyes glittered with uncharacteristic moisture. Kev was tough. It was rare for her to show girlie emotion. Seeing her friend with tears in her eyes made Addy tear up, too.

"I missed you, Addy," Kevin said, voice thick. "I wanted to be there for you. I understood why you shut me—everyone—out, but God I *missed* you. I ached for your pain. I wished you'd let me in. But what was then isn't now. Can we be friends again?"

"Yes. Please." Addison gathered her friend in her arms and hugged her so tightly, Kevin squeaked out a laugh. Putting Kev away from her, Addison choked back tears. "I missed you like hell. I'm sorry I shut you out. I missed you, too."

"Understood and forgiven," Kevin said, blinking rapidly, making the tears on her pale lashes twinkle like tiny diamonds. "I'm sorry about Sophie, Addy. My heart broke, too. I miss your beautiful baby girl more than I can say. I'm so, so, so damn sorry for your loss." Clearing her throat, she straightened her shoulders. "Okay. Subject change. Let's talk hardheaded men, and the women who want to jump their bones."

Addison laughed, letting the past year dissolve and slipping back to the time when she and Kevin had been friends and confidantes. “My mind boggles at your determination and fortitude in continuing to resist that gorgeous Italian,” Addison said. “That man is so in love with you, his heart is in his eyes whenever he looks at you.”

“I meant you and Ry, and frankly, aside from the gorgeous-Italian part of it, your statement applies to him. How can you resist him?”

“Oh,” Addison said, fire in her cheeks. “Well—”

“Hmm.” Kev narrowed her eyes as she studied Addy. “So there *is* a reason why Ry’s in a better mood today, isn’t there?”

She couldn’t help but smile. God, she’d missed having a friend to talk to. Peri and Callie were her BFFs, but she rarely saw them, and talking on the phone wasn’t the same as talking face-to-face. She and Kevin had hit it off the moment they met. Fortunate, because the older woman was one of Ry’s closest friends.

Shifting the subject, not wanting to delve too deeply into the uncertainties she and Ry faced despite their night together, Addy said, “What’s going on between you and Georgeo? Why haven’t you given him his happily-ever-after?”

The older woman scowled. On her it just looked adorable. “He loves children. I’m *fifty*.”

“I’ve heard the same song,” she reminded her friend cheerfully. “And every verse, since we first met.” Right after Addison had started dating Rydell. “You’re not too old to adopt if that’s what you want.”

“He’s a *child*.”

Amused, Addison cocked a brow. “He’s thirty-seven.”

“He should find a woman young enough to start a life with.”

"He's *found* the woman he wants to spend the rest of his life with. Thirteen years is nothing when two people love each other."

"It's not love. We have *sex*. Correction. *Had* sex. Plenty of it. That's over." Kevin pulled a face. "He said that wasn't the role he wanted, and now he keeps saying no until I say yes." She shrugged. "He's made his choice."

"Yes. To make an honest woman of you."

"Not gonna happen. Enough about me. Have you and Ry made up? I never did understand how a couple so perfect for each other—so much in love—could be married one day and divorced the next."

The sky was slowly turning mauve and delicate shades of lavender, and the calm water looked like rippled, deep-purple silk with a thin streak of apricot on the horizon. They focused on the sunset as Addy told her what she and Ry were now assuming—that her mother had orchestrated the rift.

"*That's* why Ry was shocked speechless when I spoke to him months later. I couldn't comprehend why you didn't tell him. I felt so bad for him that day, Addy. Hearing that his baby had died, and had died *three months* earlier, gutted him."

"I know." Her mouth was dry, and her heart hurt. A physical ache that would probably be with her for the rest of her life. "We talked last night."

"My God. I *hate* that bitch. What does Hollis have to say for herself? Not that there's any excuse for what she did. Damn it, damn it, fucking damn her to hell. She always did want you and the prince together, didn't she?"

Addison nodded. "If she can't have a title, the next best thing would be her daughter being a princess." Addison grimaced. "*That'll* never happen."

"Have you shared the happy news with Ry?"

Addison smiled. "I think after last night, he pretty much got the memo."

"I adore you, Addison D'Marco Case. You were always good for each other. Now, what are we going to do about the Queen Bitch of the Universe?"

"First I want to make absolutely sure she was the perpetrator. Then we'll have a little chat. Then I'll never speak to her again."

"You are *way* too fucking nice! I want to cut that bitch!"

"You'll have to stand in line." Addison lifted her head, her attention caught by a man's deep, throaty laugh. She cast a look across at the group laughing and joking with Ry. He looked so carefree, so happy in the moment.

Were his friends aware of his dire financial situation? He hadn't confided his monetary difficulties to her, but had he told *them*? Or were they, too, in the dark about the urgency and need to find this silver, and find it quickly?

"You know about *Sea Dragon*, right?" Kevin pushed her bangs off her face as the wind played with her hair. "Shit, poor, Ry. Last year must've been the worst year of his life. First Sophie, then you divorcing him, then getting his ship hijacked. Bam. Bam. Bam."

She waited to see if Kev would give a hint that she knew. Instead, Kev continued, "He's one tough hombre. He'd managed to weather each storm with his usual hardassness. Even shattered and bloody, he keeps on going. I don't know how the hell he does it."

Either Kevin was keeping whatever he'd told her confidential, or Rydell hadn't told her about his legal crap with the Cutters. He had always kept everything close to the chest; he wasn't a man who typically shared his worries or his burdens. Yet at one time he'd shared everything with her. Big and small, they'd talked. Communicated. In bed, and out of bed, their lives had been entwined. While others had been kept out of the loop, she'd always been in.

Being a part of Ry's life was like sharing secrets with a trusted friend. He'd only revealed his true self, the man of depth, compassion, and emotion, the man guided by the legacy left by his father, to her.

She suspected the only reason he'd told his sister of his financial troubles was because she was an integral part of Case Enterprises and therefore *had* to be kept in the loop. Her finances were impacted by this, too. With the information Peri had provided, Addy felt as though a giant time bomb was strapped to the ship, counting down the minutes. And if *she* felt that way, she could only imagine how Ry felt.

She felt his eyes on her, and even though she tried to resist, she turned her head. His smile sent a bolt of fiery lightning speeding through her veins. She looked away.

Kevin fanned her face with her hand. "Whew. If Ry saw how you look at him he'd come over here, toss you over his shoulder, and carry you off like a caveman."

He had seen her. And his look said he wanted to do just that. "I'd let him," Addison said softly, bringing her attention back to her friend.

"Thank God. You still love him."

With my entire heart. "There's still a lot that we have to talk about, a lot to deal with."

"Well, pull the Band-Aid off and get it done. You're not getting any younger, you know."

Addison grinned. "Talking about lustful stares, don't look now, but Georgeo is watching you like Simba eye-ing his next meal."

"He's welcome to carry me to his cave. Anytime." Kevin shot the Italian a sultry glance. He looked away.

Poor guy. “It’s not my fault the man has blue balls. All he has to do is agree to my terms.”

“No middle ground?”

“My way or the highway.”

Grinning, Addison shook her head. “That’s tricky to do when you both work aboard a ship. You’re a hard nut, Kevin Hill.”

“I’m not the one suffering,” she said airily.

“Aren’t you? I see the way you look at him, Kev.”

The older woman pushed off the rail. “Let’s see who breaks first. Coming?”

Addison shook her head, suddenly reluctant to become a part of the group. Too many conflicting emotions were still swirling as she thought of Ry, Naveen, and her mother. “In a sec. Go ahead.”

With an airy backhanded wave and a sway to her hips, Kev strolled across the deck, attention fixed on her quarry. Addison observed Georgeo’s tight expression, as if he couldn’t drag his eyes away. It would be interesting to see just which of them would gain the upper hand. Addison’s money was on Georgeo.

As if drawn by a magnet, her gaze swung left to fix on Rydell. Bare-chested, laughing, beer in hand, dark hair drifting around his shoulders in the warm breeze blowing off the water. His tanned skin looked bronzed in the waning light, and he appeared as strong and invincible as Hercules.

She’d seen him naked—physically and emotionally—and bowed in Sophie’s room this morning. Shoulders heaving with the choking sound of his sobs.

Addison turned around, facing the open water. Her knuckles turned white on the rail as the pressure in her chest built.

He wasn’t invincible.

Like other mortals, he bled and worried. And she now knew that he grieved, deeply and profoundly, like everyone else. He was just a master at masking wounds so no one saw his vulnerability. He had his pride, too. He wouldn't give a shit how other people saw him, but weakness wasn't in his DNA, and therefore any sign of it would be considered a failure to him.

So many people depended on him. He wouldn't want to let anyone down. Worries didn't create anxiety for him. They created action. He was a man who always had clear goals in mind. He was a man who usually met each goal head-on.

Life was intervening, though, teaching him the helplessness that came with facing reality.

The shit side of life had taken away his precious daughter, and the shit wasn't done with him yet.

On top of Sophie's death, if he lost his company, if he was financially ruined and lived to see the Cutters revel in their victory over him, taking everything his family had sacrificed and built—oh, God. Addy didn't know how he'd get through it.

Please God, don't give him more than he can handle.

She caught her breath and reminded herself that this was Rydell Case she was worrying about. He could handle anything. He'd find a way, come fiery hell or the highest water.

Sixteen

A man's possessive arm slid around her waist. Addison stiffened at the scent of Versace Eros cologne. Naveen, not Ry.

"You smell as good as you look, darling," he murmured against her hair.

As if nothing happened this morning? Trapped by the railing and his body, she took a step to the side and glanced over his shoulder. Jax, his pistol still visible, had been pretending great interest in rearranging salads on the buffet; now he looked up, alert to danger. She gave a slight shake of her head. She was in no danger from Naveen. Especially with everyone else nearby.

The killer was secure in the storeroom. Jax didn't need to be stuck to her like a shadow, but the security guys had been instructed by Ry to stick with her until Van Engen was taken away by the Coast Guard first thing tomorrow morning, and he was doing his job.

Still, she jerked back, out of Naveen's reach. "Don't. The only reason I haven't made a scene about you grabbing me this morning is that Ry is already pissed that you're here at all. I don't want to precipitate any violence from him. Keep your hands to yourself, Naveen."

He held up both hands in a *stop* gesture. "Good Lord, Addison. I would *never* hurt you. *Never.* That's not who

I am, and you know it. I was jealous when I heard the way you talked about Case this morning. I'm sorry if I scared you."

She held up her wrist and pushed back the sparkling bracelets, so he could see the faint marks he made on her wrist.

"Did I do that? I'm so, so sorry. Please. Forgive me?"

"Don't ever manhandle me again. I mean it." He wouldn't because she knew she'd never see him again after he left in the morning.

Since his forehead didn't move, it was hard to tell if he frowned, but his eyes darkened, his pupils growing larger and darker like a predatory large cat, and his lips compressed. "The thought of you with Case—"

"*That's* not an agreement never to grab me again, Naveen."

"Of course," he said stiffly. "I was taken by surprise. It won't happen again."

If she'd had doubts about him before Ry even came back on the scene, that brief flash of anger had shown her another side of Naveen. A side she'd never seen before, and certainly didn't like.

He'd had time to change into white linen pants and shirt, his black hair slicked back. "You were with the police for a long time."

He looked as though he'd just strolled off a *GQ* cover. Addison's gaze flicked across the deck to Ry. *He* looked as though he'd just surfed up on the beach to get a cold one. No shirt, no shoes, hair too long, body ripped and tanned. Tall, dark, and compelling. It was hard to look away.

"I don't like not being able to answer questions about my own employees," Naveen told her, dragging her attention back to him and away from Ry. "I have people for that. I gave them the phone number of my people, but they insisted I answer all their questions to their satisfaction. *Again.* They found some video footage taken several days ago, and wanted to ask me more questions this morning. They interrogated me as if I were some sort of low-life criminal. I expected them to bring out the thumbscrews before long. I had to remind them of who I am."

Addison raised a brow. "Come on, Naveen. Just because you have a title doesn't mean they wouldn't consider you a suspect—as they do everyone else on board. They appear very good at what they're doing, and they haven't been overly intrusive. They did capture Van Engen."

Naveen liked the serfs to keep their distance. A bit tricky in the real world where there weren't that many serfs around for him to ignore.

"He practically turned himself in," Naveen corrected. "All they had to do was be present."

Addison didn't have to turn her head; out of the corner of her eye she could see Ry waving his hand as he told a story. Heard the pause for the punch line. Waited. Everyone laughed. Her chest constricted a bit. She wanted to be over there laughing with them, not standing here with Naveen with a backdrop of the romantic sunset.

"However it came about, they have him," she said with a trace of sympathy.

"This is all very inconvenient, I must say. They're going to take him back with them to Mangalore as soon as we dock. Which means I'm down *two* men servants, and must wait until we reach Sydney before I feel comfortable filling those positions. I sincerely hope Case finds whatever he's trying to salvage, so we can continue our journey as soon as possible. The buyer is eagerly awaiting our arrival in Sydney. He *expects* us, Addison."

The buyer was the least of her problems. Or, she thought, possibly the *answer* to Ry's prayers. But to know that, they needed to talk about his financial situation. *That* minefield on top of the barely healed wound of their discussion about Sophia was going to be tricky. It needed time to resolve—somehow. Unfortunately Ry didn't have time. The buyer was already in place. Naveen had brokered the deal.

If between them, she and Ry could come up with the money to buy back Case Enterprises, he could get his hands on a smaller, cheaper ship until he salvaged his next treasure. Addison had seen pictures of Zane Cutter's ship the *Decrepit*. It lived up to its name. It was a junker, but it did the job and made the Cutters lots and lots of money. Millions.

Rydell could do the same.

Not that she'd breathe the name *Cutter* to him. Ever. The hatred he felt for that family was deep and bitter. She'd never been able to figure out *why*, when the ocean was so vast, they ever needed to run into each other. They sued him. Ry sued them back. It was a lose–lose situation.

But if he lost this war, it would be over. Done.

He'd be back to starting from scratch.

Addison had every faith that he could rebuild his fortune. In time. But it would be humiliating and dispiriting. Yes. Maybe a quick sale of *Tesoro Mio* was the answer. "Didn't you let the buyer know the trip was postponed?"

Withdrawing a black silk handkerchief from his pant pocket, the prince mopped perspiration from his forehead, then dabbed it over his upper lip. It wasn't that hot. Addy looked at him with concern. Crap, she didn't want to be unsympathetic, but the last thing she needed right now was Naveen getting sick. Things were complicated enough without her playing nurse to him. Because if he *was* sick, she'd feel like a monster insisting he leave the ship tomorrow.

He stuffed the scrap of silk back into his pocket. "I'd hoped that we could still make it in a reasonable amount of time."

"Rydell says it will take a minimum of two weeks for this dive, Naveen. I told you that. Not to mention that the terms of our divorce stipulate that he gets first refusal if I decide to sell." Something she'd told him when he'd brought her the offer several months ago. "Honestly, since *Sea Dragon* was hijacked, I can't see Rydell agreeing to sell *Tesoro Mio*. It's his livelihood." *More so now than ever.*

"I made a gentleman's agreement, Addison. I can't—won't go back on that."

"That wasn't your call to make, Nav." He had no right to make any kind of agreement, handshake or legal. The ship wasn't his. "Legally that agreement isn't binding. *I* didn't agree to anything. I don't think I could've been any plainer when I told you that. And Rydell would've had a fit if he'd known. I agreed only that I'd bring *Tesoro Mio* to Sydney for him to look at."

His black eyes looked cold and hard. "As your fiancé, I believed I *did* have the right to act on your behalf."

"First, even if that was true, you being my fiancé—that still doesn't give you any legal rights to make business decisions on my behalf, and certainly not for a *hundred-and-fifty-million-dollar* sale. Second, you aren't my fiancé. That's something we were going to address once we got to Sydney." Now was as good a time as any to tell him the bad news. "And since you bring that up—let me clarify my position. I can't marry you, Naveen." *There. Band-Aid ripped off.* "Not now. Not ever."

He reared back as though she'd slapped him. His

olive complexion paled, and oily sweat sheened his skin. He took out the silk again, wiping his face. This time she noticed that his fingers shook. "You don't mean that. We *love* each other, we always have. Case is just confusing you now. But once we reach Sydney—"

"No. Things have never been more clear." And she'd go to hell for lying through her teeth. Things were about as clear as London fog, but that was her personal issue and had zip to do with him. "We cared for each other, but that isn't love." He tried to pull her into his arms, but Addison held him off with both hands on his chest.

"It *is* love," he said sincerely, looking into her eyes. Unfortunately, all she saw reflected there was her own pale face, and her expression of growing annoyance. He ran his hand over her hair, then brushed her cheek with the tips of his fingers. "Let me show you how hot my passion burns for you, my darling."

Addison gave him a suspicious look, then half laughed. "Did you rehearse that line, Naveen?" Passion was the last emotion she expected from him. Where Ry held everything to his chest, he was the strong silent type and rarely showed emotion. Naveen was the cold, impersonal type. Addison wasn't sure he was capable of showing any depth of emotion at all. Scanning his features, she saw that he appeared to be shaken. Distressed. Then angry.

His expression tightened. "I don't think it should be amusing when I'm declaring my feelings for you."

Her smile slipped. "Do you really love me, Naveen? I don't think you do. You've been a good friend—which is why I didn't throw your ass overboard this morning when you grabbed me. But friends is all we can be."

"Case seduced you away from me. Again." He rubbed an elegant hand across his smooth jaw. "I could kill that man for stealing you from me *twice*."

"I wouldn't use that word when we have the Coast

Guard on board," she said drily. "And I couldn't be stolen if I wasn't willing to go."

"You . . . *love* him? After what he put you through when your child died? Do you forget that he never called you? Refused to even acknowledge that it had died? That he didn't even bother to make an excuse for not going to the funeral?"

It? Dear God, was that how he thought of her beautiful little girl? *It?* "He and I have resolved all that. And it was because Hollis tampered with my phone."

"So he says," Naveen said tightly, looking less attractive by the minute. The breeze flipped his carefully combed hair, so she had a glimpse of his receding hairline. "Are you willing to take his word for this? Have you at least confirmed what he claims with Hollis?"

"I'd believe her considerably *less* than I believe Ry." At that moment she glanced up, and her gaze collided with Ry's. He cocked a brow. *Are you okay?* She gave a small nod, her heart filling at the familiar connection. God, she'd missed him. Missed their silent communications. Missed the invisible thread that had always bound them. Missed the way he would jump in to protect her against anything at a moment's notice. "And yes." She glanced back at Naveen. "I do believe him."

"Then I have a few weeks to convince you that you've made the wrong choice, my dear. I'll prove that Case still isn't the man for you."

Oh, no, no and freaking no. Not going to happen. "I'm sorry, Naveen. When we reach port tomorrow, I'd like you to leave the ship."

He looked stunned. "You're asking me to leave you alone with the man who *abandoned* you? *Ignored* you in your hours of need? *I* was the one who dried your tears and held you when you couldn't go on. *I'm* the man who dealt with the legalities to keep your hands clean. I, may

I remind you, my dear, am the man who has loved you from the *beginning. Before* you even met Case. Before, during, *and* after Case, as it happens."

"And I will always be grateful to you for all you did. I'm sure I wouldn't have made it if not for your care and affection. But Rydell has been thrust back in my life, and I still have some feelings for him. Or I might . . ."

"So you're going to play spare-wheel ex-wife as Case spins his wheels looking for a treasure that may or may not be where he claims it is? You know damn well he'll treat you like a casual hookup because you're here and available, and then he'll just abandon you again."

She knew he was lashing out from a bruised ego, but that was damn insulting. "You say that as if I have no free will. And whether I do, or don't, is none of your business." He'd just crossed another line. "I'm asking you to leave because I don't want to string you along thinking there's any hope for us to have a romantic relationship. I've tried, but I don't love you, Naveen. Not as deeply as a woman should love a man. I enjoyed our friendship, and I'll always be grateful for the care and compassion you showed me after Sophie died. But that wasn't romantic. After this morning, I question whether we even have a solid friendship." That was as kind and compassionate as she was willing to be. Every word out of his mouth annoyed her more.

"One incident turned you against me? For God's sake, Addison—"

"This isn't because of what happened this morning. I've struggled with this decision for a long time." *Not to mention I'm annoyed at myself for not seeing this side of you before now.* "I can't spend the rest of my life with a man I don't love with my whole heart." *And one I don't even like anymore.* Insidiously, Naveen had somehow become Jekyll and Hyde.

Dark eyes ate the light, and his features tightened with anger. The same expression he'd worn that morning. It dawned on her that Naveen's anger ran just under the surface. He'd just been better at hiding it before. Or perhaps she'd never really looked deep enough before.

"And that man is Case?" he demanded, voice edged in ice.

Addison shrugged. "I don't know. But that's not your concern. It's my choice. Please. Be a gentleman about this, and don't make a scene. If you care for me at all, you'll do as I ask."

He picked up her hand from where it lay on the rail. She reflexively jerked it back, but he kept hold of it. His strength and quick move kept her hand imprisoned, yet in place of the anger in his eyes she saw only gentleness. For the first time that evening, she wondered whether she was wrong to be so harsh.

Bringing her fingers to his lips, he said quietly, "I'll give you the space you need, my darling. But don't mistake my reserve for lack of deep feelings for you. I've loved you for years, Addison. I lost you to Case once before, and you came back to me. I can be a patient man until you return to me once again." He gave her a charming, very white flash of a smile. "Third time will be the charm." He kissed her knuckles, then released her hand and stepped back.

"Captain Sharma will take you to Malé in the morning."

"You're quite serious? You want to me to disembark and not accompany you to Sydney?"

"Yes. I do." She didn't bother sugarcoating it.

After a heavy silence, he said stiffly, "Very well. Will you at least agree to meet me in Sydney when this salvage is completed? Give me the opportunity to convince you that I'm the right choice."

Not in a million years. "Sure."

He nodded, his shoulders relaxing somewhat. "I find I've quite lost my appetite. If you'll excuse me I'll dine in my cabin while Bhat packs my bags."

Relived that he hadn't made a big scene, Addison smiled gently. Maybe he really was one of the good guys. "As ever you are a gentleman, Naveen. Thank you."

"I'm not leaving the playing field, Addison. Merely stepping back temporarily to please you. We still have an interested buyer for *Tesoro Mio*."

"I'll discuss that with Rydell."

"Yes. Do," he said with a little dry irony. "I'll see you in the morning, darling." He gave her a flash of white teeth. Addy had never really noticed that his smile rarely reached his eyes. Maybe it was the Botox?

"I'll have Bhat prepare something in the galley. I have some correspondence to deal with."

Correspondence that couldn't wait until morning when he was on land? "Okay, suit yourself."

He leaned over to kiss her on the mouth, but she turned her face so that the dry kiss landed on her cheek. "Good night, darling."

As he strolled away, Addison caught Jax touching his ear, as though he was in communication with someone. Ry?

Ry would be delighted Naveen wasn't joining them for dinner, she was sure. In fact he'd be thrilled.

One problem down. It was a start.

She squared her shoulders, thought about how she might get Ry to confide in her, how she might persuade him she needed to be on his team, working with him, and drew a deep breath, realizing she'd opened the door without meaning to.

Last night's lovemaking had given her the opportunity she needed. In the past, in the midst of a challenge, whether it was a hunt for salvage or strategizing a new way to get the best of the Cutters, Ry's passions were stoked.

They'd had wonderful times in bed when Ry was facing his biggest challenges. He'd always told her he needed her there, with him, because when the world was hurtling fireballs at him, without touching her he'd die.

He'd said she was his talisman, his muse, the light that guided him to the answers that he needed. He had said he needed her with him. To touch her. To see her. To share the sleepless nights with. To ride out the storms with him, to see in the sunrise.

All needs that she'd gladly fulfilled, because Ry was a man who was careful to give more than he took. She'd always been there for him, soothing him with her body, giving him free access to work through his physical frustration, and afterward, in the long nights when he faced challenges, they'd talk. As memories filtered back to her, her body tingled with anticipation.

"That was great, wasn't it?" Ry asked Addy as they walked side by side down the quiet, dimly lit corridor to the cabins. Just like old times, they'd eaten a leisurely meal under the stars with their friends.

Three of the four Indian authorities had shared interesting and entertaining stories, and the Prince of fucking Darkness had adjourned early to wash his hair or floss his teeth for tomorrow's departure. The wine flowed, and there'd been no curry involved, thank God. Which meant Addy wasn't still pissed at him.

"It was." She smiled at him, heartbreakingly beautiful in her white dress, which showed off her smooth golden skin and lightly muscled arms. "I'd forgotten how much I missed them."

"Almost as much as we all missed you." Sure, he'd

included their friends, but really, when it came right down to it, he'd missed Addy more than all of them combined times a thousand.

When he'd found out she'd gone back to Darshi after the divorce, hell, he'd forgotten how to breathe. Now, after sharing a night with her, his chest was unlocked and his lungs filled with the warmth and freshness of a breeze he'd long forgotten existed.

Georgeo had given Ry a discreet nod, indicating they'd stay up top until a suitable interval passed for him to take Addy below in privacy.

She'd sat across from him at dinner, and Ry had spent more time watching her than he had eating. She was as much a feast for his eyes as she'd been the moment he'd first laid eyes on her three and a half years ago. He'd been starved for the sight of her for a year, and having her here with him, so close he felt the heat of her skin against his as they walked, was something he hadn't even allowed himself to imagine after the divorce.

Being with her on *Tesoro Mio* was some kind of bloody miracle.

Her bare arm brushed his. Ripples of need peppered his skin, and arousal surged through his blood. Last year, he would've stopped her right there in the corridor. Stopped and kissed her until they were both breathless and panting. When they finally came up for air he'd sweep her up in his arms and race, half naked, to their cabin.

But not tonight.

God, he was being given a second chance. *Don't blow it, dickhead. Take it slowly.*

Don't fucking assume that invitation is coming. Don't fucking assume anything.

"Who would've thought those guys had such hair-raising cases?" she laughed. "Oh, my God, I can't even *imagine* finding a . . ."

Her amused voice wove around him like silken ropes. As she recounted the dinnertime conversation, Ry's heart swelled with such powerful love that it almost brought him to his knees. He wanted to wind his fingers through the long tendrils of escaped hair drifting around her shoulders from her just-got-out-of-bed updo. He wanted to brush his mouth on hers. Wanted to sink into her and make love as though the only thing that mattered in the world was what they could do between darkness and light. Wanted to—hell. He just wanted her.

They came to her door. Ry waited for her to insert her keycard. *Invite me in.* He had the master, but he wasn't prepared to push it. Not tonight when she was mellow and had spent the last few hours watching him across the table with those gorgeous olive-green eyes filled with emotion. Over the course of the dinner, he read warmth there. He hoped he saw forgiveness. He prayed that he saw heat and longing. He used to be able to read her well. Now he wasn't quite so sure of his ability.

The cabin door swung open, emitting cool, Addy-scented air. The womanly scents of shampoo, lotions, cosmetics, and her signature perfume enveloped him in a sensory buffet. They could bottle the stuff and sell it as an aphrodisiac.

"Come in?"

Hell, yeah. His dick rose like a divining rod, and his heart picked up speed, doing a couple of double gainers of anticipation as he followed her inside. Ry shut the door behind him.

In the past, he'd have walked her backward to the bed, stripped her on the way, and entered her as he kissed her. But this was now, and he reminded himself every agonizingly small step of the way into her cabin to take this slow. Keep things at a pace that wouldn't drive her away. He owed her that much, and a hell of a lot more.

But fuck, it was hard as hell not to grab her. His fingers itched to touch her. It was a fucking miracle he hadn't stripped her naked at the door, and they weren't having sex against the wall before the door closed as they had last night.

The bedside light cast a soft golden light, which didn't reach the corners. The open drapes cast a wedge of cool moonlight across the floor to the foot of the bed. A pathway to heaven.

Seventeen

Addy turned into him. "One favor?"

"Anything," he said, voice hoarse.

Pain flashed through her eyes. "Stop treating me like I'm going to break."

He touched her cheek. "I *did* break you."

"No, Ry, you didn't. I'm strong. I'm healing after Sophia's death, but you weren't responsible for that pain. And the rest—" She waved her hand as if erasing the past. "We can't change or recoup the time we lost. We can only go forward from here. Try to put our lives back to some semblance of normalcy. Last night was a good start. I see how badly you want me. Why are you holding back when we've already taken a step forward?"

He drew a deep breath. There was no right answer. "Because I know how badly I've hurt you. I don't want to—"

"That's exactly what I was worried about." She put two fingers over his mouth. "I understand, and I appreciate it. Yes, we still have a lot to work through. But for the next few hours, can we just stop worrying about every way we did a disservice to each other? Just do. Don't think," she murmured.

Her palms flattened on his chest until she slid cool hands under his T-shirt. His belly contracted, and his dick shifted with anticipation behind the constriction of his clothes.

God, yes. Please don't stop. Cool fingers curled over the waistband of his shorts, and his heart leapt off the cliff of need. He anticipated, and braced for, the brush of her fingers on the tip of his fully erect penis. It wasn't just that Addy turned him on that fast, it was that he'd been in a state of semi-arousal all day.

Everything, every damn little thing, about this woman turned him on, turned him inside out, turned his brain to mush, and turned his good intentions to smoke. "Addy, I—"

Standing on tiptoe, she brought her mouth up to his as her fingers tightened, her knuckles digging into his abs as she tugged him closer. "Shh." She licked his lips and fused her mouth to his.

Fair enough. There were other ways of expressing themselves. For now. But he had to tell her about the situation with the Baillargeons and Cutters. The outcome would affect her, too. Still, first things first. There was no way in hell he was stopping Addy when she was on a roll. Sliding his hand up her nape, Ry freed the pins anchoring her hair in an intricate knot. The silky strands tumbled over his hands in a glossy, gardenia-scented fall as he twisted them in his fist.

Still gripping his shorts, maintaining eye contact, she walked backward and tugged him with her. Her legs hit the bed, and she fell backward, dragging him with her. He landed between her splayed legs.

"Slave?" she said, voice husky. "Pleasure me."

Oh, yeah. They'd played variations on this game many times. This was one of his favorites. "Yes, mistress." Ry thrust his hands up under her dress, fisted his hand in the thin ties of her thong at her hips, and tugged. The skimpy fabric shredded like paper in his hands.

Addy flung her arms over her head, eyes closed, and said sternly. "My favorites. You'll pay for that."

He tossed the scrap aside with one hand and shoved her dress up over her waist with the other. "I'll buy you a hundred pairs."

"Not good enough. You'll have to pay in other ways."

Ry buried his face against her wet heat and mumbled, "Gladly." Other ways were fun, too.

"Wait." She bucked to dislodge his nuzzling lips. "We have on many clothes. You know how I like it."

Bare. Skin-to-skin. Yeah, me, too. On the other hand, a quickie fully dressed was also excellent. "An oversight," he murmured humbly as he slid off the end of the bed to stand. It took him about four long seconds to strip, then he dropped back on top of her, keeping his weight on his elbows. The soft white dress bared her to the waist as she lay supine, waiting for him to pleasure her.

Now to figure out how to get her out of the dress. Modest in front, the wide straps crossed in an X over her shoulders, leaving most of her back bare. But he had no idea where or how it fastened. Ripping it off her would be more expedient. Placing a hand on each strap, he was about to do just that.

Addy opened one eye. "This dress is vintage Galliano. Do not tear it." The eye closed.

She was a Christmas package wrapped with industrial-strength packing tape. Shit, where were the fasteners? "How—"

"I don't have all night. Hurry." Hands over her head, palm up, her fingers flexed impatiently. "If you aren't ingenious enough to strip me, I can pleasure myself."

Not a threat, love. "I like that game, too. But your wish is my command, mistress." Rolling to his side next to her, he flipped her with her back to him. Had to pause because the pale nape of her neck was too sexy, too tempting to pass up. She shivered as his lips skimmed from under her hair, down her nape, to her shoulder. Her skin smelled warm and fragrant and he did it again, teeth, lips, tongue. Up. Down. Up. Down.

By feel Ry found the damn small diamond-like buttons holding the straps in place. Small buttonholes, large fingers. Frustration mounted. Fortunately she had soft skin and fragrant curves and hollows to explore as he worked at the buttons. He did it by feel because he was too busy kissing his way across the slope of her shoulder to stop and look.

When the second recalcitrant button slid free, he rolled her to her back and skimmed the dress up over her head. "Hi," he whispered as her face emerged from the fabric. She was so damn beautiful she stopped his heart.

Heavily lidded olive-green eyes opened inches from his. "Kiss me."

If he had his way he'd never stop. "Is that an order, mistress?"

Combing her fingers through his hair, Addy tugged his head down the last inch. "Damn right. Give me tongue, slave."

He teased his parted lips over hers. "Here, mistress, or . . . ?"

The heat of his skin scorched hers as he slid down her body, pausing as he got to her breasts. Addison arched her back as he licked a curve beneath her right breast, then skimmed his teeth up the curve until his lips closed around her hard nipple. "So perfect." His tongue flicked over her stiff nipple as his hand greedily explored the shape of her ribs, the curve of her hip. Hot, humid breath bathed her breast as he lifted his head a fraction to murmur, "You taste like flowers and honey."

Bringing her hands down from above her head, Addison dug her nails into the taut muscles of his broad shoulders and held on tightly as he suckled. Uneven, his breath rasped as rapid and jagged as her own as he gently closed his teeth around the nub, eliciting another moan from her. Every nerve ending in her body responded, and her hips moved restlessly against him.

With his upper body wedged between her spread legs, he wasn't exerting enough pressure where she needed it most, and she couldn't close her legs to relieve the building tension.

His fingers closed around the sensitized globe, kneading and caressing, licking and nibbling until she didn't know where he began and she ended. His hands wandered over her, exploring her breasts as if committing their shape and texture to memory. She squeezed her eyes shut as his long hair tickled across her chest while he kissed his way from one to the other.

He pressed a gentle kiss over the tattoo beneath her left breast, right over her heart. "This must've hurt like bloody hell."

She hadn't cried at the small pinpricks. It was nothing compared with the engulfing pain she'd already been in. "I welcomed every prick of the needle."

"My brave darling."

She wound her fingers tightly through the long hair at his nape, tugging until he lifted his head and she could look him in the eye. "Don't stop," she ordered, fingers lingering in the heated silkiness of his hair.

"Yes, mistress." The warm cavern of his mouth returned to her nipple and he sucked and licked until her legs thrashed and her throat arched.

"More?"

"Yes. No."

Cool air drifted like another caress over her damp nipple as he lifted his head, not to look up at her, but to receive his orders. "Up? Down?"

The width of his body held her legs spread wide open, but the weight of his chest where she needed his mouth wasn't doing the job. It was hard to push the word out as deep inside her muscles pulsed and her moisture dampened his chest. She could smell her own musk, and knowing Rydell could, too, made her even hotter. "D-down."

He maneuvered down her body, taking his own sweet time and amping her arousal so high Addison could barely lie still. He caressed her breasts, trailed damp kisses over her hip, her inner thigh, the inside of her knee.

Tightening the fingers wrapped in his hair, she demanded, "Up!"

Moonlight swirled as hard hands gripped her hips, and his mouth left her as Ry yanked her to the edge of the mattress.

His smile was all devil. "How do you like my service so far, mistress?"

Rocking her flat hand from side to side, she said, "So-so." Placing her bare foot on his chest, she held him at bay for a moment. "Less c-chitchat and more a-action."

With her leg up on his chest she was wide open for his viewing pleasure, and his gaze heated. Drawing in a deep breath, he closed his eyes for a moment, then looked directly into her own. "You're wet for me, and I haven't even touched your sweet snatch yet."

"At that rate you're going, it might never happen," she told him acerbically. "I'll be asleep before you get down to business. You don't obey orders worth a damn, you know that?"

"Ministrations too relaxing for you?" he said low, voice nothing but gravel.

She was freaking on *fire*. She didn't want to play anymore. She was so horny her eyeballs throbbed. All she wanted now was to climax long and hard. Pause. And do it all over again. Wiggling her butt restlessly, she dug her nails into her palms as her internal muscles tightened almost painfully. "I didn't say *relaxing*. I s-said slow."

"Hmm." With a twitch of his lips, his strong fingers grasped her ankle to bring her foot to his mouth. She tried to tug it away, but he ran his teeth along the length of her sole until she cried out and tried to twist out of his hold. He held her in place as he closed the hot cavern of his mouth over her toes and sucked each individually until she was mindless. "I'll p-punish you for this."

"God." His voice was hoarse. "I sure as hell hope so." He went back to tormenting each toe. Addison brought her other foot up and thumped him in the chest, using it to try to hold him away from her extremely sensitive feet, which had always been a hotbed of erotic nerve endings. Something Ry knew very well, because he didn't even pause in his ministrations.

"You are a very dear lord, Ry!" She jolted as he bit the ball of her foot. Already sensitized nerve endings shot an erotic signal directly from her foot to her vagina, then resonated to every part of her body from there. "V-*very* bad slave."

"Uh-huh."

Since he was preoccupied, Addison had plans of her own. Let the punishment begin. Knee bent, she trailed her other foot s-l-o-w-l-y down his chest, rubbing the crisp dark hair, then followed the happy trail over the clearly defined steps of his rock-hard abs. His belly contracted, and his penis lengthened. A glistening drop of moisture swelled at the tip. Addison could almost taste it. Licking her lips, she lifted her gaze to see Ry watching her. Color rode high on his cheekbones, and a muscle jumped in his cheek.

"Tit for tat?" she inquired sweetly.

"Your tits are magnificent, and your juicy tat is pretty

damn spectacular, too. Trust me." His voice, strained and thick with animal hunger, stroked over her with the sensuality of a fur glove. "You're about to get exactly what you want."

Even though the window was open, gently billowing the white drapes like sails in the moonlight, the room felt like a furnace; her skin was slick with perspiration and they hadn't really done anything. Yet. Rydell had always been a master at winding her up for the slow release. She both loved and hated it. "Hmm. Promises, promises."

Faking a yawn, Addison closed her eyes. "Wake me up when you're ready to be serious—" Her eyes popped open. "No—wait. Perhaps my slave needs some incentive?" Sliding her foot down, she paused to caress the sensitive skin right above his penis. His body jerked. She ran her toes between his belly and the stiff spar of his erection. He was as hard as steel. The muscles banding his belly flexed as she stroked.

"Bloody hell, Addy." Ry's half laugh was strangled. "Turnabout is fair play." He bit, not so lightly, the arch of her foot as if it were an ear of corn. With so many nerves clustered where his mouth was, it was as though he were nibbling on a live wire.

"It is, isn't it?" Dragging her toes down the pulsing vein on the underside of what she desperately wanted inside her, Addison delicately caressed his tight balls with the tips of her toes. "I could do this all day," she lied.

Lifting his head, he laughed. "Witch. At least you aren't whistling—" Then he yanked her all the way to the very edge so she was precariously balanced. Ry solved that problem by draping her ankles over his shoulders. "Comfy?" he murmured as he knelt on the floor at the foot of the bed between her thighs. Sweat trickled down his temple, and his sweat-dampened hair clung to his neck like chocolate flames.

His ragged breath fanned her wet heat. "Give me a minute here. The smell of you makes me drunk, know that?"

"Get drunk . . . later." Her arousal was intense and urgent. Digging her heels into his shoulder blades, Addison urged him closer. "I need your mouth on me, *now*!"

"Your wish—" His tongue lashed out, licking her wet seam as if she were a delicious ice cream cone. Panting, she whimpered then cried out as the tension ratcheted higher and higher. Grabbing fistfuls of his hair, she held on as he feasted on her. Tongue slick, teeth cool, breath hot.

His tongue thrust hard, and he found her clit. Dear God . . . Addison's back arched off the bed. Intense sensation coursed through her body as he inserted a finger into her tight sheath.

Impossible to drag air into her constricted lungs as another finger joined the first and his magical tongue danced expertly over and around her clit until she felt as tightly wound as the anchor chain. Pleasure splintered and intensified.

Almost mindless with pleasure, she panted, "Stop tormenting me! Penis! *Now.*"

Ry surged up, her legs still over his shoulders, and plunged inside her, his penis stretching and filling her as her internal muscles clenched and tightened around him.

Neither had forgotten this dance. Addison knew exactly where to touch him and when, when to hold back to prolong his pleasure, when to urge him faster for her own. And in turn Rydell played her body like a virtuoso.

They rolled across the wide bed. He on top, then under her. She came, and came and came. He shouted his release.

After a moment, arms outflung, eyes closed, he gave

a dramatic and heartfelt moan of satisfaction. "Died and went straight to heaven. You are a fine, fine, mistress."

"So not done with you," she told him, voice so breathless she wasn't sure he heard, let alone understood her. Reversing their positions, she sat astride his hips, palms braced on his chest, the damp heat of her center directly over the hard spar of his dick. "Uh-uh." She shook her head as his hands came up to hold her hips.

"This is still my rodeo, slave-boy. Lock those hands under your head."

She rode him until perspiration slicked their bodies and her muscles quivered, until her wet hair clung to her sweaty skin, and there didn't seem to be a bone left in her body. "I'm liquefied."

Her dismount was less than graceful as she fell over beside him, her breath coming hard. "*No mas?*"

Arm flung over his eyes, Rydell groaned.

Addy knew how he felt.

Spent, satiated, satisfied.

"Is that a *Yes, I give up, mistress*?"

"Ask me again in fifteen minutes," he said with an exhausted chuckle, barely moving his lips.

Addison managed to squeeze a laugh from her constricted lungs, not capable of movement, either. "Always the optimist. We'll see how perky you feel in an hour." *Or three.*

Without removing his arm flung over his eyes, Rydell snaked out his other arm and scooped her closer. "Come here, woman."

Their chests immediately became glued together with their sweat. Addison loved it. Flinging her arm over his belly, head nestled under his chin, she said quietly, "Tell me about these French investors."

Eighteen

They had to have the conversation. Now, when they were both bonelessly relaxed, and in sync, seemed like the perfect time.

A ripple of tension ran through him, and beneath her cheek his chest muscles tightened. "You spoke to Peri."

"She's worried about you." She kissed his sweaty shoulder. Making love with Rydell Case was like a workout on steroids. "So's Callie. So am I."

"God." He lifted her chin so that their eyes met. "I don't want any of you to worry. I'll work it out. I'll take care of it."

So Rydell. The man who wanted to take care of everyone and everything but himself. "I'm sure you will, and I'm going to help you. I know it's hard for you to let go, but we're three grown-ass women, you know. You don't have to protect us from the unpleasantness of life." Addy slid over his body, nudging his ankle with her foot so that he spread his legs to make room for her hips. Settling into the V of his muscular thighs, she folded her arms on his broad chest, ready for a real conversation.

"I've watched out for Peri and Callie since they were kids. My brother, too, when he was alive. You. Whether you wanted me to or not. It's hard *not* to worry and try to make sure that you're all safe, healthy, and happy."

"People aren't meant to be safe and happy all the time. Life has ups and downs for everyone. You can't stop the bad from happening, Ry. And knowing *you're* in trouble automatically rallies all of us, you know that." His sister and sister-in-law were too far away to do anything hands-on.

Addison would get the skinny, and then contact the other two and fill them in if she deemed it necessary for them to have all the details.

Ignoring his semi-erect penis as it twitched with happiness at her position, she brushed his mouth with one finger. "Start at the beginning, and don't leave anything out."

"Hard to concentrate on *talking* if you insist on wiggling around like that."

"Sorry." Not very. But she lay still.

With a wicked smile that made her heart flutter with something more powerful than lust, Rydell stroked a lazy hand down her spine, then curved his fingers around her butt cheek. She wanted to wiggle to encourage him to move his hand somewhere more intriguing. But she'd wanted to talk, and since this was important, she lay still and tried to forget that the part of him that wanted part of her were squashed together in dangerous proximity.

As the sweat dried on their bodies, and her heartbeat slowed, Rydell told her about the letter from the Baillargeons' lawyer, and the terms of the loan, and what would happen should he not be able to repay it in time.

Pretty much everything Peri had told her, and Callie had hinted at. But it was much worse than she'd been led to believe. Callie and Peri had no idea of the real dollar amount, and it was staggering.

The Frenchman had subsidized Rydell's father for years, pouring multimillions of euros into the failing salvage company. Interest had compounded, the euro had gone up in value, and the family had been unaware of the loan until after old man Baillargeon died. Now his heirs wanted the money repaid. It didn't matter that the debt belonged to Rydell's father. Case Enterprises was his company, and Rydell took his responsibilities as seriously as a heart attack.

In a gesture of comfort, Addison rubbed her palm over his heart, feeling the play of his pecs under the soft dusting of crisp, dark hair. "Is that everything?"

He made a pained grunt of amusement. "Isn't that enough?"

"Yeah, it is." She slid off him to sit up, curling her legs under her butt like a mermaid amid the rumpled leopard-print sheets. He stroked her thigh, and she plucked his fingers off her skin because she didn't want to be distracted, even though she was. Very.

"Behave for another minute," she told him sternly, clamping her hand over his when his fingers went exploring. "Clasp your hands under you head and keep them there until further notice!" She waited until he did as she asked.

He looked like a sexy, bronzed pagan god with his muscular arms over his head and that knowing glint in his eyes.

"Stop looking at me like that." *As if you're about to jump my bones and consume me in one gulp.* Then she saw what he was doing and it almost broke her heart. He was deflecting. Even though he'd shared the truth about the seriousness of his finances, he didn't want to suck her all the way in. His overt sexual playfulness was a way to sidetrack how he really felt and the depth of his despair.

It took a few moments for her tight throat to ease so that she could speak. "I know what you're doing, but don't. Please, Ry. I know you're scared. But you don't need to worry about myself or Callie or Peri. We're all big girls and can take care of ourselves if this shit ends up hitting the fan. You can't always protect us from the world. Besides, in this case we're family and we're all in it together. You're *not* alone. Let me tell you where I am on this, and you can take it from there."

Addison filled him in on her conversation with her financial adviser. "Those funds will be wire-transferred late tomorrow afternoon." When he stared to protest, she leaned over to put her palm over his mouth. "I want to do this, Rydell. You won't change my mind, so save your breath.

"I realize we'll still be short." She'd had no idea just *how* short. Dear God, the number seemed insurmountable. She didn't understand why he wasn't white-haired with anxiety. "I've been giving this a lot of thought since speaking to your sister—I don't think selling *Tesoro Mio* is an answer. You'll need her for the next salvage. Yes, I know you could buy or rent a smaller ship, but that would take money we can little afford—"

He shifted, lifting his hand to cup her cheek, eyes shining.

"What?"

"You said '*we*.'"

The way he said it squeezed her heart. "Our financials are inexorably tied." It was better to come at this in a cool, non-emotional way, if she wanted Rydell to know she was dead serious. That this wasn't a whim or a knee-jerk reaction to his dire situation. The last thing he'd want was her pity. "How sure are you of salvaging the silver from the *Nicolau Coelho*? Are you one hundred percent positive she's where you say she is, and that she was carrying such a valuable cargo?" Sometimes a salvage was just as easy as being the first person to know where the wreck was located. "That's a crazy amount of silver to be transporting just to buy *spices*."

"Yeah. It was. My theory is that they were heading to the Spice Islands to spend what they had to, then returning to pass through Africa again. This time to pick up slaves with what was left." Somehow his hands were no longer stacked under his head, but curved over the small of her back. As if touching her was his talisman.

"And yes," he said with quiet assurance, "I know exactly where she is. I was here six months ago, and again last month. She's right where X marks the spot. Seventy or so feet down. Absolutely doable. We'll have that silver on board in five days. I already have the buyers lined up. Photographic proof of what we retrieve, and the value, and the money will be transferred to my bank in London within twenty-four hours. Doable."

"It sounds too easy."

"Sometimes things *are* easy."

Not for him. He'd had adversity from the moment his father walked out on him. He'd emotionally supported his mother, practically raised his siblings, brought in Callie from her abusive parents who'd lived next door, financially and emotionally supported his brother after he was diagnosed with leukemia, and supported Callie after Adam died. He'd been lied to about his daughter's death, manipulated by Hollis and probably Naveen, and been divorced without knowing why.

Addison didn't want to think about his ship being hijacked and the added punch of the legal claim on his business. No, for Rydell, things were never easy.

"Not to be all doom and gloom, but sometimes that light we see at the end of the tunnel is a southbound train coming at us at a hundred miles an hour." This close to him and knowing what to look for, she could see the lines of strain around his eyes and mouth. The tension in his strong jaw. "Do we have contingency plans?"

"Of course, love. Don't I always? Liquidate what's left, and start over."

Oh, God, Ry . . . Her throat ached. "Can you do that if push comes to shove?"

"It depends on if you're with me or not."

"That's not fair, Ry. I don't know *where* I'll be emotionally. In a week, or a month, or a year. One thing I *can* promise you, *my* money is *your* money. I'd planned on selling *Tesoro Mio* in Sydney anyway, so if that's what you choose for us to do, I'm fine with it. We already have a buyer. She's too big for me to live on, and honestly? I would never have taken her in the divorce if I hadn't wanted to hurt you as badly as you hurt me. Petty, I know, but that's how I felt."

Needing to cover herself, she tugged at the sheet and held it over her bare breasts. She still felt vulnerable and exposed. "My book money can support me—not exactly in the manner I'm accustomed to." *By a long shot.* "But it will be sufficient for my needs."

"Hopefully it won't come to that. I saw some of the silver, Addy. It's there. The wreck is unstable, and it was too dangerous to go inside without someone watching my back. But I have the best salvage team around. We'll get it to the surface. I'll contact the buyers tomorrow after we do a prelim dive. Get that ball rolling. Barring unforeseen circumstances, we'll be fine. I might have to tighten my belt until I hit a big payday on the next salvage, but it'll work out. I don't want you to worry about money, Addy. I promise you, I'll always take care of you."

"I'm not a Victorian maiden, Ry. I told you, I can take care of myself."

He rubbed a hand along her arm. "I know you can.

You're one of the strongest women I know. But you've never had to do without. You've never given money a second thought in your entire life, Addy. You have no idea what's it like to wonder how you're going to pay your rent, or decide which is more important—eating or turning on the heat."

"No, I don't. But If it comes to that, I'll learn and adjust. Is that what happened when your father left the family?" Ry didn't like to talk about it. He'd walked out when Ry was fifteen, leaving twelve-year-old Adam, five-year-old Peri, and his wife without a backward glance. His father had run Case Enterprises from an apartment in Boston, taking his ship, their joint bank account, and Ry's mother's broken heart with him. A year later he'd committed suicide without leaving so much as a note.

At fifteen Rydell had been too young, too inexperienced, to run the business. He'd become the man of the family, the emotional and financial support for all of them. The ship was returned to his mother in London. She'd refused to sell it, holding it for when Rydell and Adam were old enough to sail her. Rydell had salvaged his first treasure and made his first million at twenty.

"There were some times I was looking up at broke, yeah. But I took care of my family, and Callie as well. Nothing trumps family, and nothing was out of bounds if it meant taking care of them. We were okay. I've been rich and I've been poor. Rich is better, but I've done poor, and by God I'll do it again if that's what it'll take to keep the Cutters' hands off my business."

Addison allowed the silk sheet to glide over her breasts to pool on her thighs. The time to need body armor was past. Now she could comfort Rydell with her body, and tell him without words what she was feeling. "Well, since it's too dark to dive tonight, let's keep ourselves busy in the meantime."

"Hmm." Rydell looked her over, a gleam in his eyes. "I believe it's my turn to choose."

"I don't have the naughty-nurse costume anymore." She'd never had a naughty-nurse costume, but it had always been a running joke between them.

"How about the hooker with a heart of gold, still have that one?"

Addison sent him a slow seductive smile. "I'll improvise.

Nineteen

Curled against his side, Addy's head was nestled beneath his chin, one leg thrown over his calf. The gentle warmth of morning light bathed his face, but Ry didn't open his eyes. He was content to lie there, Addy's hand on his thigh, her heartbeat a faint bird's-wing flutter against his chest.

"Don't go," she murmured, although he'd made no move to do so.

"I want to check my readings—"

Her lashes tickled his skin, and he felt the curve of her lips as she smiled against his throat. "For the millionth time."

Ry opened his eyes. The cabin was still in twilight, the early-morning sun barely breaching the lower edge of the windows. He stroked a lazy hand up the smooth curve of her back, feeling the bumps of her spine and the silky spill of her fragrant hair across the back of his fingers. She smelled of warm musky woman. Of sex and flowers, and half-made promises. "It's important."

"I know," she murmured, stroking his calf with the side of her foot. "Want me to come and help?"

"No, it's insanely early. Get a few more hours' sleep. Do you want me to stick around until Darshi pushes off?"

"And miss the big reveal? No way. I expect you guys

to come up with baskets filled to the brim with silver. I'm a big girl. I made my point. He'll take rejection like the prince he is."

Darshi was like a testy child. Ry doubted the guy had taken it well at all. "No man likes getting the brush-off from the woman he loves. And especially not twice."

"Yes, well, be that as it may. He knows it's over. He'll deal with it. He's far too civilized and contained to make a fuss. At least in our presence. He can be as petulant and whiny as he likes when he's in Malé."

Ry chuckled. That about summed up the last few thoughts he'd give Prince Naveen Darshi for time immemorial. He combed his fingers through her hair, the strands cool between his fingers. "Much as I'd like to stick around, I'm going—nuh-uh," he murmured, grabbing her wrist as Addy walked her fingers the few inches up his thigh toward his morning woody. "Save your strength for a celebratory fuck tonight."

She gave his erect penis a gentle pat. "Go forth and bring home the silver, my pirate."

"Aye aye, my love." Ry swung his legs over the side of the bed. God, she looked glorious lying there, a siren's smile worthy of bringing pirates to the rocky shore, her silken curves strategically covered with only her long hair.

She stopped his heart.

"Sleep," he ordered, bending to brush a kiss to the swell of her hip.

"Come and wake me before you go down, 'kay?" Her voice was already slurred with sleep.

"Sure." Ry watched her for a few moments, before he went to his cabin next door to shower and get his day started.

Excitement effervesced through his bloodstream as he shut the door to his own cabin. The silver was so close he could taste it. Last night had been . . . a relief. A blessing. A godsend. A fucking miracle he thought would never happen.

They were so close to having the happiness that grief and loss had stripped from them. So damn close. Talking had helped. But there was more to say. More wordless loving to blur the pain and help them start the process of healing.

Ry dropped to the floor for his customary five hundred morning push-ups. He'd skip his morning run since he'd be getting plenty of exercise with multiple dives throughout the day. His heart skipped several beats. Anticipation was a great motivator.

One thing at a time.

Push-ups.

Shower.

Swim trunks would be the uniform of the day.

A final—completely unnecessary—read of the charts.

A light breakfast with the team—"Four hundred and ninety-seven—crap." The carpet beneath his hands shifted, putting him slightly off balance, but he immediately righted himself with the next push-up. "Don't let a loose carpet fuck up your perfect day, Case."

He finished five hundred, then came up on his haunches to inspect the loose carpet in the corner. One of the deckhands could come and tack it down later. The ship had dozens of spaces beneath the decking for storage. The tacks must've come loose during the storm. He hadn't noticed it before. The carpet looked slightly stretched, as though it had been folded over multiple times. Perhaps Addy had stored some of the baby's things in here.

"And would *this* be a good time to prod that sore tooth, Case?" Probably not, but what the hell. He pulled the corner of the plush carpet down to expose the storage compartment in the teak deck beneath, hooked a finger in the brass ring, and tugged up the heavy cover.

The watertight compartment, two feet wide by about six feet long, ran along the portside wall between this cabin and the owner's cabin occupied by Addy. It was full of rolled-up charts.

Ry let out a huff of relief. *Not* Sophie's baby blankets and toys. Thank God.

Even though he was relieved, something about the contents of the storage area pestered him like a buzzing mosquito just out of reach. About to close the cover and get on with his day, Ry pulled out one of the canvas-covered rolled charts, curious as to why Seddeth had them in here and not in the designated area for charts in his small office off the bridge.

Taking it with him, he rose to sit on the edge of his bed to see what it was. He untied several pieces of what looked like a ripped T-shirt. Odd. Definitely not Seddeth's usual method for storing charts.

Dropping the ties to the floor, he eyed the canvas as it automatically unfurled on the mattress beside him.

Not a rolled chart.

A painting.

"Fucking, fucking bastard." Reaching over, he used the house phone and ordered Seddeth to bring Jax and Oscar down to his cabin in ten minutes.

In the meantime he needed a shower to cool off so he didn't break into Darshi's cabin on the other side of Addy's and wring his bloody neck. The shower would account for three minutes. Waking Addy would take the other seven.

Wearing a long black-and-white sundress, her hair scooped on top of her head and pinned with a tortoise-shell comb, Addy looked fresh as a daisy.

The captain's cabin, with his hastily made bed, was wall-to-wall people. Captain Seddeth, Jax, Oscar, Addy, and fifty-six priceless oils paintings. Jax and Oscar had just finished photographing all of them. Ry knew officials would do a valuation assessment. But he sure as hell was going to record the find and make his own estimate before anyone else got their hands on them.

"Wait," Addison inserted, glancing at the monitor showing the empty corridor beyond the cabin as if expecting Darshi to come bursting out looking for them. She looked back at Ry, then glanced at the others one by one before returning troubled dark-green eyes to his once again. "Are you saying *Naveen* is Procioni?"

"Isn't that the cabin he always stays in?"

"Yes . . ." She hesitated. "But his men have been in and out of that cabin for the past year. It could be any one of them."

"Do you really believe any of them capable of the greatest art heists in recent memory?"

"No," she admitted. "But it's just as hard to wrap my mind around *Naveen* being a thief."

Ry, leaning his hip against the captain's dresser, crossed his arms over his chest. "Funny, I have absolutely no problem imagining him as such."

"Sorry, Addison, but neither do I," Oscar, propping up a nearby wall, told her.

"I'm three for three," Jax said, giving Ry a meaningful glance, because over the last year he'd told Ry exactly that. At the time Ry had thought it was because his security guys knew how he felt about his ex-wife, and they were protecting his interests. "With all due respect, Addison, never liked him, never trusted him."

"Wow. Tony? Do you feel the same way?" When the captain nodded, she glanced from man to man again. "Why didn't any of you *say* something?"

"It's not for us to choose who you associate with, Addison," Tony Seddeth told her, looking slightly uncomfortable. He'd hastily pulled on shorts and a muscle shirt, his bare feet shoved into sandals. He picked up his watch from his bedside table and fastened it around his wrist as he talked. "Oscar and Jax kept close tabs on him whenever he was on board. You were never in any danger from him. We made sure of that—" He turned to open the door following a brief, discreet knock. "That should be the police officer."

Dressed in his uniform despite the early hour, Paras Sharma entered, closing the door behind him. He surveyed the serious faces around him with a small frown. "What has happened?"

Ry stepped back, and so did Addy, so the layers of paintings uncurled on the captain's desk were visible.

Sharma frowned. "What is this?"

"I just found these in the storage compartments under the floor in my cabin. There are fifty-six of them."

Taking a folded white linen handkerchief from his pocket, the officer brushed a corner of the top painting with his covered fingertip. "This looks like a Degas—" He met Ry's eyes. "It is *the* Degas stolen recently from a private residence in Prague, yes?"

"We believe so, yeah. The prince has been staying in the cabin I'm in now. We believe he's been using *Tesoro Mio* as a secure hiding place for these. No one would think to look here."

Inconsiderate, psycho son of a bitch hadn't for one fucking second considered how Addy would be perceived, if and when the paintings were discovered on board her ship. Had Darshi given a flying fuck that there was a bloody good chance Addy would be caught in the net if he was ever caught? Hell no. The prince was too inconsiderate, too arrogant to consider himself vulnerable. He thought he was almost home free.

Another week, and *Tesoro Mio* would be docking in Sydney, the paintings secure beneath the floorboards and carpet and no one the wiser.

"*Prince Darshi* is Procioni?" Sharma got it right away. He sounded just as incredulous as Addy, but *he* wasn't disbelieving at all.

"He brokered a deal for Addy to sell *Tesoro Mio* in Australia this week. Now we believe he was transporting the paintings there. Probably to sell to a private collector."

"Look," Addy inserted. "I agree with all of you that there's something . . . fishy about Naveen. Something *I* never noticed before. He's an opportunist, and Ry and I suspect he manipulated circumstances after—" She hesitated briefly as she drew in a breath before forging on. "After Sophia died. But a *thief*? That just doesn't make sense. Why would a man of the prince's vast wealth turn to a life of crime?" she demanded, clearly not buying in to the scenario.

"Just because a man's financially well off doesn't mean he doesn't get a thrill from ripping people off," Ry pointed out. "This might not be about the money at all. He might be an adrenaline junky."

"Are we sure his vast wealth doesn't come from selling the stolen paintings?" Jax asked. "May I?" he asked the captain, indicating his computer, which had been taken off his desk and put on the chest of drawers nearby so they could roll out the canvases. At Tony's nod, Jax said, without turning as his fingers flew across the keyboard, "I have a contact who'll get me into the prince's financials. Give me a few minutes here."

"This is surreal." Addy sank into a nearby chair, face

pale. "I never suspected for even a second—*This* is why Azm Kapur was killed? To protect Naveen's secret?"

Ry nodded. "Or as a warning of some sort."

"Whoever's waiting for these must be pissed as hell that the ship was diverted and they have to wait for delivery," Addy pointed out, eye glinting with anger.

"Pissed enough to kill."

"What happens now?" she demanded, fire in her eyes. "Confront him and break his face?"

"No," Sharma said quietly as Ry laughed because she sounded so bloodthirsty, vehement, and quite serious, despite standing two feet away from a law enforcement officer. "Clearly he has a buyer or someone who's been financing him. Possibly the buyer he was to meet in Sydney. Interpol will want that person or persons as well. Don't say anything at all. Interpol will want to talk to all of you after he's apprehended in Malé this afternoon."

"Fair enough," Ry agreed. "He's agreed to leave the ship. But with *this* discovery my concern is that he's leaving way too easily. A rough estimate is that these paintings alone are worth a cool billion euros. Why leave them behind?"

"I wouldn't exactly say he's leaving of his own free will." Addy's wry tone made Ry smile. "He doesn't know we found them. They've been safely hidden for all this time. He'll presume they'll be right where he put them when *Tesoro Mio* docks in Sydney. I agreed to meet him in Sydney after the dive. To talk."

"Last night I offered him a lift to Malé. Our helicopter will be here later this morning. He accepted my offer," the police officer told Ry. "I'll have Interpol waiting for him there. Can we pack these up? I'll take them with me when we leave. In a couple of hours?"

"I have a large canvas duffel bag," Oscar offered with a nod. "We'll pack them up and place it with the luggage before you go. He'll be none the wiser. I'll get the bag and be right back."

Sharma nodded. "And I must contact Interpol immediately."

"I'll go up and keep the prince company in case he has a problem packing." Jax followed Sharma and Oscar.

"I'll take Addy back to her cabin," Ry told him grimly. "Check to make sure Darshi is still in his cabin, then stick to her like glue. I don't want her anywhere near the prince. She can wave him off from the top deck."

"That's not going to work. If I do that he'll know something is off. I have to be civil, and I *have* to talk to him before he goes."

"Fine. Alleviate any misgivings he might have, and assure him you'll connect in Sydney in a couple of weeks." Ry gave Jax a hard look. "Keep her within four feet of you at all times, got it?"

"Yes, sir. I damn well do." He closed the door behind them.

"He's endangered all of us by using the ship as a hiding place for his stolen goods. I'll put in my own calls to the authorities," Tony told them, his voice tight. "He won't be falling through any cracks." The captain left through another door, this one leading up to the bridge.

Ry crossed to Addy. Wrapping his arms around her, he held her close. "You couldn't possibly have known."

"I hate it when you read my mind."

"Don't take any foolish chances, Addison. Promise me. A high-profile thief like Darshi has a lot to lose. And I'm not just talking about the loss of the paintings he stole. We don't know who else is involved, what promises he's made, and how far reaching this is. Whoever the buyer is can't be legit. We don't want the paintings to be discovered missing until Sharma and Interpol have Darshi in custody."

"I can be cool. Believe me, I'd better be cool because right now I'd like to rip his lips off." Addy stepped away from him, her back straight. "Let's get these rolled up again and ready when Oscar brings back that bag. Once they're off the ship we'll be able to breathe a little easier."

Ry tilted her chin up on his finger. Their eyes met. "I love you, Addison Case."

She shifted to pick up a handful of the rags used to tie up each canvas, handing him half. "Hold that thought."

His chest felt leaden. That wasn't the right answer, and they both knew it.

"Holy crap, man, you scared the living shit outta me sitting there!" Carrying a cup of steaming coffee, Lenka climbed down to join Ry, who was sitting with his legs dangling over the side of the dive platform. The South African was always as exuberant as a puppy, but more so when he was about to dive. "Thought I'd be the first one up."

The sky was still milky pale, the air cool with a promise of later heat. The sun, barely breaching the horizon, shone a thin line, the silver-gilt color of old Spanish eight-real coins. A good omen.

Ry had reluctantly left Addy in Jax's care.

She'd be going for her jog soon. She'd want the endorphins for her confrontation with the prince. Ry was confident that she could handle Darshi with her usual aplomb.

He wanted her here with him, safe, to share this special moment. But diving wasn't her thing. She was slightly claustrophobic and didn't like the mask or the confinement of strapping on a tank, preferring to wait for him on deck.

For now he could put aside thoughts of Addy's farewell to the prince. Goodfuckingbye. Right after breakfast. Hopefully for the last time.

Lenka folded himself down to sit beside Ry, bringing with him the smell of sunblock and French roast coffee. "Been sitting here since we dropped anchor?"

He'd been making love to Addy when they dropped anchor late last night. Ry wished he'd gone from that to this and skipped the shit that had gone down in between. He was so furious with Darshi, it was hard to focus on the dive. "About half an hour. Beautiful, isn't it?" The translucent azure water stretched out as far as the eye could see. It would become paler aqua as the light hit it later in the day, but for now the color was intense and magical.

"Is that guy leaving today?" Lenka splashed his feet on the surface of the water like a little kid. His crew-cut red hair was not as vivid as it would be when the sun hit it.

Amazing what was revealed in the right light, Ry thought, leaning back on his hands. He wanted a spotlight shone on Darshi. The prince sure as shit wasn't as oblivious about his bodyguard's actions as he pretended to be. Fortunately he was oblivious to what was about to happen to him when he reached land. That thought would sustain Ry until Captain Sharma confirmed Darshi's arrest later this morning.

Dashi was not his problem. Fuck, he had enough of his own. Let the Indian authorities do their jobs. He needed to do his and get the treasure waiting for him down beneath that azure water up as quickly as possible if he didn't want to lose everything his family had struggled for. "The prince? Yeah. They all are. After breakfast."

"In cuffs?" Lenka asked hopefully as he took a sip of coffee and scanned the water, steam drifting around his freckled face.

Ry grinned. "Maybe later."

Addy, *Tesoro Mio*, and his dive crew were all Ry needed.

This was perfection as far as he was concerned. His woman, warm and satiated from their lovemaking, asleep in his bed, and a vast ocean cradling his future in her warm embrace. His best dive team reassembled, and his dream ship. Delete Darshi from the picture?

Yeah, this was as good as it got.

He could practically hear the silver calling his name.

"Are you boys having a private moment?" Kevin dropped lightly onto the dive platform behind them from the deck above. Wearing a black bikini, she looked trim and fit. Her short blond hair was slicked back from a recent shower, and a pair of sunglasses perched on top of her head. Her bare feet padded across the deck. "Can I join the bromance?"

Ry shot her a smile. "If that other cup's for me."

She handed him the second steaming mug and sat on his other side. "Stunning."

"Just said." Ry sipped the strong brew. Nothing tasted as good a hot coffee in the cool of early morning. "But bears repeating."

Kevin matched Ry's position, legs swinging over the edge of the platform, large white mug cradled between her hands, eyes narrowed as she, like Lenka, drank in the serenity. "Suits?"

"Just tanks and masks for the first dive. I want to show you the lay of the land. Give you a feeling of what she has to offer. We've all studied the film I shot last time I was here, but she might've shifted some, especially with that storm. Hopefully she's right where I left her."

MoMo, Georgeo, and Samuel arrived in a noisy clump of excited male voice with coffee and questions, filling up the dive platform with movement, as they pulled their tanks off the racks and checked their gauges.

“Who’s right where you left her?” Georgeo asked, lifting his tank. “Addy?”

“Why do you always have to go straight to sex?” Kevin asked, sounding mildly grumpy.

“Because beauty such as yours makes all else insignificant, *amore mio*.” Georgeo’s eyes met Ry’s and the two men shared a small smile. The Italian followed up with a very insincere, “*Mi dispiace*.” Clearly not sorry at all.

Ry let the talk wash over him. Heart tripping with expectation, he waited impatiently while the others checked their tanks. Excited, anticipating seeing the wreck for the first time, their voices layered over one another as they chatted around him. There was money below. In the end, everyone would make a tidy penny.

“We’re not expecting the Cutters to swoop in and trump us, are we?” MoMo asked, looking up from his tank check, eyes scanning the horizon as if expecting to see one of the Cutter ships hovering on their port side.

“No way in hell. She’s all ours.”

It was a miracle Ry had seen the portion of a letter from one of the survivors to his grandson in Portugal. That had led to more research. The ship’s log showed the projected route of the *Nicolau Coelho* as over a hundred miles north of the location where she sank. And there was only that letter to indicate the value of her load.

Desperate, Ry had been willing to take a chance. It was about to pay off.

“No one else is aware of the shipwreck, or her treasure. Not yet anyway. Not unless they also dug into thousands of old letters and documents in the archives in an annex of the Biblioteca Nacional’s digital division in Lisbon, and went through thousands of dusty papers not yet digitized. I left registering this dive to the last second. If they follow our course, it would still take them at least a week to get here." Ry knew exactly where his enemies were located. How fast they were, and what they were capable of. He'd calculated everything out to his advantage, except for this shitstorm with Darshi.

This dive was too important to leave to chance.

"Zane's in the China Sea," he told the team. "Logan's diving near Peru, and Nick is off the coast of Ireland. Hopefully we'll be almost done with the salvage and our claim by the time those bloodsuckers show up. But they *will* show up."

"The *Nicolau Coelho* has been waiting down there for three hundred years." His look encompassed them all. The caravel had sunk in the deep waters off one of the numerous reefs surrounding the hundreds of small islands and atolls making up the Maldives.

He'd found the obscure handwritten letter with the manifest for another ship that had also sunk about the same time. He'd researched *Nicolau Coelho* for months and come here several weeks ago to register his claim. "*Two hundred tons* of silver, secretly transported by the Portuguese government to purchase spices. Probably slaves as well. They never made that return trip. The spices were never purchased. All that silver is down there just waiting for us to scoop it up. I've already lined up the buyers for it."

"Ours for the taking." Though Samuel had lived in Britain most of his life, the German accent of his youth overlaid the British when he was excited. "We can all retire."

"Never happen," Kev said. "Doesn't matter how much loot we have, we'll all be doing this until we're old and gray, right?"

They all smiled, nodded, and agreed.

For the first time in months Ry allowed himself to hope. Allowed himself to let out the indrawn breath of fear he'd been holding since receiving that fucking letter from the Baillargeon heirs.

Seven days. Seven days to bring to the surface treasure valued in today's market at close to two billion dollars and get it to his buyers. Hell, he even had a buyer for the ship's bell—if they found it—for a cool half a million. Any condition.

The blood racing through his veins felt as effervescent as the bottle of celebratory Moët & Chandon Bi Centenary Cuvée Dry Imperial Champagne in his cabin, and just as intoxicating. He glanced back to see what was taking so long.

Twenty

"I'm not getting any younger here, people. Four in, two out. Who's it gonna be?"

"Samuel and Georgeo were the last to dive on our last trip. I vote they keep watch," Kev said, sliding Georgeo a glare out of the corner of her eye.

"Good enough for me," Ry said. "You two keep the home fires burning." He looked to the others. "Let's do it."

"Race you," Kevin yelled, diving into the water with a monstrous splash. Her bikini-clad butt made a nice curve as she flipped over and went under.

Georgeo chuckled. "I love that arse, or as you Americans say, ass, which is what she's as stubborn as."

"Never give up, never surrender." Ry figured he should have that tattooed somewhere on himself.

"Words to live by, my friend. Hope you're taking your own advice?" Georgeo smiled and clasped him on the shoulder. "Is that a movie quote or a song?"

"Probably both. Ready?" Ry tuned to MoMo and Lenka. "Kev's probably filling a basket with silver while we stand here with our dicks in our hands." The two men looked at each other and bolted for the edge of the dive platform in a race. Kicking out over the side, they made a double splash as they hit the water.

The only other time in his life he'd been filled with this level of excited eagerness was that first night he'd had sex with Addison. The anticipation of discovering how to please her had kept him in a heightened state of awareness he'd been scared might lead to disappointment. He was afraid nothing could possibly be as incredible as his imagination.

Rocked to his core, he'd discovered making love to Addy far surpassed even his most fevered imagination. Nothing had changed. Making love to her for the first time, or the hundredth time, gave him the same intense wave of love and lust. He doubted that would ever change.

They'd be drinking that celebratory champagne in bed tonight.

But first things first.

MoMo climbed down the ladder. Ry dropped over the edge, just clearing his tanks from the edge of the platform. The water, crystal-clear and warm, slid over his body like silk. Adjusting his mask, he sank beneath the surface.

"I don't see anything. Am I going the wrong way?" Kev's voice came through his mask's comm unit, loud and clear.

The blue surrounded him, alive with colorful, curious fish. Just the fish and pristine sand lay directly below the shadow of *Tesoro Mio*. "It's three hundred feet that way, near the edge of that drop-off." Ry pointed to a dark smudge in the distance. The others joined him, swimming in tandem toward what looked like a hill with outcroppings of coral.

"Holy shit," MoMo breathed. "When you're right, you are right, Rydell, my man!"

In May 1498 *Nicolau Coelho*, taking her maiden voyage, was blown off the maritime trade route—between the West Indian Ocean, the Spice Islands, and China—by several hundred miles. It had sunk not three hundred miles north of their current location as reported in one hearsay version, but right here.

The last time he was here, he'd been alone. No team, no prospects, and no equipment to haul up tons of silver. With his own team, and everything *Tesoro Mio* had to offer, he had a good shot of pulling a Hail Mary and saving his company and his ship. And hopefully his marriage at the same time.

Now that things were in motion, Ry felt more optimistic. Not that he was ready to relax fully. Not just yet. But he felt lighter today than he'd felt in months. And he always felt better when he was in the encompassing womb of the water.

Georgeo swam past him, eager to get a look. "I don't see anything. You sure this is where you last saw her? Maybe one of the other outcroppings?"

He joined Georgeo, accompanied by Kev and MoMo. The hump of coral was alive with darting fish. "It's right—uck."

Right *not* here, goddamn it!

"Thank you, Mrs.—Addison, yes," The senior officer smiled when she gave him a raised brow at his formality. "You have been most hospitable. The Coast Guard helicopter will be arriving soon. We've alerted Interpol, and they will be there to meet us. You haven't let on to the prince . . . ?"

"No. I'll let you have the pleasure of witnessing his arrest. I'm just sorry I won't be there to see it for myself."

"You are most welcome to accompany us."

"No. I'll have to take satisfaction in knowing he's captured."

Sharma and one of his men were on deck with her,

meeting up after they'd had breakfast and she'd done her three miles around the deck. It was barely eight, and already promised to be a hot day, the heat intensified by the reflection on the calm water.

She heard the powerful *whop-whop-whop* of the helicopter arriving and shaded her eyes to watch its approach.

"It's a beautiful day to be out on the water. Good grief, Zikiri." Addison raced over, hands outstretched to help Naveen's bodyguard. "Let me help you with—"

"No, thank you, Miss D'Marco." Zikiri Bhat, dressed head-to-toe in black, staggered on deck lugging five heavy suitcases of varying sizes. The bespoke Louis Vuitton monogrammed leather pieces were precisely lined up before Bhat stepped away, hands behind his back as though awaiting a military inspection.

Addison mentally shook her head at Naveen's formality, and his excesses. *One* suitcase would've done him for the week trip to Sydney. He'd once been a dear friend, and she'd just accepted that his eccentricities went along with his great wealth and title. Now she knew he was a thief and a liar. And possibly a murderer as well. Just because the Coast Guard had a man under arrest—a man who'd confessed with amazingly little sense of self-preservation—didn't mean Naveen hadn't had something, if not everything, to do with it. At this point Addison wouldn't be surprised by anything Naveen did.

Even without his criminal activities, seeing the two men side by side these last few days had been an eye-opener. Naveen's polish seemed superficial and cheap besides Rydell's natural ease and charm. It was like comparing a cubic zirconia to a true diamond. While zirconia would sparkle and held no flaws, it also held no warmth, no depth as a natural diamond did.

The helicopter landed loudly overhead on the helipad, the motion of the rotors swirling her hair around her head. Addison held it back in a fist as she waited for the men to come up on deck for departure.

Rydell was still underwater. He should be returning to *Tesoro Mio* soon. She couldn't wait to hear what they discovered down there. And hopefully see some of the first treasure brought to the surface. So much rode on this salvage.

The prince came through the door several moments later, carrying nothing but a pair of sunglasses. He looked very urban and dashing, if not overdressed, in white linen pants and a light-blue shirt, his black hair perfectly styled, his gold Rolex glinting on his wrist. "Addison, a word?" His words were almost drowned out by the slowly spinning helicopter blades on the deck above them

"Sure." Addison walked around the corner to the side rail, away from the others, Naveen right behind her.

When she turned to face her, he took her hand and brought it to his lips. "I'll respect your wishes, darling," he said, clasping her hand over his heart. "But I think it would be better if I stay. If nothing else, Case will be less likely to take advantage of you if I'm here. Will you reconsider?"

Addison noticed sweat beading his upper lip, and the slight tremor in his hand. She scanned his face. "Are you ill, Nav?" *I'll be more than happy to hand your lying, avaricious ass over to Interpol and prison doctors.*

"I am quite well, Addison." He dropped her hand to reach into his pocket for his black hankie and wiped his face. "Just concerned for your happiness and well-being."

Bullshit, you son of a bitch. You brought stolen property into my own, and a killer onto my ship. "I told you Rydell and I are talking," she told him with fake compassion. "Honestly? I'm not sure where we go from here, but either way. There's no hope for you and I, Naveen.

We just don't have that . . . spark. I don't think we ever did. I hope that we'll always remain friends."

"You know you're breaking my heart." His black eyes looked—hmm, no, not sad. Annoyed? "*Again*," he said with a little bite in his voice, "I'll go. But I intend to remain in Malé as long as you and *Tesoro Mio* are here, and when you finally head to Sydney next week, I'll be there waiting for you. I hope you'll take the time to have a meal with me while you're here. One of Case's people will bring you, I'm sure."

I'm pretty damn positive one of Case's "people" will do no such thing. All Addison said was, "That sounds lovely."

The four Indian officers were nothing if not efficient. They got Naveen and his mountain of luggage secured in the helicopter, then brought out a handcuffed, and silent, Van Engen and loaded him on board as well. Having accompanied the men from the lower deck, Jax and Oscar stood on the top deck and waited for the chopper to lift off. Addison suspected it was to ensure that Naveen and Van Engen left.

"Goodbye to bad rubbish," Oscar said, shading his eyes.

"Amen," Jax grinned, tucking his pistol into the back of his pants. "Won't need this anymore."

"Thank God," Addison said with a smile. "Thanks for taking such good care of me, guys. It's humiliating to realize I didn't know Naveen *at all*. These last few days have been an eye-opener to say the least."

"He was the opposite of Ry," Oscar pointed out gently. "You needed different."

"Yes. I suppose I did. Would you like to go down and see what Ry and the others are up to? Get a first look at our wreck?"

Jax backed away with a laugh. "Not me, thanks. I'm

not fond of deep water. I'm happy to grab a beer and wait for them to come and show me what they've found."

"Oscar?"

"Not *under* for me, but a swim sounds good."

They parted ways and Addison went down to her cabin. She felt almost euphoric. If not quite *happy*, for the first time in a year she felt contentment, a lift to her step as she anticipated light at the end of the tunnel.

Learning to overcome her fears would be a start.

Where the fuck is my damn wreck?

Fish, small and large, in a rainbow of colors, swam and darted around them in the clear, warm water. The atolls making up the Maldives were home to over a thousand types of fish, and apparently they'd all swum over to check out the humans today. A six-foot-long humphead wrasse moseyed by, turning its huge, fleshy-lipped ugly face to meet Ry eye-to-eye. Predator, but not likely to take a chunk out of him, as they were too evenly matched in size. It kept going. So did Ry.

He checked his underwater GPS.

Hell.

Sand, coral, and more fucking fish than he ever wanted to see in his life.

Where's my ship?

Rippled white sand on the seafloor stretched to the coral drop-off where Kev swam, far ahead. No sign of debris. No sign of the silver. No sign that this venture was going to get done in enough time to save his ass. Maybe he'd misjudged the depth or the location when he'd been here last.

Unlikely. He was always meticulous in his measurements. He wouldn't make a bloody mistake now, when everything depended on him getting it right. He was too careful for that.

Damn it. Longitude and latitude didn't change, and they didn't lie.

Maybe the fucking Cutters had trumped him. Moved in, shifted the wreck, and were lying in wait somewhere, laughing their asses off. *Jesus.* "Paranoid at all?"

"Say what?" Lenka asked, shooting him a puzzled look through his mask. His bright-red buzz-cut hair wafted in the current like stubby orange sea grass.

"Talking to myself."

For the first time since he'd received the lawyer's letter, Ry felt a shiver of stark fear about his financial future. The no-fucking-hope-left kind of fear. He'd been freaked out before, but he'd believed the *Nicolau Coelho* with her tons of silver was his ace in the hole.

If the wreck *had* been swept over the eighty-foot cliff and now lay two-hundred-plus feet below the surface, that was a whole other kind of retrieval. Doable, but not in the time he had left. It would take months—probably *years*—to salvage. Time he didn't have.

The paintings that Naveen had stashed aboard the *Tesoro Mio* might produce something—but not in enough time. The value would have to be ascertained if there was a reward. For all Ry knew, the paintings could be high-quality fakes. Best not to count on the art producing significant financial assets.

"Storm?" MoMo suggested, staying relatively motionless beside him. His black hair, usually a cap of tight curls, was in the water dead straight and freakishly long. MoMo put out a hand as a shoal of powder-blue tang swam close enough for him to touch. They darted around him, a parting curtain of shimmering blue and yellow.

Addy would love this, Ry thought, keeping an eye on Kev as she swam way ahead. The fish were plentiful, the water warm, and visibility was great. She'd forget claustrophobia with this stunning beauty around them. He'd enjoy it a hell of a lot more if they were hauling tons of silver to the surface. Or at least fucking *looking* at it.

"Probably," he answered MoMo's question. The storm had been a bitch; it was logical to assume she'd swept the caravel over the cliff in the underwater surges.

When last Ry was here, the ship had been hovering near the edge of the drop-off; she was broken, but pretty much all the pieces seemed present within a circumference of several hundred yards. Murphy's Law, the law that seemed to rule his universe, said this was the one storm in fucking five hundred years that had pushed her over the edge. What a bloody kick in the head.

No. A killing blow to the gut.

Apparently a man couldn't have it all. He and Addy were—well, whatever they were it was a crapload better than it had been a week ago. There was hope there. A feeling of joyful anticipation. But *this*—

This would be starting over. From the bottom. Hell, lower than the bottom. He'd lose the company and *Tesoro Mio*, and the Cutters would likely sweep in snapping up all of it just to deliver the knockout punch. Bloody fucking brilliant.

"Can't see her," Kev reported in his headset as she hovered over the vast dark depths at the edge of the coral and rock cliff some thirty yards ahead. She'd always been fearless—except when it came to Georgeo. With a double flick of her fins, she went butt-up to swim down, out of sight.

The three men caught up. Ry could see the jagged, stair-step clumps of coral going down about another thirty feet; then everything became darker blue and obscured. Impossible to miss the skid marks where something heavy had bumped down the reef.

Fuck. "Not impossible," he told the others as they dropped down and passed through the thermocline, that invisible line separating the warmer surface water from the progressively cooler water below. "We'll have to use the ROV after all."

The Remote Operated Vehicle was, thank God, on board *Tesoro Mio*, and had never been used. It was one of the many upgrades Ry had ordered when he'd designed the ship, and as of a year ago had been state-of-the-art. Having it on board could very well save his ass. But possibly not in this decade.

"—et su—" Kevin rubbed her arms to indicate she was cold.

Yeah. They'd need full wet suits for deeper diving, along with high-compression helium-mix tanks. They wouldn't be able to go down more than 130 feet, and they'd need to surface more often to replenish their tanks, and stay under for shorter periods. They'd have the ROV do all the deeper work, and watch its progress on the monitors in the conference/dining room. Which sucked. They all liked to be hands-on as much as possible.

Crap. Not optimal, but still doable. Just not doable in a week's time to make any difference.

Just when things were looking too bleak and impossible to save his company, it got worse. Ry's heart sank like the vessel he was after. "There." He pointed in a straight line about twenty feet down and to the left. A ten-foot-long chunk of one of the three masts, angled down. No sign of the other two. When he'd been here last, all the masts were near the hull, broken and with large chunks missing, but within a hundred feet. Now everything was broken up and scattered across the seabed below. Far below. "Hang on. I'll be right back."

"Don't risk it," Kevin cautioned.

Ry ignored her, and swam down to check it out.

It was too deep for the time left on his tank, and almost too deep to venture in without an extra compression stop.

Ry went anyway. Could be a rock formation—unlikely with the straight length of it, but you never knew.

He swam alongside the brightly colored corals and rocks, dislodging a spotted moray eel and its housekeeping staff of six cleaner shrimp on the way down.

As he got closer, he heard the *throb-throb-throb* of his uneven heartbeat in his ears over the normal hiss-and-burble sound of his regulator. A mast, for sure. He breathed out a sigh as he swam the length of it. Broken in three—one section missing, but otherwise in pretty good condition.

"See anything?" Lenka asked eagerly. "Should we come down?"

"Sure. It's the center mast, and what looks like a rock-slide. She went skidding down here, all right." A glint on the far side of the mast caught Ry's attention. Probably a fish, but worth checking out. He headed in that direction.

A few minutes later the other three were right there. "Better than a knock on the head, right?" Lenka nodded at the mast.

"A big old box, or fifty, of silver, would be better," MoMo pointed out, running his hand down the aged wood.

"It's down there; we just have to get the ROV and go get it. Anything worth having is worth working for, right, boss?" Kevin gave him an encouraging look from behind her mask.

It would be so fucking excellent if he didn't have to work quite so damn hard. On the other hand, Ry didn't know anything else. A sedentary life on a deserted island sipping umbrella drinks wasn't his style. He smiled back at Kev, then pushed aside a little oasis of sand between two pieces of yellow coral. The Maldives had the most complex coral systems in the world, and they were all on

Technicolor display here along on the coral ridge. A glint had caught his eye, but now that he was closer he didn't see anything unusual.

Hang on. What was that?

Brushing a finger through the pale sand to retrieve what he'd merely glimpsed. Heavy. Smooth. He held the silver bar up as grains of sand floated from his hand. "A silver ingot."

It was a start. Ry glanced at his regulator. Past time to go. He indicated with a hand signal that they return to the surface.

After Naveen left, Addison took her iPad and a basket of snacks to share with the others down to the dive platform. Before checking the social blogs and society pages of her favorite publications, she said hi to Sam and Georgeo. "Patrick just made your favorite oatmeal-raisin cookies, Georgeo." She set the flat-bottomed basket on a small table beside a couple of chairs in the shade. "Help yourselves." She pulled out an apple and held up a small paring knife. "Anyone want an orange or some apple?"

She cut up the apple and arranged it on a paper plate with a few slices of sharp cheddar and some chilled grapes. Patrick had made sandwiches, too. But those could wait until the divers surfaced. She wanted to be right there when Rydell returned to the ship, face wreathed in smiles.

The Coast Guard helicopter should've reached Malé by now. Had Interpol taken Naveen into custody yet? Wasn't he going to be surprised?!

She looked down at the clear cobalt ocean lapping against the hull. It was so peaceful, calm. Did the ocean hold the answers for Rydell to achieve his goal? God, she hoped the wreck held everything he hoped for. Everything.

He didn't just salvage because it handsomely paid the

bills. Treasure salvage was his life. His passion. And Rydell did passion very well. It defined who he was. He'd been crushingly poor, seen his mother burdened by poverty, and vowed he'd never be that financially strapped ever again. He'd pulled himself—and his family—out of that financial yoke, and made good on his promises. The fact that his father had put them in that position when Rydell was a boy—and now even after his death had done it again—wasn't lost on Addison. She sent up a little prayer that the salvage was quick and easy.

He couldn't lose Case Enterprises. It would decimate him. Could it decimate them, too?

"You should give scuba another try, Addy." Sam leaned back in his hands. "Look how clear the water is. You'd love it down there."

"I can see it just fine from here, thanks." She smiled at Sam, realizing she wasn't going to get much reading done while the two men waited their turn to go down. "Oscar said he's coming down for a swim in a bit. Can you take him down?"

"Sure." Georgeo launched into a story about a dive he'd recently been on near Crete. ". . . went floating away, leaving him *scala a pioli*—"

Smiling at Georgeo's amusing recounting of a past dive and a naked diver, she glanced at the water, checking to see where *her* diver was. No sign of Ry and the others. Hopefully they'd return elated.

The throbbing sound of the approaching helicopter got progressively louder. Addison shaded her eyes to see where it was.

"Darshi change his mind?" Samuel yelled, looking up.

Addison had to lip-read. God, she hoped Naveen wasn't that damn stupid. She shook her head. Not Naveen. Unless he'd somehow evaded arrest and hired a big black helicopter for a return trip from Malé—she hoped to hell he hadn't—then this was someone else. Tourists, probably doing a flyby to see what was going on.

The helicopter was big enough to hold a lot of nosy people. She sighed inwardly. Rydell was already stressed. Having inquisitive lookeeloos buzzing them from overhead for the duration would just annoy him more.

She wondered absently who they were. People alerted to the titillation of a treasure salvage? The press? Since the project had to be documented and all the paperwork was available to anyone looking for it, it wasn't uncommon to have boats and helicopters show up to watch what was going on with a salvage. They had to stay a certain distance away, and Captain Seddeth would deter anyone from landing on the *Tesoro Mio*, but it could get quite annoying having people photographing or filming as the team dived.

The rotors whipped the air right above them, frothing the water as the enormous helicopter cast a shadow over them. Then the ship gave a small jolt as it landed on the pad on the top deck.

Rydell and the others were still down. If she hurried, she could run up to the top deck to see who it was, and get rid of them before Rydell found out strangers were on board. He wouldn't be happy. Sam didn't look too happy, either.

Georgeo indicated himself then Sam, and thumbed up, indicating they'd go and see who the visitors were.

"It *might* be Naveen," she answered Sam, even though she knew there was no way he could hear her over the din. She doubted it. Nav would be in the custody of Interpol by now. Unless . . . He'd given in *far* too easily this morning. And he was slippery. Slippery and smart enough to elude capture and double back for the paintings?

If so, he was—as Ry would say—shit out of luck. He

wouldn't know that his stolen artwork was securely on its way to Interpol.

If this was Naveen making a return visit, Addison had a few choice words for him. Given the mood and stress Ry was under right now, Addison didn't think he could be counted on to be civilized, no matter who their visitors might be. And before she confronted him, she'd put in a call to her new friends at the Coast Guard and let them know Naveen was back on board and they could come back to collect his ass. This time they could screw diplomatic diplomacy and take him away in handcuffs.

She'd just crossed the first deck and was about to take the stairs to the second when what sounded like a gunshot was followed by an even louder crash of broken glass. She stopped dead in her tracks, whipping her head around toward the sound.

Running footsteps. A yell. Another volley of shots. Oh, God. Now what . . . ?

A man, yelling, "Get down! Get down!" came barreling out of the darkness of the nearby lounge into bright sunlight.

Twenty-one

"What the—"

He shouldered her hard in the belly. With a thud Addison was down on her back on the hot wood deck. Adrenaline surged through her as surprise morphed into fear, then anger. Fighting, she tried to struggle her way out from under his oppressive weight. Punching, kicking, and biting. More so when she glimpsed the big black gun in his hand inches from her face.

"Addison! It's me, Jax."

Arms tight around her, he was full on top of her, his face inches from hers. It took several seconds of fighting him for his words and facial recognition to compute. "Are we good? Addy. Nod if you're with me."

His voice sounded muffled and distant although he was right there on top of her. Bewildered, feeling totally out of sync in a familiar place with a familiar person, but bizarre circumstances, she nodded.

He eased off. Staying in a low crouch he grabbed her arm, urging her to crouch, too. "Stay low and haul ass."

The sound of gunshots persuaded her to stay low and run with him. If she hadn't kept up, she was pretty sure he'd be dragging her behind him into the salon. It took precious, disorienting seconds for her eyes to adjust to the dimness beyond the sliding glass doors. "What—"

Still gripping her arm in a punishing hold, he pulled her across the room, leading with his gun raised, and keeping flush with the paneled wall. "Hijackers."

"No freaking way!" Inconceivable in fact.

"Your buddy the prince is with them. So's your mother."

Addison's steps halted, and he almost yanked her arm out of the socket. "Naveen is hijacking the ship? He's come for those damn paintings!"

"My guess. Our lives won't be worth squat if they find out they're gone."

"Wait. Did you say my *mother*?" Of all the improbable, downright weird scenarios. She couldn't fathom how Hollis could possibly be involved.

Jax, looking grim, eyes shifting as he watched for movement, nodded. "Yeah, I was hella surprised, too. But she's the least of our problems. There are dozens of men, and they all seem to know their way around those automatics like pros."

Maybe so, but considering Hollis's propensity for machinations and causing trouble, Addison wouldn't put it past her mother to be armed as well, or at least paying the goons very well. The thought of those long, elegant, red-nailed hands wielding a gun was mind boggling. Addison gripped Jax's arm. "We have to warn Ry and the others!"

He shook his head, not realizing how hard he was gripping her. "They've already taken over the ship. My job is to protect *you*. He'll figure it out."

The crack of a gunshot was followed by an agonized scream of pain, the splintering of wood, and more gunshots, this time in quick succession. Sick with worry about Ry and the others, Addison winced. "How can he figure it out, Jax? He's *underwater*. They could shoot him and the others as they come up. We have to go back. Damn it. We have to!"

"I'll get you stashed and go and warn him. You're my priority. Don't give me that look, Addison. I'll knock you out and carry you if I have to."

"Then for God's sake hur—"

One minute Jax was tugging her behind him at a run, the next he stumbled back into her with a grunt. It was all so quick she couldn't quite comprehend what had just happened. He righted himself immediately, shoving her hard between his body and the wall. But not before Addison saw the red bloom on his pristine white shirt over his shoulder. "Dear God, you've been sh—"

"Get down. Get down!" He jerked her arm down until she was bent double and folded down hard on her knees behind the long, sectional sofa. Whoever had come into the room was blocked by his body. *She* was blocked by his body.

Jax fired a shot over the sofa back, his hand on her back to hold her in place, facedown. A volley of shots were retuned. The wood paneling behind her head splintered, and bits of wood showered her head and shoulders.

Jax grunted, and his restraining hand went slack as he fell back away from her. Addison crawled the few feet to reach him. "Jax!"

Limp and unresponsive, eyes closed, he looked dead. God, she hoped not. She felt the base of his throat for a pulse. Then realized she had no idea how to *interpret* the heartbeat she felt there. Fast, slow? Hard, soft? Hell, at lease he had a pulse.

She had to get help.

Their first mate, Badril Patil, was a medic. Where would he be at noon? Bridge? The hijackers would be there for sure. She'd take the outside stairs and go down to the crew's quarters—

"Get the girl. Hurry."

Like hell. Jax still held the gun in one lax, outstretched hand. Addison tried to pry it from his fingers, but a man reached over the sofa and grabbed her by the hair, hauling her to her feet, the sofa back between them. "Boss wants to see you, Sheila. Come along." Pulling her by a fistful of her hair, he walked her along until they met at the end of the couch. Addison dug her nails into his wrist, but unless she wanted him to pull off a section of her scalp, it was useless to fight him.

Two other men, both cradling automatic weapons, laughed as the guy with the gun herded her in front of him. How did Naveen, a sophisticated, urbane man, know men like these thugs? On the other hand, how did a sophisticated urbane man continue to steal art worth billions of euros and think he'd get away with it?

She prayed Jax wasn't dead as she worried about the rest of the crew. The fear that Rydell would surface from his dive to find his ship overrun by gun-toting thugs made her sick to her stomach.

Her eyes watered from the sharp sting of her hair being pulled. She dug the nails of both hands into the thug's wrist. "If you want to keep this hand, let go of my hair, asshole," Addison told the guy holding her. "No need to force me along. I'm looking forward to seeing your boss and giving him a piece of my mind. Trust me, I'm quite capable of getting there on my own."

She had every intention of ripping Naveen a new one, so her steps were brisk. The guy didn't let go, just clenched his fist more tightly into her hair and jabbed her in the back with his gun. "Move."

There were headed down the polished-wood corridor toward the stairs to the second deck. A man dressed in white shorts and shirt lay on the floor. Addison gagged when she saw that he'd been shot in the head. Recently enough that blood and brain matter were still sliding down the wall.

Covering her mouth and nose with her hand she had to step over him or be brought down on top of him, because the guy hadn't let go of his grip in her hair as he walked right over him, not missing a beat.

Four men waiting at the foot of the stairs fell into step. Two in front, two behind. Addison suppressed an unlady-like snort. He had no damn idea who the hell he was going to confront. "Five guys to deliver me? We're in the middle of the ocean. Where does he think I'll run to?" No one responded as they started up the stairs. Addison's temper climbed with each step. She didn't try to break free. Hell freaking no! She *wanted* to talk to Naveen right now! This time she wouldn't hold back a damn thing. She'd show Naveen Darshi a damn show of force. Better her than Ry when he saw his beautiful woodwork shot all to hell. She was about to rip Naveen a new one and let the chips fall where they may.

The guy prodded her again. Addison stopped dead in her tracks. Yeah, he almost ripped her arm from the socket, but it brought him to a halt, too. He gave her a menacing look and tugged harder. She held her ground. "Do. *Not.* Keep dragging me, buster. If you do, you'll have to carry me kicking, scratching, and biting. Knock it off!"

"He's waiting. Get the lead out, bitch!"

Addison narrowed her eyes at him and he faltered. "You know he and I are engaged to be married, right? What do you think he's going to do to you when he sees these bruises and I tell him how you talked to me?" Drawing herself up tall, and haughty, Addison put everything she despised about Hollis into her tone.

"He didn't say nothing about you being his fiancée."

"Clearly you're not his confidant. Go ahead, really. Keep moving. I can't *wait* to see him again."

For her pains she received a bruise-inducing prod in the back, but he did let go of her hair. "Shut up and walk." This time when the guy started walking again, his hold on her arm wasn't quite as punishing. The other men fell into step with them.

No surprise, they were headed for the bridge.

The first man opened the door. The one behind her shoved her inside with a hard slam of the flat of his hand between her shoulder blades. Pain flared brightly in her vision and stole her breath for a moment. Addison staggered into the middle of the room, and had to grab the console to remain on her feet.

The room, usually large and airy, was too hot, and crowded with people. Most of whom held some sort of weapon. Tony Seddeth lay dead or unconscious on the floor.

Be scared later. Do not damn well fall apart.

Then she saw her mother and a fierceness she didn't know she had in the depths of her being emerged. It was a passion she never believed she'd feel again after her sweet baby died.

Addison narrowed her eyes at the woman seated cross-legged in the captain's chair. Long shapely nylon-clad legs ended with five-inch-high black Jimmy Choos.

"Hollis. What are *you* doing here?" she demanded. "With armed men, for God's sake?" *Goddamn it.* Addison did *not* want her mother on board any more than she wanted Naveen to suddenly return. He was there, standing beside her mother, but Addison wasn't ready to look at him.

She hadn't wanted Ry to go to jail for killing Naveen, but she didn't have the same reservations when it came to killing her own mother. Not when she knew how utterly manipulative Hollis had been.

Wearing a white dress with large blood-red flowers on it, not a blond hair out of place, her mother looked as though she'd stepped from the pages of her beloved German luxury magazine, *Deutsch*. A fashion and society publication only considered high-class because of who it featured, and the value of their toys.

It made Hollis's day if she was featured in the magazine, a handsome playboy on her arm. That playboy was frequently Naveen, who loved everything high-society, and having his picture taken, as much as Hollis did.

Her mother lifted her chin and said coolly, "This is business, Addison."

"*Illegal* business." Was her vapid mother aware that Naveen was Procioni? That he was the one stealing priceless artwork from the friends she'd introduced him to? She bet Hollis had no idea. Then again, maybe she did. Maybe she'd used Naveen to steal for her. Given Hollis's acting skills—she'd never been genuine a day in her life—her love of money, and her favorite pastime of manipulating others to get what she wanted, perhaps Naveen was just Hollis's puppet playboy in crime. "I don't give a damn what it is. Neither of you—" She cast the men a withering glance. "*None* of you are welcome."

Up close she noticed her mother's carefully made-up face had smudges of what looked like dirt on the chin and cheek, and pale tracks as though she'd sweated or—God forbid—cried, which had never happened in Addison's recollection.

Addison had zero sympathy for her.

She saw her own face reflected in her mother's large sunglasses. She looked as pissed as she felt.

Was Rydell just now surfacing to find armed men pointing their weapons at him? Shooting at him? She strained her ears, listening for gunshots. Was he of any value to these men alive? If not, they'd shoot him and the others the moment they emerged from the water.

Hollis held out an imploring hand. "Darling . . ."

"I might get over hating you with every fiber of my being for the cruel lies you told Ry and me in the next millennium," Addison told her mother, rage making her voice shake. "But probably not. And definitely not *today*. Hop on your broomstick and fuck off."

Flinching, Hollis swept off her sunglasses and sent her daughter an imploring look. "Just hear me out, Addison. This could benefit all of us—"

Whatever it was, no one but Hollis would prosper, that was a given. "Not interested." Addison crossed her arms over her waist, waiting for the slam of a bullet between her eyes.

"But darling—" Hollis continued right over her objections. Other people's objections never mattered to Hollis. Then a thought struck Addison: Her mother never called her darling. She called other people darling. She used the endearment to retain the veneer of sophisticated ennui she and her "friends" enjoyed. The word was as shallow and insincere as Hollis herself.

"I don't have one iota of sympathy for you." She shot Naveen a cold glance. "Either one of you." Her mother was in the center of a shitstorm she couldn't control. Her usual tactics wouldn't work on people who had no class or worry about society in the first place. The kind of people who only spoke in dollar signs. Well, too fucking bad. It wasn't her job to facilitate Hollis and Naveen's problems.

A man rose from the sofa to the right of Hollis and the prince. He seemed to be the only goon in the room without a gun. Dressed in a dark-blue suit and white, open-necked dress shirt, he was enormous, almost as tall as he was wide. Jabba the Hutt with gold chains and diamonds. Like Van Engen, who'd been carted off for trial just hours earlier, this guy was tall, heavyset, and Asian.

Heart beating fast, mouth dry, Addison felt the hair on the back of her neck stand up as she watched the men close in and bracket the sumo wrestler leader. They all carried heavy, military-style automatic weapons, their fingers steady on their triggers.

The big man held out a hand the size of a Christmas goose. Diamonds sparkled from several gold rings on his sausage-like fingers. "Miss D'Marco, I'm Gorou Morimoto." Australian accent. Black, reptilian eyes observed her, unblinking. When she didn't shake his hand, he dropped his arm, his small mouth tightening.

"Formalities out of the way, where are my bloody paintings?"

Goose bumps pebbled over Addison's skin. It took every ounce of control she had not to glance up at the cameras strategically placed to see the entire bridge. See and record. *Are you seeing this, Oscar?* Jax and Oscar were her bodyguards; Jax was down, but unless Oscar was compromised, too, he was somewhere planning to intervene.

Is Rydell observing what's going on, too, or have they . . .

She tried to swallow past the lump in her throat and breathe steadily, although her heartbeat thundered in her ears. *Focus, Addison. Don't even think about worst-case scenarios.*

Preternaturally aware of Naveen and her mother standing by silently, she kept her eyes on Morimoto and gave him a slightly puzzled look. "Paintings?"

He backhanded her so fast, so hard, Addison went flying backward, hit Captain Seddeth's desk, and fell to the floor on all fours. Dazed, she crouched there trying to assimilate what had just happened. The heat of her cheek and the dull, throbbing pain were nothing compared with the hard, manic beat of her heart, and the avalanche of rage she felt. She could not allow fear to immobilize her. Anger was good. Terrified was not.

"My God, she doesn't *know*—" Her mother's voice cut off with the sound of flesh meeting flesh as Morimoto struck Hollis a punishing blow.

Addison lifted her head slowly. Every muscle in her neck ached; every bone in her knees and legs throbbed. All were ignored as she narrowed her gaze to look into the evil bastard's lifeless eyes. She looked into the darkness there and saw no soul. He wasn't a man who'd care if she died, if Rydell died. Hell, he might just set the *Tesoro Mio* up in flames when he left for the fun of it. How and why was Hollis involved in the business of Naveen and this pig? Clearly her mother was in the know about the paintings.

And just as clearly, Hollis hadn't expected Morimoto to strike *her*. Blood dripped from the corner of her mouth. A deeper red than her lipstick, now smeared in a waxy streak on her chin. Hollis's eyes were all pupil with fear as she backed away from him. "Gorou, my dear—"

"Shut the fuck up, Hollis."

Her mother snapped her mouth closed, then held the back of her hand against her face, eyes welling with tears.

Addison had known the man for twenty seconds and she could've told Hollis that he wouldn't be moved by tears.

From the corner of her eye, she observed movement on the dive platform monitor where the camera faced the aft deck.

Oh, God. No. Rydell's head emerged from the water as he swam toward the platform. The beefy hand of one of Morimoto's thugs came into view of the platform camera as he lifted his weapon and pointed at the man she loved. Heart manic, Addison lurched to her feet, transfixed by the silent tableau playing out on the video screen.

Twenty-two

From behind his mask, Ry saw the blur of someone standing on the edge of platform. Sam or Georgeo. Too bulky for Addy. Not wanting to telegraph his concern, he triumphantly held the silver bar aloft. Shoving the mask out of the way, he breached the surface. "There's silver in them thar—" he yelled, then "What the fuck . . . ?"

Three armed men in black fatigues stood, feet spread, automatic weapons pointed straight at him.

Ry's first, heart-knocking thought: *Addy.*

His second came fast on the heels of the first. *Hijacked. Again.* Goddamn it to hell. Perhaps his luck hadn't changed. He'd found silver, thought he'd hit upon a miracle to save his ass, then evil Lady Luck had buggered it all up again out of spite.

Kevin swam up beside him, her faint voice an indistinct bee buzz from the mike in his mask, which was now perched on top of his head. She pushed her own mask out of the way. "What the hell do we have here?"

MoMo and Lenka surfaced nearby, stripping off their masks. Taking in the situation by following Ry and Kev's line of sight, MoMo said, "Fuck!"

Lenka swam up beside him. "How do we handle these douchenozzles, boss?"

Excellent fucking question.

With all the appropriate menacing facial expressions, a bald man the size of a refrigerator shouted, "Get outta the water."

With the stubby barrel of his semi-automatic, Baldy gestured to the dive platform ladder.

With only a knife to bring to an assault-weapon gunfight, Ry felt pretty damn ill equipped.

"I'll go first. Get your tanks off. Slow-mo. Don't get out of the water until I give you a sign." A sign to do *what* and fucking *how*? Ry had no idea. Just that, whatever it was, it'd better be done *fast*.

"No need for any more violence," Naveen said quickly, using a subservient tone Addison had never heard from him. With an aching jaw, and tamping down the urge to slug the fat man back, she reluctantly took her eyes off the monitor, and Ry, to help her mother to her feet.

Shaking as she clung to Addison's arm, Hollis whispered, "Sorry, baby."

Addison suspected by the flat look in Hollis's eyes that she wasn't apologizing for bringing danger to her only child and everyone else on board; she was apologizing for damn well getting caught. Apparently there were no depths her mother wasn't willing to plumb to get what she wanted. Oddly, this revelation didn't feel like a revelation at all. Her mother had always behaved in a self-centered, self-serving way. The knowledge wasn't a shocker. The days of wishing for the impossible—a loving, nurturing mother—were long gone.

"You're full of crap, Hollis." Addison let go of her mother as soon as she was on her feet and stable.

As for Naveen, Addison had never seen him anything but sophisticated and urbane. Completely in control of the situation, no matter who he dealt with. She couldn't fathom what the connection could possibly be among the three key players. The paintings, yes. But how had Hollis, Naveen, and Morimoto gotten together? And when?

A greasy sheen of nervous perspiration shone on Naveen's unusually pale face, and his bleached white lips were held tightly. His entire demeanor had changed from prince to deferential serf in the blink of an eye.

He was going to be a whole hell of a lot more freaking nervous when he discovered those damn paintings were gone. Addison didn't want to be anywhere near the two men when that discovery was made.

Naveen shifted his feet to face the door, but didn't turn the rest of his body. "Rest assured," he told Morimoto, "your artwork is as safe as Fort Knox. I'll go down and retrieve the paintings and this will be done."

He was in for an unpleasant surprise. And as much as she'd enjoy seeing Naveen and Hollis pinned to a board like insects, the fallout would affect everyone on board.

One thing at a time. She had to concentrate on the here and now. Casually she let her eyes roam the cabin for anything she could use as a weapon. Laughable. What could compete with a gun? With surprise, she realized that in all the chaos Tony Seddeth had disappeared. The craftily concealed door to his private quarters was close to where he'd been crumpled on the floor. None of the others appeared to have noticed the captain was missing.

"No," Morimoto snapped, his large hands fisting and flexing as if ready to punch someone out at any moment. Naveen took a sidestep, clearly aware of the other man's barely leashed temper. "*Not* done, you conniving arsehole!" Naveen flinched when Morimoto stabbed him hard in the middle of his chest with two stiff fingers. "You said this was a piece of piss." The next finger stab was harder. "I'll store your paintings on the ship, you said." Each statement was accompanied by a harder and harder prod, until Naveen was forced to step backward with the force of it. "No one the wiser, you said. Trust me, you said, you'll have it all you said. Instead, you forced me to abandon my business dealings in Sydney to fly out here and see what the bloody *fuck* you were up to. Now I'm standing here with my ruddy wang in my hand, *waiting*. Bugger that! Go get my paintings, fuckwit, and be quick about it. You. You. And you. Go with him. And you and you—bring the husband to me."

"Move it!"

Before the guy shot him in the head, and his team with him, Ry unfastened his tank in the water. Swimming over to the edge of the dive platform, he hung the tank and his mask over the ladder before pulling himself out of the water.

No sign of Addy. With any luck she was holed up in her cabin with both Jax and Oscar. Safe.

No, he realized, his gut clenching.

With Darshi gone, Oscar and Jax would've relaxed their vigilance. Addy was on her own. He prayed she was safely locked in her cabin.

Three men, armed.

Samuel and Georgeo were behind them, cuffed by zip ties to the ladder leading up to the deck, wide electrical tape over their mouths.

If these guys wanted him dead, he'd be dead. Which meant they were after something more than just the boat. Because *Tesoro Mio* wouldn't still be there, waiting for the dive team to finish their dive.

Okay. So these guys weren't simply maritime pirates, out to land an expedition yacht.

But what the fuck were they after?

The yacht *and* the paintings?

Damn it to hell.

And where the hell was Addy?

Keeping his attention on the big, bald guy closest to him, Ry gripped his dive knife and addressed him only because he looked slightly more intelligent than the other two. Which wasn't very. "Who are you, and what do you want?"

Getting the stock of an Uzi slammed into his belly was a shit way for the man to introduce himself. Surprise and pain caused Ry to grunt as he doubled over.

Fuck this shit!

If I'm going to get stuffed, I might as well go out fighting! Adrenaline surged through him. He jerked upright, dropped the knife, and grabbed the stubby barrel of the weapon with both hands, using it as a fulcrum to swing the guy over the water.

Baldy toppled over the edge of the platform with a scream and a massive splash.

"And now I have this, fuckwad." Ry righted the weapon. Heavy and foreign as hell in his hands. He'd get used to it. He swung around—had a split second to assess where Sam and Georgeo were positioned—then squeezed off several shots.

Fast. Instantly responsive. A volley of his bullets took down the man on his left, creating crimson splatter against *Tesoro Mio*'s stark-white dive platform. The guy to his right was still fumbling with his own automatic when Ry shot him high on the shoulder.

Narrowly missing Samuel just behind him, bullets pinged off metal and fiberglass, wood splintering. Samuel and Georgeo flinched as a shower of fiberglass decking ricocheted off the platform at their feet. "Shit. Sorry." Ry picked up his knife and shoved it back into the scabbard on his calf. "You okay?"

Samuel nodded vigorously as he struggled with his bound hands behind his back.

Turning to his team, who were now heading to the dive ladder, he pitched his voice so they could hear him. "Get up here pronto. We have a situation."

"No shit," said Kev, scrambling out of the water without her tank. Seeing her, Georgeo's eyes went wild and he tried to lunge forward, straining against the ties. Kev shook her head at him. "What do you want me to do with these two—oh. Good job, Ry. What do you want me to do with this o—Kick me, you asshole?" Kev jumped out of the way as the bleeding guy huddled on his knees, cradling his wounded arm, and tried to take her down with a swipe of his leg.

A red tide of blood mixed with the seawater on the dive platform.

Fine with Ry.

Right now, his priority was making sure Addy was somewhere safe. Then he'd tackle whatever waited for him up top. Kev kick-nudged the injured man's Uzi farther away from his flailing hand.

Ry kept his own borrowed weapon pointed at the guy in the water and shouted over his shoulder. "Can you tie him up and gag his ass, GI Jane?"

With a grimace Kev picked her way barefooted over the gore awash on the platform and grabbed the Uzi. "My pleasure." Pointing at the guy with the shoulder wound, she gave Georgeo a worried glance before looking at her target. "Hands behind your back, dick."

"Think there's just the three of us?" the man sneered, keeping his attention on the weapon Kevin held inexpertly to his face. Didn't matter if she knew how to hit what she shot or not. At this range he'd be dead, and he knew it.

Standing on his injured side, she pressed the barrel against his temple, then bent over to go through his pockets, looking for more weapons. "Ooh! Lookie here. He was kind enough to bring us a pocketful of zip ties. *Caro?*" she said to a hovering, worried-looking Georgeo. "Can you stand on him, please?"

Georgeo stretched out from his tied position and planted a heavy foot on the guy's chest. The man screamed in agony as he was kicked backward. MoMo and Lenka scrambled onto the platform, streaming water. "What the fuck is going on? A hijacking?"

MoMo, looking very un-MoMo-like with long, flat, soaking-wet hair, glanced around, face pale. "Holy shit!"

"Douchenozzles!" Lenka ran to use his own diving knife to cut the zip ties binding Samuel and Georgeo.

Ry didn't know what to do with the guy floundering in the water, and merely pulled up the ladder for the moment.

"Want me to take this weapon, *dolce cuore*?" Georgeo wrapped his arms around Kevin from behind.

She rested her head on his shoulder for a moment. "No. Get your own. I have a feeling we haven't seen the worst of it."

"She's right," Ry said. "Lenka, grab that tape and shut this guy up. Then hang on to the tape. We're probably going to need it. Georgeo, check the dead guy for weapons. See if he's got an ankle—yeah. That's what I thought." The man had an ankle holster with a small gun in it, and his other calf sported a lethal-looking knife in a scabbard.

"You comfortable with that?"

"*Non ci penso proprio!*" Georgeo shook his head. "I will cut off my own hand by mistake. I'll take the gun, though."

MoMo held out his hand. "I know how to use a hunting knife. Give it here."

"Are we going to just let that guy swim around hoping a shark gets him?" Samuel asked, jerking a shoulder to the man splashing about ten feet from the edge of the platform. "I'll go get him and keep him out of trouble. We can secure him by the ladder for now. Yeah?"

Ry looked for more weapons, or anything they could use as a weapon. He, Kevin, Lenka, and MoMo each had their diving knives. MoMo now had two knives, and they had three Uzis.

"Yeah," Ry said, satisfied that they could protect themselves. For now. "Sure." Samuel did a clean dive into the water. "MoMo. Help haul him up. And on second thought, grab a couple of the tanks. They're empty enough by now to be easy to carry around and use as a weapon if necessary." He didn't doubt for a second that every weapon they had would become necessary.

Anxiety beat like a metronome in his gut. Where the hell *was* Addy in this clusterfuck?

"Got him?" The guy was too busy to scream, fighting off Samuel's hold and trying not to swallow half the Indian Ocean. "Haul his ass out of the water and secure him."

Ry filled a bucket with seawater and sluiced the blood on the deck. He didn't want anyone to glance down and see it, and the men secured to the ladder. Not yet anyway.

Reasoning and second thoughts ended when these assholes boarded his boat without permission and used deadly force. He'd had his crew and divers killed just months ago in a hijacking. Fucking wasn't happening again. MoMo and Sam secured the waterlogged guy with the other one by slapping tape over their mouths and taping over the zip ties binding their wrists and ankles to the ladder. They wouldn't be going anywhere anytime soon.

"Shoot to kill," Ry told them. "Don't second-guess

yourselves. It's them or us. I vote for us every time. Anyone have a problem with that?"

"Not a problem for me." MoMo looked up. "What about the camera?"

Ry glanced at the small blinking light in the corner. The camera encompassed half the dive platform, as well as the entire outer edge, so that divers could be seen from the bridge. "Either they're watching us and are on their way down to kill our arses, or they've been too busy. In which case they'll see nothing untoward. Let's go."

"Stick together, or split up?" Samuel asked.

Ry hesitated. "We don't know what's up there waiting for us. Safety might be in numbers, but on the other hand if they don't know how many of us there are—well, we might be better off with an element of surprise. Georgeo and Kevin with me. MoMo and Lenka, go around portside." Ry pocketed a knife someone had used earlier to peel an orange.

He'd be a shitside happier if he were fully dressed instead of wearing wet trunks. The paring knife and Uzi were good accessories, however. "And for Christ's sake, don't any of you get yourselves killed."

Georgeo boosted Kevin up onto the deck above since the two bad guys were attached to the ladder, blocking their access. He patted her butt when she was secure. "Did you hear this, *cara mia*? I'll inspect every inch of you later to make sure you're healthy."

Ry blocked out the exchange. *Addy. Where are you?*

Fear torqued his pulse up a notch, while brain-fueled logic tamped it down as he stepped forward.

She had to be all right.

Had to be alive and fine, because if she wasn't, he'd just as soon figure out a way to die. Right here, right now. These assholes could have his damn boat, have the silver from the salvage, have everything that he'd once thought mattered to him. He'd just lived a year of his life without her, and if he had to enter that kind of dark abyss again nothing would matter to him.

Not a damn thing.

Addison's gaze shot to the aft deck monitor. No one on the dive platform now, just lapping azure water and endless robin's-egg-blue skies. Oh, God—was that dark blotch on the deck blood?

Fear snagged in her throat. Where had they taken Ry and the others? Realizing she was about to hyperventilate, she forced her breathing to regulate. Unconscious wasn't going to save her ass right now.

Naveen looked nervously from Addison to Hollis. "I'll take the women with me—"

"You don't have time for a ménage. I'll keep your ladies company while you're gone."

Naveen almost ran out, accompanied by five men who looked as though they hung out at an Algerian dockside bar looking for trouble. Even if you dressed these guys in suits they'd look like street toughs.

"Get these two tied up." Morimoto wagged a fat, beringed finger like a windshield wiper between Hollis and herself. "And be quick about it."

Eyes hard and impersonal, one of the men moved in front of her, a handful of zip ties from his pocket in his hand.

"Touch me and I'll—" *What exactly?* Screw that. Instead of baseless threats, Addison met the guy halfway, ramming her shoulder into his chest. Not exactly well thought out. It was as ineffective as slamming into a brick wall And she bounced backward from the impact. "*Omph*shit!"

She caught herself and staggered, bumping into her mother, who let out a shrill scream. And kept on screaming. Damn stupid considering the Australian had just backhanded her moments before.

His face turned a mottled red. "Jesus bloody Christ, shut up you *stupid* fucking bitch. If not for you I'd be—"

What he'd be was lost in the high-pitched shrieks. Clearly Hollis had suddenly figured out she'd gone to bed with the devil himself. Wiles and pleading hadn't worked worth a damn, and now she was going for hysterics. It was like throwing a match on a stack of gasoline-soaked cordwood.

"Hollis—" Addison grabbed her mother's arm and gave her a hard shake. "For crap's sake, get a damn grip." These men were capable of killing them with a bullet. Or worse. "*Mother—*"

Holy crap, her mother's voice rose in unceasingly sharper decibels. Shaking her didn't help. Addison was about to slap her, herself, when Morimoto roared, "Fuck it!" making both women flinch.

This time he swung back his fist. There was a split second when Hollis's eyes widened and her mouth snapped shut. Too late. The throbbing silence lasted only a few seconds before he put his body into the punch.

The sound of crunching bone made bile rise in the back of Addison's throat. Hollis's face seemed to explode—blood flew everywhere.

The entire situation seemed surreal, hard for Addison to wrap her brain around. The violence was shocking, and the ghost of her mother's screams seemed to hang, quivering, in the air. Addison shot out a hand as Hollis dropped to her knees, sobbing, both hands clutched to her bleeding face.

Hollis's gasping, terrified whimpers were more chilling than the piercing screams. Stunned that the blow hadn't knocked her mother out, Addison crouched beside her, wrapping her arm around her mother's thin shoulders. No matter how despicable her mother's actions were to bring this down on them, she hated seeing her physically hurt. Rocking and making soothing noises, she shot Morimoto a dark look over her mother's head.

A dozen vile accusations flooded her mind as she cradled Hollis in her arms as if she were a child. None passed her lips. One wrong word, one wrong move could inspire this man to do a lot worse than beat them.

As she rocked and murmured, she gauged the distance to the open door over a mass of Hollis's blond hair. Twenty feet. At least. Morimoto and the two men with him stood off to the side. A straight shot. If she—

No. There was no way she'd leave Hollis—no matter how she felt about her—alone with these men. She stroked her mother's narrow back.

Morimoto spoke in low tones to his men, his words inaudible to Addison over the sounds of her mother's terrified weeping and the rapid throb of her own heartbeat in her ears. As her mother's blood soaked into her shirt, hot and terrifying, everything in her screamed *Run.*

"On your feet, bitch." Morimoto jerked Addison up.

Her mother whimpered, trying to clutch at Addison's leg as she was pulled away.

"What's the point of the violence?" With effort, Addison used the calmest, most reasonable tone possible. Inside, her heart galloped. Sweat prickled her skin, and her knees and face throbbed. Fear was a living animal, racing around inside her like a gerbil on a wheel.

Tune out Hollis.

Block her fear for Rydell's safety.

The danger was here and now. Tunnel vison made the Australian the only one in the room. "Naveen will get what you want and you can all go," she told him, as calmly as she could. It pissed her off that she could hear fear in her own voice. She swallowed to moisten her dry throat. "No harm, no foul."

He nodded to the guy with the zip ties. Everything inside Addison contracted as the man wrenched her arms up.

Morimoto had her by her upper arm. Fat fingers hard as steel as he turned her. "Hands behind your back." Addison turned in his grip to present her crossed wrists for the freaking restraints. Morimoto held her still as his man looped the plastic tie over her hands and ratcheted it tighter and tighter around her wrists until the circulation in her hands was cut off. It was so painful, tears stung her eyes.

Pins and needles pricked her hands before they went completely numb.

Ry. Where are you?

Twenty-three

Addy's cabin was crowded. Out of camera view in the public spaces, Ry had gathered Jax, Oscar, and chef Patrick O'Keefe, who was armed with a wicked-looking knife and a fierce and furious glint in his eyes. Kevin, Lenka, Samuel, MoMo, and Georgeo stayed out of the way, on the far side of the room.

As they'd progressed through the ship they'd taken out not only as many armed men as possible, but also the cameras that fed into monitors on the bridge.

As far as they knew, five crew members were dead. Shot point-blank.

He'd personally killed three of the prince's men with the Uzi he'd taken from the men on the dive platform. Rage and panic roiling in his gut over the thought that Addy's life may hang on his actions made it a hell of a lot easier to do what had to be done.

Lenka took out two hijackers.

MoMo too.

They'd split up and headed down to Addy's cabin to regroup.

Ry and MoMo had found Jax, semiconscious, behind the sofa in the salon and practically carried him belowdecks. He should fucking well be in the hospital.

They'd passed Chief Engineer Omesh Chauhan, dead, in the corridor, his blood splattered on the wall.

"Did they take Addy to the bridge?" Ry demanded of Jax, whose white shirt was covered with dark, wet blood. The guy leaned heavily against the wall, but other than pressing a towel against his bleeding shoulder refused treatment.

"Was she hurt? Terrified—?" Of course she was fucking terrified. They all were. The situation was volatile and unpredictable. And at any minute things would get a shitload worse.

The dive team still wore nothing but their damn swim shorts. Worse, Addy, wasn't wearing head-to-toe Kevlar. Bloody hell. What the *fuck* was Darshi thinking bringing these men to Addy's home?

Because that's what *Tesoro Mio* was, Addy's *home*.

Dickwad. He'd disliked him before. Now he hated the bastard.

"Ry—" Kevin inserted. "Don't go there. Addison's a resourceful young woman."

He turned on her, a vein throbbing in his temple. "They have fucking *guns*, Kev."

"We noticed, but losing our cool right now isn't going to help her."

Ry dragged in a breath. "Right."

"She wasn't hurt—not before I passed out anyway. And she didn't appear to be scared," Jax told him. Glancing down at the blood-soaked towel, he slid down the wall as if his legs would no longer hold him. "She was *pissed*."

A small measure of warmth and hope unfurled in his chest. "That's my girl."

A soft, rapid tap on the cabin door made them turn in unison. Already alert, Ry stiffened and held up his Glock, indicating he'd get it. He opened the door a crack, saw the captain, and shoved it open wide enough for the other man to enter, sideways. "How bad is it?" He indicated Seddeth's seeping head wound with the barrel of the gun.

"I'll live." The captain glanced around the room, counting heads. "Just came from the bridge. They knocked me out. Addison's there. So's her mother and the prince. Who is *not* in charge, if you're wondering. Some guy named Gorou Morimoto seems to be calling the shots and brought a whole fucking army with him."

Addy's *mother*?

She was the punch line to a god-awful joke. Ry frowned. "Who is he and where does he come in? And what the hell is *Hollis* doing here?"

"Some Australian guy. Addison's mother is thick as thieves with *both* me—" He swayed. "Sorry. Need to sit down." Seddeth dropped onto the nearest horizontal surface, Addy's pristine bed. "The three of them appear to be involved with the art heists."

"Addy's *mother*?"

"Apparently."

No surprise really. The woman was vile enough to eat her young. "How many men there?" Ry demanded as Kevin rose from Addy's desk chair and disappeared into the bathroom. Water ran.

"The mother, the prince, this Australian guy, and seven heavily armed men. Semi-autos and pistols. That's who *I* saw. There are more, but I didn't see them, so have no count."

"Three on the dive platform, seven that we deleted on the way . . . There are certainly more swarming throughout the ship. And you saw—how many in the chopper?"

"Four," Georgeo told them.

"Fuck. What do we have for weapons?"

"Enough to put up a damn good fight," Jax said from his position on the floor. He sent Kevin a smile as she handed him a dry towel, some pills, and a glass of water. What he needed was a doctor and stitches.

Ry rubbed a hand over his jaw. "The prince and some of those armed men will be down here any second, looking for those painti—Fuck—" The engines kicked in. "They've weighed anchor."

Unsympathetic, Addison wished to hell Hollis would stop whimpering. It would only draw more attention, and she was afraid the next move from Morimoto would be to shoot her mother to shut her up. She nudged her with the side of her foot. Hollis didn't seem to notice.

So be it. Morimoto was her mother's buddy. Hollis would know his tolerance level to an eyelash flutter. As far as Addison was concerned, she was on her own. With her shoulder muscles burning under the strain, she attempted to uncross her wrists, shackled behind her back, without being obvious. Overlapping her wrists had seemed like a genius move, except . . . not. The guy had ratcheted the zip tie so tightly, it was all but impossible to uncross her hands. She kept trying, even though the pain brought tears to her eyes and made her grit her teeth until her jaw ached.

Morimoto took out a gun and pointed it straight at Hollis's forehead. "Bitch, if you don't fucking stop whinging, I'll make sure you never whine again."

Tears swimming, Hollis bit her lip, giving him a wounded look, which Morimoto missed as he turned his back. His girth blocked Addison's view—but it appeared he was pushing buttons on the state-of-the-art console. Oh, God. Now what? Was he weighing anchor . . . ?

Crap, yes.

The ship seemed to give a slight jerk. Addison felt a soft vibration underfoot as the winch pulled up the anchor. Her heart, already pounding, leapt out of control. This was bad, bad, bad.

Taking a small step back, she kept working her wrists. All good now that they'd gone numb and merely felt as though her skin was on fire.

Ry would be apoplectic about *another* freaking hijacking. If he was in a condition to be worried . . .

Don't go there. Do not go there.

Ry was smart, enterprising, and would do whatever it took to protect both her *and* his ship.

She needed to say that to herself over and over. A mantra to get her through this.

Ry will come.

But in the meantime, like her ex, *she* was also smart, enterprising, and determined, and she'd do whatever it took to save herself. And him.

Later they could celebrate together.

Anticipating the sound of the anchor seating in the hold, she though she heard the faint thud. Or not. Her imagination was already going haywire, not that she needed any imagination to know that moving the ship was a bad thing.

Where did Morimoto plan to go? Sydney? *Tesoro Mio* was a big ship; they wouldn't be able to hide their passage between the Maldives and Sydney. But there was over five thousand miles of open ocean between here and Sydney. And then what? Skuttle the ship? Change her name and paintwork?

Wasn't going to happen. Because surely by now the Coast Guard guys, and hopefully Interpol, were aware that Naveen was gone. Logically they must realize he'd return to *Tesoro Mio* to retrieve the paintings. Logically . . . But then when was any government anything ever logical? Perhaps they'd be dead by the time Interpol or the Coast Guard figured it out.

Her wrists needed a break. Addison stopped the torquing for a moment. "Where are we going?"

"I'm not the one going," Morimoto informed her. As he perspired in the hot room, the smell of oily garlic became more pronounced. Sweat gleamed in every fold around his jaw and neck, and darkened patches of his suit coat. He constantly mopped his face with a white handkerchief, which didn't help the steady flow of sweat. Addy wasn't going to tell him how to turn on the AC, although it was hotter than hell with the sun pouring through the wraparound windows on the bridge.

Beyond the windows the ocean shone a deep teal blue. Glittering sequins of light bounced off the deadly calm, flat surface.

Four men surrounded the helicopter, still on the aft deck helipad. She didn't see anyone else. The good news was she hadn't heard gunshots for a while.

Looking alert and ready for anything, the two thugs with Uzis blocked the door with their bulk. She wasn't going to get out that way, no matter how fast she was. If Seddeth had managed to slip through the door in back to his own quarters on the deck below, Addison wondered if she had a shot at doing the same thing? She took two more small steps backward.

It was damn hard to concentrate when her brain was going a mile a minute and she'd already lost the feeling all the way from her fingertips to her shoulders. "Where will you be?"

Was he going to kill everyone when he discovered his paintings weren't on board? Stupid question. Of course he was.

"Didn't the prince tell you?" Morimoto glanced at her over his muscled, wrestler shoulder. "*Tesoro Mio* is mine."

"If Naveen sold this ship it was without the authority

of its rightful owners. No matter what he told you, the sale's illegal."

Morimoto turned. "You gave the prince your power of attorney. I have your signature."

"I'd never sign away this ship. What you have is a forgery. Besides, my husband is co-owner so you'd have to have both signatures. Didn't happen."

"Dear sniveling Hollis over there is not only an excellent broker. She's an excellent forger. Isn't that so, my dear?"

Addison didn't take her eyes off him. "What kind of 'broker'?"

Ry where are you? Now would be a good time for you to get here.

Everyone fell silent at the sound of a key being inserted into the slot in the door. Ry doused all the lights. Addy? He shifted, eager to see her in one piece, but also aware that the ship was overrun with bad guys. This could be anyone.

The door opened just wide enough for the prince to slip inside in a wedge of light from the corridor beyond. Crap, that son of a bitch still had a key to the cabin he used to occupy? Had he hidden even more paintings somewhere? In here or somewhere else? Ry wouldn't put it past the guy to squirrel away paintings all over the ship.

Ry got a glimpse of another man before the prince blocked him from view.

"Wait here," Darshi stage-whispered to whoever had accompanied him belowdecks. He closed the door quietly, leaving his escort in the hallway.

Ry waited until Darshi was halfway into the room before switching on the light beside his chair. The prince shrieked like a girl and jumped six inches in the air. "You're *alive*!"

"Shocker."

Behind the prince's back, an armed Oscar stepped in front of the door just as someone slammed a fist on the heavy wood. "Everything all right in there?"

"Answer them." Ry got to his feet, the Glock pointed between Darshi's eyes. "Make it convincing."

"Dear God, this is a nightmare."

"Of your own choosing," Ry waved the barrel of the Glock to the door. "Answer."

"Just tripped," Darshi said in a shaking voice, suddenly realizing that far from being alone, Ry had his own backup dancers. Jax had risen to his feet, the blood on his white shirt a shocking reminder of the danger they were in. He glanced at Seddeth, who was holding a towel to the gash on his forehead, then back to Ry. Darshi raised his voice to call out, "I-I'll be right out."

"We found fifty-six paintings under the flooring in my cabin, Darshi," Ry said, cutting to the chase. "Do you have any more spirited away somewhere on board? The shit's already hitting the fan. If there are more, now would be the time to tell us."

"Aren't you the naive one," Morimoto mocked Addison, his smile not reaching his obsidian eyes. He observed her as an hunter would look at an animal with its legs caught in a steel trap, as though he was deciding whether to let her continue squirming or end her misery. "Dear, avaricious Hollis here, and your very broke, very desperate boyfriend, have been in cahoots for *years*. Right under your naive little nose."

"Naveen is neither broke nor desperate, and Hollis has nearly half a dozen husbands' alimony to keep her for ten lifetimes," Addison pointed out, keeping her tone conversational and not confrontational. She wanted to buy time, not piss off this guy more than was necessary. Her wrists stung where the zip ties cut her skin, and warm blood slicked the plastic as she worked her wrists behind her back, trying to stretch and slip the plastic so she could liberate her hands.

"No, your mother doesn't need the funds. She did it for the thrill all those young studs could no longer bring her. Isn't that so, Hollis? The prince lasted longer than most."

Addison swiveled her head to stare at her mother. "You *slept* with Naveen? That's revolting!"

"Oh, they didn't 'sleep.' They banged their way across Europe and Asia, and fucked in every major city in Australia, and even parts of Africa. Quite the pair these two—Oh, dear. You look more disgusted than shocked."

"You have no fucking idea." She looked down at Hollis. The ties seemed a bit looser. She tried to ease a hand free. No go. "Were you sleeping with Naveen when you introduced us?" That was five damn *years* ago.

"He was a perfect match." The snotty tone was just that—snotty—as her mother talked around a swollen, hopefully broken nose. Despite her puffy, bloody face, and the dire circumstances, Hollis didn't sound the least bit repentant. When she wasn't acting to get what she wanted, like now, her eyes were flat emotionless.

Dear God, the knowledge that her mother had slept—and for all she knew was *still* sleeping—with the prince repulsed Addison on every level, and she felt even less sympathy for Hollis's bloody, bruising, and swollen face. Come to think of it, she was sorry she hadn't done it herself.

"You're both disgusting. I don't know which is worse, you screwing my boyfriend, or you allowing him to use me and my *home* to transport stolen goods undetected." Would the Indian Coast Guard and Interpol come looking for their escaped prisoner? Would they think for a moment that he'd return to the *Tesoro Mio* instead of fleeing on a plane or fast ship to parts unknown?

"Addison . . ." Hollis sounded exasperated.

Addison turned her back. There was nothing more to be said. It was crystal-clear that Naveen and Hollis had conspired to destroy her marriage when she'd been at her most vulnerable. What they'd done to her proved neither had ever cared for her. Not at all.

She angled her back away from Hollis when she turned around to face Morimoto as she twisted her hands. She wasn't sure what she could possibly do in a small room with three armed men. But when an opportunity presented itself, she'd come up with *something.*

She looked at the Australian just as he glanced at the ostentatious gold Rolex on his fat wrist. He frowned.

"How long has the prince been stealing for you?" As she torqued her hands against each other the thin plastic tie became slippery. Her blood, Addison knew. That didn't stop her. Was there a little more give? Were her slippery fingers gradually squeezing free?

"Five years. I now have the most enviable art collection in the world."

"One you can never show off," she pointed out. It was harder to manipulate her hands because her movements had torqued the plastic tie impossibly tighter around her wrists as she tried to pull her thumb free. The constantly welling blood made moving the ties harder, not easier. "I presume Hollis introduced him to her wealthy friends so he could steal?" She didn't give a flying crap how the three of them had pulled off the art heists; all she was doing was trying to give herself more time to liberate her hands. She'd figure things out from there.

Looking so smug Addison wanted to punch him, Morimoto leaned his hip against the console. "Clever Hollis introduced him to her high-muck-a-muck friends.

He'd return, help himself to their priceless artwork, and hide it on board *Tesoro Mio.* Genius really. No one suspected. Your mother brokered the deal, and I sponsored both of them. Since we needed the prince, we couldn't allow your husband to take possession of this ship."

"Apparently destroying the lives of people in your way had no effect." Addison thought her left thumb was free of the restraint; unfortunately, she had to wait while agonizing pricks of sensation flooded through her nerve endings. Tears of pain stung her eyes.

"Collateral damage." He glanced at the man standing closest to the open door. "Go see where the prince is."

Crap. Time is running out.

One hand squeezed free of the tight restraints. *Owshit!* The pain went from stinging to burning like fire. Breathing through it, Addison flexed her fingers and waited for her chance. It better be soon. It shouldn't be taking this long for Naveen to go to what was now Rydell's cabin, discover the paintings gone, and skulk back to the bridge with his entourage of gun-wielding thugs.

As Morimoto turned to talk to his men, she scanned the monitors. The aft deck camera was dark. The corridor cameras leading to the cabins on all decks were dark. The camera on the dive platform was now dark.

Rydell.

It had to be. Her adrenaline hit another surge, alleviating some of the pain in her wrists and giving her a small measure of hope.

The shit was about to hit the fan.

Twenty-four

"You fucker!" Ry grabbed the prince by the throat. Darshi's eyes went wide and white-rimmed. "Where's Addy?"

The prince clawed at Ry's hands. "On the bridge with Morimoto."

Ry squeezed tighter, then let him go. Not because he didn't want to strangle the fucker, but because killing Darshi would be too damn quick. Ry flung him away, and the prince staggered back. "Did you lay a hand on her? Don't lie, Darshi."

"*I* didn't. I wouldn't—*He* hit her. She's *fine*."

Fine meant alive. For now, fine had to be acceptable. One thing at a time. "How many people came with you?"

"I don't know. A dozen? Maybe more."

"How many on the *bridge*?"

"Five or six. Maybe seven. God—I don't know. I'm *terrorized*!"

"You don't even fucking know what being terrorized *is*. Why did you fucking well think bringing this danger to Addy was okay?"

"She wasn't supposed to know! Morimoto was supposed to get the ship when we reached Sydney. Addison and I were getting married—"

"Jesus—" Ry punched him in the nose, getting some

satisfaction at the sound of cartilage and bone breaking, seeing the spurt of blood. "Not your fucking ship. Not your woman!"

"I get it." Darshi clasped a hand to his face. Blood dripped between his fingers. "Look, let me just get him the paintings and he'll leave."

Clearly terror had turned the prince deaf. "Jesus, you don't believe that. Once he has the paintings he'll kill us all."

"Perhaps I can purs—"

"The goddamn paintings aren't *here*, Darshi. Addy and I found them this morning. They were on board the chopper with you when you left."

The color drained from Darshi's swarthy skin. "No—What—How?" He sank onto the foot of Addy's bed, shooting Ry a beseeching look over the palm clasped around his nose. "What are we going to do?" His attention didn't even flicker to the others in the room.

Ry raised a brow. "'*We*'? I could kill you now. A least I'd have the personal satisfaction and save everyone the time and aggro."

"How can you joke at a time like this?"

"Not a joke. But since Interpol is probably on their way here now, I'll be saved getting any more of your blood on my hands or, in this case, Addy's bed. Too bad. I'd really enjoy beating the shit out of you right now." Ry had no damn idea where the hell Interpol might be at this moment, or what they had planned. If anything. He didn't need to look at the others to know they all had the same thought.

They didn't have either the Indian Coast Guard or Interpol's numbers on speed dial. Messages had been left all over the bloody world for people who were mere hours away.

Safe to say, they were on their own.

"Captain Sharma was aware? *Interpol* already knows? If you want a chance at saving Addison's life, you'll help me. If Morimoto finds out that Interpol has the art, you're right, he'll kill every last person on board this ship and be long go—"

There were several hard pounds on the door. "Boss don't like to wait, Prince. Get the lead out!"

Darshi gave Ry a pleading look as he shouted "In a minute!"

"Oscar? Jax?" Ry said without taking his eyes off Darshi. "Go show the prince's buddies our hospitality." They'd disabled the cameras out in the corridor when they'd come down. The two men slipped through the door so fast they were a blur. The sound was minimal. Ry snapped his fingers to draw the prince's attention to him instead of pretending he had fucking X-ray eyes and could see what was happening in the hallway beyond the closed door. "How many painting were on board?"

"This time? Fifty-four—no. Fifty-six."

Shit. "You've used my ship to store your stolen goods before?"

Darshi nodded, then whimpered as his broken nose brushed against the palm he still held over his face. "Twice. Once when Addison and I went to Hong Kong after the divorce, and—Does this really matter?"

"Same buyer?"

"Morimoto, yes." Darshi inspected the bloody hand he gingerly removed from his face. His eyes were already swelling shut, and his aristocratic nose was now off center. Bloodshot, almost swollen-shut eyes met Ry's. "Gorou Morimoto is *oyabun*. You know what that is? Top boss. *Head* of the Yakuza—the largest crime organization in Australia and New Zealand, with ties directly to Japan. There's *nothing* civilized about him. He's a violent, sick psychopath in a five-thousand-dollar suit! Morimoto considers himself a connoisseur of the arts. He's a *fanatic*, and he's already constructed the building that will house those paintings. It's taken him six years and cost over eleven million dollars! It's a place few people will ever enter. Do you understand? He paid *me* to get those painting for him. He gave Hollis a list! He was specific and precise. Just *those* particular paintings. God oh God, oh God—if he discovers his artwork was taken by the authorities he'll rip this ship apart, and everyone on it *personally*. What will I tell him?"

"I'd dive overboard," Georgeo suggested, arm around Kevin's shoulders. "Start swimming for Malé."

MoMo offered, deadpan, "Sharks. But if you can swim fast . . ."

It was no laughing matter. "You c—"

The sound of a keycard being inserted in the door had everyone stiffen in anticipation.

Oscar, and a now even bloodier Jax, entered, closing the door behind them. "We put the three guys down in the engine room," Jax informed him, coming farther into the room, then sliding down the wall to his former position. Fresh blood stained his shirt, and pain made his features stark. "Or rather—three bodies."

Oscar went to the dresser and laid down several weapons, which Ry presumed they'd stripped off the men they'd disposed of. The security guy, in his element, grinned over his shoulder. "More toys. Two Uzis, a very nice, very sharp Ka-Bar knife, a Sig Sauer semi-auto, and a Ruger. All pretty much fully loaded and ready to go."

"Enough to add to our arsenal and *finish* this fucking war," Ry said grimly. He could practically hear the clock ticking away the seconds they had left to find Abby and get these fuckers off his ship. "Good job."

"Dear God, Chase." Darshi sent him a pleading look. "What do I tell Morimoto?"

"Tell him you moved them so often, you forgot where you hid them."

"Dear Lord! He won't believe that! He knows I'm not that stupid."

"Somehow I doubt that." Ry didn't give a shit if or what Darshi told Morimoto. If he had his druthers he'd hog-tie him and toss his ass overboard. But having Darshi return to Morimoto—before the guy sent down reinforcements—seemed like a better option. For now. "If you don't think that'll work, use your brainpower. Figure out a way to convince him. You could tell him you hid each painting individually all over the ship."

Ry hated the idea. This Morimoto would more than likely rip his beautiful ship apart looking for them. It would buy them time, but fuck—his ship . . . "Hell, tell him I gave them over to Interpol. I don't give a flying fuck *what* you decide to tell him. Surprise m—Bloody hell! Are you fucking *crying*?"

Ry shook his head. He thought he'd seen everything. He'd never seen a grown-ass man cry like this. He didn't have a fucking jot of sympathy. "Oscar, you and Georgeo take and secure him in the engine room." Ry grabbed a handful of plastic ties, handing them to Georgeo.

"Hey, I wanna go, too." Kevin grabbed Darshi's upper arm. She gave him a hard yank as she started marching him to the door. "Back in five. Let's go, dick."

Georgeo shot her a proud look over the prince's head as Darshi whined, "I need *medical* attention!"

"Then try really, really hard not to die before they arrest your ass. I'm sure they have excellent doctors in pr—" Kevin's voice cut off with the slamming of the door.

Ry looked around. "No one here has to engage, that's

a given. Anyone want to opt out of what's about to be a clusterfuck of mammoth proportions? It'll be bloody. I won't allow these guys to hurt Addy, nor will I sit back while they steal my ship. But this isn't your fight. Speak fast, who's in, who's out?" The floor vibrated as his ship plowed through the water, picking up speed. Fuck them. Fuck them all. When *Sea Dragon* had been taken, he wasn't on board to fight off the hijackers. He was fucking well on board now, and they'd regret ever having boarded his ship.

His priority was making sure Addison wasn't harmed. After that he'd be out for blood, and his ship would be a fucking bonus. After the bloodshed.

"We're all in," MoMo assured him, not bothering to see everyone's nod. "Don't ask again. We have your back. Always."

Ry shot him a smile. "Good to know. Thanks, guys. Jax? Tony? How are those injuries?" Ry glanced from one man to the other. Opening a drawer in the dresser, he took out two clean T-shirts and tossed one to each man. The question was rhetorical. Other than his clothing being dirty and bloody, Seddeth looked okay. The gash in his head had clotted over a large purple knot. He probably had a mother of a headache. Jax, on the other hand, had been creased high on his shoulder. There was a lot of blood, and the skirmish with Darshi's men had opened the wound so some of it was fresh. "What do you need besides clean shirts with no holes in them?"

"A *body* with no hole in it?" Jax asked drily, pulling the wet, bloody fabric of his shirt over his head.

The wound looked worse than the blood on his clothing had indicated. Ry winced. "That looks like crap."

"Feels worse." With a grunt, Jax pushed himself to his feet and headed for the bathroom. "I'll live." Water ran.

MoMo went over to their weapons stash, laid out on

the dresser. "I'm taking one of these Uzis." He glanced over at Jax as he came out of the bathroom, pulling on the clean T-shirt, wincing as he did so. He picked up the machine gun, aiming it at the floor. "Give me a quick tutorial."

"Magazine is in," Jax instructed. "Two safety switches, one is already off. The other will go off when you hold the gun and depress the lever. Rack the slide back—yeah. Right there. Bring it back and let it slide forward. Stick the stock against your sh—Hell, you're a natural. Go full auto. Yeah, right there. Since it fires from an open bolt it'll jump when you fire, so aim lower."

Looking pleased with himself, MoMo nodded as he lowered the weapon. "Got it."

The door beeped as a keycard was inserted, and Kevin, Oscar, and Georgeo returned. "He's not going anywhere," Oscar told them. "No sign of reinforcements."

Samuel, having watched and listened to Oscar's instructions, picked up the second Uzi. Lenka took a Ka-Bar.

Ry had second and third thoughts about putting these men and Kev in danger. *Tesoro Mio* wasn't theirs to protect. Addison wasn't theirs to protect. If any of them died because of him, he'd have a fucking hard time living with himself. But since they'd all agreed to go in guns blazing, he was grateful to have backup.

"Doesn't mean they won't be down here any second to see what's taking him so long. Everyone ready?" Ry outlined a brief plan—basically shoot first, ask questions later. They tweaked, made a few suggestions, and everyone was in agreement. Although it felt like they'd been belowdecks for fucking hours, a quick glance at his watch told him it had only been sixteen minutes since they'd surfaced from the dive. It was the longest sixteen minutes of his life.

It was damn hard to push thoughts of Addy out of his mind. He was proceeding on the assumption that she was alive. That had to hold him until he saw it with his own two eyes.

"Everyone know what you're supposed to do and where you have to be?"

"Incoming," Oscar said urgently, going to the window. He held down the blinds to look out. "Three choppers. ETA probably ten minutes."

Could be the good guys. Whoever that may be. Could be more bad guys. Either way it put one hell of a countdown on getting what they needed to done. "Shit." Ry sucked in a breath. *Addy, I'm coming.* "Good thing you have ears like a bat. Game on."

Addison's hands were free. She couldn't feel them, but they were no longer bound. Even though time seemed to be ticking loudly in her head, she needed a few minutes to breathe through the burning pain before she did . . . whatever the hell she could do.

For several minutes she thought the sound she heard was her own blood pumping through her veins. It took a few more minutes to realize what she was hearing was the *whop-whop-whop* of an approaching helicopter.

God. Please let it be Paras Sharma returning with the cavalry. Interpol, Maldivian officials—anybody.

She had no idea where Naveen was, but since he hadn't bothered to return and the men sent with him hadn't come back, either, Addison presumed—no, hoped—that Ry and the crew had done something with them. Of course, it being Naveen, he might be in hiding fearing the repercussions of not returning with Morimoto's paintings.

Morimoto paced, anger seeping out of every sweating pore. His bulk blocked and unblocked the streams of sunshine coming through the windows. "Where the fuck are my paintings?" he demanded, taking up all the available floor space with his back-and-forth movements. She didn't know who he was addressing. The second batch of guys he'd sent down? She didn't see any sort of communications devices, but that didn't mean he wasn't using something.

None of the three men still with him responded. How many more of his men could she *not* see? Had they swarmed the ship? Killed Ry, the entire crew and dive team?

Someone had disconnected the cameras. And whoever it was, was just as blind as the three armed men and Morimoto on the bridge. Beyond the window four more men stayed near the big black helicopter, also pacing. Everyone was on edge. Not good.

Worse, and scary as hell, no one was piloting the ship. At full throttle, *Tesoro Mio*'s hull was carving a white, frothing path through the crystalline water, full speed ahead. Addison hoped to hell they were headed in the direction of open water, because the Maldives comprised dozens of small islands, atolls, and rings of coral reefs. Lots and lots of places to run aground and split the hull wide open.

So—three men with Uzis spread equidistant around the perimeter, Morimoto, all four hundred lardy pounds of him, waddling up and down the middle of the space, and Hollis, shoes kicked off, sitting on the floor near the chart table, head buried on her knees, shoulders heaving. Real tears, and for once she was smart enough not to be dramatic about it.

Morimoto was light on his feet for a man the size of a medium water buffalo. Back and forth. Back and forth.

Addison didn't turn when she heard the snick of a door opening behind her, or when she felt a cool draft on the back of her legs. Someone was opening the hidden door from Tony's captain's quarters and since only she, Ry, and the crew knew about it, it could only be one of the good guys. Her heart leapt.

The sound of the helicopter seemed to be getting closer, but she couldn't see anything beyond the wrap-around windows other than baby-blue sky and a few fluffy white cumulus clouds over the forward bow.

Morimoto passed within a few feet of her, and, belying his slow gait, quick as a striking snake reached out and grabbed her chin in his cupped hand. He brought her face close to his, dragging her to stand on her toes. "If the prince isn't back in five minutes," he snarled, spitting into her face. "I'm going to take pleasure in killing first your mum, then you."

His fat fingers, smelling metallically like sweat and cigarettes, painfully squeezed her cheeks. Addison looked into his dark, light-eating eyes. "How will that make him bring them any faster?" Or that was what she tried to say. God. If he gripped her face any harder, the bastard was going to break her jaw.

"Have a death wish, little girl?"

Addison whipped her hands from behind her back and grabbed his ears, one in each hand, digging her nails into his scalp. Before he knew what hit him, she brought her knee up as hard as she could and tried to knee him in the balls. There was too much fat to have any impact. Her knee hit his upper thigh. He squealed, a high-pitched shriek, more of fury than pain, and swung her around so she went flying. Her back hit the console with a painful thud, then she rolled to the floor onto her knees.

Addison lost it. She was up on her feet and running at him, head down like a Pamplona bull with a war cry before she thought it through. She almost broke her neck as she hit him full on his fat belly, taking them both to the floor hard enough to make the windows shake. Straddling him, she managed to pin one fat arm under her knee; the other she dug into his chest, and she dug her long nails into his eye.

He rolled over, smothering her. Addison pummeled everything she could reach. Years of running had given her strong legs, and she used them now to twist his body. She almost gave herself a hernia, but she got him on his back like a beached whale.

She vaguely heard one of his men laugh, having apparently too much fun watching her as they rolled and assuming Morimoto was in no danger, to try to put a stop to what was happening. Addison ended up on top. With her knees spread as she straddled him, she pummeled him in the head and shoulders with every ounce of strength she had, slapping his ears hard enough to make them ring.

Vaguely, beyond the sound of her own panting, and Morimoto's grinding teeth, she heard a loud shot, followed by another, and prayed to God whoever had just entered the cabin wasn't someone who'd shoot her in the back of the head. Yells registered, and she still didn't let go of the fat man. She kept punching Morimoto. She didn't feel any pain. Good, she wasn't the one who'd gotten shot. Yet. She'd never in her life felt this kind of black, blind rage.

"Addy! *Addison*! Stop!" Hard arms wrapped around her waist and she was plucked unceremoniously off Morimoto. "You knocked him, out, love. See that, sweetheart? Out cold."

Addison wrapped her arms around Ry's neck as he cradled her in his arms. "Rydell."

"I've got you, sweet love. I've got you." He buried his

face in her hair. “Is that his blood or yours? Are you hurt, Addy?”

She didn’t lift her face from where it was buried against his throat. “Oh,” she said with relish. “I hope it’s his.”

Twenty-five

Hours later, hips wrapped in a towel that hung to his knees, chest bare and still damp from a hurried shower, Ry went next door and tiptoed into Addy's dimly lit cabin. "How is she?"

She was wrapped in a short black silk robe, the stark white bandages on her wrists a shocking reminder of where she'd been a few short hours earlier. His heart clutched, and his mouth went dry with remembered fear. Ry drank her in like a man who'd been in the Sahara for a year suddenly seeing a lush oasis.

Kevin, seated in a chair pulled up beside the bed, swung her bare feet off the mattress and got to her feet. "Banged up, bruised, those wrists are a mess, but otherwise feeling triumphant." She shot him a grin. "I see you dressed for the party. Good man. Everyone gone?"

"Yeah. All clear."

"I'll get Georgeo to fill me in," Kevin told him breezily. "Preferably lying down with a bottle of wine, soft music, and the drapes closed. I've had enough excitement to last me awhile. I'll leave you two to play doctor."

"Hey!" Addy, leaning against a mound of pillows, sat up to wave at them. Like himself, she'd recently showered, and she smelled of sweet, aromatic rain-drenched jasmine. "I'm right here, guys." Her wet hair hung down her back, showing the pure oval of her face. No makeup, and she was so pretty she stopped Ry's heart. Dropping her hand, she curled her bare legs under her ass like a mermaid, giving him a nice view of her firm, tanned thighs and the shadowy promise of heaven.

Kev turned to smile at her. "Now that your honey's here, and you can see he's safe and sound, get some rest."

With a spring in her step, Kevin left, closing the door quietly behind her.

There were a thousand things they needed to discuss. Issues—serious issues—they needed to resolve. But right now all Ry gave a flying fuck about was affirming that they were both alive.

He rested a knee on the mattress, his towel falling to the floor unnoticed as he held her gaze. "Wanna rest?"

Her lashes fluttered as she looked down at his erect dick. Hell, he was always in a state of semi-arousal with Addy. No matter the circumstances.

With a Mona Lisa smile she lifted her gaze, slowly untying the knot of the sash around her waist. "No."

He crawled up the bed to lean over her on all fours. "Wanna play doctor?"

Turning very serious, she lay back, angling her legs between his braced arms and knees so she was supine underneath the bridge of his body. "I *do* need a full exam. Need suggestions where to start?"

"How bad are those wrists?"

"They're bandaged, Ry. They'll be fine. Just raw for now." She arched her hips against his. "Can we talk about my wrists later? Maybe you should examine the places the doctor didn't touch just now." He really did want to do a full body check. Even though a doctor had been in to see her, and he'd sent Kev to keep her company and make sure she was okay until he could get there. Still, he wanted to check her over to be sure. More, he wanted to make sure she was unscathed emotionally as well as physically.

"Hmm. This will take a while. I have to do thorough and methodical inspection. Let me see . . ." Using both hands, he slid his palms between the lapels of the robe, gliding the slick fabric slowly over her shoulders to expose her pretty breasts.

Her nipples peaked under his gaze.

"You have a bruise here." Dropping his head, Ry kissed the dark fingerprints imprinted on her shoulder. He'd like to kill Morimoto slowly and feed him piece by piece to the sharks, but considering that Interpol had him now, that option was off the table. "Better?"

"Hmm. It hurts right here . . ." she said dolefully as she shrugged the black silk off one shoulder. She used her chin to indicate her breast.

Trailing his mouth down the slope of her breast, he murmured his pleasure as her fingers tangled in his hair. She cupped the back of his head, her fingers cool as she slid them against his scalp.

I love you I love you I love you. The sweet song sang through Ry's veins like a heavenly chorus as he curled his tongue around the hard bud of her nipple, which made her back arch.

Cupping the other breast, he played one nipple with his fingers while ravishing the other with his tongue and teeth. Her breath was just as uneven as his own as he stroked a hand down her hip, following it with lips and tongue over her silky-smooth fragrant skin.

Her voice was husky as she pointed to her unblemished hip. "It hurts right here." Ry gave her hip some love as his hand curled under her to cup her ass cheek. Firm, resilient flesh filled his palm. Each place he kissed warmed as his mouth explored the hills and valleys.

Twenty-six

Moonlight, cool and romantic, flooded the cabin, washing over their tangled bodies in a play of silver and black. Addison lazily trailed her fingertips down the center of Rydell's chest, still damp from exertion, evidenced by their sweaty bodies and irregular breathing. Even after all the exertion, her touch caused his nipples to grow hard.

He caught her wandering hand, not ready for such light touches yet. She knew him so well. She threw her arm across his waist and hooked her ankle over his calf. In turn he ran his palm up and down her spine. Dropping a kiss to the top of her head, he asked quietly, "Were you worried about me?"

There were a hundred questions in the innocuous inquiry. "Not at all." She kept her voice light. "Were you worried about me?"

"Not at all." Rydell echoed her tone. "When I saw you sitting on top of the Morimoto mountain, beating the living crap out of him, bare-knuckled, I cheered."

She smiled. "You did not."

"No. I didn't." The smile left his voice and he picked up the hand she had across his middle. Ry threaded his fingers through hers. Palm-to-palm. They were already heart-to-heart. "My heart stopped. I had tunnel vision.

All I saw was my wife with her bleeding wrists and bruises—" His voice snagged. "My wife doing a job *I* should've been doing."

Addison tightened her fingers in his. "I don't need you to fight my battles for me." *No. I want you to fight* for *me.* Would he ever understand the difference?

"No, you don't," he said, his voice low and raw. "Since you beat that shithead almost senseless. But I *want* to fight your battles with you, Addy. I *want* to be the male to your female. I want to protect you from assholes like Darshi, and monsters like Morimoto. I want to lay you down on a white mink rug and shower you with scented rose petals. I want to light a thousand white candles around you, and see your skin warm and glow when I touch you. I want to brush your skin lightly, and ride you hard. I want you to allow me to do things for you—not because you're helpless and need my assistance, but because it gives us *both* pleasure. I want the sun and the moon and the stars. With you. Now and always." He brought their clasped hands to his mouth, kissing her fingers.

"I *love* you Addy. Say it," he whispered achingly. "*Tell* me you love me. I need to hear it."

God, she knew her denial was hurting him, but she couldn't say it. Couldn't allow the words to float out there. "I can't."

His entire body flinched as if she'd struck him, and she felt his physical withdrawal. "Jesus, Addy, why the hell not? You love me, I know you do. Everything else can be worked out."

She shook her head. How could she ever explain this well enough for him to understand? For him to accept? "I can't bear to feel that kind of pain again. Losing Sophie. Losing you . . ."

"You're not going to lose me. Ever."

Pulling away from him, she sat up. She moved a few feet away and tugged at the rumpled leopard-print sheet until she could cover herself. A thin piece of silk wasn't going to fix how exposed she felt emotionally. She pushed her hair out of her face, and found that her hand shook.

She met his gaze. Hurt. Bewilderment. Pain. Her throat ached. "But I did lose you. I didn't see or hear from you for more than a *year*, Rydell! You were gone. I was already in mourning, my loss unbearable. You shredded what was left of my heart."

"You know if I'd—"

"I know." If Hollis and Naveen hadn't lied. Hadn't conned both of them. If fate hadn't ripped them apart. "But I also know how it *felt*. I can't do that again. I can't. I can't give you everything in me in the hope that you'll keep it safe. That something or someone won't come between us again, and that you won't fucking . . . *fight* for me!" There. She'd said it out loud. Put it out there in the universe. "When the worst happened, you abandoned me. You didn't fight long and hard for me. You freaking *gave up*."

He sat up, all hard muscle and bronze skin. Rubbing his palm over his mouth, he watched her with haunted eyes. His hand dropped heavily to his lap. Unlike her, he was exposed, naked physically and emotionally.

She hurt for both of them. Chest tight, she returned his look with eyes burned dry from a year's worth of crying. She was cried out.

"Oh, God, Addy." He reached over for her hand, then withdrew before he made contact. A good thing, because she knew if he touched her now she'd shatter into a million pieces. "*That's* what this is about? You think I didn't fight hard enough for you?"

"If the positions were reversed I know damn well I wouldn't have stopped looking for you. I'd have found you wherever the fuck you were, and *forced* you to talk to me. Before I walked away. Before I filed for divorce. Before I—" Damn it, she felt the sharp prick of tears behind her lids. "Before I gave up. I wouldn't have given up, Ry. *Ever!* I would've been there to comfort you over our loss. I would've held you, and loved you through it all."

"I—You're right. I gave up too easily. I should've moved heaven and earth to find you. Talk to you. I shouldn't have believed that you'd file for divorce without discussing it with me first. I shouldn't have—Fuck it. I should have. Everything you just said. I should have done *all* that, Addy, and more. A hundred, excuses, valid or not, aren't good enough. You are absobloodylutely right. I fucked up."

This time he *did* pick up her hand. "I fucked up, Addy. I fucked up badly. But please forgive me. I can't go through another year without you. I just fucking can't do it. You're my life. My everything. Without you I won't make it."

As torn as she was, Addison instinctively turned her hand so that their fingers were clasped on her bare knee. Rydell's hands were cold as ice. She'd felt her own pain and grief inside herself, but now Ry's pain and grief were like a physical entity surrounding him.

She felt his isolation, his desperation, and her own body responded independently of her determination to keep the last little piece of herself, for herself. "You're not immortal. You could've been shot a hundred times today. You could have died today." Her voice broke at the thought of losing him forever, not because either of them was stubborn or didn't love enough, but because life was fragile, a gift you didn't know how long you had to enjoy.

"But I didn't." He touched a finger to one of her bandaged wrists. "You were hurt worse than I was."

A hot tear spilled over the dam of her lower lashes, and she saw him through a shiny veil. "Losing Sophie made me realize how short and unpredictable life can be." Barren. Bleak.

Pushing a strand of hair off her face with a gentle finger, Rydell slid his hand down to cup her cheek. "Then we have to suck every drop out of the life we have, right?" His thumb stroked across her lower lip, taking a tear with it. "Make every second count? Not waste a day lamenting what we don't have, but celebrate what we *do* have. I'd rather spend a week with you than have a lifetime without you.

"Not having you beside me for the past year was fucking torture, Addy, but at least I knew you were *somewhere* on the planet. I knew that, when I couldn't bear *not* seeing you any longer, I could find you, at least lay eyes on you. But today . . . Jesus bloody Christ, I realized today that that pain was nothing compared to how I would feel if you were gone permanently. *You* could've died today. No shit, I *wouldn't* make it without you, Addy."

"Sophia . . ."

"Our lives will never be the same without Sophie. We'll miss her every day of our lives. We lost a piece of our hearts when we lost her. Other children will never replace her, and we'll never forget her. But we're young. Alive. Vibrant. We love each other. We can still have a good life, Addy. Different, but just as amazing. A life filled with laughter and love, and children's laughter. *Tesoro Mio* can be the home it was meant to be."

"What about the Baillargeons?" *Tesoro Mio* was subject to being seized to cover his father's debt. She'd liquidated everything she could think of. It helped some. But not nearly enough.

"Your investment helps. As for the rest—" He gave a

c'est la vie shrug. "We can thank your ex-boyfriend and your mother for taking the pressure off. Reward money for finding the paintings will be sizable. I'll be able to secure a temporary loan until that comes through if we can't bring up the silver in time."

He knew people who'd front money based upon treasure that hadn't yet been found, people who took risks most banks wouldn't. She presumed those same people would front money based upon the recovery of stolen art. Details, she'd leave to Ry. The bottom line for her was his happiness. "You know the trappings of wealth mean nothing to me."

He gave her a full, beautiful smile. But his eyes were narrowed, and there was a gleam in them. "You'd love me even if I'm poor?"

"Of course."

"I hope we never have to test that theory."

"Will the reward money be enough?" She'd anticipated getting a reward for finding the stolen artwork. But she hadn't allowed herself to hope it could solve all their financial problems.

"Enough to take the heat off and get the Baillargeons off my back. Enough that *Tesoro Mio* remains . . . yours."

"Ours," she whispered.

"I'm glad you feel that way. We can use her as our home to travel in search of our pot of gold, and not care if we find it. But first—" Enthusiasm lit his eyes, and she felt his body start to sizzle with excitement. "—we're going to pull up the silver from than *Nicolau Coelho*."

"You sound confident."

"I feel it, Addy. The stars are in alignment for us. Right here, right now. As long as you forgive me. Can you? Forgive me? Start over? Heal—*together*, and find new purpose, new reasons to be happy? God only knows we *deserve* to be happy, Addy."

Addy wrapped her arms around his neck and pressed her mouth to his. They kissed hungrily, all the pent-up longing and despair in the kiss. When they pulled apart they were lying down facing each other. Ry's eyes looked suspiciously bright as he used his thumb to wipe away her tears.

"*I* want to fight your battles with you." Addy murmured, cupping his prickly jaw. "I *want* to be the female to your male. I want to protect you from my asshole ex boyfriends, and monsters like my mother." His lips twitched, and she placed a finger across his mouth, because she was serious. "I want to lie on top of you and keep you warm when you're cold, and shower you with kisses. I want to light a thousand white candles around you, and feel your skin warm and glow because you're brighter to me than any flame. I want to feel the brush of your fingers on my skin, and feel your hardness deep inside me. I want you to allow me to do things for you—not because you're helpless and need my assistance, but because it gives us both pleasure. I want the sun and the moon and the stars with you. I want the right to doodle your name on my binder. Now and always."

That made him blink. "My name on your . . . *notebook*?"

"Yes." Swinging her legs over the side of the bed, she padded over to her desk and pulled open a drawer. She returned to the bed where he was sprawled, hands stacked under his head, watching her. "Here." She curled up beside him and handed him her notebook. "See?"

He angled the spiral-bound notebook to the window and the flood of moonlight so he could see. Like a lovesick schoolgirl, Addison had spent months scrawling

ADDISON CASE, MRS. ADDY CASE, RYDELL CASE, RYDELL LOVES ADDISON. ADDISON LOVES RY, and surrounded each pairing with hearts of varying sizes. "I love you, Rydell Case. Now and forever."

"Ah, Christ," His face contorted. "Thank God. I love you so much, Addison. I want to make you happy. I want you to make me happy. I want babies, and a puppy, and—"

Snuggling into his arms, Addy laughed, tossing the notebook aside. "Let's concentrate on finding the rest of that silver, and just being happy for now."

He wrapped his arms more tightly around her. "Feel it?"

"Your erection?"

He chuckled. "No. Us. Our bodies, touching. The friction we create shows we're *alive*. Know this, Addison Case, every moment you're on this earth: *You* are the most valuable treasure I've ever found, or will ever find. You are the reason I wake up in the morning, the reason why I take each breath. You're more important to me than any gold medallion, bar of silver, or jewel that I have ever picked up from the ocean. I will be forever grateful that you've given me another chance. I will not disappoint. I swear it, with every fiber in my being."

"Then—anything we want. As long as we have each other, there's no storm we can't weather and no limit to our dreams."

"See, this is why I love you, Addy. When you're right, you're right."

Twenty-seven

One year later

"Is that the last of it?" Addy asked, cradling the baby against her shoulder after his afternoon feeding. Sitting in her favorite big easy chair in the common room, feet up, content and happy, Addison held out her hand for Rydell as he sat on the arm of her chair.

He'd barely stripped off his wet suit before coming inside to see how they were doing. Beyond the sliding door she could see the dive team whooping and yelling, holding the last of the bars of silver aloft and grinning ear-to-ear. Another day of celebration.

"Asleep?" he asked, using a gentle finger to move the soft blanket away from the baby's cheek.

She nodded. "Like the angel he is." Adam, named for Rydell's younger brother, had been born two months ago. So quickly they hadn't made it by chopper to Malé before his birth. He'd been born right there on *Tesoro Mio* while the ship lay at anchor over Rydell's wreck.

His very *lucrative* wreck.

Four hundred and thirty million dollars' worth of silver, to be exact. It was the biggest haul of silver ever salvaged. Steven Fenton, one of Rydell's investors, had come out to the ship shortly after Naveen and Morimoto had been hauled off by Interpol.

Fenton had dived with the dive team and, wildly excited to see the treasure where it lay at the bottom of the ocean, had upped his investment and fronted Rydell money. Which he'd used to pay off Antoine Baillargeon's heirs in time.

The reward money for the return of millions of dollars' worth of artwork had been icing on the cake. Ry hadn't needed the loan based on the reward for the artwork.

The biggest prize of all was Adam. Their rainbow baby. Their rainbow after the storm of losing Sophie. There was no moving on or recovering from her loss. Adam didn't fill that empty space, yet he filled a space all his own to the brim.

Still, the nine months Addison carried him were some of the most terrifying months of her life. Fear and doubt plagued her; she'd wake in the middle of the night in a cold sweat, terrified for the future. Rydell was always there to hold her. To talk about their daughter so they'd never forget. He helped Addison have hope. He helped her conquer the sadness and fear. He helped her by loving her unconditionally, by telling her that no matter what happened, he'd be with her.

The day Adam was born was the best and worst of Addison's life. Her emotions, fueled by exhaustion, fear, and postpartum hormones, were chaotic. She'd felt a combination of jubilation and guilt. Trepidation and euphoria.

Now they shared a look over the baby's head. "It's done, then?"

"Yeah. That's it. Not a single silver bar left for the Cutters to find." He grinned, tanned and rough looking because he hadn't bothered to shave in days. He was so sexy, Addison's heart double-tripped. The tiny white-ink tattoo of baby wings over his heart matched her own. "Ready to be on land for a while?"

She took his hand, twining her fingers with his. "I'm not sure my legs will adjust. But yes. Maybe somewhere with snow? I'm done with palm trees and beach sand for a while."

"Who gets married in Switzerland?" he demanded, not sounding happy.

"Your sister-in-law. We're going, you *will* support her, and you'll be polite to every one of the Cutters."

"Shit. We hate each other," he grumbled without much heat.

"I didn't say you have to bond with them, Ry. Just be friendly and civilized."

"They'll have heard about this salvage." He perked right up. "That'll be something to talk about."

Addison laughed as she gently punched his arm. "Don't go to a wedding and yank the groom's family's chains, Rydell! Be humble. Be nice. Be a loving brother. Then we can leave. Peri will be there."

"I'll kick her ass, too. Where's she been all these months? Why's she been so secretive? Has she told you anything?"

"No, and if she did, and it was a secret I wouldn't tell *you* anyway. It'll be nice to see her and Callie. They're both eager to meet Adam."

"Because he's perfect. And so are you."

She touched his face. Loving this man so much her heart felt full enough to hurt. Between them, Adam made little bubbly sucking noises in his sleep. They shared a smile over his little bald head.

"We'll have a party tonight," Addison told him. She'd been planning this for weeks. And the timing for bringing up the last of the silver was absolutely perfect. Callie and Jonah Cutter were marrying in two weeks in Lucerne, Switzerland. "I'll go and talk to Patrick in a bit, and see what we can come up with in celebration."

"Will you go to see Hollis before we go to the wedding?"

Hollis was in Centre Pénitentiaire de Rennes, an all-female prison in France, awaiting trial. Naveen and Morimoto were also still awaiting trial in a different French jail. From there they'd be taken separately to Italy and then Germany to face trials there for the art thefts. Addison stared at Rydell. "See Hollis? This millennium, you mean?"

He grinned. "Guess not."

Ry slipped down beside her on the wide chair, tugging her against his side. His swim trunks were wet, his body solid and welcome. Addison rested her head on his broad, still-damp shoulder. His skin was warm and supple under her cheek. He smelled of seawater and neoprene. She adored the combination. "Are you happy, Rydell?"

She felt his smile on top of her head as he murmured, "This week, month, *year* has been the best of my life, Addison Case."

Heart full, Addison smiled. She was home.

Catch up on Cherry Adair's
Cutter Cay series!

Now available from
St. Martin's Paperbacks